IN THE HOUSE
OF THE WITCH

❖❖❖❖❖❖❖❖❖❖❖❖❖❖❖❖❖❖❖❖❖❖❖❖

Brak drew up his cloak in the deepening gloom. After the dreadful night of barrow mounds, haunted stones, and this miserable shelter from the storm, he couldn't sleep.

A soft, scratching sound made him cringe. He saw the fleece nailed over the door stir slightly. Then the serving girl came creeping stealthily from her lair.

"What do you want?" he asked, his voice quaking. "Go away!"

"You're the one who must go," she whispered. "A dreadful curse abides here. If you don't leave, you'll find yourself its victim by midnight. Don't ask any questions—just go! If Katla knew I tried to warn you, she'd—"

A heavy creak from the stairs silenced her.

THE
THRALL
AND THE
DRAGON'S
HEART

Elizabeth Boyer

A Del Rey Book

BALLANTINE BOOKS • NEW YORK

Dedicated to
Capitol Reef, an oasis of peace.

Chapter I

◈◈◈◈◈◈◈◈◈◈◈◈◈◈◈◈◈◈◈◈◈◈◈◈◈◈◈

Brak shivered under the onslaught of the howling, gusting snowstorm, which had suddenly and completely enveloped the two travelers, transforming the spring afternoon into a fury straight from the dark heart of midwinter. The light failed rapidly and the storm obscured the surrounding landscape until Brak and Pehr could see little beyond their horses' flattened ears. The riders wrapped their hoods and cloaks tightly around themselves, watching anxiously for the welcoming lights of Vigfusstead. Pehr's father Thorsten, the chieftain of his Quarter, would be there waiting for them, enjoying the warmth of Vigfus' fires and his golden mead in the ancient longhouse his ancestors had built. Brak closed his eyes against a particularly hostile blast and pictured those seasoned, black beams and thick, friendly turf walls. Someone would be playing the harp and singing or reciting poetry, and all the guests would be warm and well fed in the finest traditions of Scipling hospitality.

Pehr's voice jolted him from his half-drowsing stupor. "Brak, I said do you think Vigfus will have the sense to send someone to meet us with a light? We might have been there by now, if anyone had any brains."

Brak could see nothing of Pehr but a white lump crouching in the saddle of a larger white lump. The larger lump stopped and blinked its snow-fringed eyes and heaved a reproachful sigh.

"Do you think we're lost?" Brak hated to ask, knowing Pehr would think he was a coward.

"Lost on Vigfus' road? Don't be absurd. I remember

1

distinctly when we crossed the beck, so the hall must be over this next hill. I hope you're not going to disgrace yourself and me by being cowardly. I'm supposed to be your chieftain and you're supposed to trust me, remember?"

Brak muttered a grudging agreement. Although he had grown into a tall, stout young man, a veritable shaggy bear, he still had a tendency to blush furiously for little cause and he didn't like to fight, which earned for him a reputation of cowardice.

He was of a mind to be frightened now, knowing that the cold and stony interior of Skarpsey was famous for its ability to confound the traveler with mazes of weird and desolate formations of lava rock, rendered even more inscrutable by clouds of steam from legions of smoking geysers. He was also aware of the reputed strange magic that ruled the interior of the island.

"We aren't lost, Brak. The snow makes it seem longer, and we're traveling slower, too. You know old Faxi couldn't hope to keep up with Asgrim otherwise. I feel in my bones that we're getting closer, and any moment we'll meet a thrall from Vigfusstead coming to light our way with a lantern. I refuse to be lost besides. The son of Thorsten simply couldn't do something so stupid and commonplace."

"Well, I, as a mere thrall, could manage it without the least trouble." Brak urged Faxi forward, noting how the snow had matted the horse's thick mane until he seemed scarcely able to lift his head. It also matted Brak's beard, a short, fine ruff sprouting around his face in generous growth for his early years of manhood.

"Hush!" Pehr commanded. "If you'll be quiet, I can listen for someone shouting to us."

"It will probably be a troll," Brak muttered. "I'm not too proud to be superstitious. That's one of the privileges of the lower classes."

They slogged through the deepening drifts, until both horses stopped suddenly, lifting their heads and staring with alarm into the swirling gloom ahead. With rattling snorts, they backed away, refusing to go farther.

"Barrows!" Brak gasped, catching sight of what waited ahead. Old lintels and doorposts loomed in the dimness, capped with hats of snow like grim old ghouls standing watch over the dead in the mounds.

Pehr led the retreat, halting in the lee of a scarp of lava. "Well, now we know we're slightly off the road. You might have said something sooner, Brak."

"I did, this morning before we started out," Brak said. "I told you it would probably snow; and if you hadn't been so lazy yesterday, we could have left with Thorsten to see the law-giving. But you couldn't make up your mind until the last minute, and then it was too late."

Pehr responded with a snort. "I suppose what we should do is find a place with a little shelter and wait for daylight. We can't really be too far off the track."

"I don't know why not," Brak growled, gnawing his lip in earnest worry. From their earliest childhood scrapes together, he had been expected to see to it that Pehr came to no harm; and if anything went wrong, it was invariably Brak's fault. Since Pehr had never possessed much common sense, it was no wonder that Brak had spent most of his existence in a condition of fear.

Silently they toiled up yet another hillside and stopped. Pehr gave a shout and began pounding clouds of snow from Brak's shoulders.

"Look there, Brak! It's Vigfusstead! Didn't I tell you we weren't far off the road?"

Brak saw one tiny light far below, which seemed half smothered by the storm. "That's Vigfusstead? I'd expected more lights," he said, but Pehr chose to ignore him. With rising spirits, they rode toward the faint, ruddy light. Even the tired horses walked more willingly.

The light soon showed itself to be the fireglow coming from a half-open door. Brak stopped several times to look at it doubtfully, but Pehr forged on confidently.

"This isn't Vigfusstead, Pehr," he finally announced as they approached the dooryard. "I can't imagine where we are. Whose holding could this be? There aren't any holdings this close to Vigfusstead, are there?"

"Nonsense. Of course there are, or this one wouldn't be here. Come on, Brak, quit being such a fat old coward." Pehr dismounted and approached the half-open door. "They'll be glad to let us stay the night and feed us a good meal, and I know you won't balk at anything remotely edible. Halloa! Is anyone awake in there?" He rapped at the window and waited.

A thin, pale face peered out the door warily. It was a serving girl, but she reminded Brak of a cornered fox looking at its assassins. Raggedly clad and ragged-haired, she seemed ready to bolt away at any instant.

"What do you want?" she whispered. "This isn't the sort of place for travelers. You'd better go back the way you came, quickly, before something terrible happens to you."

"What? What sort of hospitality is this?" Pehr demanded. "We're cold and hungry and lost besides and wouldn't know where to go back to if we wanted to. We were going to Vigfusstead, but we can't go any farther in this storm. Where's the master of the house?"

A voice from within sent the girl scuttling away. The door was snatched open by a heavy hand, and a large, stocky woman in poor, dirty clothing scowled out at Pehr and Brak.

For a moment she stared grimly, then said, "Well, you'll have to come in, then. I'll send my shepherd to look after your beasts. Mind you, we're not used to guests here, so you needn't expect to be treated like kings." As she turned away, she went on, muttering, "If you knew what place this was, you'd probably rather sleep in the snow. On your heads be any misfortune that befalls you here."

Brak looked at Pehr, not quite able to believe what he thought he had heard, but Pehr didn't seem alarmed. The place certainly promised an uncomfortable night. Two wretched rooms with an attic leaned against a greasy-smelling old hut where the food was prepared. A heap of untanned sheep fleeces along one wall filled the place with a strong smell of sheep, as well as furnishing the old woman a bed. The serving girl probably slept in the kitchen, and the ill-favored shepherd, who skulked out the door to care for the horses, smelled as if the barn were more home to him than the house.

The girl edged into the room with a large, black pot steaming with a muttony fragrance. Eying the two strangers distrustfully, she hurried back for two large wooden bowls, which she flung on the table with a clatter. A loaf of rather stale bread and a knife were added to the feast, followed by the grudging addition of a lump of goaty-smelling cheese.

The old woman sat down with a wad of wool at a spinning wheel, watching her guests eat their food. Her eye was grim and somehow speculative. The silence in the small house was formidable. Brak tried not to look at her lest he lose his appetite, which was already experiencing difficulties with the rubbery boiled mutton and greasy broth.

Suddenly the old woman leaned forward to inspect her guests more piercingly. "Did you pass by way of the barrows as you were coming here?" she demanded.

"We did," Pehr replied, spearing a large piece of mutton out of the pot and fussily cutting the fat off it. "A lot of people would try to tell us some frightening old tales about ghosts and strange lights and such nonsense. I disbelieve all this magical stuff myself."

The old woman snorted. "When you're as old as I am, you'll come to believe a great many things that you laugh at now, my fine young man. Ever since I've lived in the shadows of the barrows, I've seen a mort of strange things." She shook her head until her jowls quivered, and her pale eyes fixed them with a deathly glare.

"And may you live to see many more of the same," Brak said nervously, in an effort to appease her,

"Ha! I may not live out this night!" She said it with much satisfaction and hunched herself up in her shawl, pursing her lips as if no one could ever wring another word from her. Under the cover of viciously harrowing up the fire, she muttered, "And neither may one of you."

Brak's ears, sharpened with apprehension, caught what the old crone had said. He clutched at Pehr's arm and whispered, "Pehr, I don't think we should stay here. She keeps muttering under her breath about awful things. Let's leave, shall we? I'd rather sleep outside than with all the lice and ticks in those old fleeces."

"Hush! It wouldn't be polite," Pehr whispered angrily.

"Polite? Who worries about that when you're scared to death?" Brak's eyes darted around the room, lighting upon the most ordinary things with horror, as if they were instruments of torture instead of farming and weaving implements.

"Don't be so superstitious," Pehr answered, but even he jumped when the old woman suddenly uttered a loud chuckle in the midst of her scowling contemplation of the fire.

"Superstitious!" Her bright, fierce eyes bored into Pehr and Brak. "That's what you call it, eh? You young sprats know nothing about the old ways of knowledge. Superstition, indeed!" She finished with a cackle, a rusty sound that raised Brak's every hair to stiff attention.

She continued to snort and chuckle throughout the rest of their meal. When they were finished, she pointed to the fleeces. "You can sleep there as well as anywhere, I suppose, and I shall take the loft."

Dubiously, Brak measured her bulk against the rather flimsy ladder ascending through the low ceiling.

"Bar the doors, and if you've got any sense you'll bury your heads and pretend you hear or see nothing, in case anything should happen."

"What exactly are we to expect?" Pehr inquired with some annoyance, but the reply was a huffy grunt as the old woman crept up the ladder like a fat black spider climbing a strand of its web. She took the smoky tallow lamp with her, leaving her two guests in the dying glow of the meager fire.

"Now we can leave," Brak whispered, flinching when the fire popped.

Pehr prodded at the fleeces with one foot, then arranged his cloak in the far opposite corner and lay down on it. "You're being absurd, Brak. Given a basic disbelief in magic, what is there that she can do to us? I'll protect us well enough with this." He laid his short sword close at hand and looked at it proudly. Thorsten had given it to him last month for his birthday. Pehr had practiced diligently with Thorsten's oldest retainer, a one-eyed fellow Brak thought was surely ancient enough to have battled against the scraelings seven hundred years ago, when the Sciplings first set foot on Skarpsey's rugged shores.

Brak sighed, watching Pehr making himself comfortable for the night. Gingerly, Brak sat down on the stiff sheep fleeces in the deepening gloom and drew his cloak up to his chin. He had no delusions about bravery and cowardice. He knew he was a coward from his bones outward, including each carefully nurtured layer of loyal plumpness, which would someday become sturdy, faithful corpulence when Pehr was chieftain of his father's Quarter.

"You always get us into these awful messes," he grumbled, after he was quite sure Pehr was sound asleep. "Sometimes I think I might live longer as a poor fisherman. I certainly never asked to swear fealty to Pehr Thorstensson. It's been nothing but trouble ever since. Barrow mounds, haunted stones, and now a haunted house."

A soft, scratching sound sent him cringing into his cloak, except for his eyes, which glared around in terror. He saw the fleece nailed over the kitchen door stir slightly, and the small serving girl called Grima came creeping stealthily from her lair. Instantly Brak had visions of himself being murdered right before his own eyes.

"What do you want?" he asked, his voice quaking. "Go away, get back to whatever place you came out of—please!" It did him no good to notice that she was scarcely half his size and as thin and delicate as a wood shaving.

"You're the ones who must go away," she whispered. "A dreadful curse abides here; if you don't leave this house, you'll find yourselves victims of it by midnight. Don't ask any questions, just gather your things and go."

"I'd like to, but I can't. My chieftain Pehr thinks it would be a breach of hospitality—and superstitious besides. You're quite certain of the curse on this house?"

The girl nodded, her eyes lost in dark shadow. "Then you must desert him if he won't go. I assure you, the curse is as real as the wart on Katla's chin."

"I can't desert Pehr, I fear," Brak said unhappily. "Exactly what sort of curse is it, may I ask, and what kind of danger are we in?"

The girl shook her head, and pale hair gleamed under the edges of her ragged kerchief. "I can't tell you. If Katla knew I tried to warn you away, she'd—" A heavy creak from upstairs silenced her. Shaking her head and holding up a warning finger, she started scuttling back toward the kitchen.

Brak caught her wrist, dropping it hastily, amazed at his own temerity. In a whisper he asked, "Are you in some sort of awful trouble? Can I—be of any help to you?"

The girl stared at him and seemed to be of a mind to laugh. Then she favored him with a quick, sad smile, saying, "No, I don't think you can, but it's most kind of you to ask. If you only knew—no, then you wouldn't want to help me. I wish you'd slip away before it's too late." Her whisper followed her as she glided away into the darkness of the sordid kitchen.

Brak struggled between the resolve to bestir Pehr immediately and get him out of danger and the fear of the wrath and derision of his friend at being awakened from a sound sleep to listen to Brak's ridiculous and definitely backward superstitious anxieties. All the common working folk on Skarpsey possessed a healthy respect for magic and magical beings; doubt was reserved for the educated and wealthy, who had little to do with the vast, lonely fells and isolated valleys. With a small sigh, Brak picked up Pehr's sword and propped himself watchfully against the wall. The sword in his hand was as comforting to him as if it were a live, poisonous snake. Earnestly he hoped nothing would happen to prove his cowardice to an even greater extent.

From time to time he added chips of wood and dry dung to the fire to keep the room somewhat lighted. He wanted to see the menace before it throttled or murdered him, although even a vengeful, bloodthirsty draug would have second thoughts about sallying from its grave on such a night.

He pinched himself to stay awake until he was numb and almost delirious. He wished the small creaks and squeaks and sighs he heard would frighten him awake, but sleep had dulled even his overdeveloped sense of self-preservation. In spite of himself, he nodded and dozed, slumping against the wall with the sword across his knees.

For no reason, he suddenly awoke, glaring around wildly with the knowledge that something was wrong. The air felt disturbed, as if something had just brushed past him. Turning his head, he saw that Pehr was gone. For a moment Brak could only gape, listening to his heart hammering with the terror of being abandoned in Katla's evil clutches. Then he persuaded his quaking limbs to rise and creep toward the door, which was not completely closed. Fearing all manner of gruesome sights, he peered through the crack, not daring to risk breathing.

He saw a cloaked and hooded figure mounting a tall horse and turning it away to ride out of the yard. Brak fell back and began scrambling his possessions together, picking up one thing and dropping it to seize another. Deserting him in such an awful place was exactly Pehr's idea of a fine joke, which he could tell everyone back at Thorstensstead to make them all laugh. It would be a great story; the best ones always were at Brak's expense. Brak finally managed to fasten his cloak and grab his boots, letting himself outside as quietly as he could, stumbling in his haste over Katla's spinning wheel, left treacherously to ensnare the unwary, like a large, predatory insect.

Brak hurried to the stable, where no one seemed to be awake. He fastened Faxi's bridle with shaking hands, trotting his horse out without the saddle, and followed the tracks the other horse had made in the snow. The storm had left the sky clear and cold, glittering with stars and half a moon, which offered ample light for following Pehr's tracks. Pehr would tease him and complain about going back for his saddle, but Brak resigned himself to it in advance, rather than enduring a night alone in that house.

He followed the tracks to the top of a hill and down the other side, where he discovered a hodgepodge of tracks, as if the horse had galloped up and down several times. To his dismay, he couldn't decipher which way Pehr had gone. Tracks led away in all directions; after attempting to follow several sets of them, he could no longer tell Faxi's tracks from the original ones.

As he sat pondering, he heard a horse whinny behind him, toward the north. Gladly he set off in pursuit, urging Faxi to trot a little faster.

"Pehr, you're going too far for a joke!" he muttered, seeing that the tracks led straight toward the barrow mounds. Jolting and muttering along on Faxi's knobby spine, he tried to persuade himself not to follow Pehr to the barrows. He knew Pehr would be waiting to spring out at him and scare him, and even that knowledge wouldn't make the fright any less when it came. Unhappily he urged Faxi as close to the barrows as the animal would go, and then he got off and led him, cajoling and comforting the old horse.

"Pehr? Where are you? I know you're going to leap out at me with a horrible scream any moment, and I promise

I'll nearly faint, so why don't you get it over with? We can go on to Vigfusstead by moonlight."

He listened for any slight betraying sound, but he heard nothing except the hissing of the wind among the upright doorposts and lintels. With a sigh, Brak tugged Faxi after him, following the hoofprints further into the cluster of barrow mounds. Faxi shook his head and made disapproving grunts and groans as he plodded reluctantly after Brak.

The hoofprints led toward the largest barrow, which bristled with a ring of stones on its flat top. Brak shivered, suddenly feeling cold and alone in a place where he had no business.

"Pehr!" he shouted. "I'm going back now! You're going to miss out on scaring me and telling everyone about it! Do you hear, Pehr? This is no place for jokes, especially in the middle of the night!"

Still there was no answer. Brak waited, then began following the tracks again, muttering to himself. When he looked up again, he was nearly at the foot of the large barrow. The tracks led straight to the gaping, black entrance and vanished between the two tall doorposts. Unwillingly Brak approached the doorway, smelling the musty breath of the barrow and prickling all over with creeping gooseflesh.

"Pehr!" he called. "This isn't funny. I know you didn't go inside that barrow, so there's no way you'll get me into it. I'm going back, Pehr. I'll meet you at Vigfusstead."

This time he heard a faint sound in answer, an echoing clatter of stone from inside the barrow.

"I'm not going in there," Brak said to Faxi, bending his head for a look into the absolute blackness of the barrow. "I don't know why I do these things for Pehr. I'm sure he doesn't appreciate half the trouble I go to—" His words trailed off, echoing in the waiting darkness below. Brak had been forced to crawl into earthy barrows with Pehr many times to search for treasure, or merely to defy any lingering curses, but none of those sadly decayed little chambers had ever echoed. Brak made a small, quavering hoot and listened to the sound rebounding as if in a vast cavern. With an unsteady hand, he felt around the doorposts and discovered walls of hewn stone. Before his feet was a flight of steps leading down into the earth. Brak stepped back, leaning against his horse for support. Something unnatural awaited him, something more frightening than Pehr leaping out of the shadows with a terrifying yell in his ear. Pehr had already gone down into that strange darkness before him, and it was his duty to follow, however much against his better judgment.

Moving one leaden leg at a time, he stepped into the barrow and felt his way down the stairs. Faxi followed him with a little encouragement, his hooves clopping softly on the steps and his speckled nose nudging Brak along from behind.

"I don't need you pushing me," Brak muttered as they reached the foot of the stairway. A broad tunnel sloped away steadily downward, with guttering tallow lamps at intervals in little niches in the rock.

"I must be dreaming this," Brak told himself, "so there's no sense getting frightened, is there? I'm asleep, safe at home at Thorstensstead in the loft over the hall—" Accidentally he touched Pehr's sword at his belt, startling himself. Gripping it resolutely, he strode down the tunnel to the first lamp. Far ahead, the distant, sharp clipping of a horse's hooves on stone made Faxi lift his head and listen.

Brak mounted his horse and sent him trotting after Pehr, trying not to wonder where the mysterious tunnel was leading to, or how it had got there, or who had made it. He didn't feel like shouting in such a place. He wasn't at all certain it wasn't a dream; and if he was actually asleep back at Katla's, he didn't want to go shouting his head off as a guest in a stranger's house. Awakening the household would be extremely bad manners.

The tunnel ended, finally, without a glimpse of the other horse. It looked exactly like two great, half-open doors leading into a well-lit room. Brak almost chuckled, knowing for certain he must be dreaming.

He dismounted and groped his way forward in the dark, blundering unexpectedly into the other horse. It was tied to a ring in the wall and breathing as if it had galloped a long way. After the initial fright of Brak's bumping into it, the horse let its head droop again and began to shiver. Brak touched its sweat-soaked neck, wondering how long the poor beast had stood, hot, winded, and growing stiffer and colder the longer it stood. It rolled fearful eyes at

Brak and trembled as he smoothed its soaking neck and peered cautiously between the doors into the room beyond.

It had once been a large and magnificent hall, but now it looked like a forgotten lumber room. Tattered rags hanging on the walls and old sheep fleeces thrown in heaps added their own rotting smells to the natural mustiness of the cavern. Splintered timbers held up the roof in several places and were sprouting coats of phosphorescent fungus. Two small, shaggy ponies were tied to the timbers, snorting and rolling their eyes at the flickering of the fire in the center of the chamber. Brak had never seen such ponies. They were black, delicate creatures, glossy and fiery of eye, reminding Brak somehow of spiders. He shivered and poked his head a little farther around the edge of the door.

The riders of the black ponies stood on the far side of the fire, so he could see them only through the veil of dancing flame. The instant he caught sight of them, a voice shouted threateningly, "You know you can never go back now! You'll be in our power until you die, which may be very soon if you continue with such stubborn behavior. All I have to do is breathe one word to Katla's zealous and superstitious neighbors, and you'd be burned alive or hanged. I'm sure you know what that one word is, so I needn't repeat it. Even your own people would rather see you dead than allow you to return to them the way you are. Now, what is your choice? Are you going to step forward and swear your loyalty to us, or are you going to die?"

Chapter 2

◆◆◆◆◆◆◆◆◆◆◆◆◆◆◆◆◆◆◆◆◆◆◆◆◆◆◆◆◆◆

Brak gasped, staggering back against the door, certain he was going to be killed on the spot for the heinous crime of cavesdropping.

Then a different voice answered. "I doubt if I will die, Hjordis—not while I have the gift my father left me. That's what you want me for, isn't it, so you can take possession of this small object I wear around my neck? All I have to say to you, Hjordis, Queen of the Dark Alfar though you may be, is that you shall never get this necklace from me, whether I live or whether I die, and I know you wouldn't dare try taking it by force."

Brak crouched behind the door, peering around it with helpless dread and fascination. He saw a third figure confronting the other two, a smaller figure in a ragged cloak with a kerchief tied around her head. The girl reminded him of Katla's kitchen maid, Grima, only more bold and defiant. She revealed a gleam of gold at her throat for a moment, then quickly concealed the small object inside her tattered tunic.

"You'll never get it by force," a deep male voice rumbled from the blurred image of a black-shrouded figure with a long gray beard. "The Rhbus will never permit it."

Hjordis, the queen, had taken two swift strides toward the girl. Now she halted and put something back into her belt—a knife, by its flashing gleam. "Would they dare strike the Queen of the Dark Alfar?" she demanded with a toss of her lofty headdress. It was a sinister contrivance of bits of fur, bones, teeth, and other peculiar objects.

"Would you like to tempt them?" the deep voice replied

sharply. "You're already risking their anger by putting your curse on her and forcing her to stay with old Katla. She's not going to run directly back to her people, who would most likely lock her up and try to work a cure which would almost certainly be the death of her. Neither will she be able to find old Dyrstyggr to help her cause some sort of mischief; we've seen to it that he'll never get his powers back. Now all that remains is for us to convince Ingvold that her best interest lies in giving us Dyrstyggr's dragon heart. We're engaging in war on a grand scale, so where on earth could a lone, wretched girl such as Ingvold possibly thwart our plans? Those who tried to oppose us, such as her father Thjodmar and Dyrstyggr, are all happily dead or out of the way, are they not?"

Hjordis folded her hands inside the deep sleeves of her gown and stared haughtily at the girl. "Yes, but she still possesses that heart and we must have it. As you say, she is alone and insignificant, and I'd gladly kill her in an instant if not for fear of the Rhbus, who protect her, but the question is how to get the heart away from her. I believe in playing on the safe side."

"Indeed, I never suspected such a thing," Myrkjartan grunted. "I believe you're coveting that heart so desperately you'd do anything to get it for yourself."

"You'll never get it," Ingvold said scornfully. "I am the last of Thjodmar's line, and as long as I live you shall never possess the dragon's heart and the assistance of the Rhbus."

Hjordis' hand reached toward the knife at her belt. "But perhaps I can persuade you to come over to our side, willingly and gladly. You'll get tired of my curse before long, my girl. It's not pleasant to be a hag, as you have discovered. I can't say which fate would be worse, falling into the hands of the Sciplings, who would burn you alive, or into the hands of the Light Alfar, who would try to cure you. No, I daresay you won't escape from me, and one day you'll change your mind, and then the dragon's heart will be mine, freely given by its bearer. Until then, back to your miserable captivity with Katla."

"Like a bird on a tether," Myrkjartan remarked dryly. "She can fly around where she wants, until you begin to pull on the string."

Ingvold stamped her foot. "Someday I'll find a way to escape from your tether, Hjordis, and I'll return to Snowfell and tell King Elbegast about Dyrstyggr, even if the cure kills me."

"And she would, too, the little cur," Myrkjartan growled. "I think a dungeon would be a better place to reform her character, rather than letting her run loose in the Scipling realm."

Hjordis waved her hand contemptuously. "The Rhbus would regard a dungeon as infringing on the girl's free will."

"And this despicable curse you've put on me isn't?" Ingvold demanded. "I wouldn't maim and murder poor, innocent people of my own choice, although I couldn't say the same for either of you—a necromancer and a witch-queen."

Myrkjartan rose from his seat with an impatient lashing of his cloak to move it out of his way. "Get rid of her, Hjordis, and let's go back to Hagsbarrow. That idiot Skarnhrafn will get into the blackest trouble if he's not watched closely. I hope you won't trouble me again with the observation of your inept tactics for obtaining Thjodmar's heart."

"You can go," Hjordis said to the girl. "Until the next full moon, when I send for you. I hope you'll do some reconsidering, Ingvold. I doubt very much you want to continue your life among uncivilized and ignorant Sciplings."

Ingvold replied over her shoulder, "I prefer them to you, Hjordis. The smell of mutton fat and fish is far more pleasant than the smell of evil." She dived through the doors as she ended her speech, tripping over Brak, who was still crouching there, too shaky with fear to scuttle out of her way.

"You!" Ingvold cried in amazement, seizing him and dragging him out into the darkness. In the next moment the doors slammed shut with a crash, and they heard the sound of a heavy bar falling into place. "You followed me, you fool! How could you—how dare you?"

She gave him several shakes, which did nothing to restore the strength of his wobbly legs, and pushed him as rapidly as he could go toward the horses.

"I thought I was following Pehr," Brak replied. "Where is he, and by the way, where is this place? Who—"

"Never mind all that. If you're lucky, you'll never find out. There's no time for explaining, except to say that your friend Pehr is alive, if not too well, and he'll certainly be much worse if we don't get out of here as quickly as we can. Get up on this horse, not your old nag, or we'll be trapped. Dawn's not far off. Come on, poor beast, you're almost spent, but we'll take care of you as soon as we get back to Katla's barn. I swear we will. I promise you, Pehr will be all right, or I'll— Come on, come on, we've got to go!"

She was astride the tall horse and pulling Brak up protestingly behind her. The horse wheeled around and set off at a lunging gallop for the far end of the tunnel.

"But what about Faxi?" Brak began, holding onto Ingvold for dear life and limb, scrabbling for a seat on the saddleless back of the horse.

"We'll have to leave him. I'm sorry," Ingvold said over one shoulder as Faxi raised an indignant whinny. "See what happens when you go poking your nose into other people's business? Grief is all I ever cause anyone. How many times do you think I've destroyed innocent people such as you and Pehr? It's enough to make me wish I were dead, but even that wonderful privilege escapes me. I wish I'd never been born, and I wish I had the power to curse and damn Myrkjartan back to the bogs he sprang from. With my own hands I'd drive the stake through his evil heart. As for Hjordis, curse her greedy heart, I'd command lightning to strike her dead!"

The horse was racing at top speed, and Brak kept his eyes shut, not liking to think what would happen if he fell off at such a careering speed. His gentle old Faxi seldom exerted himself beyond a sedate canter, and that suited Brak and Faxi exactly.

By the time they reached the stairs up to the outside, the horse was wet with sweat and its breathing was harsh and loud. If the tunnel had seemed long before, it was almost interminable to Brak on the return trip, expecting as he was to go flying into midair at any moment, to be left behind to whatever awful fate befell those who were trapped in the mysterious tunnel after dawn.

"Hang on tight!" Ingvold warned him, and the horse went lurching up the stairs, slipping and falling to its knees more than once. With a leap and a scramble, they were out of the tunnel and into the crisp night air of the barrows. The eastern sky was dawning pink, and Brak could clearly see Katla's house crouching secretively beside a black scarp, screened by several tattered, stunted trees. It was a walk of several miles; the horse was stumbling, almost reeling with exhaustion.

"I fear you've misused your horse shamefully," Brak said, venturing a mild reproach after they had dismounted to look at the unfortunate animal.

Ingvold sat on a rock, her face hidden in her crossed arms. In a moment she raised her head to look at Brak. Her sharp little face and hunted eyes reminded Brak even more of a scruffy vixen trapped in her den.

"At least we made it out of the tunnel," she said. "That should satisfy you, if you only knew what we had missed so narrowly." She nodded to the hillside they had just come out of; to Brak's astonishment, the doorway was gone entirely. Nothing remained but the grassy side of the barrow, which hadn't been disturbed in centuries. "No questions," she added as he opened his mouth to speak. "The less you know, the safer you'll be. But as to the horse, I didn't abuse him deliberately. It's a cruel trick of Hjordis' to call and call without telling me where to meet her, until the poor creature I'm riding is nearly dead. Some have died, but if we can get to Katla's barn, we'll save this one. Come on, poor fellow, there's a nice, warm stable waiting for you, if you don't fall down on the spot and die. Then I fear it would be crows and foxes for you. Easy, now, come along. His feet and legs will be in terrible condition, I fear. We've got to hurry, or we'll not make it. If we have to carry him—"

"Carry a horse? How could we—" Brak began. Then he changed the subject. "I wish you'd explain to me what has happened here, and where I can find Pehr. Is he still down in that awful tunnel place?"

"No, no, you fool. He's—well, I can't tell you that right now. Are you as educated and clever as your chieftain Pehr?"

"No, indeed, I'm only a thrall, although we've grown up together like brothers, almost. I fear I'm quite superstitious, as we thralls usually are from lack of education." He sighed in mortification and looked at her. "But you seem different, in spite of your poor appearance, almost as if you're—you're—" He paused to frown and think suddenly, wondering what it was about her that didn't seem quite right and proper in a lowly kitchen maid.

"What about me?" she demanded haughtily. "You'd better explain."

"You're more like a—well, a chieftain's daughter, or somebody who knows she's important. You're not humbled. Now, you may laugh and say I'm crazy, which is no less than I deserve, I suppose." He looked at her sideways, anxiously, to see if she was getting ready to laugh or say something unkind. Instead, she smiled. Her fear and worry lines vanished, and Brak blushed to realize how pretty she actually was when her face wasn't pinched up by unfortunate circumstances. She touched his arm briefly, and Brak felt as if she had warmed all the dark and fearful spots in his heart.

"Thank you for thinking I'm more noble than I really am," she said, "but you and I are sharers in the great misfortune of our lowly stations in life. For you, it's lucky you're not skeptical, as your chieftain is, who was teasing you for being such a coward. I assure you, you're not being cowardly at all in fearing Katla's house. If you could but know the truth, no one would dare laugh at you."

Brak sighed. "I can't imagine that. Pehr makes great sport of my beliefs. But why can't you tell me the truth? I want to know about this curse, and who Hjordis and Myrkjartan are. What is this awful broil you're in? Why do they call you Ingvold, when Katla calls you Grima?"

"My name is Ingvold, but you mustn't call me that in Katla's hearing. She'll know you were listening where you had no business or she'll think I told you, and that would cause you trouble. No, I can't tell you anything about it. After tomorrow we'll never see each other again, and that's the best way for you." She tugged at the weary horse's bridle to urge him along a little faster.

"Tomorrow? Pehr will want to leave immediately." Brak looked across the horse's sagging head at her and caught her fleeting expression of bitter desolation. "Ingvold, can't I do anything to help? I saw your enemies and heard them threatening you with death and imprisonment. Pehr's father is the chieftain of his Quarter, a very powerful man, and a good sort besides. I'm sure he would help if something is dreadfully wrong—"

"No, you can't tell him unless you want to see me burned alive as a witch. It's a curse I'm under, and it doesn't concern you—very much, that is, except in a general sense. But you must stop plaguing me about it, because I absolutely refuse to allow you to become involved. I don't want you to be hurt, and I fear there's really not much anyone can do for me, unless he's adept at breaking spells. So don't ask me any more questions if you wish to regard yourself as my friend."

The horse began to stumble and sway dangerously as they approached the stable. Brak had to push him from behind and Ingvold pulled. The poor creature collapsed in a heap just inside the door. His eyes closed and he breathed a long, shuddering sigh. Brak made sure the horse was still alive, then found a tattered blanket and some old rags to cover him with, adding armfuls of straw.

"What he needs is a warm drink," Brak said anxiously. "Look how he shivers and shakes. Is there a bucket here?"

"Go and tell Katla what you need. I'm sure she'll understand," Ingvold said, sitting down on the straw beside the horse's head.

Brak started for the door, then turned. "Ingvold, I'm not asking questions any longer; I'm going to say something that might be important. I'm not a brave fellow, but when Pehr gets back, he'll supply all the courage and I the determination. We'll help you break this curse so that you can be free of Hjordis and Myrkjartan, if you'll only tell us what to do to help. I'd be willing to comb Skarpsey from one end to the other, or to set out in a boat, or to declare myself an outlaw, whatever it takes to rid you of that awful woman Hjordis. I know how it is to be a homeless orphan, since a whale upset my father's barge when I was a tiny child. If not for the kindness of Thorsten, I would have perished long ago, which is what might happen to you before much longer, if Hjordis and Myrkjartan were speaking the truth."

Ingvold smiled sadly. "Yes, I suppose they were. But it's no good talking about it, Brak, so you may as well go get a bucket of warm water so that we can care for our unfortunate friend. You're a stout, kind fellow, the first ever to show me any sympathy in my plight; however, when you discover the truth about me and what has happened here, you'll be glad enough to forget about me." She gave him a push toward the house, saying Katla would know exactly what he needed.

When Brak made his request for warm water from Katla, she glared at him a moment in wild surmise. "For what horse? There are no horses here but your own," she rasped, slopping water on his foot as she shoved past him roughly and hurried to the stable. "Come along, you buffoon, I'll show you what we do have."

Brak followed slowly, wondering what the madwoman meant. Gingerly, he opened the door to peer in, and Katla assisted him by seizing his collar and hauling him inside as if she were landing a stubborn fish.

"See there!" she declared triumphantly. "She's done it again, and your educated friend has reaped the benefits of a magic he swears doesn't exist!"

Brak stumbled forward, unable to believe he was actually seeing Pehr lying, pale and still, under the old rags and straw he had used to cover the sick horse. Falling onto his knees, he saw that Pehr was breathing, although he was covered with a fine sweat and shivering violently. Then Brak looked up to find Ingvold, who had vanished. Only the ugly, disconcerting face of Katla leered back at him. He administered a covert pinch to himself, a painful one.

"I must be dreaming," he managed to stammer, rubbing his eyes and shaking his head in the approved manner for awakening oneself. "The horse I thought I saw—well, I'm sure I saw—but how did Pehr—and Ingv—er, Grima, where is she?"

Katla cackled cozily. "Yes, that's right. You catch on quickly, dear boy. Grima is a hag. She changes people to horses and rides them all night whenever the full moon appears. It's a curse put on her by the Queen of the Dark Elves, who pays me to keep the girl miserable. Oh, the blisters I've seen, and the poor fellows who have died—"

"Pehr mustn't die!" Brak gasped. "He's the next chieftain of the Quarter! His father would hold me personally accountable if Pehr died!"

Katla stooped, with many grunts and creaks, to inspect

Pehr more critically. "Not a pretty pastime for a pasty-faced little chit of a girl. You're lucky it was your young master she chose, and not you, or all that lard on your ribs might have melted and gone to your brain. He's strong, though; I suppose he'll get over it, if a chill doesn't take him off first. Help me carry him into the house."

"A hag? Grima?" Brak awkwardly tried to help as Katla bundled Pehr up in her arms, leaving Brak to carry his feet. "I'd never thought of a young girl being a hag. They're usually old and ugly, like—like—"

"Like me, you mean?" Katla was so amused she whistled through her nose. She deposited Pehr on the untanned fleeces. "The young ones are the worst. Nobody suspects them, they trick you, and there you are with your legs run off and your feet worn to the bloody bone." She glowered in Brak's face a moment for effect, then hauled off Pehr's shredded boots, revealing as nice a collection of fat, white blisters as Brak had ever seen.

"I've seen far worse," Katla grumbled as she began smearing the blisters with a smelly, yellowish paste that stank like rancid tallow with some herbs in it. "There was a fellow at Brikarsnef, and before that it was at Throstrsstead. The only thing that saved this one was the fact that we're very close to the other world." Her last words were barely distinguishable from a growl as she attended to Pehr's injuries.

"Other world? I thought that tunnel was rather peculiar. Was it made by dark elves, perhaps?" Brak inquired.

Katla's head jerked up and she glared at Brak like a berserkr meditating an attack. With a sinister rattling in her throat, she snarled, "You'd better mind your own business or you'll find yourself neck over ears in the worst sort of trouble you can imagine. If you've seen something, you'd better forget it as fast as you can, and even then you'd better watch over your shoulder when you're out on a dark night. And if—" She hitched herself closer to Brak, holding him transfixed with her horrible gaze, which seemed to peer into all the corners of his being. "And if you should be so foolish as to talk about whatever you might have seen this past night, if you should decide to throw away your life and perish very unpleasantly—" She did not finish her threat; her voice trailed away to that deathlike rattle in her throat, and her stare became more piercing, more fraught with menace. Then she closed her mouth with a snap, which startled Brak into uttering a frightened yelp. She finished her job of bandaging Pehr's feet, adding when she was done, "If you ever come back to this place, you won't find us. With this sort of thing going on every full moon, we're not permitted to remain long, as you can imagine. You weren't thinking of vengeance, were you?" She leaned forward to eye Brak again.

Brak alternately shook and nodded his head, then shook it again emphatically, not daring to say a word.

Katla grunted. "Good. You may leave as soon as your friend awakens and is able to ride."

Pehr slept the rest of the day and awoke at sundown, very tired and peevish, mistaking the red glow of sunset for dawn. "Why didn't you wake me up earlier? We should have left hours ago!" He threw off the fleeces with disgust. "Brak, don't just stand there, get my boots. We must be off immediately, or we'll miss my father and we'll miss going to the law-reading, and it's all your fault, Brak. Thorsten hates to wait, and I'm starving, too, but there's no time to waste by eating." He grabbed his possessions and tried to stand up, adding a roar of pain and astonishment. Glaring at his bandaged feet, which he had instantly removed from the floor, he plummeted back into the smelly fleeces, bellowing, "My feet! What in the name of Odin's goats— Brak! What happened to my feet? And look at my boots! Worn out, right down to the very bottoms, unless some beggar has traded with me while we were asleep. Brak, why weren't you watching better? Oof! My feet! I can't walk! I can tell by your face you're not telling me the truth, Brak."

Brak's face was a constant traitor to his inner emotions. It blushed pink when he was guilty, white when he was fearful, and now it was a mixture of both. He stammered, "Not now, Pehr. I'll tell you later, when you're more in the mood. It's really nothing too serious, actually, except it's not sunrise, it's sunset, and we've probably missed Thorsten, and your feet will be sore for a while, but perhaps we should stay here another night—" He glanced around at the bulky, black figure of Katla rattling and grumbling in the kitchen.

"Stay another night!" Pehr roared. "Not another instant! Fetch me some slippers. There'll be no wearing boots for a while, I can see. Let's get ourselves to Vigfusstead while there's still a bit of light. I can't imagine why you didn't wake me up, Brak."

Brak opened and closed his mouth. It was no good explaining anything, not with Katla listening to every word; and worse yet, Faxi was lost in the tunnel under the barrow. With a despairing glance at Katla, he began gathering together their possessions, surrendering his own fleece slippers to Pehr, who growled and groaned ill-humoredly. By way of helping, Pehr hung his pouches and bags around Brak's neck and leaned on him heavily to rise to his feet.

"You're going, then?" Katla favored them with a scowl. "Well, I never promised you any great hospitality."

"But my feet are half murdered!" Pehr exclaimed. "And no one will tell me anything about it! I demand to know—"

"Where's Grima, that little wretch?" Katla muttered unhelpfully. "She should be here fixing supper, and I haven't seen her do a stroke of work all day. Come to think of it—" She cocked her head to one side and screwed up her face horribly in suspicious thought. Dropping her spoon, she hurried outside with surprising speed and summoned Grima with a piercing shriek.

Pehr paid little attention. "I must have stuck them into the fire, but I can't imagine how I'd sleep through the experience. Why won't you tell me what really happened, Brak?"

"I'm afraid you won't believe me," Brak replied in a doleful voice, considerably muffled in Pehr's saddle pouch. "In fact, I know you won't believe me."

"I don't care if I believe you or not," Pehr said. "Just tell me what happened." He leaned on Brak more heavily, and they staggered toward the door.

Katla burst into the house, glaring wildly from Pehr to Brak. "She's gone! Escaped! Vanished! What did you young villains have to do with it? I just found your old speckled nag grazing among the barrows, so I know you were there last night." She jabbed a finger at Brak. "You'll find out the price of being bold enough to poke and pry into other people's business. You'll be sorry, both of you, for what you've seen. I wouldn't be surprised if Myrkjartan himself didn't decide to pay you a call. He's a necromancer, you know, and he prefers dead things to troublesome live ones. Blast you both and that wretched girl!"

Brak cringed. "I didn't follow to snoop, I only wanted to find Pehr. Once I got there, I couldn't very well leave, could I?"

Katla gave an awful shriek and grabbed two fistfuls of her hair. "Then it's true! You followed her! Hjordis will be wild with fury! She'll come after you, too—and perhaps me for letting Ingvold escape." The thought was enough to stop her in mid-grab for her hair.

"We didn't have anything to do with your girl's running off," retorted Pehr, "and it's a shocking breach of hospitality to accuse us of it. I hope I never have the misfortune of being lost near your house again. It would be better to take our chances in a sheep shed. If you'll have the goodness to saddle our horses, we'll take ourselves out of here, with the greatest of relief on both sides, I'm sure."

Katla nodded curtly. Whirling around, she screamed out the door for the ill-favored shepherd to saddle their unwanted guests' horses at once.

Brak was delighted to be reunited with his old Faxi, who nickered at him and waggled his ears reproachfully. Brak rubbed his neck and Katla glowered.

"Yes, there he is, the old speckled nuisance," she growled. "You wouldn't get him back twice from where he's been."

"What was he doing straying in the barrow mounds?" Pehr demanded in a greater fury of mystification.

"He escaped—from—from—" Brak stopped and looked at Katla.

"Escaped, indeed!" Katla snorted. "Probably Myrkjartan let him out to see if he'd return to his inquisitive master; that way Myrkjartan would know who was spying on him last night."

Brak paled, but Pehr gave him a sharp nudge. "Help me up; I can't manage alone. Then bid our kind hostess farewell and thank her for her gracious accommodations. You'd better ask her which way leads to Vigfusstead, unless you want to wander back here again after dark."

"You needn't bother with your empty thanks," Katla snapped, her eyes darting around in fear. "Vigfusstead is straight north. You'll be able to see its lights from the fell

—all the more fools you are for traveling so close to night-fall with the Myrkriddir about."

Brak felt his blood run cold. Hastily he boosted Pehr into his saddle, nearly tossing him off the horse's far side. His legs were shaking so hard he could scarcely climb onto Faxi's back. His grandmother had told him about the Myrkriddir, bog corpses who rode ghostly horses around the skies at night, searching for hapless travelers to take captive and make them Myrkriddir—dead, but not permitted to rest peacefully.

"Myrkriddir!" Pehr said loftily. "That's just an old superstition. We don't believe in that nonsense at Thorstensstead, and you'd do well to forget it, too." He turned his horse and rode away without a backward glance.

Brak darted a last look at the lowering Katla, who stood muttering and hugging her sides. She grinned at him craftily, which made him recoil with horror.

"He'll be after you," she whispered, wagging a finger, then drawing it across her throat with unmistakable significance.

Brak suddenly felt chilled and frightened by something too strange and mustily ancient for him to comprehend. He urged Faxi ahead at the old horse's top speed, which was a rolling, complaining canter. He soon settled down to a methodical trot, overtaking Pehr. At the brow of the fell, they halted and Pehr pointed out Vigfusstead, still basking in the lingering, cheerful light of the setting sun.

"There it is, just as I told you. I knew we weren't far from the road," Pehr said.

"Do we have to stop here?" Brak inquired. "Why not just hurry on before it gets cold and dark?"

"The horses need to rest a moment," Pehr answered. "I'm not afraid of the dark. Are you?"

"I certainly am," Brak declared. "After what I've seen—" He stopped himself, wondering if he dared to tell Pehr about Ingvold.

"And besides," Pehr continued, "I want to hear your explanation for my feet being nearly destroyed. We'll sit here all night if you want to, or you can tell me quickly and we'll get to Vigfusstead before it's pitch-dark."

Brak began with a sigh. "Well, you remember the little kitchen girl who first let us in, and how she warned us to go away before something dreadful happened?" Pehr glowered at him impatiently, and he hurried on. "I was sure you'd remember her; it was only last night, after all. Yes, as I was going to say, she—she has a peculiar affliction, and rather a dangerous one, but you were fortunate, more fortunate than others, since the other world is rather close, so you didn't have to travel far."

"This tells me nothing," Pehr said, "and it's getting darker."

In a faint voice Brak said, "She's a hag—one of those who turn men into horses and ride them all night, and often the poor fellows die. She doesn't mean to—I mean, she does it because a curse has been put on her by the Queen of the Dark Elves, a most evil-looking creature called Hjordis. There's something Hjordis wants from Ingvold, a locket she wears around her neck, but someone called the Rhbus protects Ingvold, and she'll die before she gives the necklace to Hjordis. There's something about it that gives a person great power, so Hjordis is making Ingvold suffer until she gives up and joins Hjordis' cause—whatever it is. An old Alfar named Dyrstyggr is also important somehow, but I was rather frightened, and it was all so sudden that I didn't really catch it all—"

"I fear you'll catch it in a far different manner if you tell anyone else that story and expect him to believe it," Pehr interrupted. "That's the most fanciful lie you've ever told, and you're not even blushing, Brak. All these years I've been trying to teach you to lie, and here you tell a story like that without even stopping to think."

"I'm not lying," Brak said indignantly, glancing over his shoulder in the direction from which they had just come. "Ingvold changed you into a horse and went riding out to those barrows and down a long tunnel into the earth. I followed because I thought it was you trying to desert me at that awful house so you could laugh at me later. How else could a person hurt his feet so badly and never know it, unless it was an enchantment?"

Pehr said nothing to that. He wiggled his toes and grimaced. "I hope it was a fine horse, and not a nag like Faxi," he said facetiously.

"Oh, it was a very fine horse, Pehr. I can't imagine what difference it should make, unless you're worried about keeping up appearances, I suppose. If you'll only listen a moment, I'll explain."

Pehr interrupted with an impatient snort. "Then tell me how Faxi came to be wandering among the barrow mounds. That should be another fanciful story, I suppose."

"Then you have no recollection at all of—anything?" Brak looked at Pehr anxiously, and Pehr glared back at him.

"Certainly not, except what you'd expect," Pehr snapped. "I know you're going to give me some fantastic tale about magic and elves, aren't you?"

"Not exactly. I had to leave Faxi behind in the tunnel because dawn was near, and that's how Myrkjartan and Hjordis will follow us, to see who was spying on them last night."

Pehr shook his head and scowled at his slippered feet. "Hags, necromancers, dark elves," he growled. "All I can say is, you'd better keep this to yourself. Being hagridden isn't the sort of thing you want everyone to know about." He gathered up his reins and sent his horse down the fell at a reckless, plunging gallop.

Brak let Faxi pick his own way down at a casual amble. He glanced back and saw Katla's house squatting in the gathering night shadows. Unwillingly, his eyes sought out the barrow mounds, their tops still rimmed with sunlight, which deepened the shadows pooling among them. At such a great distance, the shadows looked almost solid enough to touch. In fact, they looked almost like a cluster of horses and riders advancing as the sun declined, loping silently from the barrows toward the fell where Brak and Faxi were outlined against the flaming sky.

Chapter 3

◆◆◆◆◆◆◆◆◆◆◆◆◆◆◆◆◆◆◆◆◆◆◆◆◆

A warm welcome and a generous supper awaited them at Vigfusstead. Pehr was furious to discover that Thorsten had already left Vigfusstead that morning. "We'll make an early start tomorrow," he grumbled, doing his best to stamp around and make a scene; but with such sore feet, sitting in a chair and complaining loudly was the best he could do. "We can catch my father at Hrappsrivercrossing by noon. I know he wouldn't miss a chance to stop and drink Hrapp's ale. That is, if someone will lend Brak a decent horse."

"Certainly," Vigfus said, always ready to curry favor with young fellows who happened to be the sons of wealthy and powerful chieftains. "I've got just the horse for your man; a fine strong chestnut mare I ride myself. She'll take you there, all right. Such a pity you didn't get here yesterday or earlier in the day today. Thorsten waited until midday for you. I expect it was the storm last evening that delayed you?" He looked speculatively at Pehr's bandaged feet.

"We had a slight accident," Pehr said, and quickly diverted Vigfus to the subject of the best ale in his cellar.

Brak left the talking to Pehr and the other guests in Vigfus' hall. Privately, he decided to be stubborn about keeping Faxi. The old horse refused to gallop much, but he could trot along at his steady pace long after faster horses were cross-eyed and knock-kneed with exhaustion.

Brak ate his supper without his usual appreciation of fine food, although rhubarb soup and pickled sheep's feet were two of his favorites. When he was finished, he slipped to the door without attracting attention and peered out warily at the sky, which was still light enough for him to see any Myrkriddir if there happened to be some flying around over the hall. Seeing nothing suspicious, he scuttled out to the stable to give Faxi a treat and a good scratching behind the ears, which Faxi enjoyed almost as much as it soothed Brak's anxieties. While he scratched he talked, and Faxi listened good-humoredly, shaking his head and wobbling his lips as if his night in the dark elves' tunnel had been a lark.

Still uneasy, Brak again scanned the sky for Myrkriddir and hurried back to the hall, diving in at the door of the kitchen annex because it was the closest. His mother was also the sister of Gudrun, the cook, and he was usually glad to visit Vigfusstead to exchange family gossip.

"Come in and sit yourself down, Brak," Gudrun greeted him. "You can sit by the fire and shake off those night vapors, if you'll be a decent young fellow and not fluster my girls. It's not an evening for strolls in the moonlight, if you ask me." She was vigorously punching an enormous crock of dough for breadmaking, punctuating every other word with a tremendous thump.

"Thank you, Aunt." Brak took a stool by the fire and held out his cold hands. The early spring weather was in danger of forgetting itself again and reverting to winter. "It does seem rather damp and mizzling out. And did you notice the smell? It's like a hundred moldy old cellars left open, or a barrow—" He muzzled himself swiftly and felt his face and ears turn bright pink when the kitchen girls all stared at him and tittered nervously.

His aunt nodded and grunted as she plopped the dough onto the table. "Aye, barrow mounds full of rotting bones and evil curses," she said with dark significance, burying her arms to the elbows in the brown mass. "I've had this feeling, as if something awful were going to happen, and it's well known that I've got a gift for seeing the future. Ever since I clapped eyes on that poor little kitchen girl who came scratching at my door early this morning—"

Brak's eyes flew open. "What girl?" he demanded.

"A common, scrawny girl. She came from that witch Katla, terribly abused and hungry. I gave her all she could eat and a sackful besides. She was running away, of course, but not a soul could blame her. There's something strange about that Katla, wandering in from nowhere and taking that abandoned house where the family all died; where does she get the money for the food and animals she keeps? I hope you remember the lessons your old grandmother taught you about magic and the scraelings and the secret people of Skarpsey. I hope to goodness you'll remember, as I swear it upon every stone in Skarpsey—" She raised one hand, sticky with webs of dough.

"No, no, I haven't forgotten a word she said," Brak assured her hastily, closing his astonished mouth. "You say the girl from Katla's was here, running away? Where was she going, did she say? Did you see the direction she took?"

Gudrun wrestled mightily with the dough. The battle was fairly even, but Gudrun overpowered her adversary, preventing it from escaping off the edges of the table. Breathing heavily, she tossed her hair out of her eyes and said, "The little creature didn't say, but I saw her walking east toward Hrappsrivercrossing. I wished her luck, but I fear she'll die out there. Lone travelers heading toward the inland often are never seen again. There are still scraelings out there, or trolls, or whatever you want to call 'em, but they're all hungry and mighty evil." Gudrun stopped her kneading suddenly and stared around, listening, with an expression on her face that froze the three kitchen girls into wide-eyed statues. "There, now, there it is again," she said in a deep, husky whisper. "Listen to that and tell me there's no evil in Skarpsey!"

The wind drummed and moaned, sounding almost like horses' hooves and strange voices calling out. The girls frantically made gestures with their hands for warding off evil. "Shouldn't have fed that girl from Katla's. Happen she put a curse on us!" one of the girls whispered.

"Didn't the girl say anything else?" Brak persisted. The wind's uneasy noises made him get up and walk back and forth.

"Nay, poor mite, and I'll never regret helping that one. I know, I've got a sense for these things." She nodded sagely, regarding Brak and the girls with a secretive smirk. Then her expression changed and she looked at Brak with narrowed eyes, frowning intently. "But what I'm most concerned about is you, Brak. I think something is following you. No, no, don't tell me about it; let me see it for myself."

She raised her eyes toward the roof, seeking the answers among the clusters of smoked mutton quarters and blankly staring sheep's heads and sausages.

"I think I'll be going." Brak stood up cautiously on his trembling legs, remembering Katla's half-demented raving about Myrkjartan's following the speckled horse to see who had been spying on him.

"Listen to that!" Gudrun interrupted her trance to exclaim as the wind gave the house a great buffet. "It's Myrkriddir, or I'm deaf and ignorant! Myrkriddir risen from their barrows—"

She would have continued, but one of her spellbound audience suddenly fell into a fit of hysterics, screaming and blundering wildly around the kitchen. Gudrun and the other girls subdued her by sitting on her and muffling her shrieks with a rag.

"Bera, you'd better mend your ways," Gudrun reproved. "Vigfus' wife doesn't like screwy, flighty girls. Stop that gulping or you'll be looking for a new position."

Deeming his aunt's performance to be finished, Brak excused himself and went back to the main hall to find Pehr. The other guests, all important chieftains and their retainers, were making noise enough that they seldom heard the suspicious sounds outside. Once someone commented about the restive livestock, and everyone listened for a moment to the distant squeals of the horses in the barn and the unhappy bawling and blattering of cows and sheep.

"Must be witchcraft abroad," Vigfus said with a wink, but behind his back he was making the sign.

The guests laughed and launched a series of tales that made the hair stand up on the back of Brak's neck. He could see fright in the round eyes of some of the simpler retainers like himself. By the time the tales had reached the pinnacles of terror with recitations about barrow mounds and draugar and Myrkriddir, Brak's nerves were strung as taut as harp strings. The wind outside moaned and muttered a ghostly accompaniment to the storytellers.

Brak's restless gaze traveled around the hall, suddenly fixing on the window by the porch. A face was looking in, a lean, bony face like a corpse's, shaded by a drooping hood, and Brak could swear the eyes burned in their sockets like two coals in the ash. He gasped, choked, and couldn't speak for coughing, so he pointed frantically to the window, gripped his throat with the other hand, and turned quite purple in the face.

The other guests leaped to their feet with staring eyes, and not a few made signs to ward off evil. In a babble of voices they cried: "What is it?" "Who's there?" "It's the Myrkriddir!" "House-riders!"

"Quiet!" Vigfus roared, turning to Brak and giving him a good pounding on the back to ease his coughing. "What's the matter with you? Are you having a fit?"

Brak pointed to the door and wheezed, "Someone's out there, looking in, and he didn't look—alive."

"What do you mean, you dolt?" Vigfus snorted, breathing heavily and staring at the door. "How could he—" A heavy knock interrupted him. "Well, of course. It's only a benighted traveler getting in out of the storm. Probably going to the Thing, same as you fellows." He looked at Brak in disgust. Brak shrank away in mortification at himself.

Vigfus hurried to open the door, welcoming the traveler and inviting him to share all the bounties of board and bed that Vigfusstead had to offer. The traveler stepped inside and stood holding his staff as he regarded the company in silence for a moment. Brak thought he cut an old-fashioned figure, with his long gray beard flowing down to his belt, which snugged in a shapeless garment that came down to his boot tops; a voluminous cloak covered him nearly to the heels. Modern men wore trousers stuffed into their boots, shorter, lesser cloaks, and hats rather than long-tailed hoods. The old style looked downright menacing to Brak; and what was more peculiar, Brak observed that the cloth was all fairly new—not old and rusty like the clothing of some of the ancients around Thorstensstead.

As the stranger stepped into the hall, a quirk of wind gusted in after him, revealing for a moment the rich red lining of the cloak. Brak caught his breath, remembering his indistinct view of Myrkjartan's black and red cloak through the film of flame.

"Well, old fellow, sit down and make yourself at home," Vigfus was saying jovially, not noticing, as Brak did, how the stranger was staring at the assembled merchantmen and landowners and retainers as if they were just as odd fish to him as he was to them.

"Aye, thank you," he grumbled, walking stiffly to a table and seating himself, leaning his staff nearby. The silence in the hall was rather awkward; the garrulous Sciplings for once could think of nothing to say.

"Have you a horse to be stabled?" Vigfus asked, making him comfortable with a cushion, ordering food and drink from the kitchen, and offering a set of fleece slippers, which the stranger waved away.

"The stableman showed me where to put my horse. In a stall next to a stout speckled horse, a most unusual animal."

The words struck ice into Brak's soul. In rigid terror he looked at the stranger, knowing he was unable to keep his face from being read like a book, and the stranger gazed back at him with the cold, colorless eyes of a snake. Brak knew with utter certainty that this was Myrkjartan, the necromancer.

When the food arrived, the necromancer ceased his scrutiny of Brak and began to refresh himself. Brak edged nearer to Pehr and prodded him with his foot, making signs with grimaces and facial contortions until Pehr began to glare at him. The usual genial roar of men's voices soon reached its old level as the guests laughed and tried to out-talk each other, which offered a good screen for a quiet conversation.

"Pehr, that's Myrkjartan," Brak whispered. "Did you notice how he mentioned Faxi to let us know it was him?"

"That's the man you saw underground—or thought you saw?" Pehr eyed Myrkjartan sideways and moved his sore feet uneasily on the pillow Vigfus' wife had fussed up for him. "What should we do about him? He looks like an old, dried stick to me, and I'd gladly break him if he had anything to do with that Ingvold business." He glared at Myrkjartan to mask his growing uncertainty. If one admitted to the existence of genuine hags, it opened the door for wizards and necromancers and trolls and who knew what else. Pehr's years of civilized education were beginning to totter on weakening legs.

"What's he going to do?" Pehr whispered.

Brak shook his head and shrugged. "I don't know, but I

suspect he's after Ingvold so she won't tell anyone anything about her necklace."

"What about you?" Pehr demanded, but Brak ignored him.

"Ingvold was here this morning, and my aunt said she went east to Hrappsrivercrossing. We can inquire there about her and then go after her to warn her and offer our help."

"No, we won't. We're going to the Thing."

"You might be, but I'm not. Ingvold is more important than a bunch of old lawsuits and feuds and weregild. You were more involved than I was; I'm surprised you don't want to help her."

"Help her! I never want to see her again—particularly around the time of the full moon. Brak, are you sure you're not imagining all this?" If his father Thorsten were here, Pehr wouldn't need any reassurance. Thorsten disclaimed all magic and would snort this necromancer away like a mote of dust. "I think we'd better find my father soon, because I've got some questions for him. Things like this just aren't supposed to happen nowadays."

"Something certainly happened to your feet," Brak replied.

Pehr merely grunted and looked away with a frown. "One way we might find out something more definite," he said musingly, "would be to have a look through the fellow's possessions tonight while he's asleep. As crowded as it is tonight, he'll have to sleep on the floor by the fire. As soon as we're certain he's snoring away, you'll nip down the loft ladder and take a look in his pouches."

"I will?" Brak was aghast. "I've never done anything like that in my life! I don't need to get any closer to him to tell what he is. He's a necromancer!"

Unfortunately, his last three words fell in a temporarily quiet hall. The jolly drinkers heard the piercing whisper and looked askance at the newcomer, who doubtless heard it, too. He gave no sign, however, continuing to sit, upright and silent, in a rather cold and gloomy corner. Brak didn't dare look at the man, imagining those cold, hard eyes boring right into him. He wiped his sweaty palms on his knees and tried not to think about Pehr's plan.

To make things even more worrisome, when everyone

started moving toward eiders and slumber, the necromancer opted to sleep in the privacy of the stable rather than in the warm and crowded hall. Vigfus was distressed, but the old man answered that the cold and discomfort of the stable would be as nothing to one long accustomed to far worse accommodations.

"You'll have to go out to the stable to do your snooping," Pehr whispered to Brak. "I'd go myself, but I can't." He looked at his feet accusingly. "I'll be watching from the little loft window and I'll help you climb back inside. Don't worry, old duffers like that are usually deaf as doorposts and snore so loud they wouldn't hear a berserkr raid. It'll be easy, Brak, even for you."

Brak and Pehr shared the loft with half a dozen other young blades on their way to the Thing. After a roistering straw fight and much laughter, they finally settled down to sleep. Pehr nudged Brak, whispering, "Wake up, All's quiet and it's time to get going."

Brak hadn't been sleeping. Unhappily, he squeezed himself through the small window—rather a tight fit for someone of his stocky frame—and crept softly across the steep turf roof. The wind was now so silent that he had the feeling he was being watched. Consigning himself to the hands of unkind fate, he dropped off the roof and scuttled toward the stable. The horses were still restless, not caring, perhaps, for their unwelcome guest. Brak scraped in through a low window and looked around in despair at the complete blackness inside the stable. Something suddenly gave him a shove and he almost screamed, choking himself at the last instant when he realized it was only Faxi. That meant that the horse next to Faxi was Myrkjartan's.

He turned toward it, seeing only a shadowy mass looking back at him. It was a tall horse, either white or gray. A bit of moonlight seeped through the clouds, showing Brak what he most dreaded to see—Myrkjartan's saddle and pouches lying beside a heap of fresh straw made into a pallet, with a dark shape lying upon it.

Brak held his breath, not releasing it until he was light-headed. He felt as if half the night had passed while he stood there staring, before he took a step toward the saddle. Nothing happened, so a long time later he took another step. Finally he was close enough to the pouches to touch them. His heart was thumping so loud he wondered if the necromancer could hear it. With wooden fingers he fumbled with a loop and peg fastener and tried to see inside the pouch. Reaching in, he felt something like old bones and bits of rotten cloth. Horrified, he shut that pouch and opened another, trembling in his haste to get done with an odious and thoroughly unnecessary task. The next pouch seemed to be a mixture of stones, chains, and coins—probably gold. He also felt a smooth, cold sphere of some kind that instantly gave him a wild feeling of terror and doom.

He had more than enough. As he was turning to leave, a small bag rolled off a peg and fell at his feet in a splash of moonlight. The contents tumbled out, a round lumpish thing that seemed to be hairy. Brak grabbed it and dropped it with a muffled gasp. It was a head, dried quite perfectly, so that it looked almost alive. Brak nearly wept as he tried to force himself to touch it. Trembling, he rolled it over to see the features. To his horror, the eyes were open and glaring indignantly. He knew he couldn't bear to touch it.

Then the hairy features twisted and he heard a hoarse whisper. "Put me back in my sack, you idiot, before I blast you on the spot. Myrkjartan will hear of this, never you fear."

Brak uttered a soft moan and fumbled the sack over the head so that he wouldn't have to touch it, upended the bag, and hung it on its peg. Then he fled at top speed, not caring if he was careful and quiet. As he squeezed out the window, he thought he heard a dry chuckling sound behind him, which redoubled his energy for escaping. Like the greatest of athletes, he vaulted from the window and ran toward the hall at record speed, up the wall, across the roof, and in through the loft window almost in one fluid rush. He landed inside with a terrific crash, awakening several lads who grumbled and growled at the interruption of their sleep.

"It's just Brak," Pehr said in a petulant voice, "falling out of bed. I think he was dreaming he was riding a horse."

The others snickered and went back to sleep. Brak crawled into his bed, still breathing heavily. He shut his eyes and pretended to ignore Pehr's nudging at him.

"What did you find?" Pehr demanded in a dangerously loud and annoyed tone.

"Proof," was all Brak would say, but prolonged pinching, poking, and threatening finally extorted the entire story from him. When he was finished, Pehr snorted softly and thought for a long time.

"A severed head that talks," he muttered. "A round glass thing that gave you a bad feeling. I think you'd be frightened of your own shadow, sometimes."

"Myrkjartan is no shadow," Brak retorted warmly. "You saw him yourself, if you've got any eyes in your head. He's stalking us and Ingvold, and his intentions certainly aren't of a friendly nature. We were the stupid cause of Ingvold's taking flight with that heart, and he thinks we're spies besides. As I see it, we've got to catch Ingvold and ask her what we must do to escape from him. If we can help her at the same time, so much the better."

Pehr shifted his sore foot around impatiently. "I wish my father were here to ask about it. He'd summon up an army of neighbors and kinfolks, and we'd soon see if this Myrkjartan wanted anything with us or not."

"Thorsten is too far away to be of any use to us," Brak replied.

"It seems to me," Pehr said in a solemn, musing tone, "if Myrkjartan is such a threat, it won't be long before he gets around to Sciplings, and simple weapons won't be much good against magic. Brak, I want you to tell me everything you know about magic and dwarves and elves and that sort of thing. If only my father and my teachers could hear me, they'd go into fits. You can tell me about it as we ride to Hrappsrivercrossing—and further inland if we have to, until we find Ingvold. If ever I'm going to be chieftain of a Quarter, I don't want to be threatened from a realm I can't even see. And Ingvold had better get Myrkjartan off our necks."

"Then you're going with me after Ingvold? I don't have to go alone? But what will Thorsten say?"

Pehr paused. "Perhaps he'll think we decided not to go to the Thing, or decided to go somewhere else. After all, I'm a grown man now and of an age to do almost anything I want to. I hope we'll get back home before he returns from the Thing and realizes we're missing."

In the morning Myrkjartan had vanished, leaving behind a bit of silver to pay for his lodgings. With thrills of dread, Brak inspected the place where he had lain for the night, making the discomfitting discovery that the necromancer seemed to have hardly crushed the straw and that the hay in his horse's manger was scarcely touched, as if neither horse nor master had remained in the stable very long.

Pehr and Brak set off early, riding toward Hrappsrivercrossing, intending to scout it out very carefully before approaching, in case Thorsten was still there. Pehr cursed Faxi's slowness at first, but he was repeatedly silenced when Faxi trotted past his tiring Asgrim and continued to jog along with few stops for rest.

At midday they arrived at Hrapp's house and learned that Thorsten had departed just hours before. The weather began to turn unpleasant, so Pehr and Brak were prevailed upon to stay the night. Pehr added a store of food and extra clothing to their supplies by dint of some skillful trading and subterfuge, and Brak hung around the servants, encouraging them to gossip. He soon learned that a young girl had stopped there and begged some food that morning before traveling on across the river. Brak looked at the cold, swift waters and wondered how a fragile creature like Ingvold had managed to cross without being swept onto the black rocks not far below the ford.

The night at Hrappsrivercrossing was windy, and Hrapp's animals burst from their barn and raced away into the night like mad things. In the morning Hrapp discovered that several cows and sheep had fallen off the cliffs and broken their necks or legs. The dairy was also awash with spilled cream pans and ruined cheese.

Brak shuddered, feeling responsible for the loss of the animals, but he was glad Faxi wasn't lying at the foot of a cliff with his legs broken. He wanted to tell Hrapp and his family that the trouble would be gone as soon as he and Pehr left, but he didn't dare open his mouth. He was still frightened enough that the whole business of hagriding and Myrkjartan might come flying out against his will.

As they were leaving—a very late start after helping collect all the livestock—a hired man stopped them with a message.

"From a friend of yours, or at least he said he was,"

the man said, hunching in his rough fleece coat uneasily. "Old feller with a long beard and one of those old-fashioned cloaks with the hood. Said to tell you he knew you were here but he couldn't stop. Expects to join you later at Vapnaford or Hafthorrsstead. Rather out-of-the-way places if you're going to Thingvellier, aren't they?"

"We don't know anyone of that description," Pehr said, with a startled glance at Brak. "It must have been a mistake on his part." But he passed the hired man a coin for his trouble before they rode on.

"Vapnaford. Hafthorrsstead," Brak mused. "The furthest inland settlements we know of, although I've known nothing of them but their names. If Ingvold is trying to get back to the Alfar realm, I believe she'd go inland, don't you?"

"I fear so," Pehr sighed. "If any place is the end of the world as we know it, Hafthorrsstead has to be the place."

They rode hard after leaving Hrapparivercrossing, stopping only to rest by the road that led to Thingvellier. When they left the familiar road and headed eastward into the little-known interior, their lighthearted chatter fell into long silences. Not many roads existed on Skarpsey, and homesteads were far and few—and sometimes unluckily temporary—so a map was almost useless. They knew that a road taking them eastward had a tolerable chance of depositing them somewhere near Vapnaford. After Vapnaford, the only known settlement was Hafthorrsstead, provided that the inhabitants had not starved to death during the winter, frozen from lack of firewood, or simply lost heart and given up the struggle to force a living from the harsh soil. After Hafthorrsstead, a barrier of lava flows, steaming mountains, and glaciers signified the end of Sciplings' land and the beginning of fog-shrouded mystery.

Just before sundown they arrived at the end of the road, which accommodated a small turf farmhouse nestled against the side of a green fell with hay tuns rolling out before it. Brak thought he might not see another house so homelike and familiar, so he looked around appreciatively. They were invited in cordially, as was the custom in a land where travelers were few. The farmer, Breiskaldi, immediately sent one of his sons to a neighboring house just over the fell where his brother Grim was settled, so that any news and festivities would be shared by as many as possible. Soon it was a jolly gathering, since Grim and Breiskaldi and their wives were from the same Quarter as Thorstensstead, and everyone knew the same people. Hardly anyone noticed the wind rising outside, until Pehr suggested that the livestock had better be secured.

Scarcely had the menfolks returned to the warmth and light of the hall when a loud knock sounded at the door. Brak hadn't quite recovered from the experience of groping around in the musty gloom with one eye on the sky for Myrkriddir, so he gave a noticeable start and muffled a gasp. Pehr turned pale, his eyes fastened on the door as Breiskaldi rose to open it, not suspecting the slightest evil.

A familiar-looking gray beard and old-fashioned cloak swirled in the wind as the visitor entered, accompanied by the tapping of a staff upon the floorboards.

Chapter 4

◆◆◆◆◆◆◆◆◆◆◆◆◆◆◆◆◆◆◆◆◆◆◆◆◆

"A beastly night out there," the visitor announced. Half a dozen children swooped at the old man with cries of delight, hanging themselves around his neck and prying into his many pockets.

Brak sighed noisily and squeezed his knees to stop their shaking. The old grandfather, with his tall staff and ancient cloak weathered green around the shoulders, would never know what a fright he had given the two visitors.

The grandfather disengaged his cloak from several small children and hung it to dry beside the hearth. He darted a conspiratorial glance around at his grandchildren and said, "Just as I was approaching the house, I would swear I saw the Myrkriddir flying over the roof beam. But I shan't tell people about it because they might be too frightened."

Brak and Pehr exchanged an uneasy glance. The children began to pester their grandfather for a suitably blood-chilling story, and he obligingly began to stuff his pipe with calculated leisure, while his daughter-in-law scolded good-naturedly. "Myrkriddir, indeed! Father, you're too much alone in that old hut up there on the fell."

"But I had a visitor just today," the grandfather declared, his eyes sparkling merrily. "A young lady stopped at my house, asking the way to Gnupa's pass. Her gown and old gray cloak were scarcely better than rags and her shoes were worn right out, but I had the feeling she was quality folks, in spite of her appearance. I wondered at the time if she might be from that other side, where the elves and dwarves live."

"Oh, Granddad!" the elder sons muttered shyly, looking at Pchr and his weapons and self-importance, not to mention his own thrall as represented by the bulky and mild-tempered Brak—both of whom weren't that much older than they, but were on a journey of man-sized importance from the coastlands. The young Breiskaldissons had no desire to appear like uneducated rustics.

"Young skeptics," Granddad retorted. "I've believed in magic all my life, and to this day I've never seen any evidence to the contrary. I don't suppose it's fashionable in the settlements to believe in magic, is it, my young, adventuring friends?"

"No, it's not," Pehr replied.

But Brak responded instantly, "Oh, yes, we both believe in magic and the people who work it, and we'd love to hear more about this girl who came to your house. What did she look like? Did she say where she was going beyond Gnupa's pass?"

"She was a very slight creature with pale hair tied up under a kerchief," the old man said, after drawing thoughtfully on his pipe for a moment. "She said little about her destination, except that she was traveling to visit her aunt who lives near Hafthorrsstead."

"The very place we are going to," Pehr murmured. "We shall watch for her, perhaps."

When Pehr spoke about going to Hafthorrsstead, the old

man looked at him rather strangely. "Have you been to Hafthorrsstead before?" he asked. "It's a place that is somewhat—peculiar."

"Dangerous?" Brak asked quickly.

"No, no, just a bit—well, I suppose it might be dangerous. I'm far too old to make the journey there, so I can't really say."

"Then it must be something magical," one of the children said, and everyone looked at the two travelers in wonder.

Breiskaldi stirred uncomfortably. "It will take magic to harvest our hay if this wind doesn't stop." The talk turned to sheep, potatoes, and inclement weather, which was to be expected on Skarpsey.

Brak heard scarcely a word. Ingvold had stopped at the old man's house on a fell somewhere nearby. He hitched himself closer to the grandfather. When the talk lulled, he asked, "Is Gnupa's pass the quickest way to Hafthorrsstead? We had thought to go by way of Vapnaford, but if there is a shortcut, we'd like to hear about it."

The old man's pipe had gone out, but he didn't seem to notice. "It's a path that hasn't been used in late years. Not many even know about it. Gnupa's pass, it's called, because an old curmudgeon like me used to live up there in a hut. He was a real hermit, though, and not as lucky as I am." He looked around at the ring of spellbound faces. "You'll be able to follow the faint little track to my house, but not quite all the way. In the place where I go up the side of the fell, the old road goes on around the bottom of the hill in the ravine. The way gets rather deep and narrow the further you go into the fells, but it will take you to Hafthorrsstead."

The children began pestering him for some Myrkriddir stories, so he obliged them in terrifying detail. Brak slipped away from the storytelling to listen to the adults talking of crops, harvest, and trading, and he pretended to listen until he almost fell off his chair, half asleep. That was the real signal to pack the children off to bed and say good night to Grim and his family. The grandfather stubbornly insisted on sharing the hired man's tiny, smoky hut that night, since it reminded him of his own house and was not as large and apt to creak and groan as Breiskaldi's house. Brak and Pehr were soon left with the floor beside the hearth to themselves, where they lay in the ruddy light, listening to the roar of the wind and the creaking of the roof timbers.

Pehr had a small, inadequate map which he was studying and scowling at. "Gnupa's pass doesn't even show on my map. I hope we can find it. Wouldn't it be delightful to leave Myrkjartan at Vapnaford with his teeth in his mouth while we overtake Ingvold at Hafthorrsstead? I wonder why he wanted to meet with us—to offer us gold, perhaps, if we'd stay out of his way?"

"I don't think gold is what he'd offer. Probably that shriveled fellow in the sack is what happens to people who try to interfere with Myrkjartan's plans." Brak shivered as the wind thundered outside. "And another thing—I doubt if we can fool him for long with those Myrkriddir following us."

"Oh, tush, it's just the wind, Brak. What an imaginative coward you are sometimes." He soon forsook Brak to his imaginings and went to sleep far more comfortably than did Brak, who awakened at the roars and creaks occasioned by the wind to wonder what difficulties this venture held.

In the morning Pehr extracted more directions from the grandfather, promising to visit his house on the fell on their return journey. The old man only shook his head and muttered half to himself something about those who made their way to Hafthorrsstead seldom returning. Brak wanted to ask him what he meant, but Pehr impatiently mounted his horse and urged Brak to hurry. They rode swiftly into the fells and soon found the place where the old man's path curved upward and a dim old track continued deeper into the fells. Gnupa's pass soon became little more than a gloomy crack through the fierce defile of the mountains. Icy, clear cascades poured into their ravine from the glaciers above. A narrow, damp path twisted among the mossy rocks and scrubby trees that took advantage of the shelter of the gorge, and the horses' hooves left deep tracks behind them. Often Brak spied the faint mark of a small heelprint in the dark earth, so he watched ahead alertly, certain he was going to see Ingvold's tattered gray cloak at any instant.

By the end of the day he was disappointed and worried. The way steepened and became more rocky, so he could no longer see Ingvold's footprints. The weather turned misty and wet, soaking gradually through their clothing and making them shiver. They found an old hut which must have been Gnupa's, but it looked as if the old hermit had died or gone away a long time ago. The hut was cold and damp and in poor repair. The sunlight vanished hours early into twilight. They stabled the horses in half the hut—a habit which Gnupa must have practiced also, since a bit of old hay still remained in the smoothly worn manger—and built a fire in the other side to drive away the dark and cold. The rain pattered softly on the mossy roof without a trace of wind to suggest Myrkriddir, and Brak began to feel quite cheerful to think of them howling around Vapnaford while he and Pehr were high in the mountains.

"Shh!" Pehr suddenly sputtered around a huge bite of fresh bread. He pointed to the door, swallowed, and whispered, "Someone's out there. I thought I heard the latch stir just a bit. You'd better go out and see who it is."

Brak's heart stopped cold. He crept to the door and extended one bloodless hand to open it a cautious crack. The door lurched inward as if pushed, and Brak leaped back with a muffled screech of horror. Something fell across the threshold almost at his feet, something dreadfully similar to a dead body. Pehr began shouting, but Brak had closed his ears and eyes to the terror of it and could only stare at the creature sprawling so wretchedly at his feet.

Pehr hobbled across the tiny room and hauled the body inside and slammed the door. "What a nithling you are, Brak! Leaving the door open for anybody to see the light! Now let's see what we've got here."

Brak shuddered. "Some unlucky beggar has died right at our door. It must be a warning." With great reluctance, he looked on as Pehr unwrapped the rags and shawls the poor fellow was dressed in.

"Wet through," Pehr said, "and it's cold out there. He's nearly frozen to death. We'll let him thaw a while beside the fire and see if he's alive or dead."

Brak unwillingly helped loosen the last shawl around the beggar's head and face, uncovering a face as white and unresponsive as marble. "Pehr!" he gasped. "It's Ingvold! She's not dead, is she?"

"It would spare us a lot of trouble if she were," Pehr

said. "I think we've gone somewhat beyond our usual style in mischief this time, Brak. Now that we've found her, what shall we do with her? If we try to take her back with us, Myrkjartan will find her again. She's still a hag, you recall, and that's bound to be inconvenient sooner or later."

"We'll take her to the aunt she mentioned—if she wasn't making that up. She ought to be safe there."

"Then it ought to be a safe place for us, too," Pehr said. "I only hope it doesn't take longer than Thorsten will be gone to settle this business. The old fire-breather will be mad enough as it is."

"I could go on alone, since I'm nobody important," Brak suggested.

"And leave you to do all the boasting? Never!"

Brak watched Ingvold anxiously through the night, long after Pehr had succumbed to sleep. Ingvold showed no signs of life. Solicitously, Brak dried her wet clothing and shoes, giving her his own eider for warmth. She was wetter than the sprinkling of rain merited, but her clothing was poor and worn out and was certainly no match for the tightly woven oily wool of Brak's and Pehr's cloaks. Brak was relieved to see her breathing slightly but steadily, and rejoiced in the coincidence that had placed him and Pehr in the hermit's hut before her, or she might have died during the cold and wet night in an empty ruin.

Near dawn he fell asleep, awakening with a jolt when sunlight suddenly flashed across his eyes. The door was open, and Ingvold was poised for flight on the threshold with her meager bundle in hand. Brak leaped up and raced after her as she darted away.

"Ingvold! Wait! We've been trying to find you for days! You'll never make it alone and with so little, and Myrkjartan has marked us anyway, so you may as well wait a moment for us to go with you."

She halted and turned. "Then I've already brought your doom upon you, if Myrkjartan has discovered you followed me. All I can do now is lead him away from you and hope he'll content himself with my death. A pinnacle or a crevice, somewhere steep so I can throw myself down. If you hadn't saved me last night, that would have been the end of it all." She shook her head wearily and leaned against the hut as if her knees were still weak.

"A plague on that kind of talk," Brak said indignantly. "I think you'd better have some breakfast and rest until you feel stronger. Then we shall all go and see your aunt near Hafthorrsstead."

Ingvold looked startled, then she smiled. "How did you find out about my aunt? Was it from the old man who lives alone on the fell? I fear I didn't fool him much. He has clear sight into the Alfar realm, I'd wager. Did you mention breakfast a moment ago, by the way?"

Brak gladly began putting together a wonderfully incongruent breakfast for her of cold soup, dried fish, and some strong spirits from a flask. He slapped the dried fish on a slab of bread, garnished generously with brown drippings of fat. "There, now, I hope that will last you until midday, when we can stop and eat something more substantial. I think this would be a good time to make some plans so we'll know whether to ration our food, or whether or not to reprovision as soon as we can. Pehr has a fair amount of gold, and I've got a bit, so I believe we can manage for a while, depending upon how long a journey we must make. We have two horses, and Pehr has an excellent sword besides several knives. You need better clothes if we're to make a long journey, and another horse would be welcome—"

Ingvold watched him, shaking her head. Swallowing, she said, "It's impossible, of course. You can't come with me where I'm going, although I am honored by your loyalty. It would be much safer for me to lead Myrkjartan away from you—but then again, without me to protect you, you might be easy prey for him. I'll ask my aunt Hrodney what to do with you."

"We want to help you get rid of this curse," Brak said. "And what about Dyrstyggr? Can you find him all by yourself? You'll need someone to stand guard while you sleep, someone to cook your food, or catch and kill it when necessary. You'll need someone to talk to when it gets lonely."

Ingvold ate in stubborn silence for some time. Then she shrugged. "My realm is not a good place. I don't think Sciplings could survive there for very long. What does Pehr want to do? I can't imagine he'd want to do much traveling with a hag who has nearly ruined his feet."

"He's in perfect agreement with me." Brak hurriedly gave Pehr a shake, hardly daring to turn his back on Ingvold lest she try to disappear again.

Pehr awoke with the customary groans and yawns, as if the night were scarcely long enough for all the sleep he needed. "I thought you might die during the night," he greeted her. "Finding you has been nothing but trouble from the very beginning at Katla's house. I hope if you have another inclination to go riding by midnight you'll stay away from me." He kept a wary distance from her as he helped himself to the breakfast preparations. "In the Quarter my father rules, hags are burned alive or thrown into crevices in the ice."

Ingvold inclined her head. "In my realm, hags are bound and staked down in a bog to prevent their draugar from walking. Perhaps worse, wizards often try to cure them, sometimes successfully, most fatally. For that reason I dare not return to my friends and family in Snowfell and submit to the horrors of a cure. Far better to die by my own choosing as an outlaw and an outcast from my own people."

"Let's not dwell on death, shall we?" Pehr growled. "It seems to me you have an obligation to us to get Myrkjartan off our necks somehow, and dying isn't exactly going to help any of us."

Ingvold rose impatiently to stalk around the tiny room. "I didn't injure you purposely, I assure you, or willingly. I offer you my apology and I hope you'll accept it, because I won't offer it again. I also offer you a bit of this salve I carry, which will make your wounds feel much better."

"Oh, that's all right, I'll survive," Pehr said hastily as she drew a small blue vial from a pouch on her belt. "Your apology is accepted, I promise. You don't have to put yourself out."

"But I insist. I meant to give you some, but it was such a good opportunity to run away from Katla that I couldn't resist. Now sit down and take off those bandages and put them in the fire."

Pehr's blisters and abrasions, unwrapped, revealed a loathsome red aspect and considerable swelling that must have been getting more painful by the day. Ingvold gently applied the colorless ointment, and Pehr tried to look as if it didn't hurt. "It's not serious," he said gruffly. "I don't know why you want to make such a fuss—except you do owe us a few favors."

"Yes, but I don't think taking you with me is any favor to you," Ingvold replied, corking her vial and putting it away.

"Well, you'd better not leave us," Pehr said. "We know enough of what's going on that Myrkjartan and Hjordis want us out of the way, so you've got to take us to some place safe until your wars are done with. It still seems strange to me that a scrawny little girl could know anything important enough to end a war. Why can't you just tell the right people and end it then and there?"

Ingvold sighed in exasperation. "Do you think they'd believe me any quicker than you would? They'd lock me up instantly and start their cure, which I doubt I would survive."

"Tell them where Dyrstyggr is," Brak suggested, but Ingvold shook her head furiously.

"You Sciplings don't understand. Dyrstyggr isn't just sitting in a cave somewhere, waiting to be found. Myrkjartan has concealed him, using magic. What magic has concealed, only magic will reveal."

"There must be plenty of wizards in Snowfell," Pehr said.

"But none who have this." She removed the chain from her neck and showed them the gold box it carried. Brak stared at the workmanship, which was a design of intertwining serpents and symbols he had never seen. "The necklace itself is nothing. What matters is what this little case contains. It is a dragon's heart, given as a gift of friendship to my father by Dyrstyggr after the last wars where they fought together. It has been in my father's keeping for many years, and now I am the last of the family, so I am obliged to carry it and use it when necessary. Before he died, my father gave it to me and warned me that I might have to use it against Myrkjartan and Hjordis. The draugar had been stalking and destroying the hill forts, drawing closer to Snowfell each night; then one night they came to Gljodmalborg. I alone escaped, with this last gift from my father. It is, or once was, the remains of a dragon's heart, which entitles its bearer to guidance from the Rhbus. In this way, I shall find Dyrstyggr and free him, and he will destroy Myrkjartan and Hjordis before they destroy the Ljosalfar."

"Why didn't you do it earlier?" Pehr demanded. "Escaping from Katla wasn't that hard, was it? And who are these Rhbus of yours? Relatives? Wizards? Gods?"

"Don't be ridiculous. Nobody talks about the Rhbus that way," Ingvold snapped. "The name means 'dextcrous and shining.' They are the keepers of all Alfar magic and knowledge, and very few common Alfar ever speak with them."

"Then why don't they solve your problem with Dyrstyggr, if they know so much?" Pehr asked.

Ingvold whirled around. "It's not so simple, you simpleton. If they did everything for us, what would we become?"

"But what are they good for if they just sit in a cave somewhere with all their precious knowledge heaped up around their ears? Do they hoard it like old misers, or do they pass out dragons' hearts like name-day presents? It seems to me that if they're so powerful, they ought to be worrying about Dyrstyggr and Myrkjartan and Hjordis, not a puny little girl who would fly away in a puff of wind." Pehr glared at Ingvold, who was getting angrier by the minute.

"You don't understand the Alfar!" Ingvold retorted. "Nor any of our ways. We believe in choosing for ourselves, so the Rhbus keep out of the way. It's quite plain to me that I could never take you into my realm, so the best thing to do is for me to lead Myrkjartan away from you for now, and as soon as I can, I'll send someone to help you. Perhaps the old man on the fell can hide you. The high places, you know, are safe places." She picked up her bundle and started toward the door. "I hope your feet are feeling better soon."

Pehr only grunted and attempted to stalk away, limping sorely. Then he looked at his feet. In place of the ugly, running blisters was pink, healthy skin. He gave a shout of astonishment and began to prance around in delight. "It must be magic!" he yelled. "Beautiful, glorious magic! I'm cured! They don't hurt in the least!"

Brak darted after Ingvold. She stopped and glanced at him. "You'll never give up, will you, Brak? I think you'd be safer with the old man on the fell than by coming with me. It would be so easy for you to be killed in my realm."

Brak shook his head. "You need us, whether you know it or not. My life in Thorstensstead is nothing of any great significance anyway. Why don't you persuade Pehr to start packing our things while I saddle the horses? We'll be ready to go in almost no time."

"Well—all right, just for a while. As soon as we reach a safe place for you to stay, I'll go on alone."

Brak had no time to agree or protest; Pehr came stamping out of the hut in the new boots he had purchased from a traveler at Vigfusstead.

"Splendid boots, aren't they?" he greeted them. "I'd begun to wonder if I'd ever wear them. Ingvold, I thank you and your magic salve for restoring my feet. You've certainly convinced me that I was wrong before, and a great many other Sciplings are wrong, too, for not believing in magic. Wouldn't my father Thorsten be amazed if we could show him how Ingvold's potion works?"

"No more amazed than I," Ingvold said, "if anything could induce me to stay in a realm where no magic was practiced."

When they were ready to depart, Brak insisted that Ingvold ride Faxi, while he walked behind, helped along by an occasional pull from Faxi's long tail. Ingvold insisted upon taking turns so that Brak wouldn't have to walk all day, but since she was still weak, it was Pehr who had to walk. He did a lot of grumbling and growling about it, and Brak knew it was his place to walk while his chieftain rode, but Ingvold loftily informed them that in the Alfar realm no one was too good not to walk.

They camped that night in a shallow cave behind a screen of water cascading down the face of the rock. Ingvold passed the time by telling them about her realm and people and showing them a few elementary tricks, such as moving inanimate objects, lighting fires with a spell, and finding small objects which Brak would hide from her.

"Just childish tricks," she said with a shrug, nodding a stick of wood into the fire. "Every Alfar is born with a few skills. It takes years of education to get really good at anything, and I was taken away before I could get started."

"But about these wars with the draugar," Pehr persisted,

never satisfied with what Ingvold told him. "What started the Dark Alfar fighting against the Light Alfar, and how long has it been going on?"

Ingvold explained that the exact history of the wars was lost in the mists of magic itself, and that the forces of light and dark had always vied for power over all of Skarpsey. The Dark Alfar chose to use the dark powers of necromancy and evil and fear to gain control. Allied with the Dark Alfar were trolls, giants, and various clans of white or brown dwarves. The black dwarves, superior craftsmen and dedicated fighters, were usually loyal to Elbegast of the Light Alfar, or Ljosalfar. For centuries the Ljosalfar had held their own, which was all of Skarpsey that the sun touched, and the Dokkalfar and other evil creatures moiled around below the earth, digging mines and tunnels and waiting for darkness to do their skulking above. During the winter months, when the sun lost its strength and scarcely showed itself over the horizon, the evil powers waxed stronger and worked cunning schemes to overthrow their enemies.

"But why?" Brak inquired. "Isn't there room for everyone, above and below Skarpsey?"

"Certainly, but the Dokkalfar want to destroy us and our beliefs because they know we're right. If they eliminate us, then they'll be the only ones here and can feel right about the way they kill and torture and steal from each other. They are so horrible and utterly vile that in time they'd destroy themselves for lack of anyone else to victimize. Their magic is the dark, evil kind, like necromancy and the communion with the dead. Their power comes from past evil done by their ancient ancestors. They have unholy rings and barrows where they invoke their horrible curses and spells. Our magic places, on the other hand, are always high in the fells, as close to the sun as we can get. With so much evil in Skarpsey, the ancient Ljosalfar set stones to mark the safe paths from one place to the next—although the ley-lines have fallen into much disrepair. The ancients used their stone circles for studying the heavens, but no one knows much about that science anymore. Sometimes the sites of the great stones are filled with such power that you can learn the answers to important questions and the secrets of past and future, and all without the use of necromancy. Myrkjartan has a ring which he puts under the tongue of a corpse which forces it to speak of the future."

Brak shuddered and advanced his toes a bit toward the fire. "Necromancy doesn't sound like a pleasant trade at all to me. Nor do I fancy those draugar you told us about, killed one day and alive the next, like no decent corpse ever was."

"I'm glad they're not in this realm," Pehr said, looking around him distrustfully.

"Yet, that is," Ingvold added, stirring the old patched pot they had salvaged from Gnupa's hut. "Your safe and smug Scipling realm wouldn't stay that way for long once Myrkjartan turned his covetous eyes on it. Have you heard of the Fimbul Winter, when the sun dies and the ice and bitter darkness cover the land?"

"We've heard legends about it," Pehr admitted.

"Myrkjartan and the other wizards would cast spells to cause the Fimbul Winter to return," Ingvold said. "To all realms, ice is ice and dark is dark."

"And death is death," Brak added.

"It's just a legend, isn't it?" Pehr said hopefully.

"If it is, it has been around Skarpsey for a long time— much longer than you Sciplings have been here."

Pehr answered with a huffy snort, as he always did when Ingvold reminded him that there were things the Sciplings didn't know about. The idea that the busy sea traders and sheep farmers were a comparatively recent development was particularly disturbing.

On the third day of their travels eastward they stopped beside an upright stone which Ingvold declared to be one of the stones set in the ley-lines by her ancient ancestors. She greeted it with pleasure and pointed out some pockmarks on one side which might have been carving at some long-ago time.

"This is a safe place," she said, slipping off Faxi to look around at the bleak landscape surrounding the hill they stood on. "This stone was brought from a very far place to be put here. You can see there are no other white stones nearby."

Pehr walked around the stone, studying it. "Why, it must

weigh thousands of pounds. It would take a hundred horses to drag it up here. As for standing it upright—"

"But that's only if you use horses and muscles to move it," Ingvold said, tracing the pockmarks with her finger. "I'm sure you know by now that there are other ways of moving things. Have you a piece of string, Brak?"

Brak felt in his pockets and produced a short piece of string he had twisted from milkweed fibers for something to do as he walked along. Ingvold bound one end around a pebble and began to dowse, testing several directions before pointing to the east. The rough pendulum was gyrating in tight circles. "That's the way to Hrodney's house. Hafthorrsstead is right along the way, which is a good place to stop for the night."

Pehr began to protest at once, but Ingvold interrupted, "Dowsing is so simple that Sciplings can do it, especially for water. Springs underground have a great deal of power, which may be the reason so many of our old lines cross over underground water. Brak, watch for smaller white mark-stones placed along the line to guide us."

The mark-stones led them to a single small hill and from there to a notch in the skyline of a large fell. Ingvold confidently told them that the notch had been cut by hands as another guidepost along the line. Pehr looked around bleakly and shook his head. "I think we're lost," he declared. The faint trace of a road had vanished long before.

"Nonsense," Ingvold replied, and led them down the fell into a misty, sulfurous valley where hot springs and geysers played their peculiar tricks. They stopped once for a swim in a large pool that was exactly the right temperature for bathing. By the time they had crossed the steaming, sinister place, the afternoon was far advanced. Ingvold led the way confidently, bending their course slightly to the south, while Pehr fussed over his sketchy map and wondered how they would ever find themselves again.

"We'll be there easily by supper time," Ingvold insisted.

Pehr looked doubtfully at the pebble on the end of the string and shook his head with a long, weary sigh. "Rocks," he grumbled. "Mere rocks."

They crossed two more fells, and the twilight began to deepen into the silvery light that lingered through much

of the short northern night. It was the best possible light
for Hafthorrsstead, which lay below them in neat diagrams.
Lush green hay tuns surrounded the old black house, and
flocks of sheep grazed on the opposite fell like drifting
clouds on a shadowy sea. Ingvold did not even pretend to
be anything less than smug.

Hafthorr himself was waiting to meet them when they
rode up to the house, as if he had been expecting them.
He was a short, stout fellow with a fierce beard of mingled
red and silver and a sly, twinkling eye.

"There you are at last, three strangers wandering alone
in the barrens of Skarpsey," he boomed, shaking them by
the hands as they alighted. "Are you lost, strayed, or stolen
from the comfortable roads of the Sciplings? This is not
a place where people ride up unawares. However it is,
you may make yourselves welcome for as long as you
like; there's plenty of room and plenty of food."

"Thank you," Pehr said graciously, taking it upon himself
to conduct the introductions of himself and his companions.
"We're traveling to the house of Ingvold's relatives who
live not far from here, so we won't trouble you by staying
more than just the night."

Hafthorr raised one shaggy rusty eyebrow. "Relatives,
eh? I was under the impression that we didn't have any
neighbors around here. Come inside the house and sit down
and refresh yourselves before we do any serious talking."

Ingvold shot Pehr a sharp look and signaled him to be
quiet as they followed Hafthorr into his house. It was a
pleasantly dark and smoky place, filled with tables and
benches as if Hafthorr's family were very large indeed. Six
burly fellows were already there, resting their elbows on
one table and talking together, and more were coming in.
Brak finally counted twelve youngish men and seven
graybeards, including Hafthorr. Nine women served the
dinner and took their seats on the dais at the end of the hall.

"We don't get many visitors here," Hafthorr said when
the eating was finished and the drinking under way. "In
fact, those who arrive here often decide to stay on in-
definitely. Others find the air somehow hostile and have
been known to die of strange complaints. Usually, when
we want to deal with the settlements, we send a pack train
and do our trading and selling or finding a wife for one of

my sons. But we prefer to live here in peace by ourselves, and that depends upon preventing our enemies from running back to the settlements to talk about what they found here."

Brak understood at once when he was being threatened. Ingvold began chattering blandly about sheep and wool and other nonsense while the cold perspiration trickled down Brak's spine. It was most likely that Hafthorr and his sons, as he called them, were all outlaws and very desperate men. Skarpsey was known as a haven for outlaws, who lost themselves in its hostile interior and seldom survived the term of their banishment. Hafthorr had found a hospitable place, however, and had made a home for other outcasts like himself. Their continued existence, of course, depended upon secrecy.

"You say you are traveling to the girl's relatives?" Hafthorr questioned gently, paring his nails with a sharp little knife. When Pehr nodded warily, he sighed deeply and shook his head. "That is most unfortunate. I fear you're not telling us the entire truth. My son Tostig was at Vapnaford yesterday, and a fellow there was looking for three young runaways, two lads and a girl. He seemed to know a lot about you and said you were bound to him for eight years each. I hope we haven't caught you in a lie, my young friends. Those who come lying and sneaking to this house for no good reason usually come to no good end." He flashed the little knife in the firelight.

The other outlaws listened with smiling politeness. They wore their weapons casually, as if knife and sword were everyday attire and meant to be used at any moment.

"Was it an old fellow in a black cloak?" Ingvold asked. "And did he ride a gray horse?"

Tostig nodded. "You know him, then!"

"Know him!" Pehr exclaimed. "He's no friend of ours. In fact, we're doing our best to get away from him."

"Aha! Runaway thralls!" Tostig declared. "Just as I suspected!"

"Thralls! Us?" Pehr glared indignantly, but his temper cooled as he realized no one would believe him, since they all looked rather rough and dirty from sleeping on the ground for several nights.

Hafthorr scowled. "In the morning we'll take you back

to your master, where you belong. I hope you'll learn a lesson from this misadventure, you young vagabonds, and never try to escape your duties again, or, by the bones of Thor's goats, you'll have old Hafthorr to answer to." He glared ferociously, and Brak wished he could shrivel himself completely out of sight.

Pehr looked at Brak and made covert signs for Brak to say something. Brak could barely swallow, but at last he found the courage to clear his throat with a nervous cough. "So you're going to send us back to—to the old man at Vapnaford? Tomorrow, I suppose?"

Hafthorr nodded his head emphatically. "You'll all thank me for it one day when you realize how truly generous I'm being. And since you don't look as if you appreciate the idea and may be entertaining more notions of running away again, I'm going to lock all of you in the kitchen tonight. Ha, we'll see if you're clever enough to escape from clever escapers like ourselves."

Chapter 5

❖❖❖❖❖❖❖❖❖❖❖❖❖❖❖❖❖❖❖❖❖❖❖❖

Brak looked at Ingvold, but she was busily using her bread to capture the last of the drippings on her plate. "But let us explain," he protested in a voice that threatened to quaver at any instant. "This man in the black cloak is no friend or master of ours. I'm sure you think we're lying, but he's an enemy who wishes to do us—he wants to kill us, is what I'm trying to say."

"And so would I if my thralls all ran away from me," Hafthorr replied indignantly. He waggled his knife in Brak's face. "I can tell you're one of those fellows who is afraid of work. Lazy, that's what you are, and if you belonged to me, I'd soon set you straight with short rations and long hours of hard work. You'd thank me for it later, I'm sure you would. Work is a man's friend, young fellow, and the sooner you learn it, the better off you'll be."

Brak did not dare utter another word. He shrank back as Hafthorr forcibly stabbed another potato off the platter, bestowing a fierce glare upon his three guests.

"Now see here, you don't understand," Pehr began to bluster. "My father is—" He quailed suddenly under the united scowls of the outlaws.

"Probably very angry, too, at you for running away," Tostig finished. "Nothing is worse than the crime of ingratitude in a person of your low position. You owe your master for every bite of bread you eat and for every fire where you warm your ungrateful backside. You owe him everything."

"Oh, bother on the lot of you," Ingvold said rudely, and Brak was so shocked he couldn't help making a loud gasp of fright. Ingvold faced the circle of disapproving scowls. "You've all had your sport with frightening us, so you can stop threatening to send us back to Myrkjartan. Tostig, you're a clever storyteller, but I simply don't believe you carried on such a cozy chat with Myrkjartan, or he probably would have cut your throat on the spot. We're not runaway Scipling thralls, and if you hadn't begun to badger us so soon, we might have told you earlier who we really are. I must add, if you fellows plan to continue posing as Scipling outlaws, it would be wise to avoid passing the meat without touching the platter, winking at the ale to pour it, and lighting pipes without coals. I assure you, real Sciplings would be highly astonished if they could perform such feats."

Hafthorr's face underwent a series of changes, finally arriving at a merry grin. He shrugged apologetically, and the rest of the supposed outlaws gaped at Ingvold in guilty astonishment or chuckled at Hafthorr.

"Do you mean these aren't real outlaws?" Pehr demanded, glaring around the table.

Tostig shifted uncomfortably, squinting at Ingvold. "Tell us first who this relative is you're traveling to see," he commanded.

"My aunt Hrodney, who lives east of here," Ingvold retorted.

Hafthorr said, "One of our own kind has penetrated our disguise. If she knows our aunt Hrodney, that means we are relatives also."

"You must belong to a rather large family," Brak said, still feeling weak from his past fright, and very glad to see the men at the table relaxing their hostile appearances.

"Then you're all Alfar and not outlaws?" Pehr scowled in puzzlement, as if trying to decide if someone was making sport of him, which he more than halfway suspected.

Hafthorr chuckled, once more genial. "Now you've got it. For a Scipling, you're more than half sharp."

"But what are you doing here?" Pehr persisted doggedly. "This is the Scipling realm, isn't it?"

The mead was going around again, with much laughing and talking. Hafthorr answered, "Hafthorsstead is an Alfar outpost. We're here merely to observe things that come and go and to put a spoke in Myrkjartan's wheel if we can do it prudently. Since we've lost so many hill forts to the east, Hjordis has been creeping into the Scipling realm. I wouldn't be surprised if there are dozens of Dokkalfar poking and prying and spying around the main halls of the Sciplings to see how rich they are, and whether they'll fight very hard for their hold on this troublesome island, and how many armies they have."

Pehr slapped his sword and exclaimed, "Well, I'll fight the Dark Alfar for Thorstensstead! I'm supposed to be the next chieftain there, and it shall be mine if I have to wrestle it from Myrkjartan himself."

"That may be exactly what you'll have to do if these draugar keep fighting," someone said dolefully. "Hark at that wind! I hope the livestock are secure."

At that moment a gust of wind came shrieking down the fell, rushing across the hay meadows to whistle around the corners of the stables before pouncing upon the house. It rattled the shutters on the windows and tried to draw the fire up the chimney with a whistling roar.

"The Myrkriddir!" Brak gasped. "They've found us again!"

The Alfar quickly drained their cups and began inspecting their weapons. Tostig and Hafthorr exchanged a glance.

Tostig leaned across the table to eye Brak, who was pale and obviously on the point of diving under the table. "Now what would the Myrkriddir of Myrkjartan be wanting with the likes of you, my fine fellow?"

"Never you mind about Brak and Pehr," Ingvold snapped. "I'm taking them to Hrodney, and you need know nothing more."

"High and mighty, aren't we?" Tostig cried. "Are you a princess or a chieftain's daughter, to order us around like that? You don't pass very well as a servant girl with that haughty voice and your dainty little nose in the air. Why don't you tell us who you really are?"

Ingvold was about to reply angrily when a thunder of hooves came sweeping toward the house. Gathering storm clouds had blackened the twilight sky, and the wind was chilly and restless. Brak flinched at the sudden stab of lightning that bathed the hay meadows in shuddering white and illuminated the flying mass of horsemen pounding toward the house. Brak had only a horrified, momentary glimpse of spectral faces, bare, gleaming bone, and tatters of cloth before the horsemen were upon them. Hooves clattered on the roof of the porch and drummed across the turf roof. Brak cringed from the enormity of such a stunt, and Pehr, ducking under the table, indignantly exclaimed, "That's impossible! They can't do that!" He sneezed at the dust sifting down from the turves overhead.

The Alfar dived into their positions beside the windows and began fitting arrows into their bows. Hafthorr showed his guests where to conceal themselves and bent a last lowering glance upon Ingvold. "Either you're a very important person, or you've done something dreadfully stupid to get the Myrkriddir after you. Myrkjartan isn't far behind them, usually, and Myrkjartan doesn't waste his time pursuing things of no importance to him."

"Myrkjartan—bah!" was all Ingvold could say before the Myrkriddir made another rush at the house. Hafthorr shot an arrow into their midst in a glowing, sizzling arc, and its flight was followed by an unearthly shriek. One of the Myrkriddir burst into flame like a torch, its matted hair ablaze and grave clothes flying away in flaming tatters. In a moment the white bones blackened and the creature disintegrated. Frantically, the other Myrkriddir beat at the gleaming bits of burning rag and hair, plunging their ragged horses in all directions to avoid catching themselves on fire. With a chorus of wails and howls they galloped away, climbing into the sky like a mass of rolling thunderclouds.

"A good shot, Hafthorr," someone said, and the others rumbled in agreement.

"It's not over with yet," Hafthorr said, scowling through the crack between the shutters. "The house-riders didn't go far." He had scarcely spoken when they again heard the pounding of hooves. The Alfar were drawing their bows as a huge gust of wind struck the house with an icy blast that frosted the beards and numbed the fingers of everyone inside. The Myrkriddir rode onto the porch, and the door shuddered under heavy blows. After an instant to recover, the Alfar began shooting arrows into the porch, igniting three Myrkriddir and their horses. Brak had never heard such unearthly shrieks, and the flames billowed forth clouds of black, stinking smoke that threatened to make him sick. He crawled further under the table where he was hiding, which was fortunate for him. In the next instant a bolt of ice burst through a window, shattering the wood and overturning a barricade of tables and benches, sending the Alfar defenders scuttling for cover. Splinters of ice exploded into the hall, wounding two Alfar.

Brak tumbled into the shelter of a large carved chest, with Ingvold close behind him. Pehr was somewhere in the hall with the fighters, trying to persuade someone to give him a bow and some arrows.

"I feel like such a nithling," Brak muttered, "but I don't know the first thing about fighting. Perhaps I could hit something by accident if I weren't such a coward."

"You come with me," Ingvold said. "We can help the injured more than we can harm the attackers. Don't cut yourself on the ice; it makes a very nasty gash which will not heal without magic."

They slithered toward the two wounded Alfar, stretched out stiff and cold. Brak gingerly touched the wounded flesh and realized it was frozen hard. Ingvold examined the victim quickly and thoroughly. "This one's done for, poor fellow. The ice was too near his heart. Come on, Brak, I need your help." The other Alfar was alive, but his skin was turning cold and blue. Ingvold gouged the ice from his arm with a sharp little knife and poured a few drops from her blue vial into the wound. The man grimaced and growled, but in a few minutes the blue pallor vanished and he was gathering up his bow and arrows to return to the fight without expressing any amazement or curiosity that such a miraculous recovery could be effected. Brak continued to sit and stare at the fellow until Ingvold summoned him impatiently to help another warrior who had just caught a needle of ice in the shoulder. Brak scuttled after her, slipping on the green, slimy residue of a melted ice bolt.

Before long the Myrkriddir again turned and took to the air, after four arrows claimed four Myrkriddir in fiery destruction and a fifth was struck down with a stout staff as they were leaving. The creature dropped on the front steps of the wide porch, a tangled heap of old bones held together with dried bits of leathery skin and covered with rotten clothing and straggling hair—much like a corpse removed from a peat bog.

"Are they gone?" Pehr's voice asked. Someone had finally loaned him a bow and arrows, ordinary ones made of wood and fletched with gray feathers. Although the weapons looked much the same as any Scipling's, in the hands of the Alfar the arrows glowed with light and never missed their mark unless a counterforce repelled them.

In the silence outside, a single horse approached the hall at a nervous walk. "Halloo, Hafthorr," a deep voice called. "Let's talk."

Hafthorr peered through the crack. "Is it you, Myrkjartan? What do you mean by attacking our outpost for no reason? With one of my men dead and others wounded, I'm not much willing to chitchat. Speak your piece and begone, necromancer."

"You know what I'm looking for. Tostig heard me at Vapnaford. Send out the girl and the two Sciplings and we'll never set hoof upon Hafthorrsstead again."

Hafthorr eyed his three guests speculatively. "Did you hear that? He wants the three of you. Whatever have you done to antagonize him so thoroughly?"

Ingvold gathered her ragged cloak around her. "You can send me out if you wish; I'm sure he'll forget Brak and

Pehr if he has me. I'll go willingly, if someone will unbar the door."

"No! Don't let her!" Brak gasped in horror. "It will mean the doom of Snowfell! It won't help at all; she was sick several nights ago and doesn't know what she's saying."

Hafthorr shook his head and scowled. "I've never given up any guest of mine to our enemies yet and I won't start now, but I'd certainly like to know—"

"Hafthorr!" Myrkjartan's voice thundered. "Do you know what you are sheltering under your roof? The girl has a curse which Hjordis placed upon her. The girl is a hag, Hafthorr, and she'll lead your house to grief if you keep her. Surrender her to us who have a claim upon her and be thankful her curse will never visit your house. You may keep the Sciplings if you wish, and their doom will arrive in its own time when Hjordis has swept the Ljosalfar from both realms."

Hafthorr stared at Ingvold. "A hag?" he rasped. "I don't believe it. I can't believe it. You're only a young girl and clever, like my own little daughter. How could you do anything so evil and dangerous? It's not true, is it? Myrkjartan must be lying, isn't he?"

"No, he's telling the truth," Ingvold said. "You'd better send me out, or you'll suffer the next time the moon is full. Myrkjartan won't let me leave here, now he's found me. Unbar the door before the consequences become more serious." The house shivered as a blast exploded high overhead, showering the roof with shards of ice and a spume of foul-smelling mist, worse than the breath of the rankest barrow.

Some of the Alfar were nodding and others were disagreeing. Hafthorr gave his shaggy beard a rough shaking and declared, "Nonsense. Don't be absurd, child. Myrkjartan be blasted and burned, even if you won't tell me who you are and what this is all about."

Ingvold stiffened her thin shoulders. "Very well, I'll tell you. My father was Thjodmar, and I am the only survivor of Gljodmalborg. What Myrkjartan wants from me is this." She touched the chain at her throat. "Thjodmar's last gift to me. He foresaw that I would survive to use it against Hjordis and Myrkjartan. But I have no intention of drawing innocent people into my quarrels with the dark powers. I commission you to take these Sciplings to Hrodney—"

"Hafthorr!" came a shout, and another blast shook dust from the roof in a shower. "Have you made up your mind, or will you wait until your house falls down around you? Send out the girl, or the next blast won't be so kind!"

Hafthorr opened a window cautiously, then bellowed, "Yes, I've made up my mind, Myrkjartan, and here is your answer!" He hurled his lance with all his might, adding a spell to guide it on its way. It gleamed like a red sliver of fire and exploded as Myrkjartan raised his fist and countered it. The white flash of light revealed a plunging mass of startled horses and spectral riders flinching away from the heat and flame. For a moment Myrkjartan's solitary figure blazed against the night before the darkness covered him.

A ferocious icy blast tore at the house, snatching everyone's breath away and riming every crack with frost. It was colder than the worst winter blizzard. A second, even stronger blast followed it, shattering the wood covering one window, and a portion of the weakened roof began to collapse.

"We can't survive much more of this," Brak gasped to Pehr, trying to protect himself with his cloak, but it might as well have been cobwebs for all the good it did him. Another blast caused the roof to crumble alarmingly, showering half the room with bits of turf and clouds of dust. When the dust cleared, and Brak had stopped choking, he looked around for Ingvold. She was no longer beside him, and he didn't see her anywhere in the wrecked hall. Worse yet, he discovered her dragon's heart in his pocket. He hid it quickly.

"Ingvold?" he called. "Pehr, I think she's gone!"

"What? You were supposed to be watching her." Pehr did not emerge from his safe niche between the chest and the wall.

"Gone! By all the fleas in Loki's cloak!" Hafthorr glared out into the darkness. "It was her fylgja that ran right across my back and out the window—a little white fox with a black tip on its tail. Confusticate her for a willful child! She can't survive out there alone." He made a move toward the window, but Tostig grabbed his arm.

"It's too late. Listen to them; they've seen her!"

The Myrkriddir broke into a wild cry, like a pack of hunting hounds with their quarry in view. Brak covered his ears, not caring if he looked like a nithling.

Hafthorr clapped him on the back comfortingly, growling, "Don't worry about her, lad. With a fox for a fylgja, she'll be clever enough to escape them. They haven't a chance of catching such a small, quick creature, and she knows it. This will give us the opportunity to take you to Hrodney."

"Perhaps she'll be waiting for us there," Brak said.

"I don't understand about foxes and fylgur," Pehr declared. "Do you mean to tell us Ingvold has changed herself into a real fox—four legs, tail, ears, and whiskers?"

Tostig and several others stared at Pehr. "Do you mean you can't?" one fellow inquired incredulously.

Tostig elbowed him out of the way and said, "Certainly not, you dolt, and it's rude of you to discuss it. The Sciplings have no fylgur, and they don't seem to miss them in the least."

"But how is it possible—" Pehr began, glowering around for an explanation or a twinkle in someone's eye to prove that it was all a joke at his expense.

"Never mind, Pehr," Brak said anxiously. "I'll tell you what I know about it later. Really, you're frightfully dense sometimes!"

The Myrkriddir did not reappear that night. Brak thought he would never sleep, so he sat beside the fire, nodding and starting awake at the least puff of wind in the chimney or the creaking of a roof timber. In the morning the ruin of the hall looked less sinister, and a large breakfast restored his spirits from a state of stark terror to a condition of pugnacious anxiety. He was impatient to get started, and even old Faxi was not content anywhere else but right at the heels of Hafthorr's horse, where he administered judicious nips to encourage it to hurry.

They hadn't traveled long before they once again discovered the ley-line, heading directly east. It was plainly marked and seemed to be well traveled enough that it merited a faint path. Hafthorr and the three men accompanying him jogged along as if it were nothing but a pleasure ride, singing insulting scalds at one another like the best of friends.

At midday the path ended within view of a tiny hut backed against a towering rocky fell. Moss covered the little house so completely it might have gone unnoticed by any casual travelers passing that way, and there probably were almost none.

As they approached, they could see a straight old woman clad in black waiting for them. She wore a blue shawl over her head and carried a small basket to hold the herbs and moss she had been gathering.

"Good day to you, Hafthorr," she said with no particular friendliness as her eyes traveled over Pehr and Brak, not missing a detail. "I see you are traveling with strangers. Will you all light down for a bit of refreshment before going on your way?"

Gladly Hafthorr dismounted. "It's these young Sciplings who have some business for you," he said. "It's very astonishing and something of a puzzle to me, but I suspect those fellows are going to ask you to put them through the gate into the Alfar realm. If I were you, I'd want to know more about it before I—"

"Hafthorr—" Hrodney's calm gray gaze did not falter. "You are not me, so you may keep your advice to yourself. Will you walk in, or do you want to drink tea out here with the horses?"

Hafthorr and his men were polite and uncomfortable for the rest of their short visit. When a decent interval had passed, Hrodney dismissed them with a pointed suggestion that it was time they returned to Hafthorrsstead. With a last perplexed farewell to Pehr and Brak, Hafthorr went on his way, probably lamenting that his curiosity would have to go unsatisfied.

"Well, then." Hrodney again studied her guests, folding her arms across her spare stomach and narrowing her gaze. "Why should I risk my position and reputation by sending two Sciplings into a realm where they do not belong? A realm where they would probably perish quite shortly, and most unpleasantly."

Brak shrank back in his chair away from her hostile scrutiny. Pehr gave him a sharp nudge with his foot. Brak cleared his throat. "It's because—well, no doubt you remember a girl who passed your way last night. A skinny young girl with fair hair and a ragged gray cloak and an old pair of shoes. I have some property of hers to return to her—"

"Maybe I remember and maybe I don't," Hrodney interrupted. "Why do you want to catch her so badly? Did she do you some harm? Do you wish to do her harm? What is this property you wish to return to her?"

"Oh, no—I mean, yes, she did, but no, we don't wish to harm her, we want to help," Brak exclaimed. "She needs us, or very likely she'll fall under the thrall of Hjordis and Myrkjartan, or, worse yet, do away with her own life to prevent that from happening. She's the last survivor of Gljodmalborg, if that means anything to you." He pinched the case containing the dragon's heart, wondering if he should mention it.

Hrodney's bright, predatory gaze seemed to pierce right through him. "I expect that could mean something, depending upon the property you're talking about. It's reasonable that a chieftain's daughter would entrust a precious object to a thrall to keep it safe—a trustworthy, courageous thrall who doesn't care two sticks for Myrkjartan and Hjordis, and who would sooner die than give the object over to them."

Pehr looked from Hrodney to Brak with a suspicious scowl. "Wait a moment. Brak's not her thrall, he belongs to me. What's this object you're talking about?"

Hrodney ignored him. "You must go after her, of course, and return her property to her. I caution you not to trust anyone you meet, and you won't want to be captured by Myrkjartan or Hjordis while you are in possession of the dragon's heart."

"What dragon's heart?" Pehr demanded. "Brak, how could you ever consent to such a scheme? We only wanted a bit of protection from Myrkjartan and Hjordis, not to plunge into anything that wasn't our business. I can't risk my life gallivanting around in some invisible realm. I'm the heir to my father's chieftaincy, you might recall."

Hrodney fixed him with a stern glare. "I hope the passage of time will somewhat reduce your own good opinion of yourself, young man. It may astonish you to know that there are other concerns in Skarpsey besides one small chieftaincy along one bit of coastland. It's a pity you're not half as reasonable as this man you call your thrall."

"I never said I wouldn't go, if we must, but—"

"I've made my decision." She reached for a leather bag and began to fill it with the sausages hanging from her rafters. As she worked she talked. "Here's bread, cheese, sausages, grains for broth—" She continued until she had assembled a large mound of provisions and equipment they would be needing.

"Are you sure we should take all of that?" Pehr asked nervously. "I hadn't planned on being gone for any great time. My father is expecting me at the Thing, and if I disappear long enough to use all this—"

"All this and more before you pass this gate again," Hrodney said. "I'll see to it a message gets to your father that you're safe, although it will be an outright lie, of course, because you won't be safe for an instant in our realm. Now we're ready; we haven't forgotten anything, have we, Brak?"

Brak shook his head and sighed. "Only what we shall pay you for all this. You've gone far beyond the bounds of mere hospitality. Pehr has a bag with gold and silver, haven't you, Pehr? Pay her, and we'll be on our way." He was almost trembling, wondering why he wasn't trying to get out of such a mad scheme, as common sense and native cowardice dictated.

Pehr reached for his money pouch in confusion. "Wait a moment. Who's the chieftain and who's the retainer now? Not that I object, of course," he added when Hrodney gave him a scowl.

"I expect it will do you good to be a follower for once," Hrodney said sharply. "Put your money away and listen to me. I don't want any of it. What good is it to me in my situation? I am what you simple souls would call a witch. I can use spells to turn up gold in the earth or call it forth from the barrow mounds, so I have no need of any of yours. Now, then, you may pack all this lot upon your horses, and I'll take you to the place where your realm adjoins mine. I don't believe I've sent through more unlikely candidates, and I wouldn't do it for anyone but Thjodmarsdotter. She'll be watching for you, if she's not captured. She wouldn't have given you that heart if she hadn't known you'd follow her."

Pehr looked unpleasantly at Brak. "Yes, he's a precious

fool sometimes. I've seen him go miles and miles just to repay some tiddily debt to a person of absolutely no consequence. I only hope we'll find Ingvold and get back home again before my father is too frightfully enraged, but I don't have many hopes of that."

"Then send Brak alone," Hrodney said unfeelingly. "He'd come back more of a chieftain than you'd ever be." She stalked to the door and took up an old walking staff. "Are you brave fellows coming?"

Brak looked apologetically at Pehr and shouldered one of the saddle packs. "Come on, Pehr, don't put on your future-chieftain airs. It really doesn't matter now, does it?"

"I suppose not," Pehr retorted, grabbing up the other pouch and lugging it toward the door. "You can be the chieftain and I'll be the thrall, and when you get us into a greater mess than we can get out of alive, then it will be all your fault!"

Chapter 6

❖❖❖❖❖❖❖❖❖❖❖❖❖❖❖❖❖❖❖❖❖❖❖❖

Hrodney looked a long while at old Faxi and finally shook her head, muttering something about making troll-bait before three days. When the packs were tied on, she silently pointed toward the open, green hillside and motioned them to follow her, leading the horses.

Pehr hurried to catch up with her. "If you're a witch, you must know something about our future. I think it only fair that you tell us whatever you know, so we'll know what to expect. Which way do we go when we get there? How will we know where Ingvold has gone? How——"

"You ask too many questions. Why can't you be more

like your thrall, who knows that if a way is to be opened, the Rhbus will show it to you? A clever person can travel from one end of Skarpsey to the other without danger if he knows what he is about." Hrodney took a dowsing pendulum out of her pocket. "This is the way you shall find Ingvold and answer most of your useless questions."

"I'd prefer a good map," Pehr declared, glaring pointedly at Hrodney, who paid him no attention.

She guided them to a ring of stones standing on a green hilltop. Brak and Pehr led their horses after her. Brak was silent, but Pehr muttered under his breath and glowered at Brak as Hrodney directed them to stand in the center of the circle.

"You got us into this," he growled. "You'd better have some ideas for getting us out. I thought some of my scrapes were pretty bad, but this—"

Brak paid no attention. His eyes were fastened on the black figure at the edge of the ring, making signs with her hands and drawing runes in the dust. His heart pounded and his knees were quivering, until he had to lean against old Faxi for support.

Then the circle of stones seemed to vanish into a cloud of mist. Brak blinked his eyes, and the mist began to clear as a cold wind ripped it to shreds and flapped Brak's cloak in a chilling welcome. The stone circle and the comfortable green fells around Hrodney's house were gone, replaced by a rocky landscape that looked like rotten black bone, worn away by wind and time into eerie towers and spiny crags. Tough shrubs, mosses, and lichens scrabbled for survival in cracks between stones and small sheltered pockets between the jumbled lava flows.

Pehr gasped in dismay and wrapped his cloak around himself. "Is this the Alfar realm? It's perfectly wretched, Brak. Which way do we go from here?"

Brak struggled against the wind to pull his cloak more snugly around him as Faxi danced in a circle while he tried to mount. He couldn't control them both, especially with something in one hand, so he let the cloak flap while he tried to master Faxi. Getting a good, tight grip on Faxi's speckled nose, he took an instant to shove the irritating thing in his hand into his pocket, wondering what it was, and hauling it out again at the last moment for a look at it.

Pehr was shouting at him from the bottom of the hill, and Faxi was impatient, but he was transfixed. The object in his hand was a dowsing pendulum, much like the one he had seen Ingvold use. Hrodney must have put it into his hand before the spell took effect. He remembered her clearly, crouching at the edge of the stone circle—rather anxiously, he thought—calling something after him that had been lost in the rushing of the wind.

Pehr's horse came plunging up the hill, with Pehr bellowing furiously. Brak ignored him, studying the pendulum. Experimentally, he let it swing, but it described no oscillations, coming instead to a dead halt.

"Brak, what are you doing? We've got to find some secure place, in case——"

"Shh. Watch." Brak tried another direction.

"You can't make it work. What do you think you are, a wizard? It doesn't make any sense anyway, when you think about it. A bit of a gold coin with a hole in it doesn't know anything. Give me a good road and a fast horse any day, and I'll figure out where I should go." He looked disapprovingly at Faxi, who was tearing up noisy mouthfuls of grass. "Do you suppose that grass is safe?"

Brak wasn't listening. He tried pointing the pendulum to the north. It began making a definite circular movement, strengthening with each circuit until it was swinging strongly in a circle.

"That's the way we'll go," Brak said, pointing almost due north. "I'm almost certain Ingvold has gone that way."

He led at Faxi's best trot, confident in spite of Pehr's bemoaning and complaining. Twice they halted so that he could use the pendulum to make certain they were still on the line. Brak would have gone on until it was pitch-dark, but Pehr knew when it was time to stop and make a camp.

They took turns standing guard. Brak was tired, but too excited to get much sleep. He kept awakening and peering around in the cold, white moonlight at the unfamiliar landscape. Somewhere, in some rocky little niche, Ingvold must be shivering in her thin cloak, hungry perhaps. He ignored his common sense, which told him that if she had the Alfar power of changing at will to her fylgja form, she was probably quite comfortable and warm; a good hunter like a fox could always find a rat or a bird to eat. He didn't really like to think about that.

For several days they followed the ley-line north, seldom bothering with a fire or cooking. The terrain had its own gloomy charms, Brak was beginning to admit, although Pehr steadfastly detested it. For all its filmy waterfalls, reflecting pools, and mossy beauty, the land still seemed to be watching and waiting.

They passed two empty homesteads and the ruins of a hill fort, cold and wreathed in mists on its lofty perch. Their dereliction struck an uneasy cord, particularly when Brak spied shod hoofprints in large numbers crossing their course.

"I'd almost come to believe we were here all alone," Pehr grumbled apprehensively. "Who do you think they are? Ingvold's people?"

Brak looked behind him at the shrouded hill fort. It seemed to be watching them, and following them with its eyes. "I believe Ingvold's people—the Ljosalfar—are gone. They were the ones in the homesteads and the hill fort. For all we know, that may be Gljodmalborg."

"I wonder what's up there," Pehr mused with a flicker of his old curiosity.

"No! There's nothing on earth that will induce me to go up there," Brak said with a sudden shudder. "It could be those draugar Myrkjartan uses, or dark elves."

Pehr's curiosity was promptly extinguished. He spent the rest of the day urging Brak to hurry up old Faxi and put as many miles between them and the ruins as possible.

The pendulum led them at last into a lowland which was almost pleasant. Green, rolling meadows bordered small lakes where waterfowl abounded. Further into the lowlands, however, they began encountering barrows. They backtracked several times, but it seemed each new route only led to more barrows or worse bogs. Somehow, also, the pendulum quit working for Brak, after days of cooperation. He tried not to feel frightened as the shadows deepened and the barrow mounds became more numerous and the ground more soggy. He wished they had never left the safety of the high, windy hilltops.

Pehr had been grumbling a long time when Brak finally called a halt for the night in a place that he thought might be somewhat safe. It was a low, round hill rising from the steaming lowlands like an island. When they reached its top, they found an upright stone, much blackened around its base by campfires and covered with carvings and scratchings. Messages had been left there for centuries for other travelers, but none of them were intelligible to Brak and Pehr.

"You'd think Ingvold could leave us some small sign," Pehr said. "That is, if she suspects Hrodney let us through to follow her."

"She would if she could, I'm sure," Brak said stoutly over his shoulder as he hobbled Faxi nearby. He looked at the pitted surface of the standing stone. "I wonder— perhaps some of those runic marks *are* a message from Ingvold. That one is certainly fresh, scratched with charcoal."

Pehr was trying to get a fire going, without much luck. "More likely it's a message from the dark elves saying to keep out or go back. I don't like this place, with all these old barrows and fogs and mists. Have you got that hoax of a pendulum to work yet, by the way?"

He watched very anxiously, for a skeptic, as Brak tested the directions with the pendulum. He walked around the stone several times with no results, ignoring Pehr's snorts of disgust. In quiet despair, he leaned against the stone and looked around at the unwholesome terrain sinking into darkness. Immediately to the west lay a dark stretch of marshes and burial mounds, overhung with scarves of mist which reminded him of the ghostly ruins of the hill fort they had passed. He could not believe Ingvold had deliberately chosen that way—most earnestly he hoped she had not—but he dowsed in that direction anyway, to be sure. His heart started to thump as the pendulum began narrowing its arcs into wide circles, which tightened and quickened into an unmistakable indication of the correct direction. Hastily Brak snatched the pendulum and stuffed it into his pocket. He was not yet ready to convince Pehr that they should plunge into the thickest, gummiest part of the marshes in search of Ingvold.

After supper, Pehr promptly fell asleep, in spite of the fact that it was his turn to stand watch. Brak didn't really mind; he didn't feel at all sleepy. Something about the Alfar realm kept him awake and straining his ears to hear, as if there were sounds he had just barely missed hearing and things he had just missed seeing out of the corner of his eye. He settled himself beside the glowing coals, watching and listening for all he was worth, with his cloak drawn up under his ears and Pehr's sword held gingerly in one hand.

Faxi and Asgrim had grazed themselves almost out of sight into a deep ravine where a small stream chattered in the darkness. Reluctantly Brak left his warm post to retrieve the horses, guided only by their distant munching and tearing sounds. The night was of that peculiar northern whiteness when the moon was full and the sky seemed more stars than blackness. Brak lingered, after driving stakes into the ground to picket the horses, enjoying the feeling that he was alone and fending for himself in a world of very real dangers.

He returned quietly so that he wouldn't disturb Pehr. Rounding the shoulder of the hill, he halted stock-still, not believing what he was seeing. Four short fellows in dark cloaks were standing with their backs to him, staring at the fresh letters on the upright stone. Pehr was safely out of sight on the far side of the stone, sleeping peacefully.

Brak began inching backward before they saw him, but they seemed completely occupied with whispering among themselves. Brak didn't know whether to shout and warn Pehr, or to hide. All his instincts advised him to do the latter, and under a bed if possible. Nobody needed to tell him that these were dark elves. Their mere presence inspired in him the deepest feelings of dread and terror.

The dark elves suddenly turned and took a step toward Brak before realizing someone was there. With exclamations of alarm, they sprang away like birds taking flight, regrouping with drawn swords.

"What do you want?" a rasping voice demanded. One of the dark elves stepped forward warily.

"This is where I'm camping," Brak answered, hoping his voice sounded steadier than his knees were. "I was about to ask you the same thing myself." That wasn't true, of course, but he hoped they wouldn't realize it. He edged carefully toward his fire, where Pehr's sword lay.

The dark elves peered around him, craning their necks to see beyond the standing stone. "Who are you? Did you write this message on the stone?" The speaker underlined his words with flicks of his gleaming sword. "Or are you the Brak it refers to? Who is it you're following?"

Brak coughed, hoping the sound would awaken Pehr. "Such a lot of questions. Might I ask who is doing the asking?"

"Are you by yourself?" The inquisitive one peered around with growing confidence.

"My companion is there," Brak said, nodding toward the stone.

The dark elves looked from the stone to Brak and nervously stepped away a few more paces, their confidence suddenly vanishing. Brak took advantage of their hesitation and strode quickly toward the stone and almost threw himself against it for support. For a moment he had the strange impression that the massive stone moved, as if it had rocked slightly at his touch—ridiculous of him, because the stone was solidly rooted in rocky earth.

The dark elves circled about like hostile dogs looking for an opening to attack. The leader called a whispered conference with his cronies, then advanced a wary pace. His face was indistinguishable in the uncertain light, but Brak could feel his feral eyes blazing at him. "You're an intruder here, aren't you? You might be from the other realm, for all we know. Someone is leaving these markers for you to follow. We've been following them ourselves, from hilltop to hilltop, as straight as the crow flies. Is it true that Sciplings have no natural powers to defend themselves with, as they say?"

"I wouldn't know," Brak replied truthfully, wondering what natural powers the fellow meant.

The leader drew back with a hiss, summoning his companions. "Do you think he's the one? Shall we take him?"

The others muttered and demurred. "You know what a temper Hjordis has when somebody crosses her. Better make certain first."

"We could leave him for the Myrkriddir," one suggested with a nasty cackle. "I don't like the way he hugs that stone, as if there might still be power in it. Let the Myrkriddir get sizzled, not us."

"What do you say to that?" the leader called to Brak. "Should we let the Myrkriddir have you? Or would you rather come away quietly and have a chance to survive? Hjordis would like to ask you some questions about Ingvold, nothing more. You needn't be afraid," he added, sidling a step or two closer.

Brak sidled closer to Pehr's sword, cursing the imperturbability of Pehr's sleep, as if it were his divine right not to awaken at every whisper and rustle, as Brak did. Another step, and his toe touched the hilt of the sword. Brak doubted it would do him much good, but if he was about to die, he would rather it be with a sword in his hand.

"No, thank you," Brak said, stooping and snatching up the sword. "I'm not interested in answering any of Hjordis' questions. Between this sword and this stone, you'll not get very far at all with me, so you may as well go back to wherever you came from."

The dark elves eyed his sword and were not impressed. They whispered together for a moment. "It's nothing but a rock!" one declared.

"Then you fight him," another said. "My grandfather was melted by one of those cursed stones. There's still power in those old lines and stones, you know."

"I can't do it. My stars are unfavorable until next month."

"But the fellow is obviously powerless," the leader said, raising his sword challengingly. "It would certainly look bad for us to leave him for Myrkjartan to find. We'd better attempt it and die rather than explain why we failed."

They muttered in sullen agreement, unsheathing an axe or two to bolster their courage. Brak hugged the warm, rough surface of the stone at his back and blinked at the sweat trickling down the bridge of his nose. He took a two-handed grip on the sword, flinched at the first feint the Dokkalfar took at him, then raised his weapon in self-defense. The swords clashed with a numbing impact and a tremendous burst of light. The Dokkalfar gave a triple yell of fright and astonishment as their leader suddenly flared like a torch from head to heel in an aura of blue flame. Sword, helmet, and armor dropped with a clatter as the creature simply melted away like ice. Brak blinked his dazzled eyes, and the remaining three uttered spells and vanished.

With a shout, Pehr awoke from his sleep and rushed

around the stone, snatched his sword from Brak's unprotesting hand, and prepared himself for battle.

"They're gone now," Brak said in considerable exasperation. "I've never seen a person sleep so soundly as you when something important is happening!"

"You ninny! I could have caught them! Next time let me stand guard so you won't get caught napping. Why didn't you defend yourself, Brak? Why do you have to be such a—" He stopped and backed away from the still-smoking heap of clothing and weapons, now resting in a slimy black puddle. With careful pokes with his toe he ascertained what the remains had been, and looked at Brak without an ounce of comprehension.

"What—who—" he began.

Hurriedly Brak answered, "It was the stone that did it. I only—"

"The stone! That's a nice way to talk to your oldest friend and benefactor!" Pehr turned to stalk away.

"But let me explain! The power in the stone—"

"If you don't want to tell me the truth, then you needn't manufacture a lot of implausible lies, Brak. I never thought there would be secrets between you and me, after practically growing up together as brothers."

"I'm trying to tell you, but you won't listen to me, as usual," Brak retorted. "If you won't listen or believe what I say, then there's no sense wasting my breath."

"That's right. Silence is better than deception." Pehr turned his back and left Brak to stand guard for the rest of the night.

The next day passed without either speaking to the other. That night Brak grimly took the first watch, hoping he could somehow stay awake. While Pehr slept, he alternately dozed and nodded, twitching awake with a guilty start to stare around anxiously and wonder what had awakened him. After four nervous starts, he thought he heard something in a ravine near their camp. Any drowsiness he might have felt vanished instantly, and his eyes were as hard and bright as the stars overhead. After a long time, he saw a movement in the shadows. His hair rose in anticipation of another visit from the Dokkalfar, who were probably seeking revenge for their slain comrade.

The lone intruder glided toward the camp, boldly rummaging in the packs and darting wary glances all the while at Pehr, who was sleeping soundly.

Brak crept forward, hearing the thief's teeth tearing at something with voracious energy. The fellow was so preoccupied with shoving food into his mouth that Brak approached unnoticed and suddenly seized him from behind, strangling a loud shriek.

Pehr leaped up with a shout, grasped his sword, and bared it under the prowler's nose with a pronounced tremor. "A Dokkalfar spy! I was watching for you, you sneaking rascal! Hold onto him, Brak."

The ragged old thief struggled feebly, casting his eyes over his hosts with terror and dropping a staff and ragged pouch. He gasped, "Be merciful, I beg you! I was only stealing something to eat. Such big, stout fellows as yourselves needn't fear anything from a half-starved old wanderer like me."

Pehr lowered his sword cautiously. "It's true, he doesn't look like much. Let him go, Brak, and we'll have a better look at him."

The intruder clasped his thin hands gratefully. His clothing was nothing but a bundle of rags arranged to conceal the deficiencies of one bit of clothing with another worn-out garment. Brak could see the thinness of his emaciated nose, and his scrubby beard scarcely covered his gaunt cheekbones.

"Permit me to introduce myself," the old fellow said with as much dignity as he could muster. "I am called Skalgr. In happier times I was a well-known wizard, but you now see me much abused by cruel circumstances, reduced to thievery for a bit of food to keep myself alive. I wouldn't blame you if you killed me, but even such a life as mine is nevertheless rather dear to me, if you can only spare it, please."

"You said you were a wizard?" Pehr looked more dubious than impressed.

"Why, yes, I am—when I'm not so fearfully reduced in my fortunes. I expect to become respectable again someday and repay those who were kind to me, and I shall also repay the other sorts." He shook his wretched clothes into a semblance of order, glancing all the while at Brak. "You're quite certain you're not—ah, outlaws, perhaps, or possibly even killers, eh?"

"You've nothing to fear," Pehr said, "as long as you take what we give you and move on. Brak, give the old wretch that bit of bread he was chewing on and send him on his way. I can see now my sleep was disturbed for nothing."

He started to turn away, but Brak caught him and whispered excitedly, "Don't you think it's possible he might know something about Ingvold? If we feed him and treat him kindly, he may tell us he's seen her or at least heard of her."

Pehr looked doubtful. "An old thieving scavenger like him hasn't the leisure for worrying about anything but the next meal. How much food do you think it will take to get him to talk?"

Brak beckoned to Skalgr. "Come closer. You can trust us. How would you like to warm yourself by our fire and share our food and drink? You look as if your last full belly was a long time past."

"Oh, indeed, a very long time!" Skalgr rubbed his skinny hands over the fire ecstatically, as if they were a tasty delicacy he was toasting. "Would you by chance have a small something a poor old wizard could beg to drink? I've been wandering and begging my way through life for a very long time, I fear, since no ringlord wishes to attach my services. Unimpeachable services, to be sure, but it's an ungrateful, unappreciative world. Nothing fancy; just scraps will do for poor old Skalgr."

He fixed a hopeful, ingenuous gaze upon Brak, who began burrowing through the packs to find something suitable for their visitor. The bread was tested and regretfully pronounced too stale. Leftover ashcakes were likewise rejected with much sorrow. Finally Skalgr accepted a dried herring and a bit of precious cheese, although it was rather hard and smelly.

"This is lovely," the wizard sighed, shutting his eyes and waving one hand as if he were bestowing a blessing. "I don't suppose you'd consider making some tea to soak that horrid black bread in, would you? My teeth aren't what they once were, sadly enough. Have you a knife for this cheese? I see by the toothmarks your usual method of disposition, but I, as a stranger, hesitate to take such liberties."

"Our tea is rather stewed, but a little water will relieve it," Brak said, pushing the pot back into the coals. "Pehr, won't you cut off a portion of the cheese?"

Pehr had begun to get restless from the moment Skalgr had turned down the hard bread. He glared at the old wizard and exclaimed, "Just bite off some with your own teeth! He's not exactly polite company, is he? I've seen moochers before, but none so mincing about what they beg. Skalgr, as soon as you're finished with your tea and bread, you'd better not make any more requests."

"Pehr, you needn't be unkind, even if he is only an old wanderer," Brak said reprovingly, knowing something of poverty and want. "He's not a common old beggar; you can tell he had manners once."

Skalgr elevated one eyebrow and took an uncommonly dainty sip of tea. "You're very kind, Brak, but don't be alarmed. I'm not offended by the harshness of my betters. I was once regarded as a most promising young wizard, in better days, before I ran afoul of the ale. But never mind. What I was about to propose was an exchange of services. For a very modest fee, I will take you wherever you wish to go and protect you from others like me. Have you any spirits, by the way?"

"Ale, you mean?" Pehr snorted. "Not to waste on the likes of you. I'd say that old nose of yours has already done far too much sniffing of corks in its day. And as for the notion of allowing you to set up permanent mooching arrangements, it's unthinkable. You haven't got enough magical powers to protect us. You couldn't blow your own hat off in a high wind."

Skalgr drew himself together huffily. Seizing his staff and ragged pouch, he said, "I've never been one to force myself where I wasn't wanted. I shall bid you farewell, and may we never meet again. I wish you the best of luck in your travels." His eyes glanced slyly to the great stone and the charcoal scratchings on it. "I wish you success in finding your Ingvold."

Brak dropped his cup of tea. "Skalgr! Don't go! What did you say?" He plunged into the darkness after the old wizard, who hadn't gone far.

"No, no, I know where I'm not wanted," Skalgr protested haughtily, poking his way down the hillside with determined stabs of his staff. "I never interfere, I never make useless offers—" He struggled to disengage himself from Brak's grasp.

"Skalgr—" Pehr called sternly. "I'm sorry I was so hasty. Now come back here at once and explain yourself. We know you're an old vagabond, but that's no matter to us if you know something about Ingvold. Perhaps we can talk more about an exchange of services. Brak, don't be so frightfully slow. See if there isn't something to moisten our throats with, won't you?"

Skalgr stopped his recalcitrant growling and struggling. "Oh, well, since you keep insisting, I'll be willing to reconsider."

Chapter 7

Brak quickly produced a flask and sat Skalgr down in the most comfortable spot, using Pehr's eider for a cushion. Ignoring Pehr's disapproving eye, Brak plied the old wizard with more fish and cheese and refilled his cup.

"Eat all the fish you'd like, Skalgr," he urged, "and there's plenty more tea. When you're quite finished, you can tell us what you know about Ingvold. We've come a long way to find her, and we hope to help her out of a bit of trouble she's in. She's a lone wayfarer like yourself, landless and friendless, practically, except for us. And one other, I suppose. I only hope we're not too late to help her, although we really can't be as much use as her father's old friend Dyrstyggr, whom she speaks of finding."

Skalgr was in the act of gulping ale, his head thrown back, his eyes shut in ecstasy. With a drowning snort he opened his eyes and lowered the flask. "Dyrstyggr!" He choked. "Did you say Dyrstyggr?" He glanced around as if the darkness were crowded with listening ears.

"Don't tell us you're acquainted with him," Pehr said in disgust. "It's a common enough name, I suppose."

"I'm acquainted with him," Skalgr whispered, hunching his shoulders. "I know him very well, in fact. You might say he's my employer, although no one has seen a stitch of him since Myrkjartan and Hjordis seized him and took away all his fine weapons of power—Myrkjartan his cloak, Hjordis his sword—although I hear it's not doing her any good because of a curse on it—and that bog carcass Skarnhrafn wears his helmet. And the other thing—well, what I meant to say was, what could this Ingvold be wanting to find Dyrstyggr for?"

Brak looked at Pehr, who shrugged. "You may as well tell him. I can't see any harm in it, since he'll soon drink himself insensible on our ale and forget it. You've already told him too much anyway."

Brak's eyes glowed with excitement. "I think he knows something. It'll be worth a little fish and ale if we can find Ingvold." Turning to Skalgr, he apologized. "You understand we're fearful and suspicious of strangers, even a fine old fellow like you, Skalgr. Listen carefully and don't repeat a word of this to anyone. We're looking for Ingvold Thjodmarsdotter, who is the last survivor of Gljodmalborg. She has one of Dyrstyggr's weapons of power, and she's trying to find him to give it back in exchange for his help. He's rather hard to find, however, and Ingvold is doing her best to keep the—the thing out of Myrkjartan's and Hjordis' hands. Now, then—tell us what you know about Ingvold. A great deal depends upon you, Skalgr, unless you want to see the Dokkalfar overrun all of Skarpsey."

Skalgr never removed his rapt gaze from Brak's face. At last he bestirred himself and asked, "Is there a bit more cheese? I had only enough to get my appetite for it started. If you knew how long it has been—and more ale, if you don't mind. A small flask like this scarcely goes around once before it's empty."

Pehr seized the flask and gave it a rueful shake. "Once

was about all you sent it around, indeed. Do you think he heard a word of what you said, Brak?"

Brak sliced off a sliver of cheese and watched hopefully as it disappeared down Skalgr's throat—in small bites, to savor it. "You're too impatient, Pehr. Give him a chance. I'm sure he'll tell us something we want to know." He added another bit of cheese for encouragement.

Skalgr brightened under such coaxing. When Brak returned a full flask to him, he looked positively benevolent. "For Sciplings, you're quite decent fellows," he began, but Pehr leaned over and grabbed a handful of his sparse beard and glowered into his face.

"Who was it told you we're Sciplings?" he demanded. "An old beggar like you gets around, doesn't he? Begs off anybody who happens to be nearby, eh? I'll bet it was four Dokkalfar you were begging off last—only there's just three of them now. One was imprudent, and we were forced to melt him on the spot. I hope you're not great friends with the Dokkalfar, or we may be forced to do away with you, too." He glared impressively at Skalgr, who grinned and winked.

"I've no use for Dokkalfar either. Next day, I spied the remains, but it's true I begged some food and fire from four Dokkalfar and traveled a short way with them, listening to what they said. They were following two Sciplings who had earned Myrkjartan's wrath for helping Ingvold to escape. I thought they sounded as if they needed my help, if they had come to rescue Ingvold from Myrkjartan. He has her at Hagsbarrow, according to these Dokkalfar. She did her best to leave messages for you to follow, but I suppose you can't read Ljosalfar runes, can you? I rather thought not, which is one reason you ought to hire a competent wizard to guide you. I know the way to Hagsbarrow, and I've been inside there a few times, so I could take you there quite easily. Getting her out won't be so easy, but we'll think of something, will we not?" He took another long pull at the flask. "Hah! We'll be more than a match for Myrkjartan, if there's much more ale like this in your baggage."

"Exactly what I feared," Pehr began, but Brak was too excited to pay him any heed.

"What are your terms, Skalgr? We'll hire you, if we can afford you," he added.

Skalgr shrugged with elegant disinterest. "Oh, just give me whatever you think it's worth. I hate discussing cold, hard gold when the life of a beautiful young girl is in question."

"We've got about five marks in gold," Brak said, looking at Pehr. "Would that be sufficient?"

"Oh, dear, yes, that's my going price," Skalgr responded immediately with a gleam in his eyes, holding out his hand expectantly.

Pehr eyed Brak murderously as he pulled his pouch from his pocket and slapped it into Skalgr's hand. "Well, I guess we've bought ourselves a wizard. I can't say I've made a worse bargain lately. You'd better be worth every mark, Skalgr."

Skalgr peeked into the pouch delightedly, then in a twinkling it vanished into some tattered aperture in his clothing. "This is most appreciated. I promise, you'll get results with Skalgr." He tapped his staff on the ground, and the goat's head knob spit a few feeble sparks. Even Brak was forced to admit to himself that Skalgr looked like no match for Myrkjartan's thundering bolts of ice and freezing blasts of power.

Skalgr settled himself down to sleep, contentedly appropriating Brak's eider and using Pehr's for a mattress. He shut his eyes with a comfortable sigh and fell asleep still muttering about his prowess as a wizard, cradling the half-empty flask in the crook of his arm.

In the morning, while Skalgr and Pehr were occupied in a quarrel, Brak began testing the area with the pendulum. He extended his hand westward to the steaming marshlands, silently asking the unseen powers if Ingvold had been taken in that direction. The pendulum gyrated a vigorous affirmative.

"Well!" Skalgr exclaimed behind him. Brak snatched the pendulum swiftly and shoved it into his pocket. "Fancy that! I never imagined you as a dowser, Brak. You look more like the fighting variety. I suspect there's something peculiar about you that doesn't meet the eye at the first glance."

Brak covertly drew his cloak closer around himself, as

if the wizard could discern the small parcel he carried around his neck. Skalgr, however, was evidently thinking about the melted dark elf.

"What happened? How did you do it?" Skalgr demanded.

"I didn't do anything. It was the power in the stone, I think. When that Dokkalfar tried to touch me, he went up like a torch."

Skalgr eyed Brak slyly, reinforcing his doubts with several nips from his flask, which had the effect of steadying his nerves, if not his legs. "There may have been power in these heaps of rock at one time, and it may linger there yet, but I can't imagine such a one as you being able to summon it. You're both so frightfully innocent of all pretensions to magic. You're only young fellows, for all your fierce looks, and you'll need me to protect you from unscrupulous manipulators who capture defenseless travelers and sell them as thralls. But as I was saying, the idea that you could command the old earth powers—well, Hel's kettle is more likely to boil first."

Brak only shook his head and climbed onto Faxi's back. Pehr laughed scornfully. "As long as I have a fast horse and a sharp sword, I won't be needing the protection of an old shriveled boot like you. We managed to kill that Dokkalfar without your help, didn't we? Now let's quit the useless talk. Lead on, wizard, to Hagsbarrow."

Skalgr stalked away at a brisk pace northward. Brak hesitated, then followed. As Faxi plodded on contentedly, nipping off mouthfuls of grass every five or six paces, Brak began feeling more uneasy and resentful. When they paused to rest about midmorning, still distant from the murky regions of sedge and scrubby trees to the west, he finally confronted the wizard. "I dowsed Ingvold to the west this morning," he said. "Why aren't we following her to Hagsbarrow?"

Skalgr glared at him. "What's the matter, don't you trust me? I've been there a dozen times, and it's best to approach it from the north to avoid the Myrkriddir." Then Skalgr launched into a furious argument, chiefly with himself, ending with the threat that he would leave at once if no one believed him. Brak had his doubts about the leaving, as well as about the northward direction, since Skalgr had taken another bottle of ale in lieu of breakfast and was consequently rather unsteady in his walking.

Brak allowed Pehr and Skalgr to gain a considerable lead on him while he looked at the bogs and thought. With each step, his certainty increased that they were going in the wrong direction. At the very least, he could venture a short way into the marshlands and see if he could catch a glimpse of Hagsbarrow. He knotted his reins high on Faxi's neck so that he wouldn't put a foot through them and unfastened his saddle pouch. Slinging the pouch over his shoulder, he slid off Faxi, who stopped to look at him with disapproval, knowing Brak had no business lying there in the rocks and stickers, clutching his belongings in his arms. Brak waved an arm at the old horse and growled threateningly, "Shoo, scat! Go on, you old goat! Go with Pehr, you piece of troll-bait! Shoo!" He threw a small pebble at the astonished Faxi, who tossed his head in mortal affront and trotted away in high dudgeon after the others.

Brak hurried toward the marshlands, feeling terribly guilty at the idea of deserting his chieftain. He didn't think it would take him long just to climb the nearest small hill for a quick look, and then he could scurry back to Pehr and Skalgr. However, it was rather pleasant to get away from Pehr's superior intelligence and courage, and a definite relief to be rid of the obnoxious Skalgr.

The hill was farther away than it looked. As he made his way deeper into the marshlands, he had to deviate around black pools and mud flats and, worse yet, small round barrows. It was a rotten-smelling place, steeped in foreboding silence broken only by the rattling of the wind in the dead vegetation and the mucky sound of his own footsteps. Before long he was almost tiptoeing, starting at sounds he imagined he could hear over the thumping of his heart.

He had no idea how much time had passed since he had left Pehr and Skalgr, but gathering cloudbanks in the west so diminished the daylight that he decided it was time to return to them without his look at Hagsbarrow. Retracing his path, however, was impossible. Often he saw the footprints that must surely be his disappearing into black pools or menacing quagmires he had no recollection of having crossed. He tried dowsing his way back to safety, but the pendulum would not work for him, although it pointed out the direction to Hagsbarrow almost eagerly. Unhappily, he continued in that direction, penetrating deeper into the gloomy and vaporous heart of the marshlands.

Toward sundown, he observed that the earth was a little less treacherous underfoot and that the bogs appeared fewer and farther apart. Then he recognized a stone ring on a hilltop and plunged toward it like a drowning sailor. The stones stood in a small ring, tilting at various angles like misshapen, revelous dancers. Brak sat down and leaned against one, feeling much safer, and began to look around at the terrain from his slight elevation. The marshlands gradually resolved into grasslands and hills and more barrows, some of which looked as if they had been broken into quite lately. Brak could smell musty, cellary earth mingling with the gaseous odor of the bogs, and the combination tweaked at an old, fearful memory. At once he was back in the stable at Vigfusstead, prying through Myrkjartan's possessions and smelling their awful smell. Suddenly he was convinced that the necromancer was somewhere near. His gooseflesh rose as he looked carefully all around, seeing nothing to alarm him and not feeling very much comforted.

He continued his visual search of his surroundings while the daylight lasted. The mist was rising already, and he could see nothing of Hagsbarrow to the west. Then he looked northward and saw it, a cluster of longhouses and walls and squat, round towers clinging to the feet of a craggy scarp rising from the midst of the lesser hills. A bank of mist rose from its surrounding ditch and earthwork, winding its clammy banners from rooftops to towers to pinnacles of the rock. Brak shuddered and began to wish he hadn't ventured here alone. It was going to be dark before much longer. He had several hours of Skarpsey twilight before true night descended, so he began to hurry northward, skirting toward the east in the hope that he would meet Skalgr and Pehr approaching from that direction.

The area he was crossing was dank and soft underfoot. He passed several more stones, reflecting pools, and mounds that marked the ley-line to Hagsbarrow. He detoured widely around a freshly excavated barrow and stumbled across a pit where someone had been digging peat.

He wished he hadn't come that way; it was a foul-smelling area and tended to murky fog that reeked of old barrows.

Then, to Brak's great horror, he realized he had stumbled onto a recent battlefield. He passed a heap of dead horses and encountered several dead men, frozen and blue with Myrkjartan's icy death. He knew they must have been the defenders of Hagsbarrow before it had fallen to Myrkjartan. Brak darted a glance at the fortress, wreathed in cold mist. It seemed so close that it seemed to loom over him, crouching for a pounce. Bonfires on the earthwork began appearing like the opening of sullen, watchful eyes, one by one.

Brak scuttled from one bit of cover to the next as the daylight swiftly disappeared. Hosts of frogs croaked their dismal dirges from their marshy cloisters, and the lowering sun paused to favor Hagsbarrow with a last lurid scowl before vanishing forever into a blanket of black cloud. Desperately Brak hurried along, searching for a place to hide. Then he heard a sound that froze him to the earth— the low chuckling and chattering of the Myrkriddir. As he watched, a group of them appeared on the roof of the largest longhouse, jostling their ragged horses together and greeting one another with derisive shrieks. They took to the air in a noisy, untidy mass and came flying toward him. He squeezed himself into the closest shelter and, after a rather suspenseful struggle between two slabs of rock, found himself inside a small, empty barrow. The place was narrow and musty, but he doubted that the Myrkriddir could get him out without digging him out.

They plummeted to the earth not far away and galloped toward him, their bony faces gleaming. Brak covered his face, except for one eye, as the Myrkriddir descended on his hiding place. He glimpsed their rotting grave garments and locks of matted beards and hair and their eyes that glowed like hot coals—and then they were gone without so much as a glance at him. In the sudden silence, he peered out, doubtful of his unexpected reprieve.

He saw them skimming like storm clouds over the marshlands toward the north, descending suddenly with a clamoring outcry. In a short while they came riding through the tall black reeds, cackling and jeering in triumph. When they passed, Brak was horrified to recognize Faxi and Asgrim being led behind. Two bundles tossed over the leaders' saddlebows must have been Pehr and Skalgr. Skalgr, at least, was still alive, protesting and threatening. As he passed, Brak could hear him wheedling: "Myrkjartan is a most particular friend of mine, so let me speak to him at once, you grinning ninnies, or you'll all find yourselves turned into bootblacking rags. I have influence with Skarnhrafn, too. Send word to them both that I brought this Scipling captive as a gift from Skalgr."

Brak shrank further into his hiding place, sick with fury at himself for trusting an old reprobate like Skalgr. He lay there for hours, not daring to move. The Myrkriddir reappeared and scoured the marshlands for him. Other creatures came out with the advent of nightfall, horrible beings that scrambled around in the dark, squabbling among themselves. To Brak's horror, they hauled the dead bodies from the shadows, swiftly robbed them of all valuables and equipment, and went scuttling back to the hill fort. Then others came, huge creatures, more awful than the corpse-robbers, and dragged the poor bodies away, probably to be restored as Myrkjartan's draugar.

He spent the night watching and shivering in revulsion, dozing from time to time and having grisly nightmares. When the dawn came, he had never been so thankful to see the sun. He waited until it was well up, then crawled from his hiding place and speedily took himself back to the nearest safe point he could determine. It was a slight knob of hill with a solitary stone, and he threw himself down in the grass, feeling perfectly miserable. He stared at the fortress crouching on its black fang of lava rock, wondering how he would ever summon the courage to go in after Pehr. Thoughts of vengeance upon Skalgr began to fortify his courage, however, until he was almost ready. He clutched the dragon's heart, wondering how to use it.

He spent the day advancing his position and studying his objective. The only entrance to Hagsbarrow was on its south side, on the spine of the spit of lava it rested upon. Brak approached it by subtle degrees until he found himself a hiding place in the jumble of stones surrounding the base of the outcropping earthwork. He saw no signs of life in the longhouses above, but the tightly shuttered doors and windows had a watchful attitude that made him very uneasy. The longhouses were arranged in a square, so anyone entering would have to pass through a rather narrow gateway, which was blocked by a heavy gate. A pair of round watchtowers turned their slitted windows to survey the surrounding country in all directions, and Brak felt certain a hundred pairs of eyes were fastened balefully upon him, making a mockery of all his careful hiding and skulking.

Toward dusk, the shadows in the rocks around Brak began to stir. To Brak's fright, the corpse-robbers and body-haulers came to life around him, unfolding like bats from their dark niches for another night's work. Brak remained still, hoping to escape the notice of their gleaming eyes and ferreting noses. Some of them even possessed sharp, upright ears tufted with hair, and he was certain he saw some with long, ropy tails. Trolls, he decided with a thrill of dread.

He escaped their notice in their eager rush to get to their work. They carried their booty up to the gate, where they were rewarded with bits of food which they consumed at once, viciously rebuffing any usurpers. The reward for an entire corpse seemed pitifully small to Brak—a piece of bread the size of a fist and a bit of dried fish.

Brak looked at the gatekeepers, who were Myrkriddir, and despaired of slipping in unnoticed. The heap of corpses and equipment grew slowly, with much wrangling over the payments. The smaller scavengers had scarcely a chance, Brak noted; the larger trolls or whatnot either seized the objects they had salvaged or stole their food from them when they did manage to reach the gate with some small object.

With a sudden scattering of the scavengers, the gate opened and Myrkjartan rode out on his gray horse, followed by a black, hulking Myrkridda. Instantly, the scrabbling and snarling of the scavengers was silenced, and they melted away into the shadows to watch, their eyes gleaming in the twilight. The Myrkridda raised the visor of his helmet, and fiery light raked the battlefield. Brak crouched further into his niche. The eyes of Skarnhrafn were like twin scythes of fire, searing all their glance touched. Brak recoiled, quaking in fear as the fiery beams swept over his hiding place. Then a clank of metal signaled the end of

Skarnhrafn's inspection of the battlefield. When Brak dared to look up, he saw a dark, brooding hulk, with tiny glimmers of fire showing through each rivet hole and seam of the helmet. The great draug and his master were so close that he could hear them when they spoke.

"Gljodmalborg—Hagsbarrow—we're yet a long way from Snowfell," the draug rumbled. "Eleven hill forts stand between us and our goal, Master."

"Ten, if Hjordis successfully takes Miklborg."

"I don't trust Hjordis. What are Dokkalfar good for, except peat for fires? Hjordis would be better use to us dead, Master. Much more cooperative as a draug."

"I'd have it done in a moment if I could arrange it decently. Dyrstyggr's cloak and helmet and sword should be in the same hands."

"And the dragon's heart also, Master."

"You'd better not mention that if you want to keep me in a good humor," Myrkjartan snapped.

"Humors are unhealthy," Skarnhrafn growled. "Much better to be dry and dusty, like us draugar. Nothing to trouble you but an occasional moth or rat. We'd better be leaving Hagsbarrow soon, or your army will be chewed to pieces. With the help of the Rhbus, we could make the draugar indestructible."

"The Alfar girl is still unrelenting, is she not?"

"Perhaps she'll never surrender it of her own free will, Master, before she dies."

Brak strained his ears to hear more about Ingvold. He crept a bit closer, unable to straighten his back without stabs of pain. While he was in this awkward predicament, a pair of scavengers suddenly rounded a boulder and took one look at him and attacked. They pounced upon his good cloak with shrieks of glee, and one seized the pouch hanging from his shoulder. Brak buffeted the first scavenger away and flattened the one fastened to his pouch with a single blow. Two others backed away when he straightened himself to his full height, and took to their heels in terror when he lunged at them. Their shrieking attracted the notice of Skarnhrafn, who swept the area with his gaze until all the scavengers lurking there ran for their lives. It was getting much too hot for Brak also. Rabbitlike, he bounded from shelter to shelter, encountering knots of scavengers who instantly recognized him for something unusual and began pursuing him with a great clamoring outcry. The fire of Skarnhrafn's eyes passed overhead, illuminating his fleeing form almost to perfection.

"It's the other Scipling! Fetch him, Skarnhrafn!" Myrkjartan commanded. Skarnhrafn replied with a wild howl, echoed by Myrkriddir in the hill fort and others prowling the battlefield. Excitedly they dived at the scurrying scavengers, spying anything that moved, so Brak wedged himself into a crevice and watched for an opportunity. Raucous Myrkriddir galloped through the sky overhead, taking care not to incinerate themselves in Skarnhrafn's raking gaze. Presently their gleeful screeching turned to baffled howls. Brak crept warily from rock to rock without being detected, until he reached the edge of the rocky skirt of Hagsbarrow and contemplated a dash across the battle plain to the relative safety of the marshes.

Drawing several deep breaths, he glanced around. The Myrkriddir were busy ferreting out the wrong specimen on the other side of the ramp leading up to the gate, so he leaped up and sped out onto the battlefield. When he was halfway across, he heard a wild, clamorous shriek behind him that provided him with an extra burst of speed and bathed him in cold sweat. Myrkriddir came swooping from the hill fort, too far away to do more than scream in frustration.

He had nearly reached the safe hill when his foot slogged deep into soft mud, nearly pulling his boot off as he lurched and almost fell. The foot came out of the muck, but the other foot sank deep into soft, squelching mud and refused to be pulled out. Brak floundered and struggled, but the bog had its hold on him and had no intention of letting him go. The Myrkriddir howled in triumph and soon swarmed around him like a flock of motley ravens eager to peck out the eyes of their bog-mired victim.

Chapter 8

Cursing at them, himself, and his situation in general, Brak lashed at the hateful creatures with a small knife, and the Myrkriddir howled with glee. They buffeted at him, mocking and jeering, until at least thirty of the awful things had gathered to torment their captive.

A shout halted their antics instantly, sending them skulking away with hoots and snickers. As they departed, Brak recognized Myrkjartan approaching. He banished the Myrkriddir with a sharp gesture and stared doubtfully at Brak. He nudged his horse as near as it would approach and offered Brak the end of his staff, which Brak was loath even to touch. The knob was carved into the shape of a grinning skull.

"Come along, it's better than dying in the mud, isn't it?" Myrkjartan snapped, turning the horse and drawing Brak out of the mud with a loud, squelching pop and nearly pulling his arms from their sockets. Then the necromancer stared at Brak. "I can scarcely believe that even a young and stupid Scipling would be so foolish as to wander deliberately into Hagsbarrow alone. Or into an open Dokkalfar tunnel to spy upon Hjordis. Why is it you insist upon being so fatally inquisitive?" He poked Brak along in the direction he wanted him to go, as if herding an errant sheep.

Brak stumbled miserably in his mud-covered boots, maintaining a stubborn silence.

"Won't talk, eh? Well, it's no matter. I know everything I need to know about you and that wretched Ingvold. A most tiresome individual, that girl. I hope you'll make yourself useful and help me persuade her to give up the dragon's heart to those who can use it to a greater extent than she ever could, even with the assistance of old Dyrstyggr." Myrkjartan laughed and prodded Brak a little harder with his staff. "What curious friends Ingvold chooses—an old rag like Skalgr and a great timid lump like you. Her plans to thwart me are doomed at the beginning. Hjordis, too, will suffer some slight disappointments," he added slyly with a chuckle.

A grinning group of Myrkriddir waited for them just inside the gate, raising a chorus of hisses and cackles at the sight of Brak.

"Put him in my workroom," Myrkjartan commanded. "I want him left alive, so don't waste any time torturing him unless you want to be used as spare parts for better fighters than you'll ever be."

Two of the creatures seized Brak's arms and hauled him away into one of the longhouses. It was musty and gloomy, with the central corridor littered with what Brak first assumed was firewood cast in untidy heaps; but as his eyes became accustomed to the gloom, he saw that it was heaps of corpses, still peaty after their recent extraction from the bogs. The Myrkriddir hurried him along, not allowing him time to choose his footing with more care, so that he was stumbling over the dry husks of men much against his will. On either side of the corridor, the long rooms seemed crowded with more corpses, but Brak soon became aware of a rustling and stirring among them. Several times shriveled hands shot out at the intruders, but the Myrkriddir struck them away with angry growls, or took a thrust at the draugar with the staffs they carried.

The last chamber in the longhouse was partitioned off and set apart with a stout door, which the Myrkriddir hammered upon until it was opened by a dark, shuffling creature that beckoned them in and quickly closed the door. The room was lit by a low fire and two lamps on a large table. The doorkeeper glided back to its place beside the cavernous hearth to tend the meager fire, by the light of which Brak took his first good look at a draug. It was covered mostly with scraps of rags which did little to hide its fleshless limbs and leathery hide, dyed a deep brown by the peat. Brak's hair lifted in horrified fascination as he watched the creature mechanically adding sticks of peaty fuel to the fire. As the light burned brighter, with a sullen red gleam, Brak realized that the fuel was discarded pieces of draugar that were apparently too broken up to be mended for service. A few peaty old skulls waited patiently for immolation, dry and withered as old toadstools.

The Myrkriddir shoved him toward a dark corner, where something suddenly stirred in the shadows. A voice shrilled, "Who's that? Who's here? You don't dare annoy us, you know, or it'll go the worse for you!"

"Skalgr!" Brak exclaimed. "It's me, Brak. It is you, isn't it, Skalgr? You cheat, you nithling! You tricked us! How much did you expect to get for us from Myrkjartan?"

"He didn't get anything," Pehr said with a chuckle. "Nobody believed his protestations of undying loyalty to Myrkjartan and Hjordis. I hope they cut you up for dog meat, Skalgr—except it will probably make the dogs sick."

The Myrkriddir made a few threatening gestures and retreated to guard the door. Brak sat down on a bench, after warily pushing away what he supposed was a corpse.

"I am desperately sorry," Skalgr continued, sounding genuinely sorrowful. "I confess I was at first motivated solely by the prospect of immediate gain, since my old lord Dyrstyggr is in lamentably dire straits at present. I knew Myrkjartan was looking for two Sciplings, so I decided to offer him my services, which he rather unkindly rejected. I greatly overestimated his sense of honor, I fear. I'll never again be tempted by the dark side. In fact, I have a marvelous plan for getting my revenge upon him—"

"Just be quiet, won't you?" Pehr invited. "We're not interested in your marvelous plans, or anything about you. Brak, you can't imagine what it's been like locked up with this old windbag for two days. What happened to you anyway? How could you have gone off like that without telling us? I was worried sick!" Pehr launched into a lecture, which Brak scarcely heard. He was looking around more sharply at their prison and liking it less the more he saw of it.

"What sort of place is this?" he demanded. "All that stuff stacked along the walls and under the table certainly isn't firewood, is it?"

"Bless you, no, it isn't," Skalgr replied with a cackle. "This is Myrkjartan's workshop, where he puts draugar together and brings the dead back to life. He commands them to do his bidding until they're too battered to repair, and then it's into the fire with them. They make a very pleasant blaze." He rubbed his hands appreciatively, then added, "Brak, you haven't anything to eat in that pouch, have you?"

"No! You can starve for all I care!" Brak snapped. "We'll all probably die here anyway."

"No, no, trust me once again," Skalgr said. "It will all work out most agreeably if we watch for our chance. We can even take Ingvold with us when we escape. From outside, freeing her would be much more difficult. And you do agree we mustn't leave her with Myrkjartan and Hjordis."

"Ingvold! Then she is here, for certain?" Brak asked.

"Oh, yes, and she hasn't given the heart to Myrkjartan either," Skalgr replied with a conspiratorial snigger. "Listen, I really do have the cleverest plan for getting out of here—"

The door burst open suddenly with a scattering of Myrkriddir who capered into the room and swooped at the prisoners menacingly, until Myrkjartan strode into the room and silenced them with a shout. His cloak swirled from his shoulders, where it was held by two skull-faced brooches. He glowered at his prisoners, then beckoned toward the door. Another Myrkridda dragged Ingvold forward, stiffly resisting with all the dignity she could muster in spite of her ragged appearance.

Myrkjartan glowered from Ingvold to his other prisoners, eyeing his most recent acquisition with a moody scowl. "You see where your curiosity has brought you now, Scipling? I shall be forced to kill you presently, I fear, unless you can convince Ingvold to give up that dried morsel of old meat which someone has invested with such outlandish powers. You'd rather she gave it up, wouldn't you?"

Brak shook his head, acutely conscious of the little case inside his shirt. "You'll never get it," he said with a dry swallow.

"That threat won't work," Ingvold declared in her clear, fearless voice. "If you harm my friends to force me to give it to you, the Rhbus won't consider it a gift of free will. One touch, and you'll suffer a curse like that of Hjordis. You've seen her hands, haven't you? And lately she's kept her face covered a lot; don't you rather wonder why?"

Myrkjartan flicked at a fold of his cloak with his staff.

"I haven't noticed any ill effects from the cloak, and most assuredly it was not a gift of free will, since I left its owner for dead."

"But Dyrstyggr isn't dead," Skalgr interrupted.

"No matter," Myrkjartan retorted. "He's nothing without his weapons. Even if you managed to take the heart to him, wherever he's hiding and nursing his disgrace, he can't do you any good with it."

"I don't believe you!" Ingvold's eyes flashed and filled with sudden, angry tears. "My father told me if ever I needed help I could rely upon Dyrstyggr. Perhaps you have beaten him for now and taken his treasures, but he's not dead, he's not defeated, and I know he'll come back to avenge himself on you for taking that cloak and making such a mockery of his powers." She gestured contemptuously around the room at the evidence of Myrkjartan's necromancy.

Myrkjartan's calm was unruffled. "Bid your friends farewell. I can't tell you if you'll ever see them again. That is for you to decide, in your misbegotten pride." He motioned to the Myrkriddir to take her away. She resisted long enough to get the last word.

"If I don't see them again, Myrkjartan, you'll never get this!" She clutched a chain around her neck and waved a small dark case at him in triumph.

Brak looked after her in astonishment, wondering which of them actually carried the decoy.

Myrkjartan angrily stalked up and down the room, kicking parts of draugar out of his path and bending venomous looks upon his captives. Pehr was transfixed, and Skalgr was keeping prudently quiet. Again Myrkjartan singled Brak out, glaring at him in distaste. "I'm beginning to dislike you more each time I see you. For a fat, stupid coward, you certainly manage to trifle with my wrath—following Ingvold on her hagride, searching my packs at Vigfusstead, and standing between me and the dragon's heart. You are a most unlikely, unlucky star rising on my horizon. I shall have to get rid of you soon, I fear."

Pehr found his tongue and protested. "I don't appreciate such threats being made against Brak, if you don't mind. He's been my own thrall since we were children, and I'm as fond of him as if he were my brother. My father

Thorsten is a chieftain, a man of considerable power in the Scipling realm. I'm sure you wouldn't like to cross him if you knew him."

Myrkjartan transferred his glower from Brak to Pehr. "A thrall you say? A small, wretched girl and a mere thrall attempting to defy me! And you, you conceited son of a Scipling chieftain, dare to threaten me with your father's power? What sort of power does he have? Can he compare with my skills at ice magic or necromancy? Is he a fire wizard?" As he spoke, he moved his hands, writing on the air with frost, conjuring a mighty power into the room that chilled everyone to the bone and caused the turf and timbers to tremble. He pointed to an old skull on a shelf, and it opened its eyes to look around with lively interest and began to mouth and mutter.

Abashed, Pehr shrank back a little behind Brak. "Well, my father's power is more of the money nature, rather than —than—" He looked at the skull and couldn't finish, except with an uneasy cough.

"I thought as much. Faugh! It looks as if I'm stuck with you, for a while at any rate." Myrkjartan stalked up and down again.

"If I might venture to offer my services again, my lord—" Skalgr began, grinning and sidling after Myrkjartan a very little way.

Myrkjartan halted. "Services? How do you feel about digging? Ha, it makes no difference; that's what you'll be doing. Digging into barrows for more corpses to fight against the Ljosalfar. You in particular, thrall, will be most useful, since you know what it means to work for your keep." He beckoned to the waiting Myrkriddir and directed them to take the prisoners to another room.

"But I had in mind something quite different—" Skalgr began indignantly, but a Myrkridda seized him and bore him away before he could finish, except with a screech or two of protest.

They were put into a dreary cellar of a room with only a smoky lamp and scores of hungry rats for company. They attempted to sleep and rest, but it was a distinct relief to be summoned forth to begin their digging. Sometimes they dug by moonlight, under the watchful supervision of a pair of Myrkriddir, or by daylight, with the assistance of several draugar. Frequently they had to work inside when they ran out of that sort of work. Guided by the hisses and snorts of the Myrkriddir, Brak and Pehr learned to sort the musty old arms, legs, and skulls that had been dug in a mess from the bogs. They soon discovered that being outdoors, even in a peat bog, was infinitely preferable to watching Myrkjartan gloatingly assemble his draugar.

They saw Skalgr less frequently, but he was forever hobnobbing with the Myrkriddir and bowing and scraping fatuously before Myrkjartan. The perverse old wizard seemed to rise in favor, drawing easier chores for himself, more and better food, and his own place to live apart from Brak and Pehr, which suited Brak and Pehr to perfection.

In the days to follow there was no significant change in the routine. Brak never ceased to think about Ingvold, wondering where they kept her and how he and Pehr would ever escape. He became accustomed to the sight and company of draugar and Myrkriddir, but he never lost his horror for the grisly occupations of the necromancer. Myrkjartan ignored Brak and Pehr with lofty unconcern, except for an irritable shout now and then. Sciplings were evidently beneath his attention. A nearly intact corpse was of far greater interest.

After almost three weeks of captivity, they were summoned unexpectedly into the sacred precincts of Myrkjartan's work chamber. Their first warning of impending trouble was the large number of Dokkalfar lolling outside the door, picking quarrels with the draugar and Myrkriddir. The Myrkriddir escorting Brak and Pehr shoved them through the crowd and into the chamber beyond, where they saw Hjordis in possession of Myrkjartan's large black chair. The shadow of her headdress kept her face well hidden, and her hands were concealed within the sleeves of her cloak.

Myrkjartan gestured impatiently. "These are the prisoners in question, I believe. You may have them if you wish."

Hjordis retorted, "These aren't the ones I'm interested in. I heard you had captured Ingvold, and I've come to take her back with me to Hjordisborg. I'm sure you haven't the time or the patience for wearing down her resistance and convincing her that her greatest interest lies in giving up Dyrstyggr's heart. Your draugar occupy too much of your time, Myrkjartan. Turn her over to me and we'll have that heart very promptly."

Myrkjartan's eyes narrowed to gleaming points. "Ingvold is well guarded here at Hagsbarrow. I've perceived that there is some sort of bond between the girl and the Sciplings, and I've been threatening her with my killing them until I believe she's almost ready to give it up. Your devious hag spell simply takes too long to work. She's a stubborn, sullen creature. I wonder why she wanted to bring these Sciplings into our realm?" He gave Brak a sharp poke and looked at him disapprovingly.

"She needed help," Brak said stolidly.

"Yours? Ha!" Myrkjartan replied.

Hjordis laughed scornfully and tapped the sword at her waist with one hand. "Perhaps she knows they are the only ones who can touch Dyrstyggr's weapons without fearing curses and corruption." She turned her face toward the light, and Myrkjartan looked away with a disdainful snort. "Believe it, Myrkjartan. You see what Dyrstyggr has done to me. Something just as bad will happen to you."

"What dismal croaking," Myrkjartan said. "You weren't half so gloomy when the sword enabled you to crush Gljodmalborg."

"I want Ingvold," Hjordis resumed in a deadly tone, "and I shall take her from you if you don't give her up, Myrkjartan. Don't try to thwart me."

"Don't try to threaten me," Myrkjartan returned acidly. "I'm no servant of yours. We are equals in our opposition of Elbegast."

"But Skarnhrafn has the helmet, and Skarnhrafn is your creature. I demand Ingvold and that heart, or very soon we'll no more be equals, but enemies." Hjordis angrily threw back her hood, her eyes blazing from her swollen, discolored face.

"You need me and my draugar too badly for that. Alone, you're not moving very well against the Ljosalfar. You should have attacked Miklborg by now, and you haven't. When Miklborg is taken, we'll discuss who is to possess Ingvold and the heart. I'm at the point of moving my draugar north to Miklborg, and I shall bring the girl and the Sciplings with me. We'll renew this discussion at a later date." He turned back to his work on the table.

Hjordis looked at his back a moment, then at Brak and Pehr with an icy smile. "We shall see about that," she said, and walked toward the door with a slight limp. "Beware of the full moon, Myrkjartan. My astrologers tell me it might be an unfavorable time for you."

"Astrologers!" Myrkjartan growled as she closed the door behind her. "What do I care for her or her wizards? Look alive there, you dolts, can't you see I'm running out of extra parts? Full moon, indeed, as if I had cause to fear any of her useless spells."

"The hag spell isn't a useless spell," Brak said, keeping a wary distance, and a long leg bone in his hand in case he needed a weapon. "I doubt that you'll be able to hold Ingvold if Hjordis sends for her. She'll escape somehow and return to Hjordis with the heart."

Myrkjartan examined a skull and hurled it angrily away. "It makes no difference to nithlings who holds Dyrstyggr's heart. Tend to your own duties or I'll give you to the scavengers."

"Begging your pardon, Master—" Someone scuffled a moment with the Myrkriddir before approaching with much deferential sidling and scuttling. "It's Skalgr, my lord, ever grateful and eternally faithful old Skalgr, but I'm forced to agree with the Scipling. Hjordis is likely to call the girl and the heart right out of Hagsbarrow, whether you wish it or not. I have an idea, however—"

"Silence! It'll be a desperate day when I need the advice of an old vagabond like you!" Myrkjartan roared furiously. "Take yourself away, and take the Sciplings back to their cell while you're at it. If you don't want to become a draug, you'd better stay out of my sight for a few days."

"Thank you, thank you, my lord!" Skalgr exclaimed, hurrying Pehr and Brak toward the door. "I'm always grateful to do your bidding, my lord, always faithful, always—" The door slammed shut, cutting off any further effusions.

"Skalgr, you disgust me," Pehr declared as they picked their way through the longhouse to their gloomy cellar lodgings. "Look at you—new clothes, boots, cloak, and even a knife—"

"A very small knife," Skalgr added hastily. "Barely big enough to eat with. They know a wretch like me can't be any threat, living as I do on my stomach and gullet."

"I'd say they have you pegged pretty close," Brak said gloomily. "As long as there's food, you won't betray them."

"Move aside there!" Skalgr called officiously to a knot of Myrkriddir. "Prisoners coming through! Out of the way, you dustbags!"

"Ever faithful, aren't you, Skalgr?" Pehr demanded as Skalgr bowed them into their cell.

Skalgr winked and hauled a parcel out of his cloak. "To be sure I am, my dear friends. Here's a lovely feast for you —mutton, bread, and cheese. I never stop thinking of you for a moment. I've made friends in high places, such as the kitchen and the guardroom. There are only a few of us in Hagsbarrow who are alive, you know, so we have to stick together as best we can. I hope you don't mind my scraping along as I do—you see, you'll benefit from it. That's a nice bit of mutton, isn't it?"

"You're the mutton, Skalgr," Pehr growled, sinking his teeth into the meat with great relish. "Now just go away, won't you?"

Skalgr closed the door and locked it securely, checking it twice to be sure. "I won't go far, my friends; you can count on old Skalgr!" He scurried away, chuckling to himself and rallying the Myrkriddir as if they were on the most intimate of terms.

Brak watched the phases of the moon closely each night through a small gap in the stonework. Feeling helpless and angry, he noted it waxing toward the apex of its career.

"Myrkjartan can't hold her," he fumed. "If she escapes, then we've got to follow her."

Pehr looked horrified. "My feet won't stand for another hagride, Brak. Not to mention the fact, of course, that escaping from here is almost as likely as a whale that flies. How do you propose to do it, just burst through that door?"

Brak brooded in silence, his eye upon the moon through the niche. "It's almost full, wouldn't you say? Do you think this will be the night when Hjordis calls?"

Pehr only shook his head and lay down on his thin pallet of straw with a sigh. The rattling of a key in the lock revived him suddenly, and a hoarse voice announced, "Here's your supper."

"It's about time, too," Pehr declared. "Late again, you dolt. Why can't you—"

He was about to take the ungenerous offering from the stooping, skinny figure of the draug that brought them their food every day when Brak suddenly launched himself from the corner, falling upon the creature and pummeling it in a fury. Pehr was too astonished to do more than smother its shrieks with a wadded cloak while Brak pounded it insensible.

"What do you think you're doing?" he whispered in a scandalized squeak as Brak shoved the draug into a corner and snatched up their supper to stuff into his pouch.

"Escaping, you idiot. Now come along or I'll leave you here!"

"A fine way for a thrall to talk. Wait just a moment, I'm coming with you. Is that draug coming around?" Pehr eyed the draug nervously as he pulled on his boots. "Brak, look! It's old Skalgr. I wonder what he was about, disguising himself as our draug?"

"More mischief, no doubt." Brak led the way out of their cellar and up some earthy stairs; a short dash through a longhouse, and they were outside.

Chapter 9

❖❖❖❖❖❖❖❖❖❖❖❖❖❖❖❖❖❖❖❖❖❖❖❖

They crept along the turf wall in the darkness, crouching behind heaps of dismantled draugar or firewood as the Myrkriddir screamed overhead in great excitement. Pehr and Brak exchanged a rueful look, thinking their freedom was apt to be short-lived if their escape had been detected so soon.

"I knew this was the night," Brak whispered exultantly.

"All we have to do is follow her. We'll go to one of the old safe hilltops when we need protection."

"Brak—I think you've lost your wits," Pehr retorted, cringing as several Myrkriddir took flight from the nearby roof.

"The next time the gate opens, we'll make a dash for it," Brak said. "Maybe they'll think we're only scavengers."

"Brak—" Pehr began in protest, but Brak whirled in the other direction.

"Someone's coming!" Brak whispered. "If it's a draug, we'll have to take his skull off. Get ready!"

A dark figure crept toward them, hugging the wall as more Myrkriddir and draugar noisily assembled in the open ground inside the longhouses. The creature stooped low and slithered directly after Brak and Pehr. At an unspoken signal, they rose up and seized it and bore it down underneath them, smothering any cries it might make. Brak laid hold of its crown and jawbones and gave a mighty wrench, but was disappointed of the desired effect. His quarry gave a muffled, indignant yell and threshed around furiously. Then Brak realized he was wrestling with a living creature, not a shriveled dead one. He took a swift look at the fellow's face in the moonlight and exclaimed in disgust, "It's only Skalgr!"

"Let's kill him," Pehr suggested, releasing his hold reluctantly.

Skalgr collected himself, coughing and wheezing and chuckling. "I was coming to help you escape," he whispered. "A clever disguise, wasn't it? You didn't need to beat me so thoroughly, however."

"What are we going to do with him?" Pehr demanded. "The moment we turn our backs on him, he'll yell to the heavens where we've gone. We'll have to kill him, or at least tie him up where he won't be found for a while."

"There's no time," Brak replied urgently. "They're opening the gate again for these draugar—searching for us, no doubt. We've got to get out with them, now or never." He grabbed a handful of Skalgr's cloak. "We'll have to take him with us and get rid of him later."

They bolted out of the shadows barely in time to tack themselves onto the end of the stream of draugar shuffling out at the gate. None of the draugar or Myrkriddir gave them a second glance. When they were well outside the gate and descending the winding ramp, they took the first opportunity to dive into the surrounding rocks and crevices.

"Very well done, fellows!" Skalgr exclaimed. "I'm proud to know such excellent skulkers and escapers. It would have been easier if you'd let me help you, which I was going to do, in my own time."

"Hush!" Pehr said. "Here come Myrkjartan and Skarnhrafn! I never once supposed a thrall could make an effective escape. I wonder if we shouldn't give ourselves up before Skarnhrafn comes searching with those eyes in that helmet of his."

"Why, whatever would you want to do that for?" Skalgr inquired. "They have no idea you're even missing. It's Ingvold they're after. She worked the lock on her door somehow and nipped out and over the gate just like a goat into the granary. You wouldn't see Myrkjartan looking so grim for a pair of mere Sciplings."

Myrkjartan came spurring down the ramp, with Skarnhrafn loping behind. The necromancer's horse plowed to a halt, prancing and pawing with as much impatience as its rider.

"Skarnhrafn, hurry yourself! She's getting farther away each moment you dawdle and delay. After her, you fool, and don't come back without her. Bring her to me, Skarnhrafn, if you want to keep that helmet and its powers!" Myrkjartan gestured angrily at the draugar gathering around him. "Not here, you mindless lumps of dust—go search for her! Away, Skarnhrafn! Find Ingvold!"

Skarnhrafn's rivet holes blazed with a burst of light. "I hear your command, my lord, and I shall do it. I swear to bring the girl back, with every atom of dust in this carcass." He slapped himself proudly on the chest with an eruption of dust and spurred his draug horse into the air with a horrendous shout.

Myrkjartan and the draugar began scouring the battlefield, turning out the scavengers and harrying them from place to place. Skalgr urged Brak and Pehr to follow him, and they fled northward in advance of Myrkjartan's depredations. The lights of Hagsbarrow were soon behind them, along with the dismal howling of the scavengers, so Skalgr permitted a brief halt to rest and look around.

"Brak, you still have your dowsing pendulum, don't you?" he asked, rubbing his hands. "See if you can dowse her out, my boy. She isn't far ahead of us—if she's still afoot, that is."

"Let's hope we don't encounter her if she's still looking for a horse," Pehr growled apprehensively.

Brak attempted to compose himself sufficiently for dowsing. His thoughts were over-lively with reflections of Skarnhrafn and Myrkjartan and Hjordis, and the pendulum refused to indicate anything.

"We can't wait any longer," Skalgr finally said. "Don't be cast down, Brak; we all fail now and again. If I'm not mistaken, we're on a ley-line this instant, and perhaps Ingvold will find a safe place and wait for us. I told her we'd be directly behind her as she was working that lock— with only a little help of mine."

"You helped Ingvold escape?" Pehr demanded. "I don't believe it. Brak, you'd better not believe it either."

Skalgr shook his head vigorously. "You'll see, then, if you'll just follow me." Beckoning impatiently for them to follow, he led the way at a jerky trot from shadow to shadow. Pehr brought up the rear, grumbling about the last time they had trusted him to lead them and what had happened.

The moon was a watery gleam just beneath the horizon when Skalgr pointed out a higher hill with a ring of stones on its crest. Panting and wheezing, he whispered, "She'll be there waiting for us, but we'll be safe in the old ring— I hope. I've got a few spells that might do us some good. We'll just hide here a while and try to see her." He edged into the shadow of a large boulder, darting wary glances on all sides. Pehr also looked as if he intended to take no more chances with his feet.

"There's not much more time—" Brak began in exasperation, but Skalgr suddenly laid hold of him and hauled him into the protection of the boulder with astonishing strength. Silently he pointed toward the hill, making all sorts of frantic gestures.

A darker silhouette stood on the side of the hill, near the base. All Brak could see were the pricking ears of a horse and a shapeless bulk crowned with a distinctive helmet. Brak swallowed his protests hastily and crouched lower as the helmet slowly turned in their direction. He could see tiny points of red light around the seams as Skarnhrafn watched a moment, then turned the horse toward the far side of the hill and silently disappeared.

"She must be here," Skalgr whispered hoarsely with great glee. "And you see Skarnhrafn's afraid to go up there. He knows the magic still lingers in these old places. Now wait a moment, Brak, what are you doing? Let's not be hasty—"

"We're going up there," Brak replied, rising to a stoop. He shook off Skalgr's restraining hand and moved carefully to another shadow, ignoring the intense whispered arguments that followed him. When he was about halfway up the hill, Skalgr and Pehr joined him. Skarnhrafn circled the hill below them, silent and dark, occasionally uttering a hollow chuckle or moaning to himself, a sound that made Brak shudder. When he went out of sight again, they rose and hurried upward to the stone ring. It seemed empty. They circled it, looking for Ingvold in the shadow of each stone.

Brak saw her first and dashed ahead. She was crouching beside a stone, her eyes fixed on the moon, which had just cleared the horizon.

"Ingvold!" he gasped. "Are you all right? Is Hjordis— doing whatever she does?"

Ingvold looked at him a little wildly. "It's too late. You shouldn't have come after me. Run away—flee from me and my curse, if you value your life." She walked away from the ring a few steps, saw Skarnhrafn waiting, and reluctantly returned to the stone. "She's not strong yet; the moon isn't high enough. You've got time to save yourselves if you hurry, Brak, so why don't you go?"

"Isn't there something we can do? Skalgr, come here, you old cur, and tell me there's something we can do to stop Hjordis from taking her." He dragged the old wizard forward impatiently.

Skalgr composed his rumpled clothing and looked at Ingvold for a moment. "Well, there may be time," he said slowly. "She seems to have most of her own will left, so far. If we can awaken the magic in this ring, we might thwart Hjordis' curse. Or at least postpone it for a while."

He didn't sound hopeful. "Let's take her to the center of the ring and try it anyway."

The moon emerged from a nest of clouds on the horizon and began its climb into the sky. Ingvold gasped, as if in pain. "It won't work—it's too late!"

She resisted weakly as they led her to the center of the ring, where her strength seemed to dissolve and she collapsed, much to Brak's consternation.

"She'll be all right, it's nothing," Skalgr assured him in a very worried manner. "What we've got to do now is run—no, Pehr, I don't mean run away, you great ninny. I mean run around this ring, or dance, if you're in the mood. Sometimes three circuits is enough to start it, and sometimes nine is the magic number. Come along, let's get started before the moon gets any higher."

"Not me," Pehr growled. "This is absurd. I won't—"

"You will, Pehr. Come on, run!" Brak urged, giving him a shove. "This is easier than running all the way to Hjordisborg, isn't it?"

In single file they trotted around the ring, with Skalgr calling a reedy cadence. After nine revolutions they were all quite warm and out of breath, but Brak felt no inclination for stopping. Several times he glimpsed Skarnhrafn skulking around the bottom of the hill, and three times the draug darted fire at them, bathing the old ring in flickering light, but none of its heat reached them as they ran.

Skalgr began to sing and skip, crowing exultantly, "It's working, it's working! Can you feel it?"

"I feel a blister forming on my heel," Pehr retorted, puffing.

Skalgr darted to the center of the circle, humming a bit of a dancing tune. "Come along, Ingvold, and dance with us. You needn't languish for want of partners, with twenty-two great stones waiting for so many years for someone to dance with them."

Brak heard her voice protesting, but in a few moments she joined them with a faint laugh at Skalgr's ridiculous capering and singing. He lifted his knobby old knees in high prancing and made up insulting scalds about Skarnhrafn lowering from a nearby hillock. The moon climbed higher and still they ran and danced. Brak no longer felt rather silly; he felt as if he couldn't stop if he wanted to—not that he did want to stop. With each stride he felt as if he were soaring, his weariness and exhaustion and anxiety forgotten. The pitted faces of the stones became familiar faces, friendly faces that seemed to glow in the moonlight. Ahead of him he saw Ingvold running with a long, floating step, as if she were leading him down a long, dark corridor, looking back from time to time and beckoning him on toward a dim, silvery light which seemed to increase bit by painful bit.

He was still staring at the silvery light when he became aware of himself lying face down in some prickly grass with his head cradled between two scaly boulders. He blinked and did not move anything except his eyes, which traveled slowly around the silent circle of stones, looming dark against the dawning day. Without moving, he could tell that his feet and legs were exceedingly weary. His eyes lighted upon Skalgr, lying like a discarded heap of rags, twitching and snorting occasionally in his sleep. On one side of him slept Pehr, curled up in a suspicious knot and scowling, and on the other side of Skalgr slept Ingvold, looking very pale and forlorn, with her ragged hair matted with dew and her fingers wound around the small case about her neck.

Brak sighed and closed his eyes. Their mad dancing around the circle of stones seemed to have worked. He fell into a doze and didn't awaken until the sun warmed his face. His friends had not changed their positions, as he ascertained by opening one weary eye. Shifting his head from its grinding proximity to the boulders, he became aware of a slow, steady sound not far from his position in the ring. His heart hammered a sudden warning and he raised his head warily, ready to sound an alarm.

To his astonishment, old Faxi looked back at him a moment, munching a mouthful of grass, and went back to his grazing with a shake of his mane and a contented flutter of his nostrils. Brak sat up slowly, looking around cautiously for a trap, and saw nothing but Pehr's black horse cropping on the side of the hill.

Brak gave Skalgr a sharp prod with his foot, enjoying the old wizard's wild gasping and thrashing as he awakened. With frightened eyes Skalgr stared around, seizing upon the two horses with separate and distinct shocks and coming to rest upon Brak.

"That's a horse to behold," he announced in a somber tone, shaking his head. "He left the other horses of Hagsbarrow and brought Asgrim with him to follow his master. Uncanny creatures are often speckled or ill-assorted."

"Much like yourself," Pehr interjected with a yawn. "Are we all here and still alive, more or less?" He looked suspiciously at Ingvold, who was stretching and rubbing her eyes.

"We all survived the night quite well, I'd say on first inspection," Skalgr declared, hobbling to his feet with the aid of his staff and grimacing with the effort. "We have escaped from Hagsbarrow, and the spell of Hjordis over Ingvold is broken—perhaps." He looked closely at Ingvold, with not a little anxiety. "I'd hate to do this again tonight. I'm not sure my old joints and bones could take it. Let's hope the spell is broken completely."

Ingvold sat combing her hair with her fingers and studying Skalgr with a frown. "So this creature is our rescuer."

"And our betrayer," Pehr added. "If not for him, none of this would have happened."

"And Ingvold would still be locked in a room in Hagsbarrow," Skalgr rejoined triumphantly. "I rescued all of you, didn't I? Who was it that worked the lock on Ingvold's door? And who was it that came in disguise to the Sciplings' cell to let them escape—and who was rewarded with a beating and a muffling and later a near decapitation? But I'm of a forgiving nature, so we'll let bygones be bygones."

"I wish you were a bygone," Pehr grumbled.

"I, too, have my doubts," Ingvold said. "You were awfully thick with our jailers and the Myrkriddir, weren't you? You seemed to talk your way into rather more freedom than we enjoyed. A most adaptable old beggar, aren't you, Skalgr? I'm wary of a person who seems to make himself fit in wherever he is. One never knows his true loyalties, it seems to me."

Skalgr was not in the least deflated. He tapped himself on the chest proudly and declared, "Skalgr knows where Skalgr's loyalties truly lie, Ingvold Thjordmarsdotter. Dyrstyggr is my master, and I'll serve him until the day I die. He sent me to see if anyone survived the destruction of

Gljodmalborg, and he is most concerned about the dragon's heart, which he gave to your esteemed father as a token of friendship. When I learned that the heart was indeed in the hands of his daughter and serving as a great bone of contention for Myrkjartan and Hjordis, I hastened to find you, kind lady. Now I shall take you and your friends to Dyrstyggr for his advice."

Ingvold cut him short with a rude snort. "I can't believe that any friend of my father's could employ a miserable wretch like you. Dyrstyggr is a noble and heroic warrior, much admired by the Alfar for his past glories. He's almost as venerable as Elbegast, and his four weapons make him very powerful—"

"But, alas, no longer," Skalgr said. "He was captured and treated most cruelly, and his cloak, sword, and helmet were taken from him. He is an old fellow, too, and his days of battle are past history. He was weakened also by the absence of the dragon's heart, which he gave to your father, my dear."

"I am no dear of yours," Ingvold retorted. "I regret to seem ungrateful, Skalgr, but we must part company with you. I can't find any trust in you in my heart."

"Nor I," Pehr added with great satisfaction and malice.

Brak looked around thoughtfully at the circle of stones and the quiet green countryside surrounding it. "I think we ought to give him another chance. He did go to a lot of trouble to get us all out of Hagsbarrow. That certainly is no way to curry favor with Myrkjartan."

"I simply can't believe Dyrstyggr would hire such a rag-bag of a servant," Ingvold said. "You can tell by looking at him what a shifty character he is. It would take a large amount of proof—"

"Proof!" Skalgr exclaimed. "Now why didn't I think of that earlier! Look, look here, if you don't believe me. I should have shown you this earlier, but it slipped my mind somehow." He fumbled for a grimy string around his neck, pulling at it as if he were landing a difficult fish. At last he hauled out the elusive object attached to a cord, after pulling out an inordinate amount of string. "Here, look at this, my dear, and tell me what it is."

Ingvold stepped closer. "It looks like a gold ring. Let

me examine it more closely," she commanded, giving the
string a hard tug which nearly choked him.

"Mercy, you needn't strangle me," he croaked, sawing
at the string with his knife. "Here, take it and welcome."

She took the ring, polished it a bit, and held it up to
the new sun to read a runic inscription. Then she gave
a terrible cry, clutching the ring in her fist. "It's my father's
ring! I'd know it anywhere!"

Chapter 10

❖❖❖❖❖❖❖❖❖❖❖❖❖❖❖❖❖❖❖❖❖❖

Skalgr nodded sadly and patted her ragged head
gently. "I thought you'd recognize it. Thjodmar gave it to
Dyrstyggr as a token of his friendship. Dyrstyggr told me
this ring would prove who I say I am. Would you like to
have it? Keep it if you wish, since it was your father's."

Ingvold nodded and thanked him. For a long time she
sat turning the ring around and around in her fingers, lost
in thought.

Skalgr unfastened a bag from around his neck and began
laying out some rather battered articles of food. "I knew
we'd be needing some provisions. It's rather a long way
to Dyrstyggrsstead, and since we've got off to such a poor
start, we'll be living on our wits most of the way."

"Then we'll probably starve," Pehr said gloomily. "Your
wits especially wouldn't fill a thimble." He hacked off a
large slice of the cold, greasy mutton and began chewing
the resilient stuff arduously.

Brak also helped himself and sat considering the old
wizard as he ate. Skalgr darted sly winks at him and cheer-

fully urged a flask of ale upon him repeatedly, as if they were old friends.

At last Ingvold pocketed the ring and rose to her feet. "Well, we can't stop so long this close to Hagsbarrow, trying to make up our minds about Skalgr. Skalgr, I don't know how you could have acquired this ring, either by fair means or foul, except that it was indeed given to you by Dyrstyggr. Myrkjartan's and Hjordis' ruffians certainly wouldn't allow such a prize to escape their notice. However you came by the ring, you have earned for yourself another opportunity to serve us—or trick us. We shall accompany you, trusting that you are telling a semblance of the truth."

Skalgr grinned, hugging his knotty elbows to his sides. "I am delighted, my dear. I knew you'd recognize the truth when you saw it. You won't be sorry, this time. I shall be undeviating, faithful, and honest down to the last bedbug in my beard—"

"Never mind the promises," Ingvold snapped. "Where are we going?"

Skalgr laced his spidery fingers together. "North to Dyrstyggrsstead, but first we must stop at the nearest hill fort to beg, borrow, or steal—no, no, we won't do that— but we need some supplies. As near as I can figure, we can be at Langborg in three days. I have an excellent map of this area here in my satchel." He delved back into the shabby pouch tied around his neck and juggled two large sausages, several hard loaves of bread, and a small bag of grain before turning up the map. He spread it on his knee, and Brak leaned over his shoulder for a look at it. The map was a hodgepodge of ley-lines and crosses and stains, as if Skalgr had used it more frequently for wrapping fish. Something had nibbled away all the islands on the west coast and made a considerable inroad into the mainland.

Pehr sniffed hungrily. "Let's eat the map. It smells like pickled herrings."

"This is a fine and expensive map, you young cannibal," Skalgr snorted huffily. "You haven't a better one, have you?"

"I think the rats had the right idea," Ingvold said. "In

a nice soup, perhaps, it wouldn't be bad. I've eaten worse, lately."

Skalgr began to grumble, and Pehr couldn't resist a few more gibes at the old wizard's expense. Brak attempted to conciliate the combatants, to no avail. They set off, still insulting one another, after improvising halters for the horses and managing to agree upon who would ride and who would walk.

Skalgr chose their camping place early, despite Pehr's complaints. It was a large hill similar to the one they had camped on the night before. Ingvold silently agreed with Skalgr by stationing herself at the foot of the ring's central stone and gazing around watchfully until sunset. Brak was too anxious even to eat. When the moon began to rise, he could scarcely bear to sit still and watch. He alternately peered at the pale, silent image of Ingvold waiting beside the stone and gazed at the moon rising with leisurely, maddening deliberation.

"Hjordis is calling," Ingvold said suddenly, causing him to jump.

"What shall we do?" he demanded. "Reawaken the ring magic? There's still time, isn't there?"

"Yes, a great deal of time. The hag spell is broken. Hjordis has lost her power over me," Ingvold replied triumphantly.

Pehr sighed and relaxed against one of the stones. "My feet are grateful to hear it," he said. "You're quite sure, aren't you?"

Ingvold chose to ignore him. Brak clapped Skalgr on the back and shook his hand. "It was all your doing, Skalgr. I can almost believe that your capture at Hagsbarrow was an unfortunate accident. Perhaps we were too ready to be suspicious of you."

Skalgr expanded and beamed. "Oh, tush, I'm an old lizard with a thick skin. It's a pleasure to be of service to you. As I've said before, it's an ungrateful and unappreciative world—" He was warming up for a long speech, but Pehr suddenly muzzled him with one hand and pointed with the other into the surrounding darkness.

"It's Skarnhrafn!" he husked, still grasping Skalgr. "There, on the next hilltop, watching us!"

Brak and Ingvold dived into the shelter of the central

stone and looked around its edges. A black shape like a horse and cloaked rider stood there silently for a long moment, then descended to pick a course slowly toward them. He approached no closer than the ditch and earthwork surrounding the hill. Several times he rode around the hill, moaning and muttering to himself. Three times he blasted fire up at them, but it flickered away by the time it reached the ring of stones.

"It's me he's after," Ingvold whispered. "He won't stop following us until he captures me to take back to Myrkjartan." She paused. "It might be a good delaying tactic. You three could hasten on toward Dyrstyggrsstead with the heart. Myrkjartan is probably advancing with his draugar even now, moving toward Miklborg. If I could slow him down somehow, or stop him—"

Brak said, "No, we should stay together."

"Why don't we summon these marvelous Rhbus to blast old Skarnhrafn and set fire to Myrkjartan's army of draugar and drive Hjordis so far underground we'll never see her again?" Pehr demanded. "What's the sense in possessing this heart if we don't use it? Why save it for Dyrstyggr to use if we're the ones in danger? He's probably quite well off, wherever he is, snugged up in some cozy cave somewhere with his feet before the fire, while we're out here freezing and dodging the flirtatious winks of Skarnhrafn. I say it isn't fair, nor very smart either. We ought to—"

"It's simply not the way of the Rhbus to interfere," Ingvold interrupted. "If we get into an impossible situation, we'll ask for their help, and they'll help us if they think it wise."

Pehr continued to argue and simmer for the rest of the night, while Skarnhrafn prowled around their hilltop, uttering unearthly chuckles.

Finally Ingvold ended the argument by retorting, "It isn't I who possesses the heart. I gave it to Brak long ago. I suggest you nag and harry him for a while, Pehr."

Pehr shrugged. "Oh, well, Brak's still only a thrall, after all, and he'll give it back to you whenever you want it."

"No, he won't," Skalgr said gleefully. "It's his now, and he needn't give it up simply upon demand, even if he was a thrall in your realm. Things are different here, particularly if one is possessed of a dragon's heart."

Pehr glowered at Brak, who looked back at his chieftain with a rather defiant scowl. "Well, Brak, why don't you use it, then?"

"The time isn't right," Brak replied.

Pehr turned away in disgust. "You're sounding just like them!"

By the end of three days, with nightly appearances by Skarnhrafn, the argument was buried in grim and exhausted silence. Their food supply was gone, except for a small bag of ground meal, which was made into mush for supper, and water extended it into gruel for breakfast. They swallowed the stuff with little enjoyment, to preserve their strength. On the fourth day Brak killed a hare with a stone, which almost made a meal for them at midday.

Toward evening, Skalgr seemed to look at the map more often. He dowsed feverishly, with no observable results. The course on which he was leading them turned rocky and steep, descending into glacier-choked valleys and winding high into windy scarps where the horses picked a perilous footing.

"I think we're lost," Ingvold announced at sundown, glaring at Skalgr as he tried to dowse.

"I'm sure this is one way to Langborg," Skalgr replied. "All we have to do is get on the eastern side of these fells. I fear it will take us closer to five days than three, but we've got enough of this meal to keep us alive—"

"Provided Skarnhrafn doesn't find us first," Pehr interrupted, shivering in the cold wind.

As if in answer, a far-distant sound drifted to their ears on the wind, a chilling wail echoing across valleys and scarps of ice and stone. They slogged onward on numb feet until it was dark, too cold to be hungry, too cold even to talk. The course they took angled downward, leading perhaps into a lower and warmer valley eventually, where they could catch birds and hares for sustenance. The hope kept them going until dark, when they suddenly arrived at the end of the lead they were following. A vertical barrier of stone rose before them, so steep and jagged that not even snow could cling to it. The wind whipped viciously at their numb faces and froze their hands around the horses' reins. In silence they contemplated the sheer scarp.

"If we stay here much longer," Skalgr said, his speech slow and blurred from stiff lips, "we shall certainly freeze. I propose we walk southward to see if we can't get around it. I shall endeavor to create a light to help us."

He blew on his fingers and held his staff before him. Eyeing it with a fixed glare, he began to mumble spells to it, entreating his power to show itself. After a long time, a faint glow suffused the tarnish, flickered a moment, then died.

"Skalgr's only fire is in an ale bottle," Pehr croaked bitterly.

"A small drop right now would certainly help," Skalgr sighed, and began his spells again.

This time the watery glow strengthened and became a light. Slowly it gathered in strength, making a rather dim and wavering beacon. Skalgr straightened and held it up a little unsteadily, as if the effort of maintaining the light were all he could manage.

"Brak, you lead the way. You'd better lead the horses in case one of them slips and falls over a precipice. I'll follow you with the light, such as it is."

"It's splendid, you old thief," Ingvold said. "I didn't know you had any remaining particles of power left in you."

"Nor did I," Skalgr said solemnly.

They picked their way around the rocky scarp, slithering, stumbling, and hearing rocks falling down unseen chutes and slides, crashing and shattering far below. The horses scrambled for their lives, plunging and straining over places where no one would dream of taking horses, even in broad daylight.

"They'll be troll-bait before this is over," Skalgr growled anxiously.

"Not Faxi," Brak said stubbornly. "He'll go anywhere I can go."

The moment he said it, Faxi stopped short, almost sitting down on his tail. He lifted his muzzle and sniffed, his eyes growing bright with alarm. A fearful snort rattled in his throat and he began to tremble.

Brak gazed around, searching the darkness, but the glare

of Skalgr's torch had dulled his vision. "Skalgr, put out the light."

Instantly the light was extinguished. Pehr grumbled, "I'll bet he never gets it lit again."

The other horse snorted and danced skittishly. Brak's eyes adjusted quickly, but not before Ingvold's did. She looked up the face of the scarp as a large black shadow glided overhead and alighted.

"Skarnhrafn!" she exclaimed.

A moaning sound answered her, and small bits of rock pattered down almost in their faces. Above leered the fiery mask of Skarnhrafn, his visored glare glowing through the slits of the visor in a brilliant, maniacal grin.

"It's useless to run," his voice rumbled. "I have been commanded to return the girl to Myrkjartan. A draug never forgets an order."

He raised the visor halfway, and the tail end of his glance brushed over Brak and Faxi in a scorching breath of flame. Faxi lunged away, dragging Brak after him, and plunged down a steep chute like a cramped staircase. Asgrim charged after Faxi. Brak dropped the reins and grabbed Faxi's tail to keep from being scraped against the walls or trampled underfoot.

In a few moments the steep incline ended abruptly in soft sand, instead of in midair, and before Brak could disentangle himself from the horses, the others came tumbling down the chute.

"Where are we?" Ingvold gasped. "It's darker. It feels like a cave. It's sand under our feet."

"Skalgr, can you get that thing lit again?" Brak asked.

"Where's Skarnhrafn?" Pehr demanded.

"Up above on the scarp, probably wondering where we went," Skalgr replied, between cajoling and cursing his staff. "I hope he's lost us. More likely he'll wait for us above to come out again." He got the staff glowing again and held it up to take a look around. "No one in his right mind would follow a troll tunnel very far, and this looks like a troll cave, or I'm a troll's uncle."

Brak poked at some bones in revulsion, recognizing blackened human skulls among the rubble, all cracked and picked whisker-clean.

"Plenty of fresh tracks," Ingvold reported after a brisk

survey of the cave. "Recent bones. And a tunnel leading off this way, which we could follow and hope it leads to the valleys below, provided we don't run into any trolls. Or we could stay here and climb out in the morning and no doubt meet Skarnhrafn again at night up on the glaciers and scarps."

They considered for a moment, listening to the dead silence of the cave. "Are draugar afraid of trolls?" Pehr asked.

"I wouldn't be if I had that helmet," Brak replied, nervously clutching the small case that hung around his neck.

"But we do have the dragon's heart," Pehr replied. "If the trolls discover us, we can summon the Rhbus to defend us, right? And if trolls are anything like badgers, they always have more than one entrance to their burrows. This tunnel probably opens farther below, which will put us that much closer to Langborg. I certainly don't relish going back the way we came."

"Nor do I," Skalgr agreed.

In the dim light of his staff they all looked at Brak, waiting for him to decide. He wanted to protest that he was only a thrall and not much accustomed to making decisions even for himself, let alone for three other people and two horses.

"Shall we go on, then?" he finally said.

Skalgr gave him a patting push forward. "You lead the way, Brak; you're the one with the dragon's heart. You're doing a fine job leading us, so just go on ahead."

The tunnel dived downward, a deep, slanting fissure in the mountain above. In places, rocks had fallen from above, but years of being scrambled over had worn them smooth. Brak waited anxiously for the one that would be too big for the horses to get over. The tunnel had narrowed enough that a horse could not swap ends and go back the way it had come. Perspiring, Brak began to realize how awkward horses were and how right Skalgr was to grumble about them.

With Faxi's insistent nose nudging him along, Brak walked at a faster pace than he would have chosen. Skalgr's staff lit up only a short bit of the tunnel ahead. Worse yet, he began to imagine that the damp air smelled faintly smoky, and from time to time he thought Faxi acted as if he heard something ahead in the tunnel. Whenever Brak tried to stop to listen, Faxi shoved him impatiently, and Asgrim crowded into Faxi and everyone grumbled. Pehr in particular berated him angrily, since he was the one smashed between the two horses.

The tunnel narrowed further, and Faxi's well-padded sides began to scrape occasionally on the walls. Once or twice he had to scramble and squeeze to get through. During one of their halts, they all heard a distant noise, muffled in the dead air of the cave. It sounded as if something were following them down the long fissure.

"Skarnhrafn," Ingvold said grimly. "I only hope this tunnel comes out somewhere soon. I don't fancy the idea of him coming up behind us in these cramped quarters."

Brak said nothing about the distant singing and yammering sounds he had been hearing ahead of them. There was no choice except to hurry on and hope the tunnel became no smaller.

Suddenly, with a final lunge and snort, Faxi halted, stuck fast in the narrow shaft. He lunged and pawed ineffectually, then relaxed with a resigned sigh, a horse-sized cork in a bottleneck. No amount of pushing and cajoling from behind would help; he was stuck and he knew it. He flattened his ears and looked obstinate. No one could climb over him or through the fence of his legs. Faxi was rather prickly about his heels, even wedged so tightly.

"Now what?" Ingvold wailed.

Skalgr noisily scratched his untidy scalp. "Well, we can't wait for the horse to starve so he won't be so fat, not with Skarnhrafn behind us."

Pehr's voice sounded as if his teeth were clenched. "Let's kill the stupid beast and carve him out of the way!"

Faxi kicked at Pehr, settling himself more tightly in the tunnel. Brak patted Faxi's nose to soothe him and sat down in a small niche to try to think. Skalgr and Pehr began a disagreement, so Brak decided to venture down the tunnel a short distance, as far as Skalgr's light would reach, at least. He felt his way along carefully, noting that the tunnel widened appreciably. As he groped along the wall, his hand suddenly touched something that felt like coarse fur. It jumped away with a startled snarl, and Brak froze for an electrifying moment, then he whirled and ran, yelling a warning. In an instant he was overrun and brought down under a crush of hairy bodies and clawed feet. They seized him and dragged him first one way, then the other, shrieking in unspeakable depravity. While several trolls sat upon Brak and gouged at him with their claws, probably to see what sort of pot they would need for cooking him, the others went clamoring up the tunnel toward the travelers.

Faxi greeted them with a warlike squeal, and they surged forward with a delighted roar. Brak heard the sound of iron-shod hooves pawing on stone, and the vicious shrieks suddenly were punctuated with solid thumps and screams of pain. The trolls came pelting back, followed by Faxi's triumphant squeals and the yelling of Pehr and Skalgr and Ingvold. Brak's captors abandoned their post and joined the retreat.

Brak scuttled back to Faxi, tripping along the way over three trolls whose skulls had been battered in. Faxi's snapping teeth were at the moment fastened in the skin of a shrieking troll, tossing the creature around like a rag. A litter of knives proclaimed their owners' lost hope of dining that evening upon horseflesh.

With a final rending, the remaining troll freed itself and ran down the tunnel, gibbering.

Brak steadied himself, gasping for breath. "Halloo, Pehr! Are you all right back there?"

"Brak! You're there?" Pehr demanded.

"Yes, they forgot about me, I guess. Is everyone all right?"

"Of course," Ingvold answered. "We have half a ton of horse blubber to protect us. I can't believe you survived."

"They'll be back," Brak said faintly. "Ingvold, you'd better take the heart, hadn't you?"

Ingvold stamped her foot. "Not with Skarnhrafn breathing down our necks!"

Skalgr suddenly yelled. "Listen to that! Trolls behind us, too!"

They listened, scarcely breathing. The sounds were distant, but unmistakable as the quick patter of many feet accompanied by shrill yelps and yammers. Then they heard Skarnhrafn's familiar bellowing voice, and the trolls burst into full hunting cry. Their uproar became louder and louder as they galloped toward the travelers and their horses. The trolls poured into the tunnel from a side passage, bearing a few smoky torches to light their way. Without glancing toward the travelers, the trolls turned the other way and churned away in search of Skarnhrafn.

"That should keep both trolls and Skarnhrafn occupied for a while," Skalgr said with a pleased cackle.

"Time enough for you to summon the Rhbus, Brak," Ingvold declared.

Brak was aghast. "Not me. I'm nothing but a thrall, a base-born nithling. I'm not worthy to talk to your Rhbus."

Pehr roared, "There's nobody else to do it, you great stupid idiot! I, as your chieftain, command you to do it, do you hear?"

"I hear," Brak growled resentfully, taking the case from inside his shirt and opening it with trepidation. "What do I do with it?" He held it in the wavering light of Skalgr's staff glowing through Faxi's legs. The thing inside the case was a lump of dry, black meat the size of a small egg. It smelled pleasantly smoky, which made Brak's mouth water.

"Tear off a small shred and chew it," Ingvold said. "Hurry, Brak. We don't know how long those trolls will detain Skarnhrafn."

Brak listened for a moment to the furious worrying sounds the trolls were making, and to the booming shouts of Skarnhrafn. He began to smell the distinctive odor of singed fur. Resolutely he tore off a thread of the dragon's heart and began to chew it.

"Well? What's it like?" Pehr demanded.

Brak put the case away and stalked down the tunnel to a more private spot. He sat down and swallowed. The more he chewed, the more resilient the meat became, and his mouth grew hotter and hotter. Swallowing the burning juice made his throat burn, too. Presently its effects reached his stomach, which took a definite dislike to dried heart of dragon and made its owner acutely uncomfortable. He felt sweat bursting out on his forehead and palms. His vision, already limited in such a place, became distorted, changing rocks into leering faces with knobby noses and twisted grins.

Red and black nightmares danced just inside his eyelids,

which he fought to keep open on that very account, but his struggle was futile. He felt himself sliding sidewise into an untidy heap, totally helpless in the grip of the nightmares pounding wildly through his head. He saw the faces of Myrkjartan and Hjordis, and they appeared to be quarreling again. He saw a terrible fire with Ingvold's face in the midst of it, and himself a puny little figure compared to the fire, beating at it helplessly while the face of Hjordis leered and laughed. He felt as if his entire body were being consumed, but his arms and legs were like useless lumber. He tried calling for help, but all he could manage was a faint whisper, a feeble word that quickly lost itself in the gloomy cave.

Despairing, he abandoned himself to the tortures of the nightmares, seeing Myrkjartan scowling at him and Skarnhrafn's eyes pursuing him relentlessly, burning and withering. A great black-cloaked figure he took for Myrkjartan bent over him. He tried to shake his head and thrash away from him, but Myrkjartan had a hold on him and wasn't letting go. The nightmares faded, but the hands became more real. Terrified, Brak stared into an unfamiliar face.

"Let me go," he gasped.

Chapter 11

❖❖❖❖❖❖❖❖❖❖❖❖❖❖❖❖❖❖❖❖❖❖❖❖

"I came to help you," the stranger said. "I am the Rhbu, Gull-skeggi, and you sent for me, so I came. It was not wise of you, however, to swallow so much of the heart on your first attempt. Do you feel better now?"

Brak felt life gradually creeping back into his arms and legs. With a great effort, he sat up to prop himself against a stone so that he could see the Rhbu. The light came from a large, rugged opening in the rock, beyond which he glimpsed a green valley. He looked at Gull-skeggi wonderingly, seeing an ordinary-looking Alfar of undetermined age clad in an ordinary black cloak fastened with an elaborate brooch on one shoulder. Brak had never seen a face so serene and pleasant, framed by a light-colored beard braided into two forks.

"I've got a great many questions," Brak began, "but I hate to trouble you more than I have already. Such an exalted being as yourself has little time for a mere thrall. I and my problems are terribly common and stupid, I fear."

"A fat old horse stuck in a tunnel is not a common problem," Gull-skeggi said with a smile. "The other Rhbus and I have been observing your progress and we decided to intervene, since Skarnhrafn would surely kill you otherwise and capture Ingvold. The heart would be stupidly lost if that happened, because Myrkjartan does not yet realize you possess it. As for your other questions—" He paused, and Brak experienced another fiery burning in his throat, and the red and black nightmares rushed at him again from nowhere. This time, however, they were not frightening images. He saw a party of horsemen striding over a hilltop with sunlight twinkling on their metalwork and weapons. He could hear the thunder of hooves and the frequent clink of a shod hoof on stone and the squeak of leather. The cave seemed to be filled with men and horses, and to Brak's astonishment, he saw himself among them, and Pehr and Skalgr and Ingvold also.

"They'll take you safely to Langborg," Gull-skeggi continued, "and that is all you need to know for now. What we must attend to now is the job at hand—unsticking your horse from the tunnel. It's not really so difficult; you must convince him that he can do it before it is possible. What you must do is whisper these words in his ear, and he'll follow you directly. Then you will simply go along the tunnel to this place and proceed westward toward Langborg until the Alfar warriors overtake you. Good luck, Brak, and farewell."

"Thank you, sir. I hope we'll meet again?" Brak stammered, still rather confused, after the Rhbu had whispered the words to him.

"You may never actually see me again, but I assure you, I'll be aware of what you are doing. If ever you feel truly desperate, send for me and I'll help you." He raised one hand in farewell and smiled benignantly, very quietly vanishing before Brak's eyes.

Brak looked away nervously and rubbed his eyes, wondering if this was another species of dragon-induced hallucination. The Rhbu was gone, however, although the words he had whispered for Faxi were etched in Brak's memory. Brak reluctantly turned back into the darkness of the tunnel, soon leaving the dim daylight behind and knocking his shins and his head against outcropping rocks. Judging from the number of bruises rising in those sensitive spots already, he assumed that he had passed those painfully familiar outcroppings of rocks before and was now renewing old acquaintances. He supposed it was the Rhbu's doing, to show him the way out of the cave.

The distance back to Faxi and his friends seemed interminable. He knew he had arrived when Faxi suddenly neighed ringingly and pawed and snorted eagerly.

"Pehr! Ingvold! Are you still there?" he gasped, seeing no light from Skalgr's staff. For a moment he was panic-stricken, thinking Skarnhrafn had carried them off, in spite of the Rhbu's best intentions.

"Brak? Is that you?" Ingvold asked in an odd voice.

"Yes, it's me. I guess I sort of wandered off while I was—"

"You've been gone for hours," Pehr said, angry and relieved. "We had no idea what was happening to you. Trolls might have eaten you, or the dragon meat might have killed you, for all we knew. What happened anyway?"

"Did you see the Rhbus?" Skalgr demanded, trying to summon a flicker of light from his staff and failing.

"I'll tell you later." Brak pushed away Faxi's inquisitive nose and found one ear. He began whispering the words, and Faxi at once ceased his restless fidgeting and tail-lashing.

"What? What? Don't whisper!" Skalgr exclaimed. "Wait! What's happening?"

Faxi squeezed his ribs against the rock and heaved

mightily. Pehr gave an excited shout, and he and Skalgr put their shoulders to the horse's haunches and shoved. The horse shot forward so fast they went sprawling, and Ingvold leaped over them to pounce on Brak.

"I want to hear all about it," she demanded. "Did you see one of them? What did he tell you? Are we going to get out of here?"

Brak sidled away, suddenly reluctant to share his experience. "I'll tell you later. It's not far to the outside, and I'm sure Skarnhrafn isn't far behind." He gave Faxi a whack and sent him scrambling through the tunnel, still scrubbing his sides on the walls where they narrowed. "I won't really feel safe until we're out of this tunnel. I've had a bellyful of trolls." And dragon meat, he added to himself with a shudder.

Faxi and Asgrim began to hurry, snuffing hungrily. After another fifty yards of darkness, they came into the dim light of the opening. The shaft widened into a deep cleft in the mountainside, overlooking a narrow green valley. The two horses crowded ahead, anxious to get at the grass. According to Skalgr's reckoning, they had been in the tunnel two nights and a day. After putting some miles between themselves and the troll caves, Brak could suddenly believe he had gone that long without food. Near midmorning they stopped to cook an enormous batch of mush, and spent the remainder of the day resting and looking at Skalgr's map.

Ingvold could stifle her impatience no longer. She captured Brak as soon as he awakened and demanded to know what had happened with the Rhbu. Skalgr and Pehr listened with interest. Brak only twitched his shoulders and stared at his feet. "I can't really explain it," he said, his hand closed protectively around the heart. "I'm not a clever person, like you or Pehr."

"I see. You don't want to talk about it yet." Ingvold said. "But the Rhbus did answer your summons?"

Brak nodded reluctantly. "There may be ears listening. We know Skarnhrafn isn't far behind."

They spent a cold and watchful night among some large boulders. No trolls attacked, although Brak was sure he heard their distant voices. He was warmed by the hope that the trolls had caught Skarnhrafn in their tunnels—a temporary situation, but enough, perhaps, to let them get ahead of him again.

In the morning they feasted on marmot and a hare. Even Pehr, the finicky, devoured his share of the marmot and pronounced it delicious. Somewhat heartened, they gathered up their meager belongings and trekked westward at Brak's heels—not without complaint on Pehr's and Skalgr's part.

"There's nothing to the west but bogs and more mountains," Skalgr growled. "We'll be so far from Langborg that we'll never find it."

"It is going to find us," Brak replied, refusing to elaborate further, much to the ire of Pehr.

"He's been addled in the wits since he ate that wretched meat," Pehr muttered, "and he won't tell us a thing about it. We've always been like brothers, Brak and I, and now he turns against me and won't talk, except in riddles."

Brak scarcely heard; he was looking around at the fells and valleys, hoping to see ones that looked like those he had seen in his vision in the tunnel. They all looked so similar that he despaired of recognizing specific hills, so he jogged onward, trusting that if they were to be found, then they would be found.

It was late in the afternoon when his mouth started burning. He stopped his weary slogging and looked around swiftly. Faxi, with Ingvold on his back, came up behind him to give him an encouraging shove with his nose, but Brak continued to look around at the hills in the red light of evening.

"We'll stop here," he announced, knowing Pehr would protest that they had several hours of twilight yet. He quickly added, pointing to a nearby hill, "Alfar horsemen will be riding over that hill, and they'll take us to Langborg. We'll stop here and wait for them."

Pehr was too incredulous even to complain. "Brak, you're not the same thrall I thought I knew so well. Something's come over you since you ate that dragon meat."

Everyone stared in silent curiosity at Brak. Then Ingvold spoke up stoutly in his defense. "I'm sure an encounter with a real Rhbu would change almost anyone, and in some cases—" She glared at Pehr. "—the change would be much to the better."

They waited for nearly an hour before Brak's stubborn resistance softened to uncertainty. Morosely he stared at the hill, wondering if his imagination had been playing tricks on him. Ingvold attempted to console him with some highly plausible excuses, but a part of him refused to deny the fact that he had seen Alfar riders while he was under the influence of the dragon's heart.

At last Pehr stood up and declared, "It would be a good idea if we were in the shelter of those hills ahead for to-night. I, at least, intend to get there before it's pitch-black, and I hope the rest of you will realize—"

Brak didn't listen. He kept his eyes on the hill, remembering how plainly he had heard the squeak of leather, the rattling of arrows in quivers, and the thudding of many hooves on the soft earth—and suddenly he could see them, bursting over the crest of the hill at full gallop, manes, tails, cloaks, and beards flying in the wind. The leader gave an astonished shout and brought his horse to a skidding halt within a few feet of overrunning Skalgr. With drawn swords, the horsemen surrounded the strangers. Skalgr dropped his staff as a sword was thrust under his nose and a gruff voice demanded, "Are you from the Fire Wizards' Guild? Speak up, your life depends upon it!"

Skalgr recovered his aplomb quickly and glared at the horsemen. "Certainly I am, you dolts. You should be able to tell by looking that I'm not a troll or a Dokkalfar. Now who are you? Ljosalfar, I presume?"

"Aye, that we are. My name is Smidkell, and these other fellows are my brothers and neighbors. You haven't seen any signs of Myrkjartan, have you?" The sword was sheathed and Smidkell began to look more friendly.

"None this side of the mountains," Skalgr replied.

"And who are these young fellows with you?" Smidkell turned his attention to Brak and Pehr. "I say, they're the tallest Alfar I've ever seen, particularly the brown-bearded one. Where do you hail from?" he asked Brak with interest.

"My thralls," Skalgr interrupted hastily. "I believe they originally came from the north. Nobody really knows what one may find in the north, you know. We were going to Langborg to help fortify against Myrkjartan and Hjordis, but, as you see, we've run into a dreadful lot of bad luck.

All we've eaten in the past three days is one small hare, a marmot, and some very thin gruel."

"Is that so? Well, we can remedy that easily enough. We were about to pitch camp for the night anyway, and you shall join us and share our provisions. Nothing too delectable, I fear, but you certainly won't be hungry when we're done. I thought this little fellow here had a half-starved look." Smidkell tweaked Ingvold's ear, which was less of an outrage to her than being mistaken for a boy. Brak saw her open her mouth to put Smidkell in his place, since she was a chieftain's daughter, but a thoughtful expression came into her eyes and she remained silent. With her ragged hair and castoff boots and trousers, she would have difficulty persuading anyone she wasn't a scruffy, skinny young thrall.

The Alfar busied themselves with taking the horses and setting up their camp. In a very short time, enticing aromas were steaming from the kettles.

"Will you be staying long in Langborg after you re-provision?" Smidkell inquired of Skalgr.

Skalgr rubbed his disreputable chin. "I'm not certain. I'm simply aghast at the supplies it takes for three thralls, even on short rations. At this rate, I'll have to sell off a couple of these fellows."

Pehr glared indignantly, but Ingvold poked him covertly and frowned.

"You'll get a good price for them in Langborg," Smidkell said. "In fact, I know a wizard who needs a good thrall or two to help him take supplies to Miklborg. Since the wars with Myrkjartan and Hjordis started, trade has been down considerably. Most of the pack trains simply can't get through. Plenty of freemen and thralls have been killed."

Brak darted an apprehensive look at Ingvold. She whispered, "Miklborg is north, not far from Dyrstyggrsstead. Don't you think it's a good idea to let someone else worry about the food for a change?"

"But Skalgr's going too far," Pehr protested. "He's tricked us again! And I'm no thrall to be bought and sold!"

"Yes, but we're well rid of him," Brak answered with a wry smile. "You must try to look more humble, Pehr. Good thralls don't glower."

Pehr would have argued it further, but the food was ready, so they joined the Alfar fighters in a feast, or so it seemed to their starved bellies. The Alfar were amiable, generous fellows, and they were curious about Brak and Pehr, but Skalgr posted himself close to them so that he could answer the questions in his own fashion. Repeatedly he darted winks at Brak and Pehr and Ingvold, as if to say it was all a ploy, and they looked back at him very coldly.

Pehr was still dissatisfied. "How can we be sure he'll sell us all? And to the same person? Isn't this rather chancy, Ingvold?"

She shrugged. "Just wait and see what happens. We're not exactly helpless as long as we've got Brak and the heart."

Brak shook his head. "We must stay together, then."

Skalgr officiously poked at Brak with his staff. "Mind there, sir, and stop that whispering. Remember what happened last time."

Brak favored him with a piercing look. "I remember, Skalgr."

Smidkell laughed. "You'd better be careful, Skalgr. He's more than twice your size."

"Which isn't saying much," Skalgr agreed with a broad grin, rubbing his hands together. "It's an ungrateful and unappreciative world, and I'm much reduced in more ways than one." He continued to chuckle and mutter to himself as if he considered it a great joke.

A guard was posted on the hillside, and everyone else settled down in eiders and cloaks for the night. Skalgr selected a spot somewhat removed from his so-called thralls. When they were certain everyone else was asleep, Brak, Pehr, and Ingvold crept over to Skalgr, surrounding him and pinning him inside his eider. Ingvold seized his staff and dealt him some terrific whacks, while Pehr muffled him with a cloak. Then Pehr removed the cloak and snarled into the old wizard's face, "If you make one sound, I'll twist your wretched head off as if I were wringing a chicken's neck, and I'll do it right gladly, too. The only reason we didn't kill you was because we'll be glad to get to Langborg and be rid of you."

"Have pity—oh, my joints and bones—"

"What we came to tell you," Ingvold said severely, "is

that we know you've betrayed us again, and you deserve much worse punishment. You'd better sell us together, or, by the beards of Thor and Odin, we'll get even with you."

"I shall, I shall! I only—"

"We'll continue this miserable game only as long as you do as you're told," Pehr continued. "You'd better sell us to a wizard of good repute who can help us find Dyrstyggr."

"Don't worry, I'll be very glad to," Skalgr gasped. "I'm truly sorry to trick you again, but the prospect of money and ale and food is more than I can resist, even for Dyrstyggr's sake. Please forgive me—ha, perhaps we can trick them all together and join each other afterward—"

"Never!" Brak growled.

"But maybe you'll never find Dyrstyggr without me," Skalgr suggested slyly.

"We have the heart and the Rhbus to help us," Brak said. "We don't need the likes of you, Skalgr. After we part in Langborg, I hope we never see you again."

They released him and glided back to their beds, leaving Skalgr testing his sore spots and muttering to himself.

In the morning, the three thralls were assigned to ride behind the riders on the strongest horses, and Skalgr rode Asgrim. Faxi was left to his own devices, since he was obviously an elderly horse of very common ancestry with an unfavorable aspect. To Brak's distress, Faxi was at once left behind, looking very forlorn. However, at the next stop for rest, Faxi soon came trotting into view, searching for Brak, and although they left him behind again, he always reappeared. Smidkell laughed, then marveled, then admired that night when Faxi trotted into camp almost as fresh and strong as he had been that morning. Smidkell rubbed Faxi's wide, stubborn forehead and patted his thick neck.

"This is a heroic little horse," he declared. "I'd pay a good price for a horse that can trot all day. Is he for sale, Skalgr?"

"Oh—ah, not that one." Skalgr darted a worried glance at Brak.

"One hundred kronur," Smidkell said.

Skalgr's eyes began to gleam. "One hundred—"

"That horse kicks and bites like a demon," Brak said. "I'm the only one he really likes."

"Oh? A pity," Smidkell said. "I'll have to think about it."

In the afternoon of the next day, the Alfar horses trotted across the wide green plain that surrounded Langborg. A vast earthwork rose around the foot of the scarp on three sides, and on the fourth the land fell away in an abrupt drop hundreds of feet to the inlet below. Turf longhouses clustered inside the earthwork, and men, women, and children went about their business while the sentries patrolled the earthwork. Smoke from many cooking fires whetted Brak's appetite.

"That's the warlord's hall." Smidkell pointed out an ancient mossy edifice of turf. A ring of fires burned among the encampments surrounding it, illuminating rows of shields and weapons hung on the hall's venerable sides. "Skalgr, you can take your thralls and beg the warlord's hospitality, which is always generous, and he'll be glad to hear anything about the situation to the east. You'll have a few inches of hard boards to sleep upon and share with dozens of soldiers. Or you can come with me to my humbler home with my family, where you'll be our honored guests. My wife Hidi will give you a feather tick, and the thralls will have clean straw in the beasts' stable. Come, what do you say, old wizard? Have I convinced you?"

"Sounds splendid," Skalgr said graciously. "It's been eons since this wretched old spine has encountered a feather bed."

Smidkell's kinsmen dispersed cheerfully to their various homes, or sought the warlord's hospitality if their homes were distant. Pehr, Brak, and Ingvold trudged behind Smidkell's horse, exchanging angry glowers.

"Feather bed!" Pehr grumbled. "While we get straw!"

A warm welcome awaited them at Smidkell's house, a scrupulously neat longhouse designed to shelter man and beast under the same roof, with room for a knarr to be stored besides when the winter sea was not navigable. It was in the beasts' part of the house that Brak and Pehr and Ingvold were expected to sleep, which was none the less inviting for the sharing of it with several horses and a friendly family of goats.

After a most agreeable supper and a long evening of ale and poetry, the household went to bed, including a long row of chickens on the rafters overhead with their heads tucked under their wings. Brak found the clean straw wonderful, after so many nights of curling up between cold, sharp rocks and expecting to be awakened all too soon for his turn at standing guard.

Early in the morning, entirely too early, the house was awakened by a strident hammering on the door and several impatient shouts. The voice was loud and self-important.

"Halloa, Smidkell! What are you doing in bed so late in the morning? I want to see those thralls your friend has for sale. Open up! I haven't got all the rest of my life to wait for you!"

Brak and Pehr and Ingvold looked at one another and listened.

"I only hope," Ingvold said, "that our new master is not as disagreeable as his voice is."

Chapter 12

The wizard Kolssynir stalked haughtily into Smidkell's house, a tall, lean fellow with a magnificent silver-and black-streaked beard. He wore a long cloak over one shoulder of a short, high-collared coat cinched with a wide ornate belt. Bands of fancy weaving and embroidery embellished his coat and cloak, and he wore a very arrogantly poised bonnet-type hat with four flopping ears on top, which showed what area he was from. His trousers were the most flamboyantly baggy trousers Brak had ever seen, and were stuffed into reindeer boots made of the heads of the reindeer, with the snouts forming the upcurling toes. As if all this splendor weren't enough, he also carried a pair of magnificently stitched gauntlets under his belt.

He stared down his nose at the three thralls when they were presented for his inspection, then eyed Skalgr with obvious distaste.

"So these are the thralls in question," he declared. "Not much to look at. Rather like yourself, Skalgr. I knew a horse thief once who ought to have been your twin brother."

Skalgr nodded and shook his head and twisted his hands. "But I never had a twin brother. You see, it's an ungrateful and unappreciative world, and I've had such hard times—"

"Bah!" Kolssynir barked into Brak's face, despite the fact that Brak was taller by several inches. Brak did not flinch, and he and the wizard exchanged a measuring glance.

Then Kolssynir gave Ingvold a push. "This is a puny one. Skinny fellows like this usually die without the least provocation, and blame the lack of food and proper shelter for it."

Skalgr eagerly interposed himself again. "But big, stout lads like these two can work twice as hard chopping wood and hauling water and can stay up half the night working with no problem. Not to mention, of course, that good labor is rather scarce nowadays, since the traders are staying away and the Dokkalfar are killing or stealing your thralls from time to time."

Kolssynir gave Ingvold another disparaging poke with his staff. "So what you mean to say is, I'd better take what I can get and like it, or you'll just peddle your wares elsewhere and demand an extravagant price merely because you can get away with it, right, eh?"

Skalgr writhed, managing a sickly grin. "Why, whatever is wrong with that? Good business, is what I'd call it. I'm prepared to make you a very fair bargain for the three of them."

Kolssynir scowled at Pehr, who scowled back. "I don't want three thralls. I don't have enough horses for three."

Ingvold spoke up haughtily. "We have two horses of our own."

"Indeed! Who says thralls have the right to own horses?" Kolssynir demanded, outraged. "Such a notion could throw our entire system of government and social order into chaos! I knew from the moment I set eyes upon the lot of you there was something gravely amiss, and my powers warned me that dark schemes were lurking below the surface like poisonous snakes, ready to strike in an unguarded quarter. You, Skalgr, are not what you seem, not at all."

Skalgr's grin became wider and more forced. "Perhaps I should confess and be done with it, but I wish to remind you, I took no pains to deceive anyone. I merely came here to disburden myself of three thralls I can't afford to keep any longer. It's true, I'm no Guild wizard, nor ever was, and doubtless never will be, since a Guild wizard needs to be sober at least half the time, and I've a dreadful fondness for the aged, fermented spirits. Once I had powers and aspirations and dreams of doing much good for my fellow Alfar and much harm to those with evil intentions, but you now see before you the sad wreck of all those treasured hopes, a miserable creature who seeks only a moment's shelter and food before returning to the cold, wretched world of the homeless and the lordless vagabond. All I ask is a fair price for these thralls who cast their lot with mine, hoping for something better and failing to find it. Let's say one hundred marks for the three thralls and the two horses?"

Kolssynir snorted. "They aren't the last thralls in the world, Skalgr. For a moment you almost deceived me with that heartrending nonsense of yours. What I'd like to know is where you got three thralls in the first place, you old thief. Stealing thralls is almost as serious a crime as stealing horses."

"Oh, no, not I," Skalgr protested, feigning righteous indignation. "I may be unscrupulous from time to time, I may even be what you'd call a thief, but I never stole anything of that size."

"Then where did you get them?" Smidkell inquired, looking much distressed and apologetic for harboring such a creature.

"We're runaways," Ingvold said casually, as if no penalty existed for thralls seeking their freedom.

"Indeed!" Kolssynir exclaimed, whirling around to look at her with more astonishment than he could hide. "Then those horses must be stolen and you fellows are the next best thing to outlaws, and here's this old thieving deceiver trying to turn a profit for himself on thralls he doesn't own and who are very likely to be sought out by their rightful masters and properly punished, if not hanged!"

"You needn't worry about that," Ingvold continued in the same calm voice and demeanor that must rightfully belong to chieftains' daughters. "We came from the Scipling realm, and no one is looking for us—not here anyway. We joined this old wanderer Skalgr for his protection, such as it was, and we'll gladly go our separate ways, provided you're not a terribly unkind and ungenerous master."

"Well! This is new to me!" Kolssynir exclaimed, stalking up and down, thumping his chest and waving his arms as if he were about to burst with too much indignation. "Thralls who give their masters conditions! Thralls who own horses! Thralls who desert their masters and slip into the Alfar realm!"

"Well, perhaps you'd better think about it for a few days," Skalgr said soothingly.

Kolssynir gave another great snort. "I don't have a few days. I need some help immediately, if I'm ever going to get to Miklborg before Myrkjartan and Hjordis lay siege to it. I need at least two good men to help me run the pack train, and a third would be useful, even if he were a pale skinnybones. Fifty marks, you old thief, and that's more than they're worth, even in wartime." He brought out a heavy little pouch and began counting gold marks.

Skalgr's eyes gleamed, although he pretended to be unimpressed. "Well, I shouldn't give them up so cheaply; after all, they're almost like friends to me, after everything we've gone through. I wouldn't like to think I'd sold them cheaply to a wizard who might be—less than adequate, shall we say? I did promise them I'd find someone of great power and intelligence—"

"Well, then, that's me," Kolssynir said shortly. "I expect I'm the best wizard in Langborg, perhaps the best on the entire west coast. At least no one has disagreed with me for very long after I said so." He conjured a sudden, crackling aura about himself. Fire seemed to leap from every hair on his head and to glow like globes of gold on his fingertips. With a twitch of one shoulder he banished the illusion and tossed his pouch down on the table. "Here's your money, you old wretch. Take it and your scheming carcass out of Langborg. I'd prefer not to see you again—

you understand?" He looked narrowly at the old wizard, who was slyly winking and grinning and nodding as he hung the heavy pouch around his neck.

"Goodbye," Skalgr said, sidling toward the door. Bestowing a last conspiratorial wink upon Brak, he took himself and his gold away.

Smidkell looked embarrassed. "Perhaps we should go after that old rogue. I don't know if we should believe what they tell us. It must be a scheme of some sort, I fear."

Kolssynir stalked up and down, looking at his new workers. "Yes, I rather thought so myself. Got a mind like a vise, that old thief. Even I could not trick him into revealing his true intentions. He's a very deep one, isn't he, my lad?" He turned to pounce upon Pehr, who looked incredulous.

"Skalgr, a deep one? Not that I ever noticed," he said. "Why do you say such a thing?"

Kolssynir winced and shook his head. "The thralls in the Scipling realm must think themselves quite as good as anybody, to ask such questions. I only hope your appalling sense of freedom isn't highly contagious, or all our Alfar thralls will be demanding horses and fine halls of their own." He glared at each of them in turn. "I shall warn you now that I am a difficult fellow to work for, although not unkind or ungenerous. I expect the maximum effort from all of you, and the situations we get into may not be at all pleasant. We shall be taking a pack train of ten ponies to Miklborg, where the fighting is. We are the only hope Miklborg has of surviving the winter, which will be upon us before we know it. Hjordis and Myrkjartan have taken Thrombsborg and Hagsbarrow—"

"And Gljodmalborg," Ingvold added. "Miklborg will be the next one they attack."

Kolssynir raised one eyebrow. "I suppose you'll tell me next that you've been on the east side of the Slagfells, since you seem to know so much."

"That is correct," Ingvold stated. "We may be from the other realm, but we are not strangers to the situation here. I am, in fact, probably the last survivor of Gljodmalborg's destruction."

Kolssynir grunted. "I see. Then only the two Sciplings are runaways." He bent a threatening glare upon Brak and Pehr. "I hope you both have the good sense not to run away again. Not from me, you'd better not. I need all the help I can muster to get those supplies to Miklborg. If you should happen to feel tempted, you might think about several hundred good Alfar starving and dying this winter in the darkness while the Dokkalfar are howling around them. Now, then, there's nothing more to be said about your fate, so let's have a look at those horses of yours and get started packing."

Kolssynir passed approval on Asgrim and Faxi with considerable brow-arching and significant snorting. He and Smidkell exchanged knowing glances over Asgrim and muttered, "Stolen, beyond a doubt." Asgrim was clearly a fine horse, unlike old Faxi, if he were judged by appearance alone. Kolssynir shook his head, but Smidkell said, "That's a horse that can trot all day with scarcely any rest. He might look like butter, but he's more like iron."

"Hah, we shall see. They say speckled horses are lucky. Did you steal him in this realm or the other, hey?" Kolssynir snapped at Brak.

"I didn't steal him anywhere," Brak replied. "He was given to me by my old chieftain in friendship. You needn't worry about him slowing you down either."

Kolssynir nodded emphatically. "He'd better not, or we'll leave him for the trolls to find. Come along, we've got a mountain of work to do today." He saluted Smidkell and stalked away at the head of the procession.

His house was built into the hillside on the highest part of the hill fort, where the sentries climbed onto his roof to watch the plain below. They hailed him through the smoke hole in the manner of old friends and frequently stopped for a drink of something after duty. The house was small, dark, and extremely cluttered. Mounds of foodstuffs and equipment ascended to the roof beams and were heaped everywhere, so that there seemed to be little space for people or horses. Brak put the two horses in a large paddock with eleven others, then attempted to penetrate the gloom and tumbling mounds of supplies in Kolssynir's house. On the far side of a tremendous pile of ground meal, he heard the wizard's voice directing Pehr and Ingvold to put everything into wax-treated parcels and make packs for the horses.

About noontime two sentries on the roof shouted down. "Kolssynir! What are the chances we can share with you whatever's in that pot? We've got ale and cheese and stale bread to go with it."

"You needn't ask, you numbskulls!" Kolssynir roared. "Get yourselves down here at once, or there's likely to be nothing left, with three hungry thralls who would eat fried troll as long as it kept coming. You there, give that pot a stir. What's your name anyway?"

Brak straightened and looked into the pot. He had thought the wizard was boiling a batch of dirty clothes and old boots—not dinner.

"Brak is my name, sir." He cautiously stirred the mess, recognizing turnips still clad in their gray skins, unpeeled potatoes, and stalks of rhubarb, all floating in a greasy gray broth that smelled rather muttony.

The sentries climbed over the heaped supplies, exchanging insults with Kolssynir and seating themselves on bundles of stockfish. Brak served up the stew in large crocks and sat down with his share beside Pehr and Ingvold. It wasn't dainty fare, and the bread certainly was stale, but at least it was plentiful.

"We heard all about your thralls from Smidkell," one sentry said. "Rather a villainous lot, from the looks of them. Runaways and thieves are often likely to repeat themselves, you know. I wouldn't trust them with any weapons if I were you."

"Well, you're not; you're only a sentry and I'm a wizard," Kolssynir retorted good-humoredly. "I've dealt with Dokkalfar, trolls, jotuns from both north and south, ice wizards, and hostile draugar, so I expect to manage three thralls quite handily."

"Speaking of draugar," the other sentry said, with a potato impaled on the end of his knife, "did you hear about my brother-in-law Veili last night?"

"Is Veili the one with the short, fair beard?" his friend asked.

"No, that's my other brother-in-law, who married—"

"Just get on with what happened last night," Kolssynir growled.

"Speaking of draugar," the sentry continued in a lowered voice, "my brother-in-law Veili, who was riding last night with the Thordssons, got separated from them in the dark—he insists on riding that old half-blind nag of his wife's; you know the one I mean. While he was finding his way back to Langborg alone, he rode up behind someone, thinking it old Njal, and he even shouted out some sort of nonsense to the fellow before he realized it wasn't old Njal, but a draug instead. He said it was a great tall fellow with a wicked helmet of a strange design, and he said the draug had eyes like a fireship and a horse that looked as if it had been dead for a century, with mane to its knees and hide coming off in patches as big as your hand, and nothing but bone underneath." His voice fell to a shocked whisper, and he glanced around as if expecting to see the draug and his horse come stalking out from behind one of the piles of staring stockfish.

"Is that all? What did your cousin do after saluting this creature on such familiar terms?" Kolssynir inquired.

"Brother-in-law, not cousin. I believe he turned that old nag of his wife's around and whipped it all the way back to Langborg, feeling the hot breath of that draug on his back until he was safe inside and the gate shut. It was a wonder his horse didn't fall and break both their necks. If it had been me there, I would have—"

"Oh, hush yourself, you wouldn't have either," the other sentry interrupted. "Kolssynir, have you ever heard of a draug such as this one described by Veili?"

Kolssynir meditatively pared a mouse-gnawed corner from his bread, allowing a silence to tantalize his audience, during which Pehr poked Brak with his elbow. Kolssynir caught the movement and looked sharply at Pehr and Brak. "Perhaps you fellows have heard of a draug such as he describes. Perhaps you even know his name, eh? I suppose Sciplings can be made useful to the Dokkalfar, or to Myrkjartan, just as well as I might, so I shall warn you three." He flicked his hand, and a finely honed knife appeared in his palm. "In this realm, we deal with spies in only one way. We cut their throats and leave them unburied."

"We're not spies," Ingvold said indignantly. "It would be better to be dead than to join forces with Myrkjartan or Hjordis. Of course we know the draug you are talking about. Anyone who has been east of the Slagfells knows about Skarnhrafn. He leads Myrkjartan's draugar and wears Dyrstyggr's helmet."

The sentries looked at each other in dismay. "Skarnhrafn! West of the Slagfells! Could they be coming after Langborg instead of Miklborg?"

Kolssynir put his knife away with another flick of his hand. "Veili saw only one draug, not an entire army of them. Yet isn't it strange how visitors often come in batches to Langborg? Strange visitors in particular. I shall get at the truth one day when I'm not so pinched for time. Speaking of which, isn't it about time you fellows got back to your posts?"

The sentries departed with gracious thanks, and Pehr, Brak, and Ingvold also returned to work, avoiding the eye of Kolssynir, which watched them very thoughtfully. For the rest of the day he wore a preoccupied manner, absentmindedly humming bits of songs and staring at nothing in particular. He lurked around the piles of goods as if hoping to overhear some interesting conversation among his thralls. Late that night, Brak was awakened by the stealthy approach of the wizard, carrying a horn lamp. For a long moment the wizard studied his three charges, then withdrew with a short, impatient sigh. Brak then heard him go out to the horses and ride one away toward the wall. He debated awakening the others to discuss an escape, but he fell asleep while he was thinking about it, grateful for a full stomach and a roof over his head, however briefly those luxuries might last.

In the morning Brak covertly observed Kolssynir, who was again observing his thralls covertly. The wizard stalked around with a truculent, uneasy attitude, and he even climbed on top of the house to stare out at the surrounding fells and meadows. At midnight he rode out again and returned after several hours, smelling of burned wool cloth. The next morning Brak noticed Kolssynir wearing a new cloak, and the old one was stuffed under the roof beams. At the first opportunity, Brak snatched it out for inspection. As he suspected, it was badly charred, which confirmed Brak's suspicions about what Kolssynir had gone out to seek at night. After the experience of getting his cloak set afire, Kolssynir discontinued his nighttime expeditions and doubled his previous exertions to prepare the pack train for Miklborg.

When they did depart, they were anything but ill-prepared. Worn-out clothing was replaced and everyone was fitted with reindeer boots, which were stuffed with coarse, porous grass to keep his feet warm. Ingvold rode the extra pack horse, and Kolssynir appeared with a fine, fiery black horse with a graceful head and neck and long, slender legs —very unlike sturdy, hairy old Faxi and the common pack horses. Kolssynir was well aware that he cut a dashing figure, capering at the head of his long procession of horses and goods as they rode out the gate of Langborg and took the northward road.

They traveled at a brisk pace for four days without seeing a sign of Skarnhrafn. Pehr was certain that they had left the draug prowling and groaning around the earthwork of Langborg, not realizing his quarry had escaped. Brak was not so hopeful; the further they rode into the Slagfells, the more uneasy he became, and it was not merely because of the trolls that stalked them each night. Kolssynir handled the trolls with fire spells and cleverly hidden traps, which amounted to a passion with the wizard. Nothing pleased him more than to find half a dozen trolls hung up by their heels from rocks or trees when he awakened in the morning. The magic rings he drew with his staff around the entire camp always seared ten or more trolls a night, and other devious traps turned the trolls to stone with a great flash of light. Kolssynir always left the grim remains as a warning to other trolls.

On the fifth day of travel Kolssynir announced with his usual confident aplomb, that they were more than halfway to Miklborg. He pushed the pace all day and past the customary stopping time in the evening. The days were growing shorter with the ending of autumn, which meant less daylight traveling time for the creatures who preferred the sun, and more dark hours for the creatures who preferred the cloak of darkness for their pursuits.

As the day darkened, Brak watched the shadows with concern. At last he rode up beside Kolssynir and said, "I think it's past time we stopped for the night, Kolssynir, while there's still a bit of light to see what we're doing.

Before much longer it will be pitch-black, and we're likely to lose a horse over a precipice, or to trolls."

"Indeed. And you don't suppose there's something worse out there in the dark, do you?" Kolssynir demanded. "Something following us?"

Brak looked up sharply, thinking at once of Skarnhrafn. "There may well be," he said cautiously. "You're the wizard, however, not I."

"Don't be impertinent. We shall stop here, but I don't want to unpack until I walk a short distance back and see what's to be seen and what's not to be seen. You may want to be rather vigilant while I'm gone." Dismounting as he spoke, he opened a pack and produced a sword and an axe for each of his thralls.

"I'd prefer a good bow and arrows, if you have them," Pehr volunteered, fastening the sword belt gladly and hefting the axe with approval.

Kolssynir provided him with the bow and arrows. "I needn't ask if you're acquainted with weapons, I see, in spite of the laws that prohibit arming thralls, as a general rule. What do we care for the general rules, hey?" Grumbling and shaking his head, he slipped away on foot into the deepening darkness, striking occasional sparks with the metal tip of his staff.

The pack horses sighed and shifted their weight from leg to leg with reproachful snorts and groans. They were tired and wanted nothing more than to roll their sweaty backs in the grass and receive their daily dole of grain. A chill wind stiffened everyone's muscles and made the wait for Kolssynir seem twice as long as it was.

The night was fully gathered when they heard a distant shout. In a few minutes rocks clattered on the trail, and Kolssynir came plunging down the last hill in a controlled skid. Gasping and staggering, he flung himself onto his horse and began whipping up the pack horses into a scrambling gallop.

"It's Skarnhrafn!" the wizard croaked, still breathless. "Following right behind us! Hurry! Fast!" He gave Faxi a whack with his staff and lunged off to harry at the heels of the slower horses.

Faxi jumped away indignantly, slowing almost at once to a fast trot in spite of Brak's urging. Brak knew it was useless to insult him further with lashing or swearing, despite Kolssynir's shouts and threats. Considerably behind the others, Brak was the first to see the distant red glow bobbing over the glacier below them, circling for a surprise attack beyond the next scarp. Skarnhrafn vanished into the crags; just as the horses surged around a shoulder of stone, he appeared only a bowshot above them, glowing like an overheated kettle. The horses milled about in fright, but Kolssynir drove them relentlessly forward. Skarnhrafn's fire swept over them, singeing manes and tails and blackening the packs they carried, but they rushed on gamely, with the riders shouting encouragement.

Faxi, however, took one look at Skarnhrafn and jammed to a halt. The other horses scrambled down a steep, icy gully onto the glacier, where a small thermal spring steamed eerily, forming a cloud which all the others vanished into, leaving Brak and Faxi facing Skarnhrafn across a small ravine. Kolssynir was shouting furiously from the other side of the trickling stream and the fog, but Faxi refused to go forward. When Brak tapped his ribs gently, he backed up quickly to show he had no intention of getting any nearer to Skarnhrafn. Brak dismounted to try leading him across the water. Running water, his ancient grandmother had told him, was a sure way to elude evil beings if they were pursuing you, and Brak did not pause now to wonder if her sources for that information had been reliable or not. He hauled at Faxi's bridle, cursed him, and gave him a sharp crack with the flat of his sword. Faxi danced in circles around Brak, refusing to be led. Brak could no longer hear Kolssynir shouting for him. Probably he had gone on with the pack train, thinking it was better to lose one thrall than everything.

Brak began to retreat, and Skarnhrafn turned his horse and followed. A row of fiery slits gleamed through the visor of the helmet as Skarnhrafn studied his prey. Brak drew his sword and took refuge behind a large rock, determined to delay the draug as long as he was able, allowing Kolssynir to escape.

Skarnhrafn unsheathed his own sword and urged his horse forward with a sepulchral chuckle. "Is it a Scipling, then, one of those troublesome intruders who helped Ingvold to escape? Myrkjartan would like to see you roasted, my friend."

Brak retreated as the draug advanced. "You're nothing but dust and old bones," he said. "What you need is burning, like firewood that has been cut too long."

"Old and rotten, that's true," Skarnhrafn wheezed, "but I will serve Myrkjartan until every atom of this old carcass is dust. A draug never forgets an order, and I shall capture Ingvold if I have to kill a thousand Sciplings to do so—beginning with you. You have done things which are not allowed."

"Things which Myrkjartan and Hjordis did not think possible, you mean," Brak replied, "and that isn't the end of their surprises. In a very short while the Ljosalfar will put you all back where you belong, and the draugar will be destroyed."

"What nonsense. We have the cloak and the helmet and the sword of Dyrstyggr. What power can stop us?"

"You don't have the Rhbus, and without them you'll fail." Brak held the heart in his hand, inside its case. His mouth and throat burned slightly when he even thought about sampling the meat again.

"Enough of this useless talk. I must go after the girl." Skarnhrafn raised his visor partway, letting fire swathe the darkness. "Can you defy that, Scipling? Can you escape from your doom this time? Where are your precious Rhbus when you most need saving?"

"They are here," Brak said, removing the blackened heart from its case. Holding it before him, he stepped out of the shelter of the rock with his sword at the ready.

Skarnhrafn's fire swept toward him eagerly. He held out the heart to meet it, and the fire suddenly dwindled, shrank, and disappeared, immersing Skarnhrafn in a cloud of choking black smoke. The draug raised his visor to its fullest extent and glared out at Brak with eyes like two red coals dying on the hearth.

"This is only a trick," Skarnhrafn wheezed. "It is not allowed to happen. You are the one Myrkjartan wants, not the girl. You are the one who has the heart. I must tell Myrkjartan—but a draug never forgets an order. The girl—she must go back to Myrkjartan." He turned his horse as if to follow Ingvold.

Brak leaped after him, swinging his sword as if he knew exactly what to do with it, and cut the hind legs from under Skarnhrafn's draug horse as if they were nothing more than rotten wood. With a terrible bellow, Skarnhrafn took his maimed steed to the air, raking the sky with fire and sending bolts of it down toward Brak without touching him.

Chapter 13

◆◈◆◈◆◈◆◈◆◈◆◈◈◆◈◆●◆◈◆◈◆◈◈◈◆◈◈◎◎◎

Brak waited until Skarnhrafn was gone, winging southward over the Slagfells to the tune of furious screeches and bellows that echoed from the silent fells. Long before Brak's courage returned, Faxi was cropping grass contentedly and doing his best to rub his bridle off against a rock. Still feeling shaken, Brak captured his horse and returned the heart to its box, concealing it inside his shirt and silently thanking the Rhbus for the sudden impulse to attack Skarnhrafn's horse. Without four legs, it wouldn't be able to carry him around on the ground as Skarnhrafn required, so the draug would be forced to replace it. Returning to Myrkjartan for another horse would also give him the opportunity to tell his master who indeed possessed the heart, a circumstance which gave Brak no little disquiet.

As he was mounting his horse, a shadow suddenly moved in the ravine, stealing toward him without a sound. Quickly he brought Faxi around as he pulled the axe from his belt, a weapon he felt more comfortable with than a sword.

"Who's there? Speak your name, or, by the Rhbus, this axe will find its mark!" Brak spoke in the fiercest growl he could muster, poising the axe for a throw. Many hours of clandestine practice with an ordinary, wood-chopping axe ensured that any axe thrown by Brak would stick its blade into its target.

The shadow halted. "It's only I, Kolssynir, your master, as I may jokingly assume," the wizard's exasperated voice replied. "I returned to attempt to rescue you, or at least to find the remains of you, but instead, I see a first-class exhibition of a lowly thrall summoning the powers of the exalted Rhbus and quenching Skarnhrafn as if he were a small candle. That little object you held up in your hand and returned to a small box inside your clothing is the dragon's heart once possessed by Dyrstyggr, is it not?"

Brak put away his axe and nudged Faxi toward the ravine. "I doubt if you could convince anyone else of that story, Kolssynir," he said cautiously. "What would a mere thrall know about the Rhbus, and how could he come to possess a dragon's heart?"

"Gljodmalborg was the last known location of the heart. Your small friend confessed to having been there, so perhaps one of you discovered it among the ruins and pocketed it. Most likely, however, the three of you aren't even thralls at all and never were."

"I am indeed a thrall, and I was born as such," Brak said. "You may assume that I am a great dumb ox and a coward, but if you try to take that small object you observed away from me, the Rhbus won't be as kind to you as I was to Skarnhrafn."

"Hoity-toity! Maybe I only dreamed it, after all!" Kolssynir exclaimed in a huff. "I'll ask you no questions as long as you consent to help guide my pack train to Miklborg. At the moment, my concern for Miklborg outweighs even my burning curiosity about you and your friends and that heart. Traveling together is a sure way to become truly acquainted with someone, and I've formed some opinions of my own, but I shall keep them to myself until we have taken these supplies to Miklborg. After that, we shall all sit down and answer some interesting questions, agreed?"

"Agreed," Brak said willingly. After Miklborg, he intended to leave Kolssynir far behind as soon as possible.

Following their brush with Skarnhrafn, they traveled onward to the north for another four days without event. That was not to say there weren't strayed horses and an alarm or two about trolls, but Kolssynir thrived on problems. He tracked down the missing horses with magic and entertained himself with new and devastating traps for the trolls. He cajoled the utmost limits of strength and endurance from the horses, his men, and himself, and seemed to regard each obstacle surmounted as a personal enemy defeated.

They rode into the hill fort of Miklborg like heroes. The fighting men swarmed around them eagerly, asking for news, coveting the horses, and hauling the supplies away for rationing.

"It's a miracle you got through the Slagfells," their chieftain declared. "Trolls, draugar, and Dokkalfar have kept us cut off from the other hill forts since Hagsbarrow was taken. The Rhbus must have led the way for you and protected your flank, or you wouldn't be here now."

"The Rhbus have their higher vision," Kolssynir said gravely. "If we were protected by their magic, it must be for a cause. Miklborg must not be defeated."

They spent three days in Miklborg to rest before starting back. Kolssynir was at his best, rushing around importantly, sending off small, sly groups of the best archers to seek out the hiding places of the advancing Dokkalfar and showing the wizards of Miklborg some of his favorite traps, guaranteed to strike terror into the hearts of the enemy. The chieftain of the hill fort urged him to stay, but he regretfully begged off because of responsibilities to other hill forts that showed signs of being surrounded by the Dokkalfar threat. He left all the horses but four, which made a handsome gift of nine to Miklborg, courtesy of the warlord in Langborg, who did not even suspect himself of such generosity.

They began the journey back through the Slagfells, feeling curiously unencumbered. Even old Faxi trotted along with the other horses, his large round feet plopping down in a businesslike manner. Near midmorning, Kolssynir called the accustomed halt for resting the horses and eating whatever odds and ends were left over from breakfast. Brak assisted Kolssynir in building a small fire and putting on a pot of water for tea. The wizard hummed to himself and seemed to be in excellent spirits as he consulted his maps.

"We shall be back in Langborg in half the time it took us with the pack horses," he announced. "All things permitting." He looked distrustfully at old Faxi, who was tearing up mouthfuls of grass behind him. Then he looked significantly at Brak.

Brak got hastily to his feet, muttering something about standing guard, and climbed to the top of a scarp where Kolssynir wouldn't follow with his questions. Ingvold soon climbed up after him and perched on the edge of a breathtaking drop.

"It's time we went north, Brak," she whispered. "I have a marvelous plan, since he already knows about the heart."

Brak had told her about his encounter with Skarnhrafn, and she had agreed that he had done the right thing, particularly when he maimed Skarnhrafn's horse, although she did say that if it had been she, it would have been Skarnhrafn's head she would have removed.

"It won't be easy escaping from him," Brak said, remembering Kolssynir's devious traps and snares.

Ingvold smiled. "We won't. We'll take him with us. A wizard of his rank would be very useful to us. We shall abduct him."

Brak gaped at her. "And also very difficult to abduct, particularly if it's against his will. I wouldn't be surprised if the penalties for thralls abducting their master weren't rather severe, Ingvold."

"I'm not a thrall, I'm a chieftain's daughter," she retorted with a toss of her ragged hair. "Pehr's not a thrall either, and you belong to him, not to Kolssynir. Now don't interrupt me, Brak, I know exactly what must be done if we are ever to find Dyrstyggr."

Brak shook his head, trying to repress a shudder. "Well, tell me what we must do, then, and how you plan to subdue a wizard such as Kolssynir, who certainly won't submit to it willingly, if I know him."

"It will be very simple. I've been going through his satchel when he wasn't looking—don't interrupt—and I found some sleeping powder. All we need to do is slip some in his tea, and by the time he wakes up—"

"He'll be very angry," Brak said, "and unwilling even to listen to us. Let me have a chance first to convince him, Ingvold. If I can't persuade him to come north with us instead of dragging us all back to Langborg, then you can try the sleeping powder on him. Do you think it's quite wise to prowl in his satchel, considering his great fondness for surprises and traps?"

Ingvold shrugged and looked downward at their trail. "There's no time like the present for approaching him, Brak. Let's go drop the bolt on him and see what he says."

Kolssynir was waiting for them. He motioned them to sit down and handed around cups of scalding tea. "The questions," he prompted gently in the tense silence, looking at Brak and Ingvold and Pehr.

"I can see you've guessed I'm no thrall," Pehr began haughtily. "I am Pehr Thorstensson, and my father is an important chieftain in the Scipling realm. You have heard of Thorsten the Lawgiver, haven't you?"

Kolssynir shook his head. "Never, but I shall assume you're telling the truth for now and go on to the others." He turned at Brak and Ingvold.

"Brak is my thrall," Pehr continued. "We've been raised together since we were infants, and I gave him Faxi after I acquired a faster and better horse, so you see no horse thieves before you, nor runaway thralls either. We've helped you get your supplies to Miklborg, and now we wish to continue with our own journey—northward."

Kolssynir scowled and shook his head. "Fifty marks of my gold says you are all thralls, in spite of what you may have been in the Scipling realm. My fifty marks says that you have sold your freedom—or rather, Skalgr sold it for you and pocketed the money. You ought not to have done that if you wanted to remain freemen."

Pehr was about to leap hotly into an argument, but Brak swiftly interrupted. "But this isn't the most important matter, whether we're Kolssynir's thralls or not. The real concern is Ingvold Thjodmarsdotter and the dragon's heart—the only two survivors of Gljodmalborg's destruction."

"Yes, the dragon's heart, which you carry in that case inside your shirt," Kolssynir said. "But wait—what did you say? The chieftain's daughter is the last survivor? I thought—" He looked at Ingvold.

She nodded her head. "Yes, he said I was the last survivor. I am Ingvold Thjodmarsdotter. My father gave the heart to me at the beginning of the last attack, and I hid where the Dokkalfar and draugar would never find me. Or so I thought—I was captured and taken to Hjordis. When I refused to give her the heart, she decided to punish me. She put a curse on me and sent me to the Scipling realm under the care of an evil old worshipper of hers, Katla. When she wanted to summon me to see if I was penitent yet, she caused me to change men into horses and ride them to the place she wished. Sometimes they died."

Kolssynir eyed her with interest. "A hagriding spell. I am quite confident I can cure you, if you'll cooperate. Cures for this sort of thing are not pleasant, but the curse is worse, is it not?"

"No, no, don't bother," Ingvold exclaimed as he began rummaging in his satchel. "Skalgr cured me; I'm all right now. Let me finish—"

"Skalgr! Skalgr couldn't cure an everyday wart, let alone a—a curse—a hag spell created by Hjordis, the Queen of the Dokkalfar. Skalgr couldn't—"

"But he did," Ingvold interrupted sharply. "The point is, we have this heart of Dyrstyggr's and we plan to find him and return it to him so he can smash Myrkjartan and Hjordis and send them back underground, where they belong. At the time, it suited our purpose to allow Skalgr to sell us to you, since it rid us of him as a nuisance and led us to you as a competent, practicing wizard. We are in need of a wizard if we are ever to find Dyrstyggr, particularly in time to do something to save hill forts like Miklborg. We can't offer you any payment except the satisfaction of striking back against Myrkjartan and Hjordis in a most worthy cause, but we wish to ask—no, require—that you join us and assist us in finding Dyrstyggr."

"Require! Few people have required me to do anything lately," Kolssynir replied, looking down his nose at them coldly. "Since I became well known in the powers of magic and the cause of Elbegast, people usually address me in terms of humility and respect, and they are never penniless scruffy-looking—"

"I am a chieftain's daughter, no matter how I may look," Ingvold cut in, in tones no less chilling. She pulled Thjodmar's ring from her neck and held it out for Kolssynir to examine. "That is my father's ring, and you may keep it as a promise of future payment. Your rewards will be great if you are the one to assist Dyrstyggr in driving out Myrk-jartan's draugar and Hjordis' Dokkalfar."

Kolssynir looked at the ring, tested it between his teeth, and rang it against a stone. "It's real gold," he announced in surprise. "A beautiful piece of workmanship, truly worthy of the possession of a chieftain's daughter. You may have it back, and you may consider me enlisted in your cause. I am convinced that I now know some of the truth, at least, and I live in the hope that other things will be explained as we go on, such as Skarnhrafn's following you, and why you have given the heart to Brak."

"We shall tell you all you need to know," Ingvold replied with lofty solemnity, holding out her hand to Kolssynir. "We are pleased to accept the offer of your services. I shall also return your property to you. I'm glad we came to this understanding, rather than being forced to resort to trick-ery." She removed a small vial from an inner pocket and gave it to him, ignoring his expression of outrage and astonishment. "Haven't we delayed here long enough? Let's put this fire out and turn back toward Miklborg. Dyrstyg-grsstead isn't far from Miklborg. My father used to visit there often, but I never went with him. Somehow my mother thought I would do better to learn weaving rather than riding and fighting." She smiled a grim, dark smile and touched the axe in her belt.

"Surely you have some relatives somewhere," Kolssynir began, "or we could leave you at Miklborg or someplace safe—"

"No one's leaving me anywhere," Ingvold snapped. "The heart was my father's, and mine before I gave it to Brak, and I intend to see it used against the enemies who de-stroyed my family and my home. I won't hear of any such talk of leaving me behind. Haven't I done well enough so far? I don't complain nearly as much as Pehr, and I cer-tainly ride better than Brak does."

Pehr started to protest that he was accustomed to having thralls do his hard work for him, but Brak interrupted him with a hiss, listening intently.

"What's that sound? Someone's coming!" Brak scuttled to the cover of a large rock and studied the path below. Ingvold stamped out the fire, and Pehr fitted an arrow in his bow. Kolssynir swallowed the last of his tea, which was stone-cold, and joined Brak at his position. After a few moments, they saw a lone traveler plodding along the path with the aid of a staff, which he leaned upon heavily with a frequent sharp sound of metal against stone. While they watched, he stopped several times to rest himself dejectedly before resuming his journey more slowly than before.

"We've got an hour before he gets here," Ingvold said. "He's as slow as a glacier. Look at that, he's sitting down again. Why wait for him? Let's just leave him behind while our horses are fresh."

Kolssynir wrapped his cloak around his shoulders and sat down. "We'll wait for him, mostly because he went to a great deal of trouble to follow us. The least we can do is have the courtesy to find out who he is and either reward him for his faithfulness or kill him if he means us harm."

While they waited, Kolssynir looked at his maps. After a long period of considering and sighing and scowling, he rolled the maps up and climbed a high pinnacle for a look through a small pocket spyglass at the solitary figure toiling along after them. When he came back, he was chuckling, and his eyes sparkled with the delight reserved for his better troll traps.

"My lads—and lady," he said with a pleasant, malevolent grin, "you are in for a surprise. An old friend has come to visit you."

"Friend? In this country?" Pehr shook his head and held up his bow and arrows. "These are our only friends."

The traveler finally approached their camp, not seeing it or them among the rocks. He sighed, moaned, talked to himself, and seemed miserable enough to walk right into the hands of the Dokkalfar and never notice.

"Halloa!" Kolssynir roared, adding a fearsome laugh.

"Spare me, merciful gods!" the poor wretch shrieked, dropping his staff in his confusion. "I haven't a thing worth taking. In fact, I'm almost starved to death, so poor and miserable am I. Have pity on me; I'm only a wretched wanderer."

Kolssynir chuckled and twirled his staff. "You're a poor liar besides. I know you've got fifty marks sewn into that wretched cloak of yours. Such an unappreciative and ungrateful world, eh?"

"Kolssynir! Is it you?" the traveler gasped, tottering forward. "I can't believe my eyes and ears! What good fortune! What a miracle to find a friend in the Slagfells!"

"It's not so remarkable, considering that you followed us," Kolssynir said pleasantly, disengaging himself from Skalgr's grateful handshaking. "It's a pity the trolls or the Dokkalfar didn't get you, Skalgr, but since you're here, let's discuss my fifty marks."

"Gladly, gladly. You're not satisfied with your thralls?" Skalgr grinned feebly and darted an apprehensive glance at the unwelcoming faces of Brak and Pehr and Ingvold. "I can explain, you know. It's quite understandable—a mistake perhaps. If you could spare an old beggar a bit of something to eat, I'd—I'd be your grateful servant to the last of my days."

"Fetch him something, Brak," Kolssynir said with an exasperated snort. "First he robs me, then I must feed him, too."

Skalgr brightened at once and scuttled into camp, where he sat down expectantly upon a rock as Brak set out the remains of their breakfast. He seemed rather disappointed when Brak poured out fresh milk from a clay jug.

"Ale is for fighting men," Brak said, "I suspect your long walk has rather dried you out and cleared your wits. What have you done with Kolssynir's money? You have to give it back to him. He knows everything—almost."

Skalgr assailed half a loaf of bread and couldn't speak until it was safely eaten. "It was wise of you not to tell him everything," he whispered, spluttering a few crumbs. "You are the master now, and he is the servant. It won't hurt to grind it in a bit, now and then. I picked a very fine wizard to help us, did I not?"

"Help us? Us? You're not coming with us." Brak reached menacingly for his axe. "Twice you've betrayed us. As soon as you've finished eating, I'll point you toward Miklborg, where you can beg for your dinner and perhaps find something useful to do with yourself for a change. We've seen the last of each other, Skalgr."

"You have a kind heart, Brak, to concern yourself with the fate of an old thief like me," Skalgr said, shaking his head. "I shall never forget what you've done for me, and I shall repay you with interest someday. I shall make you your fortune, perhaps."

Kolssynir ceased his pacing up and down and swooped at Skalgr, impaling the last slice of bread on the point of his staff just as the old wizard was reaching for it.

"That ought to be your false and treacherous heart, you old rogue," Kolssynir growled, waving the bread under his nose. "How dare you attempt to break a hag spell, and no doubt lie about it later? Then you come sneaking after us, plotting more mischief. What are you up to, Skalgr? Trying to steal them back and sell them again?"

"Ha, I'll bet that's it!" Pehr declared, glaring at Skalgr.

"Certainly not!" Skalgr exclaimed. "I've accomplished my objective. And if you don't believe Ingvold's curse is cured, you may ask her." He turned to her, waiting for his vindication.

"It's cured," she said reluctantly. "He used the magic in one of the old standing rings."

"See there? I told you so." Skalgr snatched the bread from Kolssynir's staff and took a large bite. "I do have some small bits of honor and integrity remaining in this worthless carcass you see before you. My sense of justice is crying out to make retribution for the gold I accepted from you in payment for these three false thralls. I hope you see we had to do it this way, since you were so intent on packing those supplies to Miklborg. Most good wizards, as you know and exemplify, tend to be of a rather suspicious nature, and you might not have believed a word we said. Ingvold might have been seized for being a hag, in spite of the fact that I broke the spell; but no one would have believed it in Langborg any more than you believed it when I first told you."

"And I'm convinced of it now?" Kolssynir demanded. "Skalgr, I'm rapidly losing what little patience I have with you. I greatly doubt your share in this test to find Dyrstyggr, unless it's to make certain nobody ever finds him as long as you can deceive people somehow. I don't like you, Skalgr."

The skinny old wizard merely grinned and rubbed his hands. "Good, good, we're off to a promising start, then. I assure you, Kolssynir, you shall never find Dyrstyggr unless I help you. Dyrstyggrsstead is destroyed, so it won't do you any good to go there. If you want to find Dyr-styggr, you must trust me." He stood up, fastening his disreputable satchel on its strap around his neck. "I'm afraid, my friends, you have no choice."

"No choice, indeed! We shall make a choice!" Kolssynir reached for his sword, but at that instant they heard a feathery hiss, a sharp sound of impact, and Skalgr uttered a terrible shriek. He stood rigid, trembling, with a black-and-red-fletched arrow protruding from his back. Then he fell forward without a twitch and lay still.

"Dokkalfar!" Kolssynir snapped, diving into the shelter of a stone as more arrows rained around them, striking sparks on the rocks and rebounding in all directions.

From the scanty shelter of the rocks they could see about ten Dokkalfar arching flights of arrows toward their intended prey. Pehr pounded on Brak, urging him to summon the Rhbus to their defense and not waste any time about it.

Chapter 14

◈◈◈◈◈◈◈◈◈◈◈◈◈◈◈◈◈◈◈◈◈◈◈◈

Brak clenched the heart in his hand, flinching at the deadly hiss of an arrow narrowly missing his head. He ventured to peer around a rock at their assailants, but all he could see was dark shapes keeping well back in the shadow of the jutting cliff.

While he hesitated, the arrows stopped abruptly, probably on command, and a lone dark figure appeared more distinctly against the rocks. Kolssynir made a move to raise his staff, but thought better of it and bided his time. The Dokkalfar was swathed in dark garments from head to toe to protect him from the effects of the weak and autumnal sun. Somewhere in the black folds were two eyes, warily scanning the target.

Kolssynir made a motion for silence, scowling down Pehr's impatient scowl and shaking his head threateningly. Presently two more Dokkalfar joined the first, similarly swathed and cloaked. They kept themselves close to the shadows, moving with a bent-over, furtive gait that bespoke a preference for the dark safety of an underground passageway. Before long nearly a score of Dokkalfar scuttled from their hiding places, like a pack of ferrets, and stood arguing and peering across the intervening space in wary speculation. Brak supposed they could see Skalgr lying stretched out on his face with the arrow in his back, and that they hoped, perhaps, that the rest had met a similar fate.

Kolssynir waited until the dark elves were gathered in a bold knot, arguing and strutting back and forth, staring toward their enemies' hiding place. Finally several seemed to find the courage to investigate their kill when a particularly black cloud obscured the pale sun. Kolssynir raised himself on one elbow and, with a whisper, sent a great bolt from the ends of his fingers hissing into the midst of the advancing Dokkalfar, where it burst with a roaring explosion. A few saw it coming and sprang away; the bursting of the blast added impetus to their flight.

Kolssynir leaped atop the rocks to watch, letting his cloak swirl and flap in the stray gusts of power. "Cowards! Ambushers! Secret murderers! I dare you to combat the powers of Kolssynir of Langborg! See what your puny arrows can do against me!"

The dark elves dived for cover, leaving the singed and gravely wounded to fend for themselves. Then, obligingly, a single arrow came arcing wickedly toward Kolssynir, its owner keeping well out of sight.

Kolssynir snorted with contempt and waved his hand. The arrow vanished in a small *pftt!* of flame without his so much as glancing at it. He stalked forward, ignoring the wounded Dokkalfar, several of whom made some desperate efforts to slash at his legs with their knives as he stepped over them. One blackened fellow made a surprise rush at him, but Kolssynir melted him to ice water almost instantly.

"And so shall the rest of you perish if you don't take flight at once!" Kolssynir looked around him like an ill-tempered bear, and the Dokkalfar shrank back into their hiding places.

A thin voice called out, "Wait, Kolssynir. Give us plenty of room and we'll clear off, as long as you give your word not to blast us before we get away."

Kolssynir propped one fist on his hip and sighed impatiently. "Well enough, go, then, if you don't care to make a decent fight of it. The second time we meet won't end half so pleasantly—you with the red pantaloons, and you with the patch on your cloak, I shall know you if I see you again, and all of you will be nothing but empty cloaks and melted ice."

The Dokkalfar hastily saluted him and disappeared into the rocks, leaving behind the remains of five totally destroyed dark elves, three who were melting fast, and six badly singed fellows who were hobbling away as fast as they could go after their companions.

Kolssynir poked among the various cloaks and weapons left behind by the Dokkalfar, freely pocketing anything that suited him and pushing the other junk aside. Pehr made it plain that he did not approve of such cannibalization, regarding anything once in the possession of the Dokkalfar as an object of horror.

Brak and Ingvold approached the small heap of old clothes that was Skalgr. After a moment of searching for signs of life, Brak called to Kolssynir. The wizard finished examining a fairly passable pair of boots and strode over for a look at Skalgr. He prodded the remains experimentally with his staff, then knelt on one knee for a closer inspection. Rolling the old wizard partway over, he put his ear to Skalgr's lips. "He's still breathing, but I can't say how much longer he'll be doing it. I don't expect he'll survive, but we'll have to take him with us anyway."

Pehr started to protest, but Kolssynir interrupted. "I have no great regard for the old carp myself, but if he died here, abandoned by us, the draug he'd become would certainly pursue. I don't think any of us would fancy that.

Skarnhrafn is enough draug for a hundred of us. Let's patch him up somewhat for now and hope for the best."

The patching up elicited some piteous moaning and groaning from Skalgr, although the wound was not particularly serious. When they were done, they packed him onto Faxi, who was the least likely to bolt or shy, and took turns walking throughout the day so that the old wizard could ride. Skalgr's spirits revived enough for him to apologize and thank everyone a thousand times.

"What a relief it is to know that you have joined our cause, Kolssynir," Skalgr declared with a grateful sigh as they lifted him off his horse that evening. "I'm most delighted that my young friends convinced you that I am indeed an emissary of some importance who can lead you to Dyrstyggr—unless I perish in the effort."

"You'll live, no doubt, to plague us a great deal further," Brak said gruffly, good-naturedly rallying the old fellow as he had done throughout the day to keep him in spirits.

Kolssynir strode around the campsite, directing where to build the fire, where to tether the horses, and where the sentry should sit. "One of my better facilities has been my remarkable ability to make the best of a bad thing," he said, bending a frown upon Skalgr. "I don't embark upon this venture with optimism, nor do I foresee much future in the five of us alone assailing Hjordis and Myrkjartan, even with the assistance of the dragon's heart. It seems to me that the Rhbus are drawing me onward to my death —or to tremendous glory, if by some means Hjordis and Myrkjartan are defeated. I can't foresee the means, nor can I foresee if any of us will even survive. The territory to the north of here is probably the most dangerous terrain in Skarpsey, and it gets more dangerous the nearer we approach to Hjordisborg. Hence, how can I resist? This will be my ultimate challenge." He made several fiery cuts in the air with his staff and clapped Pehr on the back. "Don't look so glum; we'll have you and Brak back to Thorstensstead safe and sound by next summer at the latest."

Pehr was not reassured. The frequent sighting of prowling groups of Dokkalfar during the night added to his disgruntlement. In the morning Skalgr directed their course due east, which occasioned two encounters with suspicious

Dokkalfar before noonday and left Pehr in a state nearing mutiny. The day was foggy and dark, and the audacity of the Dokkalfar kept Kolssynir alertly on guard. They made very little progress in three days, which was partially attributed to a lengthy retreat they were forced to make when their course seemed to be leading them directly into a large encampment of draugar.

"Fancy that!" Skalgr exclaimed indignantly. "Who would have supposed they'd be so bold as to stop so close to Miklborg? I wonder if Myrkjartan has actually advanced his position to Hjalmknip?"

Brak looked over his shoulder at the hilltops wreathed in spectral fogs, feeling with cold certainty that Myrkjartan was there somewhere, watching perhaps. He would not have been very much surprised to see Skarnhrafn's fiery grin watching them through the mist.

"It's an ideal place for draugar," Skalgr continued. "It used to be an ambitious Dokkalfar mining project, but now it's a maze of old tunnels and collapsed caverns that even the trolls avoid. It's just as well we're not going anywhere near it."

"But Dyrstyggr," Brak began, "where is he?"

Skalgr gave a discomfitted start. "Oh, Dyrstyggr, of course. I thought you meant something else for a moment. Don't worry, lad, I'll lead you to him—unless, of course, we get caught in the middle of a battle between Hjordisborg and Miklborg, which certainly seems to be an imminent possibility, wouldn't you say, Kolssynir?"

Kolssynir certainly did say, and spent a considerable period berating Skalgr for leading them into such peril. They retreated straight south and took shelter in a small cave for the night. Kolssynir and Skalgr pored over the maps with little satisfaction, since Skalgr either was unable to pinpoint Dyrstyggr's location or refused to. Their arguing went on far into the night, which became progressively foggier and more dank. When Brak was called to stand guard in the early hours of the morning, the air smelled as if it had come straight from the bogs of Hagsbarrow. As Ingvold left her post, she whispered, "I've seen hundreds of draugar passing us on their way to Hjalmknip. Once I thought I heard Myrkriddir, and where Myrkriddir are, Myrkjartan isn't far away. I only hope Skalgr knows where he's taking us. I swear, if he betrays us one more time, I'll have his life if I have to squeeze it out of him with my own hands." Her face in the dark was pale and determined.

"I don't like the looks of it either," Brak said. "This time I doubt if we can fool Myrkjartan. He'll know from Skarnhrafn that I have the heart, and not you."

"Perhaps you'd like to give it back?" Ingvold asked. "I could slip away with it again."

"No, no, not alone in this country. I shall keep the heart for you until we give it to Dyrstyggr, so that Myrkjartan will have no further interest in you. Coward that I am, I can withstand anything he might try to do to me to make me surrender it. A thrall can be a very stubborn creature."

"And so can a chieftain's daughter. I won't have you dying on my account, do you hear?"

Brak settled himself to watch, wrapping his cloak around him against the bone-chilling damp air. "If you're waiting for me to give you back that heart, you may as well go to bed now and forget about it. My mind was made up about the heart quite a long time ago, Ingvold. What I do from now on won't be on anyone's account except my own."

After Ingvold had left him to his lonely vigil, Brak began the longest and most dismal watch he could remember. The air was thick with the smell of old barrows and graves, and he frequently heard groups of draugar passing nearby, rustling like dead leaves and sighing and muttering to themselves.

When morning finally came, it brought little relief from the gloom. Cold dew from the fog covered everything, and heavy mist rained on them gently as they tried to light a fire and find something to eat. The fire wouldn't burn properly, so they all huddled miserably in the grudging shelter of an overhanging rock, gnawing on hard bread with nothing to moisten it except half-tepid tea that tasted like hay in cold water. Very soon everyone was anxious to start traveling. Kolssynir indicated a northwesterly route and they proceeded cautiously through the fog, which lifted near midday, only to descend more thickly than before late in the afternoon.

The travelers were forced to make a camp quickly. They longed for a fire, but whatever sticks and tinder they could find were soaked with dew and refused to burn. Kolssynir conjured a small flame to heat a pot of tea, cajoling and cursing it when it spluttered and threatened to expire.

"Wretched fog," he muttered. "Ice magic, I wouldn't doubt, conjured by Myrkjartan and Hjordis for their attack on Miklborg. I hope those fellows are ready. I wish I were there to help them. I'd make a blaze of those cursed draugar such as the heavens have never seen, and Myrkjartan would find Skarpsey far too hot for his liking."

Skalgr pushed his damp hood away from one eye. "But a spell such as this rather dampens fire magic, does it not, Kolssynir?"

"You'd better hush," Pehr growled. "It's all your fault we're wandering around aimlessly, looking for someone we don't even know for certain is still alive. Ever since we got to those mines and caves where Myrkjartan is probably hiding, I haven't experienced a moment's peace. Now we're going back toward that place, and I don't fancy it one bit."

"I assure you, it's the proper direction," Skalgr insisted. "We certainly can't wait here, or the battle will break over our cars, and I don't imagine you'd care for that either."

"And I'm beginning to wonder if you don't have another trick planned for us," Pehr went on angrily. "It seems that whenever we come anywhere near Myrkjartan, you have a way of switching loyalties for your own profit rather suddenly."

"That's not entirely true," Skalgr said in an injured tone. "We'd never have found Kolssynir if I hadn't pretended to sell you as thralls at Langborg."

"Who was pretending?" Ingvold put in. "What about Kolssynir's fifty marks, then? And before, at Hagsbarrow—"

Brak stood up wearily. "I'm going to stand the first watch," he said into the midst of the argument, doubting if anyone heard him.

Tempers in the morning were scarcely improved by another night of restless draugar and heavy, chilling mist that made fingers stiff, numb, and easily pinched as horses were saddled and packed. Brak soon learned that Faxi was in a recalcitrant mood and refused to let Skalgr get near enough to put one foot in the stirrup, so Pehr had to give up his horse to Skalgr and take the first turn walking, which never put Pehr into an agreeable humor. Kolssynir hurried around, snapping at everyone, and Skalgr made himself objectionable by complaining that their course was taking them too far to the west.

Brak urged Faxi after the other horses, but the contentious old horse could not be hurried and seemed to take a perverse pleasure in lagging behind, despite Brak's threatenings and coaxings. When Brak whacked him, he halted in his tracks and flattened his ears, bunching his hind legs under him as if he yearned to pitch Brak over his head. Brak leaped to the ground impatiently and stamped away. Faxi began to graze, keeping one eye upon his master all the while and occasionally taking a few steps after him before resuming grazing. Brak knew the old brute wouldn't let him out of his sight for long and would soon come trotting anxiously after him.

Brak strode along alone, enjoying the absence of Pehr's caustic complaints and Skalgr's crafty, bright eyes observing everything around him, whether or not it was his business. Ahead, Kolssynir's voice, ordering Brak to hurry up, came eerily from a bank of fog rolling down the steep side of a rocky fell. Brak eyed the fog, astonished and wary. The sun had vanished like a candle under a snuffer. A thick, dark mantle was settling over the landscape, filling small valleys with darkness and the earthy smell of open barrows and draugar. His heart began to pound with the uneasy certainty that something was amiss. He whistled for Faxi and began to hurry after his friends while he could still see their tracks in the soft earth. Too soon he plunged into the misty darkness of the fog, stumbling over rocks and scraping his hands raw on cold, wet stones as he groped for hoofprints in the turf. Faxi followed him closely, assisting by treading on his heels and shoving him anxiously with a long nose.

Brak was unable to estimate how long he groped and blundered through the fog. His hands were raw and bleeding and his knees were scarcely aware of any new shocks and scrapes. Gasping, he stopped frequently to hold his breath and listen. Once he thought he heard horses' hooves and a shout, but in the fog it was impossible to guess which direction to take. He could see nothing but dim, dark shapes looming around him in the unnatural twilight. Again he crouched and explored the ground with his fingers for hoofprints. After crossing a small, ice-cold streamlet and some punishing rocks, he found the tracks of horses. Anxiously he groped his way after them, seeing the right direction during moments when the fog lifted slightly.

Suddenly his hand touched something soft and warm—the folds of thick fabric. He drew back hastily, whispering, "Hello! Who's there?" His heart hammered in his ears, but there was no other sound. "Pehr? Ingvold? Kolssynir? Skalgr?" He whispered each name into the silence and heard no response. Reluctantly he tugged at the fabric, exploring; then his fingers encountered flesh—a hand outstretched, as cold and stiff as marble.

Brak hurled himself away with a muffled shout and fell into a nest of sharp rocks. Shuddering, he scrambled away, blundering into Faxi, who was snorting and trembling with alarm. For a moment, he collected himself, somewhat reassured by the feel of warm, living horsehide, knowing he had to discover whose corpse lay in his path. When he had collected his nerves and hardened them into resolve, he crawled back to the corpse. Extending one hand gingerly, he felt the back of a cloak, crisped into something like frost that burned his fingers. Exploring, he found a hood and the head turned partially to one side. Very cautiously he touched wiry hair, a stout masculine nose, and a liberal, bristly beard. Gritting his teeth, he pushed the body over and tried to determine by touch what sort of clothing the fellow wore. It seemed like a short, belted jacket with a high collar and embroidery done in silver and gold wire. Pouches were fastened to his belt, which was wide and ornate. Nearby lay a satchel, and a staff was clutched frozenly in one hand.

"Kolssynir!" Brak breathed incredulously, sitting down to stare numbly at nothing for a few moments. Then he searched unsuccessfully for the other bodies he was certain must be there somewhere, but finally he gave it up and crept back to Faxi. He stumbled through the fog for a short distance and took refuge against a shoulder of wet stone, unwilling to wander any further until the fog lifted.

He must have slept, because he suddenly woke up cold and shivering. It was night, but he knew immediately that the black fog was gone and normal darkness was covering him. He could even see the stars. Faxi was scraping his saddle against the rocks with alarming grinding noises, as a hint that he would like to have it taken off. Brak unsaddled him and tethered him where he could graze. He took his eider from his saddle pack and began munching from a bag of dried fish, which was very much like eating rotten wood, but he felt half starved. Still hungry, he put the fish away, wondering how long his meager store would last.

He spent a very cold night trying to sleep. When morning came, he was so relieved he scarcely missed the night's rest. He ate more of the fish for breakfast and, steeling himself, walked back to the place where he had found Kolssynir. He knew it couldn't be far, but he could not find the place. He did find quantities of footprints, as if a disturbance had occurred. Someone had come in the night and carried away the body of Kolssynir—and the three others as well, if they, too, had perished with Kolssynir of Dokkalfar arrows or spells.

Puzzled and despondent, Brak studied the tracks of men and horses. He had no idea yet what to do or where to go. If Skalgr had died, the secret of Dyrstyggr's whereabouts had died with him.

"The dragon's heart," he murmured to himself and Faxi, rising from his stupor of shock. "Gull-skeggi, if ever I needed you, it's now." He opened the small case and tore off a shred of the black meat and chewed it, waiting for the burning and numbness. Closing his eyes, he invited the nightmares to begin, and they arrived with horrifying clarity. Gull-skeggi showed him the merciless attack on his friends, confused by the black fog and easy prey for the waiting Dokkalfar. He saw nothing but dark figures struggling with one another, frequently illuminated by a fiery, silent blast, like summer lightning. Then the scene shifted without warning to the sinister caves and mines where the draugar lurked, and he saw lurid visions of Myrkriddir capering through the air and beckoning to him. He also saw Gull-skeggi pointing inexorably toward the old mines. Brak shook his head, refusing to believe what he was seeing. He struggled to overcome the effects of the dragon meat and escape from the awful visions of Myrkjartan and

Hjordis materializing out of the black fog, searching for him with thousands of eyes glowing malevolently from every shadow. In horror, he withdrew as the haunted hills and deserted mines loomed at him, larger and more frightening. Then he heard a faint voice calling his name from inside the maw of a crumbling portal inscribed with letters that twined and curled like snakes.

"Brak! Help me!" the voice cried.

Brak regained consciousness with a sudden jolt, hearing Ingvold's voice still ringing in his ears.

"Ingvold! Where are you?" he called, leaping up unsteadily and looking behind the nearest rocks with the vague notion that she might be there, somehow. Instantly realizing he had dreamed the voice, he felt rather foolish and sat down again before his quivering knees deserted him. Reflecting on what the heart had shown him, he felt even worse. Twice he convinced himself that going to the old mines couldn't be the right thing to do, but in the end Ingvold's voice won out. With great reluctance, he saddled Faxi and turned him toward the east.

During the rest of the short, gloomy day, he saw none of the ominous black fog and no Dokkalfar, although he was certain they must be watching him. He made his camp in a crevice in a lava flow and treated himself to more of the dried fish, rendered slightly edible by the addition of cold water. He did not dare light a fire.

Brak could think of little else but Ingvold, certain one minute she was still alive in those mines and cast into gloom the next minute with the certainty that she must be dead. Remembering when she was the wretched captive of Katla and how her cheerless fate had touched him with its contrast and similarity to his own condition, Brak knew he would never rest until he had scoured the abandoned mines of Hjalmknip one by one.

Faxi lifted his head from his meager grazing, looking and listening intently toward the west. Brak at once seized his axe, his heart thumping. He glided to Faxi's side, ready to muzzle any incautious whinnies. Faxi snorted and stamped, flicking his ears as if he heard something beyond Brak's capabilities. Brak doubted that it was another horse, which Faxi would salute with a loud whinny of greeting. This creature seemed to be disliked—an enemy, perhaps, from the way the old horse stamped his hoof and lashed his tail. Pausing often to listen, Brak stepped cautiously away from his camp, keeping his axe ready. He heard nothing while he was standing still, but he was certain a multitude of significant noises was concealed under the slight sounds of his breathing and walking.

Something moved, straight ahead. Brak froze as it slithered toward him, not half a bowshot away. He was certain he distinctly heard cloth scraping stealthily against the stone. Then the creature uttered a terrible moan, and Brak promptly retreated back to Faxi. Cursing himself for a great stupid coward one moment and praising his own prudence the next, he waited in a horrible state of suspense to see if the creature followed him.

Follow him it did, although it took quite a while to approach his camp. He heard it panting and moaning just beyond Faxi's tether range. Oddly enough, Faxi was not much perturbed; he seemed more curious than alarmed. Brak stood up, vowing not to be more cowardly than an aging horse, and went stalking forward for another look.

"Who's there?" he demanded gruffly, treading around noisily to sound like two or three men instead of one.

"Help!" a faint voice implored, off in the rocks to his right.

"I won't be fooled that way," Brak retorted. "Show yourself if you really want help and not a fight."

After a lengthy period of groaning and scraping around, a dark figure crawled wretchedly from the rocks and collapsed with a last, desperate effort to rise to its feet. Brak edged closer, still wary, for a good look at the unfortunate fellow. With his axe he turned him over, face up in the moonlight. Although the light was pale, it was ample to show Brak the familiar features of old Skalgr, much the worse for dirt and bruises.

"Skalgr, old thief! Are you and your bad luck at an end at last?" Brak felt his neck for a heartbeat and listened for his breathing. Smelling onions rather strongly, he suspected that Skalgr was still somewhat alive. With a grunt he lifted the old wizard, carried him back to his camp, and put him on the bed of moss he had made for himself. He scratched together a small fire and made hot fish soup in a large cup. Skalgr revived to an amazing extent when

Brak held the fragrant fluid under his nose and shook him gently.

"I must be dreaming!" Skalgr exclaimed. "Is it really you, Brak? You've saved my life, you know. I would have died by morning, I'm sure."

"Oh, nonsense. Just drink this abominable stuff and you'll be right again soon enough." Brak extricated himself from Skalgr's grateful grasp. "A tough old boot like you isn't discouraged so easily, and you know it. Now tell me what happened to Pehr and Ingvold, and how you got here. I already know Kolssynir is dead."

Skalgr stopped his grateful slurping and knit his brows. "Dead, is he? That's a shame. We needed him desperately. It was Dokkalfar, of course, lurking in that cursed black fog. We held them off for a moment or two, then they blasted him and overran the rest of us, quite delighted with themselves when they realized they had captured Ingvold at last. They hauled me along until they discovered what a useless old cripple I really am, instead of anyone important, and they dumped me in a ravine, presumably to die. However, the desired effect did not occur immediately, so I departed at my own speed, which became slower and less erect by degrees, until I was merely crawling, nearly expired from exhaustion and hunger. I had it in mind to find you and Kolssynir, if you had survived, which I see you have—"

"But Pehr and Ingvold are still alive?" Brak interrupted.

"Certainly they're alive. Hjordis wouldn't want them otherwise, although Myrkjartan isn't particular about it one way or another."

"Do you have any idea where they are being taken?" Brak asked, trying to hide his impatience.

"Yes, indeed, I do. I overheard everything they said. I'm sure they never suspected I wouldn't die, grievously wounded as I was to start with, and then shaken around and beaten up in this last encounter; it's a wonder I didn't die. They could have murdered me in that ravine—"

"Skalgr, I'm very happy they didn't, but I'd like to know—"

"Of course. They were going directly to Hjalmknip, where Hjordis and Myrkjartan have set up temporary joint headquarters."

Brak drew a deep breath and exhaled it in a long sigh. "Then the Rhbus were right. I'm going in the proper direction."

Skalgr's eyes were bright with anticipation. "Then you're going after them, my lad? Myrkjartan and Hjordis are certain to quarrel over the possession of that heart. That's a battle I'd hate to miss, even if it means forgetting about Dyrstyggr for a little while." He settled himself with a comfortable sigh on Brak's improvised bed and pulled the eider up to his chin snugly. "We can split them and defeat them. Let them tear into each other, encourage them to attack themselves, not Miklborg—" He yawned and muttered more nonsense, already half asleep.

Brak curled up in his cloak close to the coals, alternately dozing and waking until dawn, when a mizzling rain mixed with snow began falling. He roused Skalgr from a deep and comfortable sleep. After a hasty breakfast with no fire, they turned toward Hjalmknip and its draugar-haunted, crumbling tunnels. Brak walked ahead and Skalgr rode Faxi, despite the old horse's subtle efforts to discourage him, such as rubbing Skalgr's kneecaps against rocks and biting him everytime he started to mount. They traveled slowly, spending much time hiding and listening to unseen draugar moving past in the rain. During the nights they heard Myrkriddir carousing overhead, and more draugar filed toward Miklborg in doleful processions. Skalgr was never more encouraging and cheerful, assuring Brak that thousands of draugar would be arrayed at Hjalmknip by the time they arrived.

The rain and snow still persisted. When they reached the bare hills and heaped-up tailings from the mines, it seemed too sudden for Brak, who would have preferred to see Hjalmknip at a distance first so that he could study it as he approached. Instead, it loomed suddenly at them through the mist and snow, and they were into it before they realized it. They plodded forward cautiously, seeing no sign of Dokkalfar or draugar. Open portals gaped at them from the sides of fells, and great sinkholes had eaten away the surface of the earth as old tunnels collapsed below, leaving horrifying vertical pits with no visible bottom. They picked their way around these immense traps and descended into a lower valley similarly deformed by unnatural heaps of tailings from the mines and the remains of scaffoldings that reminded Brak unpleasantly of gibbets.

Faxi pricked his ears forward and began to inhale deep breaths. With a friendly nicker, he walked forward more obligingly.

"Horses," Brak said, discerning their snowy shapes grazing or standing in the lee of boulders. He caught Faxi's bridle and led him into the cover of a large heap of rocks. Not far beyond the horses lurked another mine portal, braced by stone lintels inscribed with runic. "This is the right place," he said, recalling what the Rhbus had shown him. "Now, Skalgr, I suppose you have some ideas for getting in and getting back out with Ingvold and Pehr—alive?"

"You're quite sure this is where you want to go?" Skalgr inquired uneasily, gesturing toward a heap of rubbish outside the portal. Bones and rags comprised most of it. Brak's practiced eye discerned piles of unsorted spare parts of draugar, and his nose recognized the familiar smell of Myrkjartan's workshop.

"This seems to be Myrkjartan's side of the camp," Skalgr continued. "I think we ought to find the Dokkalfar—no, no, perhaps you're right. We may be able to drive another wedge between Myrkjartan and Hjordis. I'll go in there, begging for a scrap of food, and I'll get a good look around. One ragged old wretch looks much like another; no one will pay me the slightest heed, particularly if I disguise myself." Skalgr squinted up one eye in a gruesome fashion and hunched one shoulder higher than the other, walking up and down, dragging first one leg, then the other. "I limp better on the left," he said pridefully. "It's almost a genuine limp, you know. Isn't it wonderful the way I can assume these different characters and deformities? I wager Pehr and Ingvold won't even recognize me."

Brak watched him dubiously. "But Myrkjartan might remember you. And what about those Dokkalfar who caught you? They might be in there and recognize you, mightn't they?"

"Oh, they won't be there. This is Myrkjartan's workshop, and nothing will be with him except draugar. I assure you, those Dokkalfar wouldn't recognize me if they saw me. They think I'm dead."

Limping and squinting, Skalgr advanced upon the portal. With a furtive glance around, he scuttled inside and disappeared. Brak sighed and sat down, watching the early darkness descend in a most disheartening gloomy manner, with the snow whispering away with the same dull insistence.

Skalgar had not been gone very long when Myrkriddir came flapping out of the cave in great excitement, filling the air with gleeful shrieks and chuckles. Brak pushed Faxi further into the shadows, glad the old horse's white coat with its black speckles looked very much like a large, snow-covered rock. Anxiously Brak watched the foul creatures careering around the sky like insane nightmare images. They flew overhead several times with mirthful cries, and Brak armed himself with his axe, knowing they must see him.

Suddenly, with no warning, while his attention was on the sky, six Dokkalfar sprang from the rocks around him, advancing with axes and swords in hand and grinning in unpleasant good spirits.

"Welcome to Hjalmknip!" the leader declared, arrogantly knocking Brak's axe away with his own fearsome axe and motioning two Dokkalfar to collar him, which they did promptly. "Fancy your coming here so directly and obligingly, after we so carelessly neglected to find you when we captured your friends. We can't express how glad we are to see you and your skulking friend Skalgr!"

"That fool," Brak growled. "So he gave himself away directly, did he? I knew he wouldn't fool anybody."

"He didn't even try. He pranced right in and told us that the Scipling was outside trying to rescue his friends, and he mentioned exactly where to find you."

"I hope you've rewarded him properly," Brak said between his teeth. "You treated him rather shabbily the first time around, I believe."

"Oh, yes, we've made that as right as we could with him. All the food he can eat, all the ale he can hold, and a warm place to sleep. Clever old rascal. He'd sell his own grandmother if it were in the least bit profitable." The Dokkalfar chortled and gave Brak a shove toward the mine portal.

Brak could only agree; how well he knew. Silently he nourished some plans for suitable revenge.

Chapter 15

◇◇◇◇◇◇◇◇◇◇◇◇◇◇◇◇◇◇◇◇◇◇◇◇◇◇◇◇◇

Brak's captors pushed him inside the mine portal and hauled him, stumbling, down the tunnel toward a smoky fire. Seven Dokkalfar huddled around it, feeding bits of old, dried corpses into it and looking rather dissatisfied and melancholy with their surroundings. Farther down the tunnel, more light gleamed on the sweaty walls, and someone or something was stirring around. The Dokkalfar took a brand from the fire and pushed Brak down the tunnel. As they approached the source of the light—a large fire and beyond it lamps and candles on a long table—the darkness around them stirred and rustled. Ranks of gaunt, ragged creatures crept toward the intruders, some with parts of limbs missing and others with great jagged wounds sifting dust. The Dokkalfar sidled around the restless creatures, evidently not caring for their company in the least.

A tall, dark figure strode forward with an irascible shout. "Halloa, you brigands! What do you mean by disturbing my work? Haven't I told you often enough that if you must guard me, as Hjordis so kindly insisted, do it without bothering me and keep yourselves well away!"

The Dokkalfar leader stepped forward, eyeing the workshop and its contents. The place was littered with bones and scraps of draugar; a heap of spare parts stood beside the door. Several partly assembled draugar scratched around with blind malevolence, each one missing an arm or leg or more; and one wretched creature with no head crawled about, searching with awful patience for its missing member.

"We've taken a prisoner, Lordship, and don't rightly

know what we should do with him," the leader of the Dokkalfar muttered, shifting his feet nervously.

"Prisoner! Why bother me with these trifles? I ought to——" He turned back to his table and took up a large knife. The Dokkalfar stepped back quickly. "Take him to Hjordis. I'll be glad of your absence, and you may tell your queen so, if you dare."

"Begging your pardon, sir, wait a moment!" A scruffy figure stepped from the shadows, leering hopefully and rubbing his old hands together. "This is the other Scipling. The one who got away, you recall, and cut Skarnhrafn's horse from under him."

Myrkjartan whirled around. "The one with the dragon's heart!"

Brak bestowed a murderous look upon Skalgr, who anxiously signaled to him with propitiatory gestures and almost melted with conciliatory grimaces. "That's him," Skalgr declared. "Begging your excellent pardon again, sir, if an old, homeless wanderer's opinion is worth anything, I'd say you oughtn't send him with these fellows to Hjordis. He might escape, you know, and you'd lose the heart forever."

Myrkjartan looked at Brak and nodded. "Perfectly right, of course. Leave him here, you fellows, and get back to your guarding or spying, or whatever it is Hjordis wants you to do. I urge you not to disturb me again unless I should send for you."

The Dokkalfar lingered, scowling. Their leader growled, "Shouldn't the queen be told of the capture of the dragon's heart?"

"Not by anyone who wishes to live very long. If any of you tell her I have it, I'll send you home to your families, pickled in crocks."

Hastily the Dokkalfar withdrew, in the process dealing the disabled draugar several subtle kicks. Skalgr drew nearer to the light, as if in anticipation of a reward, but Myrkjartan banished him with a threatening stab of his staff. Then he turned to Brak, his eyes glowing in their sockets like those of a hungry animal.

"Well, at last we meet, with nothing but you between me and the dragon's heart." Myrkjartan almost chuckled. "You look as if you've been through hard times—not as soft and buttery as you once were, which is a pity for the trolls, eh?"

Brak measured the necromancer—thin and stringy, but no doubt as strong as rawhide and loaded with evil spells as well. "Where are Ingvold and Pehr? I came to get them, and I doubt that you can stand against the Rhbus."

"Who said anything about bringing the Rhbus into this?" Myrkjartan asked. "This is a personal matter between you and me. We worked together once before at Hagsbarrow, you recall, and I propose we go on as if nothing had changed, although I won't require you to dig for corpses or to sort parts anymore. Since you have the dragon's heart and won't relinquish it, I shall have to take you as part of the bargain, alive and troublesome, as you can be. But I have a plan—swear your loyalty to me and I'll see to it that Ingvold and Pehr are brought here at once. Hjordis has them now, no doubt cursing her luck, if she has discovered that Ingvold no longer has the heart." He almost chuckled again with glee, watching Brak intently.

"I won't swear fealty to you or anyone else," Brak replied.

"That is unfortunate," Myrkjartan said with a sigh. "But perhaps you'll change your mind when you come to know me better. Come over here and watch what I am doing."

Brak reluctantly stepped closer. Myrkjartan busied himself among his crocks, jars, and dusty pouches. He ground something to a powder with a mortar and pestle and sifted it carefully into a small phial. He peered into a large crock with a heavy lid, where some live thing sloshed and slithered around, flipping out a slimy appendage very much like a human hand with no bones. Myrkjartan struck at the wriggling tentacle with a bone from the workbench, and the thing quickly withdrew. Adding a pinch of powder and a bit more water, Myrkjartan shut the lid as the thing inside started a burbling wail. He moved on to other jars in which other live things waited for their daily sustenance.

Brak folded his arms across his chest. "What are these —your pets? I'd never have thought it of you, Myrkjartan."

Myrkjartan methodically opened all the jars one by one. "Pets! These are all my enemies who tried to thwart me," he said, patting a dried, leathery skull fondly. It snarled, its eyes gleaming with hatred. "Old Sigfus was my teacher.

He never forgave me for becoming greater—and more dangerous—than he. We necromancers never apologize and never forgive, do we, old fellow?"

Sigfus snarled horribly, and Brak recognized the same head he had inadvertently spilled in the stable at Vigfusstead. Myrkjartan patted Sigfus' skull again. "He's furious that it is I who shall one day possess the dragon's heart. He's as jealous as a defeated rival, or more so, even yet."

Brak moved away from the table. "I suppose you'll threaten me with a similar fate if I don't swear loyalty to you and do what you wish with the dragon's heart."

"I never threaten," Myrkjartan answered pleasantly. "All I require right now is that you think about my offer. We'll make you quite comfortable here until we quit the place. First we shall make an end of Miklborg as planned, particularly since a battle will rid us of a large number of these wretched Dokkalfar and provide us with some new draugar. You will stay, won't you?" He tapped his staff gently on the ground, and the figure on its top exuded a streamer of the cloying black fog.

Brak glanced behind him at the Dokkalfar crouching around their fire, honing their weapons and appearing as watchful as jailers could be. He sighed and lowered himself to a stool beside the fire. "First send for Pehr and Ingvold so I'll know if they're unharmed," he said.

Myrkjartan considered and began to scowl. Then Skalgr sidled from the shadows again. "Would you care for more advice, Myrkjartan? Send for Pehr and Ingvold, or Hjordis will have an advantage over you and Brak. She'll hold them as hostages and use them against you."

"Get away! Do you think I can't think for myself? If I see you again, or hear you again—" But Skalgr was already gone, and Myrkjartan prodded the shadows in vain. After a few moments of muttering and poking, he summoned one of the Dokkalfar with an angry roar and sent him away to demand the prisoners of Hjordis.

Hjordis did not respond immediately to Myrkjartan's request. She kept him waiting for nearly two days. Myrkjartan paced up and down and made several more vaguely threatening appeals to Brak to join his cause and destroy both Ljosalfar and Dokkalfar, which Brak refused to listen to. Skalgr, however, listened from the shadows with chortles of delight, taking care to flee Myrkjartan's wrath when the necromancer plunged after him or darted ice bolts at him in supreme irritation.

When Hjordis finally did respond, Myrkjartan was attending to the creatures in the crocks. He did not even glance around as ten or so Dokkalfar marched into the tunnel with self-important pomp and clatter. Myrkjartan ignored them as they glared at his back, shuffled their feet, and rattled their weapons, until finally they became uncomfortable and shrank back against the walls.

"Well? What do you want?" Myrkjartan growled finally, still without looking at his guests.

Their leader stepped forward. "We're to fetch you to Hjordis, along with your prisoner—if you please, that is."

Myrkjartan turned and looked at the messenger with a chilling expression. "I have no intention of being fetched to anyone. I don't wish to speak to Hjordis. I sent word for her to deliver her prisoners to me, and you may return with that message at once."

"But we have our orders from the queen herself—"

A black-cloaked figure pushed him aside. "Let the queen speak for herself," the voice of Hjordis said. "I feared something of this nature would occur, so I followed my messengers to make certain my will was carried out." She stepped forward with a slight limp, her hand on the hilt of a sword. Her face was wrapped in strips of black cloth, and her eyes gleamed angrily through a small slit as she confronted Myrkjartan. Her Dokkalfar gathered behind her, leering speculatively at Myrkjartan and Brak.

Myrkjartan lowered his eyes to look at her hand on the hilt of the sword, but she quickly hid it in the fabric of her cloak. "You've sadly abused my faith in you, Myrkjartan," she said in a murderous tone. "I am the queen and ruler of the Dokkalfar, and you have your authority only as far as I grant it to you. It was presumptuous of you to seize this prisoner from the guards I loaned you. I hope you have repented of this folly now and are ready to make an apology to me."

"I need not apologize when it is my thousands of draugar who are doing all of the fighting for these hill forts which we have captured," Myrkjartan replied coldly. "I am not your servant to be ordered around. When we divided Dyrstyggr's weapons between us, we agreed that we were to be equals, did we not?"

"But Skarnhrafn is your servant," Hjordis snapped. "Thus you have two of the weapons to my one, and now you have designs to have the dragon's heart also. It should be mine, so that we each will possess two of Dyrstyggr's weapons."

"You have Ingvold, which has been your object from the beginning—" Myrkjartan began, but Hjordis cut him off with a sharp retort.

"Treacherous old fool, do you think I don't know she no longer has the heart and hasn't had it since she returned to the Alfar realm? She gave it to this Scipling at Hafthorrsstead, so he had it all the time at Hagsbarrow, when you had him digging in the peat. Hah, I can see that makes you angry, and well it should because of your own stupidity, Myrkjartan. Then you sent that mindless dustbag Skarnhrafn after Ingvold, which was one of the more useless things you've done, since he can't get it out of his head that he is supposed to carry her back to you. He's making himself a frightful nuisance outside my cave, and unless you chain him up or destroy him, I may do it myself and keep his helmet." Her eyes flashed through the bandages challengingly.

Myrkjartan appeared unmoved. "I shall be forced to destroy Skarnhrafn, perhaps, to get this notion of Ingvold out of his head. I don't advise your trying it, even with that sword."

Hjordis interrupted with a harsh laugh. "Why ever not? It's destroying me, isn't it, and I'm more powerful than that draug. Come, Myrkjartan, this is enough chatter. You're trying to frighten me into surrendering my power and leadership to you, and you've been defying me in a hundred subtle ways since I enlisted you in my cause."

"Your cause? It seems to me that the cause belongs to the one who possesses the most fighting men and the most power," Myrkjartan said. "Don't underestimate my power, Hjordis. I happen to know how the curse of Dyrstyggr's sword is weakening you. I know what you're trying to hide under that cloak and those bandages."

Hjordis clutched her sword, and Brak saw that her hand

was swollen and discolored. She and Myrkjartan exchanged a fiery stare across a deadly silence. "As for you, necromancer, don't overestimate my patience. I am taking your prisoner, whether you wish it or not." She beckoned to her escort, and they drew their weapons, assuming defensive positions around their queen.

Myrkjartan lifted his staff and motioned to the draugar slinking around in the shadows of the tunnel. They shuffled forward, drawing their rusty weapons. "Then shall we fight for the dragon's heart?" Myrkjartan inquired grimly, putting his hand on his own sword.

"You are badly outnumbered, Myrkjartan, and I don't really want to kill you with this." She drew the sword partway, shaking her cloak aside. Brak looked at her arm in horror. Knobby accretions had deformed it so, it was scarcely recognizable as a human limb. The skin hung in dark, baggy folds, like the scaly skin of a lizard.

Myrkjartan, too, stared at her forearm, and she laughed. "You never thought it was as bad as that, did you? I warn you, Myrkjartan, this affliction does not improve my temper, which was never very good. The curse is in my blood; I will not be thwarted."

She motioned her men forward, indicating that their object was the removal of Brak from the tunnel. Myrkjartan made no move, but the draugar advanced to block the Dokkalfar. The ill-assorted, ragged creatures loomed menacingly, watching with dead eyes and clutching their weapons with blackened claws. The Dokkalfar hesitated, knowing the horrible creatures would fight until nothing of them remained but shreds of dried flesh and broken bones; and even then something malevolent would remain, unseen and bitterly resolved to seal the doom of the draugar's enemies.

Hjordis stepped forward. "You think I'm afraid of your carrion fighters? Watch this!" She lashed out with her sword and hacked the head off the foremost draug. Immediately the Dokkalfar plunged forward and chopped the remaining six draugar into pieces until Hjordis commanded them to stop. "Now you see how determined I am, Myrkjartan. Would you still care to fight with me?"

Myrkjartan looked away from the burning gaze of Hjordis. "Your fury has a certain terrible fascination,

Hjordis. I can see there's no use appealing to your common sense or your reason, both of which have evidently deserted you with the onset of Dyrstyggr's curse. You may take the Scipling and begone—but don't think for a moment that I will forget what you have done."

Hjordis beckoned to one of her men, who edged past Myrkjartan and indicated to Brak with the tip of his sword where he was expected to walk. Brak made no objection, since the purpose of his journey to Hjalmknip was a reunion with Pehr and Ingvold, although he couldn't help looking askance at Hjordis in her fury and affliction. Once Pehr and Ingvold were safe, he would waste no time in summoning help from the Rhbus to escape. As he glanced back at Myrkjartan, who was again unconcernedly attending to the creatures in the jars, the necromancer's expression reminded him of what Myrkjartan had told him about necromancers never forgetting a wrong.

Outside the mine portal, Hjordis directed part of her men to bring Brak to her headquarters in the old mines to the north, and the others she commanded to remain behind with Myrkjartan. Judging by their faces, her order was little to their liking. Hjordis then departed in the company of a large, evil-looking Dokkalfar who appeared to be as near to the Dokkalfar wolf-fylgja as humanly possible. The prisoner and his guards followed more slowly, arriving at a large, busy portal near dawn. Great numbers of Dokkalfar were returning from whatever mischief they had been up to all night and were taking shelter in the nearby tunnels, where cooking fires winked in the darkness like wicked red eyes peering from the bowels of the earth.

Hjordis' ill-favored attendant waited near the largest portal.

"Take him in to the queen," he directed the other Dokkalfar with contemptuous curtness, and looked at Brak with hostility and disdain. "My name is Tyrkell Blood-Axe, and you'd do well to remember it. If you try to escape, I promise you won't leave here alive, Scipling."

"Empty threats mean an empty head," Brak retorted. "You're much like Skarnhrafn in that manner."

Brak's captors quickly pushed him past Tyrkell, taking him down a tunnel to a large, smoky gallery where several women were cooking various delicacies over fires. Two

Dokkalfar were grooming Hjordis' horse, knee-deep in fresh straw, and six more men were guarding a large booth. The flaps were closed, and a lamp glowed from within with a ruddy light.

"We've brought the prisoner," Brak's attendants announced, halting before the tent. "What does the queen wish done with him?"

"Send him in," Hjordis commanded from inside the booth. "Send in Tyrkell also, and then the rest of you take yourselves outside. Any listening ears will be cut off."

Tyrkell slouched forward with an offensive grin for his fellow Dokkalfar and a threatening lower for Brak. He opened the tent flaps and beckoned Brak to go in. Brak did not remove his eyes from Tyrkell as he did so, wondering suspiciously why the fellow's hatred was so obviously personal, as if Brak were a direct threat to him somehow.

Hjordis waited for them, lounging in a large, elaborate chair where her face was comfortably in shadow. Before she could speak, Brak seized the opportunity to make his own demands. "Where are my friends? If you don't want to suffer some very dire consequences, you'll return them to me at once and allow us to depart unharmed."

Hjordis sat up straight with an angry laugh. "Listen to him, Tyrkell! His first words to me are a threat. He's rather bold, don't you think?"

Tyrkell swelled and bristled with menace. "I can kill him for you at once, if you wish it, and put an end to all threats and boldness."

"Don't be stupid," Hjordis said coldly. "He has the heart and must not be harmed." In a more pleasant tone she continued. "Now, Brak, I assure you that your friends are quite comfortable—as comfortable as one can be in a place such as this, with slime on the walls or dust sifting into everything. You needn't glare at me so wickedly. I brought you here for no other purpose than to restore your companions to you."

"What?" Brak exclaimed, echoed by a surprised grunt from Tyrkell. "Or I suppose I should ask why, instead. What do you hope to gain from it, if you do this?"

"I have no wish to anger the Rhbus and turn them against us," Hjordis replied. "Myrkjartan is a greedy, impulsive fellow and a threat to everyone in the realm, so it was essential that I prevent him from taking the heart from you. Once we finish with this disagreement with Miklborg, I shall be able to offer my honored guests whatever they wish—horses, gold, clothing, land, honor, positions. I hope you'll allow me to be generous with you."

"Generous?" Brak slowly shook his head, scowling suspiciously. "I don't want gifts from the Dokkalfar. In fact, there's nothing I want less. All I want is the safe return of my friends so we can leave."

Hjordis put her hand on her sword, drew it from its sheath, and laid it across her knees. Tyrkell looked from Hjordis to Brak several times, squinting in angry confusion. Brak could not take his eyes from Dyrstyggr's sword, thinking what an asset it would be if he could get it for Dyrstyggr, when they found him.

"I know you covet Dyrstyggr's sword," Hjordis continued gently. "It seems that the brotherhood of Dyrstyggr's weapons is an envious lot. You'd like to have this sword, wouldn't you? It won't hurt you to admit it—don't you yearn to possess it?"

Brak refused to do more than scowl and look away haughtily. "I don't know much about using a sword," he said.

"With this sword, it doesn't matter. It fights for you just as if Dyrstyggr's hand were on the hilt."

"It's also cursed," Brak added. "I wouldn't take it as a gift."

Hjordis did not lose her complacency. "But its curse is against Alfar, Dokkalfar, jotun, and all other creatures of Ymir, such as the dwarves, trolls, and so forth. No mention of Sciplings is made in the curse. Do you see?"

Brak nodded his head slowly. "Yes, I think I'm beginning to," he said cautiously.

Hjordis leaned forward, her eyes glittering triumphantly over a fan she used to hide most of her face. "The Rhbus are mysterious to us, and their ways of accomplishing their objectives are often too deep for us ordinary folk to understand. Perhaps it was their working that brought you to Hjalmknip. Perhaps they don't want you to leave just yet." She leaned farther forward and whispered, "Perhaps they want you to stay and obtain all of Dyrstyggr's weapons, beginning with this sword, which I am soon going to offer to you."

Brak could find nothing to say for a few moments. He glanced at Tyrkell and realized the fellow was almost tied up in knots with hatred and envy at the thought of Hjordis' giving the sword to Brak. He also realized that Hjordis was bargaining with all her might to entice him to stay and use the powers of Dyrstyggr's weapons in her behalf. It was a tempting snare—or else a cleverly planned stratagem of the Rhbus.

"But what am I expected to do in return?" Brak growled, assuming a certain attitude often adopted by thralls to conceal their true intelligence—a dogged scowl and slumping shoulders. Hjordis relaxed and began to smile in triumph.

"Don't worry about that yet; it's not dreadfully important," she replied almost genially. "We'll discuss it later, after you have seen your friends. Tyrkell will escort you to the place where they are being kept." She gave them a nod of dismissal.

"Come along," Tyrkell growled venomously. "It's outside and down another tunnel." He stalked behind Brak with his hand on his axe, directing their course with snarls and grunts. He indicated the largest and smokiest entrance, which was also the muddiest, and they slithered down its sloping maw past clumps of Dokkalfar huddling around small fires and trying to cook or sleep. Tyrkell strode through them with no regard for common courtesy or the resentful glares he earned from his companions.

The muddy tunnel widened abruptly into a large chamber shored up at intervals with splitting, rotten timbers. More fires and groups of Dokkalfar camped here, casually breaking off bits of the timbers for their cooking fires. The place reeked of wet wool, boiled fish, and sweaty horses, which were tethered in long lines across the back half of the chamber. The dozens of small fires created a lurid, choking atmosphere that reminded Brak strongly of the effects of dragon meat.

"This is worse than a stable," Brak said, meeting Tyrkell's lowering glare. "What sort of place is this to keep a chieftain's daughter?"

Tyrkell grinned wolfishly. "You're finally beginning to

understand. There isn't any chieftain's daughter down here. Hjordis keeps her hidden very well indeed, and if you behave yourself and do as you're told, no harm will come to her. If you try summoning the Rhbus to rescue her, she'll be dead by the time you find her."

Brak clenched his fists, realizing he had been tricked. "I want to talk to Hjordis again—right now," he said in a deadly, even tone.

"I'm not allowed to disturb the queen for something so unimportant as a complaint from a prisoner," Tyrkell replied, twisting his ugly face up in a sneer. "You may talk to her when she sends for you, and not until then. Now come along quickly, Scipling." He drew his axe and smiled, as if yearning to make a dent in Brak's skull with it.

"I'm no one's prisoner," Brak replied stubbornly. "I can leave here any time I choose."

"And it will be the death of your precious Ingvold if you do," Tyrkell said, with a menacing gesture of his axe. "I strongly urge you to remain with us for a while—although I myself would rather see you hanged. Hjordis has doubts about Myrkjartan and his draugar, and we may need the assistance of that dragon's heart of yours if we are to crush Miklborg."

"You'll never crush Miklborg if I can do anything to stop it," Brak said, almost too angry to speak. "You're all nothing but thieves and murderers, greedy savages who would drive out every decent living creature until nothing was left but stinking trolls and a plague of Dokkalfar. You're the maggots of the earth, digging tunnels through it and ruining it just to get at more gold to fight over and more metal to make weapons from. And you, Tyrkell, are a great, fat rat with slime for blood and the heart of a lying traitor."

"Hear, hear!" someone muttered from a nearby group gathered around its fire, watching with interest.

"If it comes down to a fight, I'll bet my money on the Scipling," another voice remarked.

Tyrkell dropped his axe and began to circle. "We'll see if your precious Rhbus care to save you this time," he snarled. "I've broken many a neck with my bare hands, as any of these dolts can tell you. For the sake of Hjordis, I shall be lenient with you and leave a fragment of life in your useless carcass."

Brak made the first rush and they grappled like two angry bears, flailing and kicking and rolling, scattering the spectators and all their possessions. Fights were common enough in the Dokkalfar camps to be more of an annoyance than entertainment, particularly to fellows who were trying to sleep. The fighters garnered plenty of kicks and buffets from exasperated Dokkalfar who merely wanted to find a dry spot in the mud to sip their tea and elderly Dokkalfar who thought they deserved a little consideration on behalf of their advanced years.

Thus it was that a very ancient Dokkalfar ended the fight without ceremony by pouring hot water on Tyrkell, scalding him soundly. When he leaped away, howling like a singed cat, Brak scrambled after him and got a perfect hold upon his throat. Just as he was beginning to throttle Tyrkell, the curmudgeon with the teakettle brained him senseless.

Before Brak's consciousness deserted him entirely, he was aware of the old fellow with the kettle hobbling away, muttering something about a perfect waste of hot water, what a nuisance it was to have fights, and why more people couldn't be peaceful souls like him. Brak's last impression was a double blurry vision of the much-battered teakettle, with a vague speculation on how many skulls it had similarly cloven; then his senses lapsed into blackness.

Chapter 16

Brak awakened with one hand clenched around the dragon's heart in a grip like death itself. His hand ached almost as much as his head, which his other hand told him was caked with dried blood and endowed with a handsome lump.

"Well, he *is* alive, after all," a voice declared argumentatively. "That's a flagon you owe me, Svagi. No one knows as well as I do what a thick skull Brak has."

Brak rubbed his eyes, which were still seeing double. Pehr's image floated before him, accompanied by a squat hulk of a Dokkalfar with a greasy tunic who kept a large axe across his knees. By some undoubtedly violent means he had lost the use of one eye and the greater part of one ear. His method of communication was grunts and growls and menacing flourishes of his axe.

"Pay no attention to him," Pehr advised Brak, helping him to sit up and offering him a drink of water. "I've tried to draw him out for three days, but he's still shy. I've never seen such a timid fellow, nor such an ugly one either. It's quite a relief to see you again, old friend, since I assumed you were either killed or safe somewhere else and plotting to rescue us. But I realize you couldn't hope to manage alone. You still have the—the object in question?"

"I have it," Brak said. Speaking made his head throb worse than before. "And I wasn't alone. I came upon a mutual acquaintance of ours."

Pehr groaned. "Skalgr. And he betrayed you again. You

needn't say it. If I could get my hands on his neck for only a moment—"

"Have you seen Ingvold?" Brak interrupted.

"No, but I hear she's kept under heavy protection. How did you come to deserve such a splendid crack on the head, Brak? When they dragged you here by the heels, I thought you must be dead, or near to it. I tried to make a friendly wager with old Svagi, or Grunt or Glum or whatever he's called, but talking to him is like knocking on the door of a house where no one is home but the dogs. You are feeling a little better, aren't you?" His voice betrayed his anxiety as he tried to make Brak more comfortable against the stony wall.

"Much better," Brak said. His vision had cleared, and he recognized the underground gallery with the rotting timbers supporting the roof. The fires still burned in the darkness, but the place was stirring with activity. Horses were trampling past, and men were hurrying back and forth with a rattling of swords, arrows, and lances. "They're going to battle against Miklborg, and there's nothing we can do to stop them, Pehr."

"Summon the Rhbus," Pehr whispered. "Tell them to get us out of here and to do something for Miklborg!"

Brak slowly shook his head. "We have to stay here for a while."

"What? Don't be absurd! How can we ever find Dyrstyggr if we stay here? We're in peril of death every moment we remain, and hundreds of Ljosalfar are going to be killed! What do you mean, we have to stay here for a while?"

Brak closed his eyes and tried to shake his head, but the motion was excruciating. "I'll tell you about it later, when my head doesn't hurt so much."

Pehr could scarcely remain still. "We could be out of here in a matter of moments. This lump of grease and filth could be melted like old tallow." He exchanged a hostile glower with Svagi. "If we had the help of the Rhbus, all the Dokkalfar in Hjalmknip couldn't stop us from leaving."

"Unless Hjordis realizes, as she does, that we don't intend to leave," Brak said wearily. "Otherwise, why would she have only one guard for us, and a one-eyed, one-eared one at that?"

The excitement and activity in the old mines increased

to battle pitch, and Brak's and Pehr's spirits sank accordingly. Men and horses hurried away eagerly. A sparkle illuminated even the eye of old Svagi as he fondly cradled his axe and watched the preparations.

Then through the noise and confusion rode Hjordis in a white cloak and polished tunic of mail, with Tyrkell lurking behind her. As she stopped before the two prisoners, Tyrkell scowled bitterly at Brak and shook his fist threateningly.

Hjordis was carefully bandaged in black with her hands hidden in gauntlets. She drew Dyrstyggr's sword, letting it flash in the red firelight. Pehr moved back from the expressionless queen, but Brak had the feeling she was smiling in triumph.

"I came to give you a glimpse of Dyrstyggr's sword before we go into battle." She held it aloft for a moment, where it gleamed with the color of fresh blood, then extinguished it in its sheath. "I shall lead the Dokkalfar to victory tonight. With this sword before them, they wouldn't be afraid to assail the sacred halls of Asgard. If you are clever, my Scipling friend, this sword will one day belong in your hand and the Dokkalfar will be united at your back."

Brak replied, "Only if the Rhbus wish it."

Hjordis reined her horse around to depart. "They will, I feel certain. At the very least, it's an innovation they will have to become accustomed to." She set spurs to her curvetting horse and sent it plunging after the long lines of Dokkalfar riding away into the night. Tyrkell followed, after glaring at Brak with murder and jealousy in his expression.

"I don't understand this at all," Pehr said, folding his arms and scowling at Brak. "She wants to give you Dyrstyggr's sword? What have you promised in return?"

"Nothing—so far," Brak said. Rather than endure Pehr's glares and questions, he told him about Dyrstyggr's curse on Hjordis and her various promises, and also how the Rhbus might be guiding him toward the recovery of Dyrstyggr's sword. "And now, unless you have any more questions, I'm going to try to sleep, if you don't mind," Brak said by way of finishing his report and hinting to Pehr that he was actually very tired.

Pehr strode back and forth a few paces with great impatience, closely watched by Svagi's suspicious single eye. "Well, I can't sleep, with Miklborg about to be attacked. I hope it will withstand them, what with the supplies we helped carry there. I can't believe you'd ever use that cursed sword for Hjordis against the Ljosalfar, not even if Ingvold's life is in question. I can't imagine her being very pleased with you if you did such a thing. I'm sure she'd rather die, Brak."

Brak was also certain of it. Nothing could equal her contempt, if ever she found out that he had sold himself and the dragon's heart to Hjordis for so paltry a sum as her own life, which she would gladly and fiercely sacrifice for the cause of her people. However, since Hjordis was bargaining for a thing she desperately wanted, and since he could bollix up her plans best by simply delaying, he decided there was no immediate action necessary—except a good, long rest.

Near midnight, his sleep was terminated by the first clash of battle. Old Svagi and the remaining handful of unfit warriors pricked up their ears, and most of them hobbled to the portal to listen and to try to judge the progress of the battle by its distant din. Presently the wounded and the dead on litters began straggling back to Hjalmknip. An infirmary was hastily set up in the cavern where Pehr and Brak were waiting, and the litter-bearers deposited their cargo before a half-dozen harried Dokkalfar healing physicians, for them to patch together hastily, or dumped it in a heap outside with a casual, "Here's another for Myrkjartan." Soon the chamber was as bloody a battlefield as the real one, strewn with the wounded, the dying, and the dead.

Shortly before dawn, the battle was finished, with the Dokkalfar in retreat. They arrived at Hjalmknip in total rout and took refuge in their respective grottoes, like hosts of wounded, tattered rats, to nurse their defeat. The Ljosalfar had significantly advanced their position, greatly at the expense of the Dokkalfar.

Into the midst of their misery rode Hjordis on her horse, surrounded by her chieftains, who were loudly complaining about the heavy losses of their neighbors and kinsmen, despite their own rather desperate-looking injuries. Hjordis dismounted and pushed her way through them with the ready assistance of Tyrkell, whose looks were not enhanced by a fresh wound over one ill-favored eye.

"We have lost nearly a hundred men tonight," Hjordis declared, breathing harshly and clenching her fists. "If we'd possessed the dragon't heart, we would have been successful in capturing Miklborg. Perhaps you think you can delay in making up your mind and play games with the lives of the Dokkalfar, but I assure you the time is drawing very short, and so is my patience. I have Ingvold Thjodmarsdotter to use against you. Surely you would not like to hear of her being hurt in any way."

"I'll destroy the heart if you hurt her," Brak said, his wound beginning to ache anew as his anger stirred.

"Then do what you must to preserve her," Hjordis snapped. "The draugar of Myrkjartan deserted us at the critical moment. Without them and without the heart, we had no chance of taking Miklborg. It seems they were ready for us. Myrkjartan and the ravens will be very pleased." She clasped her hands to keep from tearing at her hair and her face bandages. The bandages were beginning to come unwound, revealing more folds of blackened, scaly skin and an unsightly growth beneath one inflamed eye. Brak couldn't help looking away in revulsion.

"It was our doing that made them ready for you," Pehr declared. "We helped Kolssynir get the necessary supplies to withstand your attack. Messengers have also been sent to the other hill forts near here, so your attacks on unsuspecting settlements and isolated farmsteads have come to an end."

Hjordis replied with an ugly laugh. "Well, it's villainy for villainy. You may have just put Ingvold out of your reach for a very long time—if not forever. If you wish to save her from the slow, icy death of the fires of Hjordisborg, you'll begin to beg for my terms."

"I don't even know if she's alive or dead," Brak retorted, meeting Hjordis' furious eye. "Show her to me and I'll consider doing something to help you."

Hjordis looked at him calculatingly and finally nodded her head. In a much more pleasant tone she said, "I think I can arrange it—depending upon how the fighting goes tomorrow night. If it goes well, perhaps you can talk to her.

But if it goes poorly again, all you'll see is a glimpse of her as she is taken to Hjordisborg and a long, cold sleep. You needn't look so menacing, Brak; she won't be harmed. I give you my word of honor."

"I suppose you can afford to, since you already have everything worth having except this heart," Brak said bitterly. "If you did kill her, I wouldn't hesitate to call on the Rhbus to destroy all of you."

"I hope you don't think I don't know that," Hjordis answered. "One doesn't become Queen of the Dokkalfar by being stupid or by being weak. Remember what I said about the battle going against us tomorrow night." She saluted him with one hand, taking care to hide as much of the curse's evidence as she could with her sleeve, which only served to enforce the illusion in Brak's mind of the knots, knobs, and strange discolorations of her skin. She strode off with a slight limp, Tyrkell slouching in her wake to shove away the angry chieftains, who were clamoring for her attention.

When the uproar had died down somewhat, leaving only the general growling of the defeated Dokkalfar and the groaning of the wounded, Pehr whispered to Brak, "How do you suppose the fighting will go tomorrow night?"

"Very badly for the Dokkalfar, I hope," Brak snapped. "Let her find out where it gets her to threaten us. If she takes Ingvold to her fires at Hjordisborg, I'll follow and pull it down stone by stone until Ingvold is free, and if the Rhbus won't help me, I'll do it with my bare hands."

"Yes, but I hope you'll be prudent about it," Pehr said anxiously. "She won't kill Ingvold, nor will she let her go. If we attempt a show of force, however, Hjordis is liable to react like a cornered weasel and attack anything within reach. I'd say you're both at loggerheads with each other as long as neither of you will budge an inch."

"Well, I won't give in to her," Brak said. "I may lead her to believe I am giving in, but when I've given her enough rope, she'll hang herself." Brak's eyes blurred again and his throat burned, as if the dragon's heart were in agreement with him.

The proximity of the infirmary and the horse lines made sleeping difficult, but by the end of the day Brak awoke refreshed and less troubled by his injury. Someone brought the captives a generous supply of food, which was most welcome. Brak watched with anticipation as the Dokkalfar prepared to depart again, this time with considerably less enthusiasm. Hjordis did not pay him another visit before she led her warriors toward Miklborg.

The fighting began around midnight, and before long the first of the wounded and dead were returned to Hjalmknip. Presently Pehr poked Brak excitedly and nodded toward the tunnel, where the dead were stacked. Only a few torches illuminated the area, but Brak saw a bent, scuttling form searching among the corpses, skillfully removing rings and ornaments, a pair of boots, a cloak, and a sword.

"That fellow reminds me of Skalgr," Pehr whispered, but before Brak could get to his feet, with the idea of lunging after the old thief and attacking him, the corpse-robber had scurried out of sight with his plunder. Brak sat down slowly across from old Svagi again, who was shaking his axe and beetling his brows with silent threats.

"I have a feeling you are right, Pehr," Brak said with a sigh of resignation.

The fighting went as badly as Brak had hoped, and Hjordis was furious, which they learned from the disgruntled warriors who came trailing back near dawn with more tales of defeat. Although Brak expected her, Hjordis did not appear. He and Pehr spent the hours enticing Svagi into playing wagering games with them, which he lost with unfailing regularity and unimpaired bad humor.

At last dawn brought the remaining warriors home, after a long night of grimly holding their own at the unrelenting behest of Hjordis in spite of all losses and weariness. Their efforts ultimately resulted in an unfruitful stalemate, resolved only by the imminent arrival of daylight. Brak prepared himself for an angry confrontation with Hjordis, but again she did not appear. He paced up and down, growing more distraught by the moment from wondering where she was and when she was coming.

"I have to talk to her again," Brak said uneasily, looking at Svagi each time he passed. Finally he halted before the suspicious old Dokkalfar. "Svagi, you must send word to Hjordis that I demand to see her as soon as possible."

Svagi's response was to raise one hairy eyebrow and to

snort disparagingly. His head seemed to retreat into his
shoulders, much like an old tortoise that had been offended.

"I mean it, you old lump of ignorance," Brak insisted.
"Send one of these fellows with the message, if you can't
manage it yourself. If you don't, I'll be forced to disgrace
you, Svagi, and simply walk away. You can't really suppose
you're much of a guard, you know."

Svagi scowled and pouted, clutching his axe in both
hands and resting it on one shoulder while he began the
laborious process of reconsidering. Finally he heaved a
great sigh, as if it were too annoying to endure, and beckoned to a nearby warrior, who carried away Brak's
message very dubiously. Brak sat down to wait with more
anxiety than he could conceal.

"What if she really does take Ingvold to Hjordisborg?
Would Hjordis dare gamble much further and do some
harm to Ingvold?" Brak demanded, pacing up and down
before the watchful eye of old Svagi.

The messenger returned with the news that Hjordis
wouldn't consent to see the prisoner. Brak crouched against
the wall and began to worry in earnest, despite Pehr's assurances that Hjordis was only playing a game of cat-and-
mouse with him and that the more he demanded to see her,
the more impossible she would be to see.

Brak shrugged his shoulders and muttered, "I suppose
you're right, Pehr."

"She's no doubt angry about her losses. Maybe she's
planning a new tactic to trap you into conceding to her.
She might be—"

A voice coughed gently behind him, and he whirled
around as if expecting to see Hjordis herself standing there.
Instead, it was Skalgr, grinning and shuffling in the most
propitiatory manner he could muster. Deferentially, he offered Svagi a small, greasy parcel, steaming with a delightful aroma. Svagi snatched it, smelled it, and glared at
Skalgr as if he had been betrayed. Skalgr thereupon offered
him a shining gold arm ring. Svagi's hairy face broke into
an astonishing happy grin, and he allowed Skalgr to hustle
him aside so that Skalgr could talk to the prisoners privately.

"You shouldn't have troubled yourself, Skalgr," Pehr
said. "We have nothing to say to you, except—get out of

our sight! This is a fine atmosphere for a murder. One more body wouldn't attract much attention."

Skalgr nodded and shook his head and tried to soothe them down with desperate fluttering motions of his hands. "Shh! Shh! That's all very well, and no doubt you think I deserve it, but let me tell you what I came to say. Tomorrow we're going to rescue you and Ingvold. We've been most wondrously successful in dividing Hjordis and Myrkjartan at last. He refuses to send the draugar into battle to help her, and you see what happens to the Dokkalfar alone, who are, beneath it all, mortal fellows much the same as you and I and have the goodness to stop fighting once they are dead, unlike those wretched draugar—"

"Skalgr, hush!" Brak commanded. "I don't know what you're talking about, and neither do you. Nobody is going to rescue us from this place, let alone you. There's no face except Myrkjartan's that I'd sooner punch than yours, so take yourself away."

"I won't warn you again," Pehr added menacingly.

"But listen—you're going to be rescued—taken out of here—saved, you fools! You can't possibly want to stay here, can you?" Skalgr spluttered, his eyes glazed with distraction. "I thought—what are you planning anyway?" A light dawned in his eyes and he began to grin.

"As if we'd tell you—you of all the vermin we know!" Pehr exclaimed. "Get out of here, Skalgr, before I choke you!"

"But, Brak, Pehr, wait a minute and let me explain," Skalgr began, but at that moment Svagi's sense of duty overcame his admiration of the arm ring, and the horse meat was gone, so he returned to direct a kick at Skalgr. Still protesting, Skalgr retreated under a flurry of axe-swipes.

"Very good, Svagi!" Pehr declared, and Svagi showed one yellow tusk at him in a condescending manner and sat down beside his smoky little fire.

"I wonder who the 'we' is that Skalgr was mentioning," Brak said. "I hope he doesn't do anything foolish."

"How can he help himself?" Pehr demanded. "He's probably found another old, scrounging thief like himself, and they've concocted a plan of some sort to get money from somebody. You don't suppose he really could get us out of here, do you?" he added anxiously.

Brak shook his head. "Not unless we get that sword and Ingvold."

The day passed uneventfully, and the Dokkalfar began preparations for the third night of fighting. They were rather grim and dispirited preparations, and the Dokkalfar marched away in silent resignation, instead of boasting and rallying. Brak waited impatiently for Hjordis to renew her threats and promises, but she stayed away. He thought he would lose his wits if he didn't find out what she was thinking or planning and was debating a mad charge from his tunnel to accost her before she rode off to battle, but he was saved from his rashness by the arrival of a messenger sent to fetch him.

Hjordis waited outside, flanked by torches and covered to the eyes in black wrappings. Brak could see that her eyes gleamed redly, like a beast's eyes glowing in the firelight. For a chilling instant, he wondered how he could ever expect to out-threaten and outmenace such a dangerous being as she was.

"I promised you a last look at Ingvold," she said offhandedly. "After yesterday's debacle, you certainly can't expect any pity from me. Over a hundred Dokkalfar lost, and rumors that the draugar killed some of them. There you see her—on her way to Hjordisborg and the magic fire at the bottom of the royal catacombs." She waved a bandaged paw toward her own cave, where a group of mounted Dokkalfar were leading Ingvold forward on a white horse. Brak tried to struggle through the throng around Hjordis to get to Ingvold, but her chieftains held him back.

Ingvold saw him and raised one hand to wave. "Don't worry about me, Brak," she called. "You know what you must do. The Rhbus will help you." She looked pale in the torchlight and she was dressed like a stranger in proper women's clothes instead of ragged castoffs.

Brak nodded, scarcely able to speak. At last he burst out, "You won't die. I'll be there to save you when—when I've done these other things. You're—you're dressed warmly for the journey?" He at once felt foolish, but with the hated Dokkalfar on all sides he could say nothing that he might have wanted to say.

Ingvold nodded. "I'll be all right, Brak. Don't worry about me."

Then she was led away, looking back several times. Brak was about to turn back to Hjordis with a furious warning not to harm Ingvold when a fiery blast swept over the Dokkalfar, sending them scurrying for cover.

"It's Skarnhrafn!" Hjordis shouted furiously. "Attack him, you fools—don't run for shelter!"

Skarnhrafn rode his ragged horse over a hilltop, taking the same direction as Ingvold's captors. The Dokkalfar rode after him and hailed him with arrows and a few spells; but all he had to do was pause and look back at them, and they scattered before his fiery gaze. With a triumphant cackle, Skarnhrafn launched his horse into the air and swooped overhead exultantly several times. Hjordis stood her ground, defying him with terrible shrieks and threats. Finally he lumbered away after Ingvold, still convinced his master required him to bring her back.

Brak quickly abandoned his shelter behind a rock and hurried after Hjordis. "You're not leaving without speaking to me first," he said, catching the bridle of her horse. "It's not too late to send someone after Ingvold and your Dokkalfar. Bring her back now, or you'll have a worse defeat at the hands of the Ljosalfar tonight."

"My answer to you is this: Command the Rhbus to make us victorious tonight, or you shall never see your Ingvold again!" Hjordis yanked at her horse's head, but Brak held on.

"I don't believe you," he said. "If you don't preserve Ingvold's life, not a single Dokkalfar will leave the battlefield alive, and you yourself I will personally stalk until I find you. The curse of Dyrstyggr will be a minor affliction compared with what I can do with the help of the dragon's heart."

Hjordis spit and fumed furiously, then drew Dyrstyggr's sword. "I could easily kill you! Perhaps I should before you get too much power!" She feinted with the sword, rather irresolutely.

"Then we'll know which is the most powerful, the heart or the sword," Brak replied grimly.

Hjordis sheathed the sword. "Come, now, let's be more reasonable. Neither of us will get what we want if we continue in this manner. I have said that I will give Ingvold back to you at once if you'll help me in some small way. It's only your stubbornness that makes me threaten. I'll see to it that she's safe and unharmed at Hjordisborg if only you'll call upon the Rhbus to turn the fighting against the Ljosalfar. You can have this sword and even Hjordisborg itself in exchange for the assistance of the dragon's heart."

Brak released the reins of her horse. "First bring Ingvold back here, where I can see she is safe. And you must be the messenger."

"I can't do that; they've already gone. It would take time to catch them, and we've got to reach our positions around Miklborg or it will be too near dawn. I am the only one who can lead the Dokkalfar—unless you will," she added cunningly.

"I won't. Keep them in camp tonight, then. All I will promise is a thundering defeat for you if you go to battle tonight."

Hjordis sawed at the mouth of her prancing horse, starting first in one direction, then another. Her eyes gleamed furiously, as if her thoughts were also disordered and half wild. Finally she shrieked, "I am the queen! *I* have the power to threaten and take away, not you! If my Dokkalfar are defeated again tonight, then Ingvold will die! That is my last word! I, Hjordis, swear it!"

She set spurs to her horse and galloped away, angrily calling to her warriors to follow her to battle.

Chapter 17

◆◆◆◆◆◆◆◆◆◆◆◆◆◆◆◆◆◆◆◆◆◆◆◆◆◆◆◆◆◆◆

Not knowing if the situation was better or worse, Brak returned to Pehr and Svagi and found them both sleeping. Svagi sat embracing his axe and snoring earnestly, until his one eye fluttered open and rested upon Brak in dismay.

"You may as well go back to sleep," Brak growled, sitting down dejectedly. "You won't be able to later."

Svagi bared one tooth at him, very truculently, and took a firmer grip on his axe, as if to say he would do his duty until someone had to pry the axe out of his cold, lifeless fingers.

Brak paced back and forth until Svagi's suspicions were somewhat allayed. Then he sat down and wrapped himself in his cloak as if he intended to go to sleep; but he was actually using the cloak to hide the fact that his hands were opening the small case that held the dragon's heart. Unnoticed by Svagi, he began to nibble a small thread of the meat. When it started to burn, he lay down and shut his eyes as if he were asleep, drifting easily into the red and black visions. He saw the Dokkalfar and the Ljosalfar battling furiously, urged on by the twisted figure of Hjordis, and he saw Myrkjartan and his draugar covering the hilltops with forests of spears and arrows, waiting with silent menace. Over it all were superimposed the images of three bearded men who watched the proceedings with great gravity. One of the men was Gull-skeggi, who seemed to bend a look of sad compassion toward Brak as he said to the others, "We must not interfere for one or the other. How easy it would be, yet how deadly for the one we

196

favored. Our tools must be small and weak lest we overwhelm where we would help."

"But what about Ingvold?" Brak asked with difficulty, dimly aware of muttering something that caused old Svagi to awaken and glare at him.

His visions began to melt one into another, and he had the feeling he was floating above it all, looking down unconcernedly into a mêlée of ants battling. He saw a hill fort perched high on the rocky shoulder of a steep fell, as if it had been hewn from the native stone. Fires surrounded it like a sea of jewels winking in the night, lapping around the foot of the fortress and threatening to overcome it. The scene darkened gradually, all the light drawing together in one spot and beginning to blaze with an intense flame that leaped at him hungrily as he was funneled helplessly toward it.

He felt desperately cold, imagining that the narrowing walls around him were coated with ice. The flame crackled with a sound much like Hjordis' voice when she laughed. Behind its noise he thought he heard Ingvold calling to him in tones of fear. He writhed around, trying to stop the inexorable plunge into the heart of the fire that waited below. It laughed at him again, and he saw the face of Hjordis leering at him through the darkness, growing closer and more distinct by the moment. With a tremendous effort, he tore away from the power of his descent and leaped at Hjordis with a triumphant yell. His fingers found her throat, and she uttered a frightened screech that startled Brak back into consciousness.

To his surprise, he discovered that he had Skalgr by the neck and was shaking him as a dog would shake a rat. Skalgr did not submit gracefully to being strangled; he lashed and kicked and yelled ferociously. Brak sprang away quickly, muttering something about being asleep and having a nightmare. Svagi capered around, snarling, gnashing his tusks, and swinging his axe to the peril of everyone within a range of twenty feet on all sides of him. It took Skalgr four arm rings to lure him finally away and soothe his emotions into complacent greed.

"Are you all right?" Pehr demanded, gazing strangely at Brak. "You look positively fierce and gritty, like a berserkr. With a sword or knife in your hands, you might have killed old Skalgr."

Brak shook his head to clear the last of the red images away. "I'm sorry, Skalgr. It was a nightmare, and I thought you were Hjordis."

"A pity I wasn't, or I would have let you strangle her," Skalgr said with a nervous chuckle. "Not to be overly curious or indelicate, but was it perchance a bit of smoked meat that set you off, Brak?" His answer was a resentful stare, which he pretended to ignore. "I wonder what the Rhbus are going to do to resolve this dispute between you and Hjordis? I was watching when they took Ingvold away and I'm not ashamed to say I did my best to overhear every word you and Hjordis said to each other. Imagine a thrall talking to a queen in such a haughty manner. The Rhbus must be helping you, wouldn't you say?"

"He wouldn't say to the likes of you," Pehr retorted, with another anxious look at Brak. "Now what do you want with us, Skalgr? We're not fond of your company, you realize."

Skalgr grinned and winked, hitching himself closer to whisper, "When Hjordis returns from tonight's fighting, you must be ready for a journey. I'm sure you'll be very glad to go to Hjordisborg to rescue Ingvold, won't you?"

Brak shook his head in exasperation. "Skalgr, we're not going to Hjordisborg after Ingvold until I—perhaps we never will," he amended bleakly, thinking of the fire with a shudder. "When we leave Hjalmknip, it will be when we think it best. We don't want your help, even if you don't have any evil intentions this time. It seems that the good in you is easily misdirected into harm for someone else."

"Misdirected! Of all the ungrateful, unappreciative—" Skalgr began with an angry twitch of his shoulders.

"We've you to thank for all our problems," Pehr snapped, "so let's not talk about ingratitude. None of this would have happened if we hadn't had the misfortune of being discovered by you. I'm still not certain you're really a servant of Dyrstyggr's."

Skalgr stamped his foot. "What cheek to speak to me like that! I'm trying to tell you that you're going to be rescued and Ingvold is going to be rescued, and you refuse to allow me to do it. This is my venture as much as it is yours, even if you don't realize it. You can't imagine how hard I've worked for our success and how difficult it has been—"

"You, at least, seem to maintain your freedom remarkably well, while we are detained," Brak said. "You always seem to do rather well for yourself when it comes to food and drink and a warm place to sleep. I don't imagine Ingvold is very comfortable right now."

Skalgr hitched himself a bit closer. "I'd planned to do this as a surprise for you, my two dear young friends, but I can see that you've become ungrateful enough to be suspicious of my intentions, so I shall tell you exactly how it will be done. I realize you're resolved not to leave without Dyrstyggr's sword, although there will be more opportunities to get it. Very well, since you're so determined, tonight when Hjordis returns from the fighting will be the time to challenge her. We'll come for you and we'll—"

"Just a moment," Pehr said. "Who is this other person you keep talking about? You'd better mean someone else besides the fleas in your beard, Skalgr."

"Just be quiet a moment and let me tell you!" Skalgr exclaimed. "You don't give me a chance to—" A great, heavy paw clamped his shoulder and hoisted him away, and Svagi stuck his face into Skalgr's with a wicked growl. Skalgr twisted aside, delving into his pouches for another ring, but Svagi's sense of honor prohibited him from being bribed twice in the same evening. He drove Skalgr away with several expert jabs of his axe, thwarting Skalgr's efforts to mouth something to Brak and Pehr.

The Sciplings looked at each other doubtfully. Pehr shook his head. "I just can't believe Skalgr could," he whispered. "I don't like the idea of confronting Hjordis either. If we let her, she'll give you the sword. But of course she'll expect something in return, unfortunately for us."

Brak only nodded and retired further into his state of gloom and impatience. Before much longer, either he or Hjordis would be forced into conceding something to the other. Knowing that the Rhbus would not intervene made his resistance even shakier; yet it seemed that he alone carried their hopes—a very small and weak tool indeed. They could only point out the way to him and let him stumble along as best he could. He hoped Hjordis wouldn't realize the truth.

The fighting proceeded worse than he had expected. From the reports of the wounded and dying, he learned that the Ljosalfar of Miklborg had advanced on the Dokkalfar and would soon push them back to Hjalmknip. The situation became even more grim an hour later, when word arrived that Myrkjartan's draugar had pitched themselves into the battle against the Dokkalfar. Hjordis at this point had abandoned her men and fled, probably to avoid capture.

"Then the battle is lost! It's all up with us!" someone exclaimed, and in a moment those who were able began preparing for the retreat. Those who were not able were loaded into carts and wagons. Anyone with at least one good leg was expected to look out for his own welfare on the long trek back to Hjordisborg.

"And what are we expected to do?" Pehr demanded, eyeing Svagi, who appeared to attach himself more firmly to the spot where he sat, as if all the wars of the Ragnarok could not disturb him in the dispatching of his duty. "I don't fancy the idea of being captured by the draugar. What could have possessed Hjordis to desert her men at such a critical hour?"

Brak smiled wryly and touched the dragon's heart. "She's going to Hjordisborg to make certain Ingvold is all right. She's beginning to understand that Ingvold is the linchpin of her ambitions."

"Well, what about us? Aren't we important?"

"Most certainly. Let's start putting our things together and getting ready for a journey, shall we?"

Pehr looked even more glum. "To Hjordisborg, no doubt, to pull it down with our bare hands. Shall we take Svagi with us, or do you have a better idea for getting rid of him?" He glanced at Svagi with distaste and was rewarded with a vigilant snarl.

"There are more troublesome things than Svagi to worry about," Brak replied. "Horses, for example, and some food. Not to mention weapons, but I think we can find—" He turned around and looked up, remembering a heap of weapons belonging to the wounded and dead, and found himself facing a dark figure in a long cloak carrying a drawn sword. The meager light was behind the fellow and his hood was pulled close around his face, so that it was hidden in shadow. His cloak was the fine black sort lined with red that was worn by Hjordis' chieftains and other important Dokkalfar. Brak faced their new threat with a scowl.

"You there, get to your feet," the stranger addressed Svagi in a deep rumble, poking the sword at him. "I'm relieving you of your responsibility with these prisoners. You are ordered to report to the chieftains of the front lines. You prisoners get your kits together and come with me at once, if you have any regard for your lives."

"Are you from Hjordis?" Brak asked, hiding his dismay.

"No questions. Hasten!"

Svagi hoisted his axe to his shoulder and stumped away, looking for the chieftains of the front lines. Brak and Pehr had very few possessions to gather, so they were finished quickly.

"Over there, by the horses." The Dokkalfar motioned with his sword and followed behind them, glossy boots creaking with self-importance as he strode past groups of wounded warriors, who found the strength to glower after him, knowing it was the fault of him and others like him that they were in such miserable straits.

A half-crippled Dokkalfar waited with three horses. With a shock Brak recognized old Faxi, looking as ill-tempered and unprepossessing as ever. He greeted Brak with a delighted nicker and tried to bite the Dokkalfar groom.

"These are the best you can do?" their captor growled. "I demand the best if we are to escape from Myrkjartan. My prisoners are important to the future of our kingdom."

The old groom sidled away warily, like a huge, hairy crab clad in an assortment of rags and castoffs. "It's the best that's left," he muttered. "The decent ones was took." When he was safely out of range, he added, "Drat and blast all of you, and anything like you!" Then he scuttled away into the blackness of the tunnel.

Their captor chuckled darkly. "Fetch that lamp over there, one of you, so we can see one another and become better acquainted."

Pehr fetched a small soapstone lamp and held it for a moment. "We're not really prisoners, you must know.

Brak has the power to escape from you any time he likes, so you needn't think—you needn't try to—to frighten us with a lot of—of fancy Dokkalfar finery and swords that never saw a battlefield. We're not bluffing, you know."

The Dokkalfar took the lamp at arm's length, then drew it close to their faces, so that they had to squint in its brightness. "What a lot of idle threatening and chatter," he growled, bringing his own face into illumination suddenly. They saw a fierce mat of black and silver beard, a rugged beak of a nose somewhat disfigured by a purple, healing scar, and a tremendous set of grinning teeth. For an instant Brak was unnerved by the grin, which had a maniacal quality in such a place. The hair bristled in his scalp as he was suddenly struck by the fellow's similarity to Kolssynir, except for the purple scar.

"Why are you staring at me so strangely?" the Dokkalfar asked.

Brak looked away. "For a moment you resembled someone I used to know, but I was mistaken."

"Is he dead? You thought I was a draug, perhaps?"

Pehr clutched Brak's arm tightly, whispering, "Don't you recognize him, Brak? It's Kolssynir!"

Brak looked at the grin again. "But is it Kolssynir alive or Kolssynir dead? I want nothing to do with his draug, even if he was a good friend."

"Draug, indeed!" Kolssynir said in his own voice. "Shake this hand and see if you think it's dead flesh or living!"

Brak's hand was crushed in Kolssynir's grasp, and Brak crushed it back, feeling healthy muscles and bones. "Kolssynir!" he gasped. "Kolssynir alive and breathing, in a Dokkalfar cloak!"

"Skalgr stole it for me. It was going to get us close enough to Hjordis tonight either to kill or capture her, but as luck would have it, she's already flown."

"Skalgr helped you? You're the one?" Pehr asked incredulously.

"After the Dokkalfar attacked us, he escaped from them and came back to find you and me. He spent most of the night dragging me to Miklborg to be healed by their physicians and, before the Dokkalfar could catch him, he went back looking for you, Brak. When you were captured, he returned to me for help. We had an excellent plan. I'll tell you more about it after we get out of Hjalmknip."

They mounted their horses and rode through the tunnel with only the dim light of the little lamp to guide them around heaps of bodies and small knots of invalids pegging their way gamely toward the outside. Carts and sledges rumbled past, filled with more wounded and with a dozen clinging to the sides for dear life. Everyone was too intent on escaping from the advancing draugar or busily robbing corpses to pay much attention to the horsemen. Once outside in the starlight, they saw the survivors straggling away to the northeast and heard the fury of the battle not far from the outlying heaps of mine tailings.

"We can't wait for Skalgr," Kolssynir said after a quick, surmising look around. "I've great faith in his ability to look out for himself."

They rode toward Hjordisborg at a fast trot, passing the deserters and stragglers, who were too anxious or dispirited to do more than gape and scurry out of the way. By dawn, they were safely into the mountains with the battleground of Hjalmknip far behind. They stopped to rest and feasted on the hard sausage Kolssynir produced from his satchel to accompany the flask of ale he passed around.

"How did you ever survive it, Kolssynir?" Pehr asked, stretching out comfortably. "When I saw you catch that blast, I thought you were finished. Almost anyone else would have had the good sense to die."

"It was near, very near," Kolssynir admitted proudly. "But with all modesty, I confess I am a more determined, braver fellow than most. A coward knows his life is worthless and he is powerless to defend it, but a brave man fights with every atom of his being, knowing he is more worthy to survive than his opponent. With the assistance of such a force of will as mine, the healing physicians at Miklborg were able to put me together in almost no time. So here I am before you, restored by their magic and ready to fight again. Life is more dear and precious than it ever was before, because I very nearly lost it." He tapped the purple scar on his nose and swelled his lungs with a great breath of beautiful, life-sustaining air.

Brak and Pehr exchanged a grin. If any of the creatures

walking the earth deserved to live, it was certainly Kolssynir. Kolssynir himself was convinced of that opinion early on, but his conceit did nothing to destroy his charm.

"Now about Skalgr," Brak began seriously.

"I expect he'll catch up with us somehow," Kolssynir replied. "We needn't worry about losing him, or hadn't you noticed?"

"I'd like to notice it a lot less," Pehr answered. "Permanently."

Kolssynir rubbed his chin. "I owe my life to the old rogue. I suppose he sold you over again, eh?"

"Just as fast as he could," Brak said. "His loyalty depends upon how full his stomach is, I think. When we fall into a bad situation and the outlook is a little bleak, he betrays us to Hjordis or Myrkjartan. Sometimes I think he's playing us against the others, and whoever comes out victorious will be Skalgr's champion."

"I hate to agree, but I fear you're right," Kolssynir said. "He carried me and dragged me all the way to Miklborg. It was heroic. He'll never do anything more worthwhile."

"But he'd better not show his face around me," Pehr said. "He's tricked us once too often."

They rested several hours that morning, listening to the scattered battles. It sounded to Brak as if the victors were hunting down the remnants of their vanquished foes and dispatching them. Hjordis had paid a high price in her gamble for power, and she must be furious. Only her fear of something worse happening stood between her vengeance and Ingvold.

Kolssynir took a watchful position on the hillside above them with his staff across his knees. Pehr fell asleep immediately, but when Brak closed his eyes, all he saw was unpleasant recollections: Skarnhrafn in his fluttering grave clothes following Ingvold like an apparition of death; the twisted face of Hjordis; and the blood-spattered victims hauled from the battlefield. At last he fell into an uneasy doze, awakening at the smallest sounds and imagining that the Dokkalfar had found them.

Finally he drifted into a sounder sleep, and it seemed he had scarcely relaxed when a scuffling sound awakened him. He leaped to his feet and plunged toward Kolssynir, who was struggling with someone near the horses. Kolssynir had pounced on the intruder from the rear, locking one powerful forearm around the throat and holding his knife in his other hand.

"Speak and identify yourself, or we'll see what color your blood is!" Kolssynir growled, with an anticipatory flourish of the knife. "Or perhaps we'll take off that hood and see what the sun does to you!"

"Spare me! I'm not a Dokkalfar! I'm only a miserable beggar! I was going to steal only enough to keep me alive for one more wretched day of miserable— Halloa! Brak, is that you? I don't believe my eyes! Who's this choking me? Kolssynir! It must be!"

Kolssynir released his hold hastily. "Skalgr! We were just talking about you, and how our luck turns as sour as old beer whenever you're present. Thus it is that we give you rather a cold welcome."

Skalgr clasped their hands in a near-ecstatic greeting, scarcely able to speak coherently in his delight at their escape from Hjalmknip and the wonderful coincidence of their meeting so promptly. He dragged a dirty sack from a bush and triumphantly pulled a stone bottle from it. "And here's a jolly breakfast for us, and there are more victuals of a solid nature, such as some first-rate horsemeat, done to a turn, and fresh bread and some nice cheese and more, much more. I knew we'd all be fairly starved, and it's three days to Hjordisborg."

"Have you any idea of honor?" Brak demanded. "You turned me over to those Dokkalfar without a moment's hesitation. If you weren't such a shriveled-up useless old nithling, I'd kill you. Perhaps I should, anyhow, but the first blood I intend to shed will be that of a more worthy enemy than you, Skalgr."

"Don't be so particular," Pehr said. "You're still only a thrall, Brak, and not bound to our codes of honor. Go ahead and kill the miserable old thief and traitor."

Skalgr looked at Brak in alarm. "You'll give me one more chance, won't you? These captures I've caused have done you more good than harm in the long run, haven't they? Why, if you hadn't arrived at Myrkjartan's cave to cause that quarrel between him and Hjordis, Miklborg would have been destroyed!" His eyes snapped and he stiffened his back with pride.

Pehr chuckled. "Then Miklborg owes its success to one scroungy old nithling who sold his friend to the Dokkalfar because he was cold and hungry? No, the credit belongs to Brak, who frightened Hjordis into deserting her men to race after Ingvold. That's what saved Miklborg."

"It doesn't look good for you, Skalgr," Kolssynir said gravely. "In spite of everything I owe you and the great service you've done by saving my life, I have to agree with Brak and Pehr. You're a sneaky old rat who ought to be hung."

"Yes, but let's eat before we discuss it further," Skalgr said. "Maybe our humors will be kinder after they're fed. I haven't exactly had an easy time of it myself, you know."

It was a surly, silent meal. When the meat was gone, the flask was passed around, and Skalgr seemed to relish each moment of delay. Finally Kolssynir thumped the stopper in and flung the bottle at Skalgr. "Enough time wasted, you old thief. We've got to be on our way—without you."

"Let me say one final word," Skalgr said, scrambling to his feet.

"We'll listen only if it's goodbye," Pehr replied.

Skalgr glowered at him and went on earnestly. "I know you have a perfect right to feel a little dismayed with some of the things I've done, but I want you all to know I've never once wavered in my loyalty to our cause of finding Dyrstyggr. Would I dare to keep coming back to beg your forgiveness if I weren't loyal? You forget how I helped you escape from Hagsbarrow, and you know best, Kolssynir, what I have done at Hjalmknip. At Langborg I never deserted you; I was there watching to see if this wizard was any good, and I followed your pack train to Miklborg, making certain nothing went amiss. Rough going, it was, too; some fool left traps and snares practically every foot of the way. You see how determined I was to keep you in my sight, how fixed I am upon the objective of seeing Dyrstyggr reunited with his precious weapons? These Dokkalfar aren't discouraged by their defeat; they'll be back at Miklborg again with twice the fury, and how will you manage to engineer a second defeat for Hjordis? How will you find Dyrstyggr without me? I alone can guide you to him in his exile. Please don't be hasty, my dear friends. Forgive an old troublemaker once again, won't you?" He looked at each of them anxiously.

Pehr began a vigorous protest, but Brak interrupted. "Skalgr, let us talk about it by ourselves for a moment. Wait for us by the horses. I promise you we'll try to be fair."

"I know you shall," Skalgr replied. "You're a generous, good-hearted creature, Brak, and I know you have infinitely good sense." He retreated to the horses, and the argument erupted with Pehr protesting the fiercest.

He finished angrily by saying, "If Skalgr goes, then I'll stay behind and take my own chances with the Dokkalfar, because I'm certain he'll give us up to them at the first opportunity."

"Then, to say it briefly, you vote no," Kolssynir said. "I, too, vote no. Brak, is it unanimous?"

Brak had scarcely listened to Pehr's long tirade against Skalgr. His thoughts carried him back to their first meeting with Skalgr, and how at the time Skalgr had seemed like no ordinary, desperate old beggar or thief. Most of all, he remembered how Skalgr had broken the hag spell of Hjordis' over Ingvold. Skalgr had gone to a lot of trouble for them and put himself through a great deal of misery that would have discouraged a stouter, younger man, even if his intentions had been solely greedy and treacherous ones. The only possible motivation strong enough to keep Skalgr going had to be sheer loyalty to his master Dyrstyggr.

Brak slowly shook his head. "We'll take Skalgr with us to Hjordisborg. I believe he is what he says—that last remaining key to finding Dyrstyggr."

Chapter 18

❖❖❖❖❖❖❖❖❖❖❖❖❖❖❖❖❖❖❖❖❖❖❖❖❖❖❖❖❖

Skalgr expressed his gratitude to Brak in an astonishing fashion. He merely bowed once to him with a manner of deep respect and bestowed his delighted and guileless grin on them all. Then he scuttled away toward the bottom of the hill, where he had hidden a horse appropriated from the battlefield; numbers of the poor creatures, many of which were badly wounded, were wandering in skittish groups through the vapors of melting Dokkalfar. As they rode toward Hjordisborg, Skalgr told them what he had seen, and how the draugar and scavengers had returned to the battlefield to carry away the dead to Myrkjartan.

"So the more Hjordis loses, the more Myrkjartan gains," Brak said wryly. "It looks as if we'll have to fight the same enemies twice."

"Don't worry about Myrkjartan," Skalgr said reassuringly. "He's probably too intent on punishing Hjordis to remember us. We're going to take him by surprise and get that cloak from him before he knows what has happened to him. We'll teach him that we're a force to be reckoned with, just as we're cracking the whip over Hjordis and putting her through her paces. We're not anyone's fools, are we?"

"No one's except yours, if you think I'm going to try snatching Myrkjartan's cloak," Pehr said vehemently. "Let Dyrstyggr demand his own clothes back from Myrkjartan; that's not our job. I don't know why you're so cheerful, Skalgr. We may be riding right into the jaws of our own death by riding up to Hjordisborg. If only we'd sent Ingvold back when we had the chance—" He glanced sideways at

Brak. "—before our enemies realized what a spell she's put on Brak."

"It's nothing to joke about," Brak retorted in a nettled tone. "Besides, she's entitled to seek revenge for her family's death, and we'll help her get it, if the Rhbus are willing."

"They will be, they will be!" Skalgr chortled.

At sundown they stopped to rest where they had a good view of the country behind them. Brak sat watching as the shadows descended across the fells and folds of the rocky landscape, listening for any more sounds of battle. Skalgr joined him, smelling of the boiled onions he had had for supper. Brak rather resented sharing his solitude with the old wizard, but he made a space for him on the rock where he was sitting, and Skalgr sat down beside him, still wrought up with gratitude. He had seized every opportunity to thank Brak for his generosity, assuring him he would never regret it. After performing the expected effusions, Skalgr gazed around and remarked, "How peaceful it looks right now, doesn't it? Nothing to make you suspect thousands of draugar are hiding in every shadow, and Dokkalfar in every crevice, waiting for darkness so they can travel. Very desperate creatures by now, I'd say, and they're behind and before us and on all sides. It might be safer to turn aside to Miklborg and wait until these wretched fellows either die or regain the safety of Hjordisborg."

"I can't wait. I must keep after Hjordis so she won't forget she promised me that sword, and so she won't attempt to hurt Ingvold. If I'm there before her to taunt and threaten, I can see to it that she doesn't seize some advantage in this maddening game of ours." Brak sighed and leaned on his fist. "It's difficult to know how far I can bend to deceive her without losing my balance."

"Bending is a very good exercise," Skalgr observed slyly. "You've seen the way I do it continually and where it's got us. Wait and see if my luck doesn't change. Old Skalgr will do something right for you yet. I can insinuate myself into almost anywhere. I want to do something to prove my great loyalty and friendship to you, Brak, so don't be afraid to ask anything of me. I can get into the dungeons and look around for Ingvold, or I'll listen at doors or start the servants gossiping, and I'll find her for certain. Just allow me to prove myself, Brak, and you'll never have cause to distrust me again."

"Yes, well—we'll see what opportunities present themselves," Brak said doubtfully. While they talked, the darkness deepened, and they discerned distant fires on hilltops, winking like multitudes of red sparks against the black velvet sky. Brak rose and turned to go back to the fire, but he paused suddenly to listen, motioning Skalgr to be silent. He heard the sound of horses' hooves approaching at a fast gallop, ringing over the flinty fellside and plunging into a ravine not far below their campsite.

"Dokkalfar, or I'll eat my boots," Skalgr whispered. "They're fleeing for their lives, and I'll warrant Myrkjartan is at their heels in a most vengeful frame of mind. He'll be pressing toward Hjordisborg, sweeping all in his path before him, or grinding them to powder. I doubt that we could reach Miklborg now, even if you decided to change your mind."

While they saddled their horses, two more groups of survivors came flogging by without seeing them and plunged into the ravine at the foot of the fell. The ones with horses were the fortunate ones; there were many more toiling along on foot in scattered clots, some of whom could barely creep from shadow to shadow. They hugged the shadows and watched the horsemen pass, often shaking their fists and reviling them for their cowardice.

Kolssynir repeatedly assured Pehr and Brak that no one would give them a second glance if they were riding toward Hjordisborg, but Brak kept his hood pulled low and remained watchful. The Dokkalfar around them were too intent upon escaping to say much, but most of their terse remarks concerned the draugar coming up on their rear. Myrkjartan had advanced to the Dokkalfar position in Hjalmknip and would soon overrun the small force who remained there to defend it staunchly rather than retreat in disgrace, even if it meant to die.

Toward dawn, most of the Dokkalfar searched out dark crevices in the lava flows to lie in and wait for nightfall. A few wrapped their faces, buried themselves in thick cloaks and hoods, and hurried on, with their weapons ready in their hands.

By nightfall the draugar had advanced farther, assisted

by the cloudy, dank weather and Myrkjartan's added clouds of darkness. Soon after the last of the lowering sunset had faded from the sky, the travelers heard sounds of fighting. The fleeing Dokkalfar scurried away more desperately, trying to save themselves, leaving the wounded and exhausted scattered along the way, filling the night with their hopeless cries. From the comments of other riders, Brak learned that the draugar had captured Hjalmknip and were pressing inexorably toward Hjordisborg with untiring draugar compulsion, marching until their ragged carcasses fell apart and were trampled into dust by the draugar behind them. All during the night they shuffled forward in the direction Myrkjartan commanded, chivied on all sides by the Myrkriddir, like grisly sheep dogs herding macabre sheep.

During the following day the companions had to rest. Although they had started out near midday, after stopping for the morning in a safe place, they had to call a halt within only a few hours. Faxi began to limp, nodding his head painfully at each step. Dismayed, Brak searched his hoof for signs of a bruise or swelling, but he could see no damage. Faxi leaned on him patiently, glad for the help in supporting his considerable weight. When Brak released his foot, Faxi held it up delicately, as if it were too tender to rest upon the ground.

"We'll have to leave him," Kolssynir declared, glaring at the old horse. "Why he'd pick this particular moment to go lame is more than I can comprehend and remain sane. He's had plenty of opportunities when we would have been grateful for some fresh horsemeat, but he waits until the most critical moment to betray us."

"I wish you had taken Vigfus' mare when he offered it," Pehr said gloomily. "I always knew that old beast would break down and we'd end up eating him."

"We can all do with a little rest," Brak said. "We may as well take it while we can." He didn't spend much time resting, however. He stood Faxi in a cold running stream for several hours, then bound up the hoof in a poultice concocted by Skalgr. Faxi seemed to enjoy all the attention, but the limp remained unchanged for as long as the pale sunshine was warm and cheerful. Kolssynir spent the afternoon honing his knife to deadly sharpness and discussing the best ways to cook horsemeat with Skalgr, despite Pehr's protests that a good Scipling would die before eating his horse.

Toward evening, they all began to hear sounds of the approaching draugar. Short battles erupted on all sides of them, beginning furiously and coming to a quick conclusion. The other horses were saddled, and Kolssynir gave his knife a few more loving strops on his whetstone.

"There's no sense in leaving him to suffer," he announced. "Or to make a nice supper for a bunch of Dokkalfar. We'll push him down a crevice where he won't be found and recognized as a Scipling horse and therefore yours. His speckled hide is quite famous, now that the word of the dragon's heart has gotten out."

Brak stroked the old horse's nose despondently. He and Faxi and Pehr were all very nearly the same age, having grown up almost together. "You'd better do it quickly, then," he muttered. "The Dokkalfar are beginning to come out of hiding. We'll be going slow tonight with two on one horse." He and Skalgr would pair up on the stout Dokkalfar horse and trade off when that horse tired under its double burden.

"The Rhbus will send us another horse, perhaps," Pehr said in a discouraged tone. "If you care to trouble them for something so insignificant as a horse."

Brak closed his eyes a moment, feeling a sudden rush of fear and hope. He remembered when Faxi had wedged himself in the tunnel with Skarnhrafn close behind. Faxi had been the cause of Brak's first occasion to seek the advice of the Rhbus, and the words of that advice had not deserted him. He began to saddle and bridle Faxi, ignoring Pehr's exasperated remarks about wasting time. When he was finished, he led Faxi away a few limping steps and took hold of one speckled ear to whisper into it. Faxi stopped lashing his tail in pain and irritation to listen. By the time Brak had repeated the words twice, the sore hoof was resting firmly on the ground, with an occasional stamp of impatience. Brak walked him up and down a few times and saw no trace of a limp. On the contrary, the old horse pranced and shook his head like a fiery young colt that couldn't endure merely standing

around much longer and being gaped at by a pair of astonished wizards.

"Speckled creatures," Skalgr said with a sly chuckle, "are
thought to be somewhat inclined toward the magical. The
Rhbus might take a special interest in them, perhaps?"

His only answer from Brak was a noncommittal shrug as
he swung into his saddle. Kolssynir put away his knife with
another shrug and hurried his tired horse after Faxi. Pehr
followed watchfully, predicting dourly that the old horse
would be lame again within the hour and they would
have to abandon him yet.

The rugged trail inclined more steeply and they passed
more worn-out refugees. Most were too tired to be covetous
of their horses, but a few attempted to waylay them in
desperation. Kolssynir returned their arrows with spells and
bolts, and twice Pehr used his sword to discourage would-
be horse thieves.

Their objective came into view at moonrise. Hjordisborg
was built high against the side of a steep, rocky fell, surrounded on three sides by vast frozen bands of glaciers
that gleamed like rivers of ice in the moonlight. The few
lights and fires from the fortress beckoned with scant welcome through the winding sheets of fog that enmeshed the
mountain.

After a slithering traverse of one glacier, they gained
the rocky pedestal of the mountain and began the upward
climb, keeping their eyes warily on the scattered groups of
disgruntled warriors returning to Hjordisborg. From what
they overheard, only the fear of Myrkjartan's pressing forward at the warriors' heels kept them from rising up against
Hjordis and attacking her for her treacherous desertion.

As they approached the main gate into the fortress, Kolssynir instructed them to assume their former roles as captives, drew his hood lower on his face, and struck a haughty
pose with his sword across the pommel of his saddle. Skalgr
assumed his most natural position as a skulking scrounger,
keeping a respectful distance and looking as craven and
ragged as possible.

They rode up to the gate and halted. One of the guards
put his head out at the top and demanded to know who
they were and what they wanted. Kolssynir moved forward
impatiently to shout up at the guard. "Where are your

eyes, you blundering fool? Don't you see by this black and red cloak who I am? Open this gate immediately and send word to Hjordis that I have brought the captives from Hjalmknip. I wish to present them to her at once, with no further annoying delays."

In short order the gate was opened and they were greeted by none other than the surly Tyrkell, who commanded that the horses be taken away and stabled. Then he glared at Kolssynir.

"Who might you be?" he growled, poking a torch a little closer to Kolssynir's face. "Another of her favorites, I suppose, or she wouldn't be so anxious to see you and these Sciplings while more faithful retainers are kept out."

Kolssynir knocked the torch from Tyrkell's hand with a deft sweep of his staff. "I'm not here to stand in the cold talking to vermin like you. Either get out of the way or take me to Hjordis before I become impatient." He motioned with his drawn sword to indicate in what direction his impatience might take him.

Tyrkell's eyes gleamed wolfishly and he showed his teeth in an obsequious snarl. "I beg your pardon, most certainly. Follow me and I'll take you to her."

He led them across a narrow, musty-smelling enclosure to a turf hall built with the mountain shouldering it on one side and the barns and stables adjoining on the other. Prows of ships and other war trophies adorned the doorposts and roof timbers, and the large front door was shut. The hall was surrounded by a crowd of angry Dokkalfar shoving to get in against a smaller number of angry Dokkalfar who were keeping them out. The uproar was menacing in tone, particularly on the part of the newly arrived remnants of the armies deserted at Miklborg.

Kolssynir took a firm grip on his staff in one hand and on his sword in the other, prodding his prisoners forward despite their very realistic hesitation. Pehr looked downright mutinous, but Brak gave him a covert shove after Tyrkell, who cleared a path through the objectors with much kicking and swearing and returning of dire threats. The door opened a bare crack to admit the prisoners and Kolssynir, who hesitated long enough to allow Skalgr to slip in behind him, like a skinny old cat in search of a handout.

The inside of the hall was dim and dusty, as if unaccustomed to much use. A small fire burned in the far end hearth to light its vast gloom and populate the place with eerie, jumping shadows that might have been the ghosts of past generations of Dokkalfar warriors who had eaten and drunk in the great hall. Now it seemed ominously empty, except for a small knot of Dokkalfar hovering protectively around Hjordis and frequently shoving back a crowd of angry chieftains. Many sported wounds and bandages, and all wore ugly scowls, as if they restrained their tempers only with difficulty. When any shouting broke out, the guards stepped forward to restore order with menacing flourishes of their axes and swords.

Hjordis dismissed her angry petitioners, who stumped from the hall with mutinous grumbling. When they were gone, Hjordis beckoned to Kolssynir. "You may approach with your prisoners. Allow me to express my gratitude to you for bringing them here." She rose to her feet, keeping her hands covered with her cloak and her face shrouded in the shadow of her hood. "Tyrkell, you and these others are dismissed. Stand guard outside and try to convince those fools that what I'm doing is for their best interest."

Tyrkell obeyed with a painfully jealous growl and a murderous glare at Kolssynir. Brak stared at Hjordis, waiting until the last of the guards had shuffled outside and the door was shut. Hjordis glared at him, clenching the back of her chair with one scaly hand until she remembered to hide it.

"I saved Ingvold from any lasting harm," she said in a hoarse voice, "at a cost very great to myself and my Dokkalfar. Unless you use the powers of the dragon's heart quite soon against Myrkjartan, the price is likely to become much higher. I urge you not to goad me too far, Scipling, or both of us will lose everything. Don't be too haughty, my fine fellow; I have a large amount of pride myself."

"Where is she? I want to see her and make sure she's safe." Brak took a step forward, trying to see Hjordis' eyes.

Hjordis lumbered a little farther from the firelight. "You shall see her, but not just yet. I was certain you'd be coming here soon, so I've planned a small entertainment. You've had a long journey, and you must take the time to refresh yourselves with the hospitality of Hjordisborg. We are not enemies, after all; I've made you a handsome offer in exchange for your advice and your protection from Myrkjartan. Who is this fellow in the stolen cloak, by the way, with such a brazen attitude? Whoever you are, put away your weapons and hold your tongue unless you have something useful to say to us."

Kolyssnir sheathed his sword and made a low bow, uncovering his features at the same time. "I am Kolssynir, the wizard your Dokkalfar left for dead when Ingvold and Pehr and this scavenger Skalgr were captured. Without troubling you with an explanation of the particulars of my miraculous survival, let me say that I am here to protect Brak and his companions from any unseemly coercion. I shall be his adviser and something of an arbiter in this dispute between the two of you. My first bit of advice is to let this matter rest until we've had something to eat and drink and some rest ourselves. Then we shall expect to see Ingvold, safe and unharmed."

Hjordis inclined her head in agreement, and Skalgr fervently added, "Hear, hear! Let's eat!" Hjordis summoned servants from the adjoining rooms to begin the preparations. The servants set up tables and benches, bestirred the fire to cheerier heights, and killed a goose in the kitchen, darting nervous glances all the while at Hjordis, shrouded from head to toe in her black cloak.

Brak and Pehr joined Skalgr beside the fire, where he was soaking in the heat with a kind of ecstasy. "Isn't this splendid? Who would have thought I'd be an honored guest in Hjordisborg?" he chortled. "Old, wretched Skalgr, the outcast, the despised. It must be a sign of the times, don't you agree?"

Pehr never agreed with anything Skalgr said. Brak smothered his impatience and stood glaring at Hjordis, realizing he could not ignore the rules of hospitality, no matter how much he might detest the hostess.

"I hadn't really expected this hospitality from you," Kolssynir said to Hjordis. "It makes me curious—or suspicious. Something must be softening your former position."

Hjordis answered with an afflicted sigh and a shake of her head. "This curse is a grievous thing to bear. I realize my life will be short, so if I am to have time to enact the changes I want to see, I will be forced to compromise. With Myrkjartan's draugar almost upon us, I know that the time has come to concede in a few ways, perhaps. If I could but guess the final outcome of this course—but never mind. We won't discuss unpleasant topics before eating."

Hjordis delayed for hours over the eating and drinking, poetry-reciting, and harp-playing; all of which was excellent in quality but sadly lacking in spirit. The black figure of Hjordis in the shadows dampened everyone's jollity like a specter of death. Brak could scarcely endure the waiting, knowing that Hjordis was enjoying the delay, like a cat lazily dallying with a tortured mouse. Finally dawn arrived and she rose to depart, saying that they would see Ingvold at dusk. Again Brak stifled his impatience, too proud to give her the satisfaction of knowing how much he hated the delay.

"I shall wait," he said stolidly. "We thralls have learned to wait, if we have learned anything at all."

Hjordis favored him with a long, silent stare before irritably calling for a woman to help her walk to her rooms. "I can't understand why a mere thrall would have to possess Dyrstyggr's heart. It's almost more than I can tolerate when I contemplate the injustice of it."

"If it's injustice you want to contemplate," Brak retorted, "then contemplate what happened at Gljodmalborg."

"Yes, indeed, I frequently do. A wretched little starved cat of a girl was spared, when she could have easily been killed, and that is the cause of your being here now with that cursed heart to threaten me. If only Ingvold had died then, how simple it would have been!" Hjordis stalked away with the help of her servant, giving the poor woman's arm a twist and a dig with each word.

"I believe she'd have you boiled in an instant if it weren't for that heart," Kolssynir observed. "What an extraordinary talent you have for infuriating her."

"She must know when she's come up against someone more stubborn than she is," Pehr said with a sigh. "And of course being such a cheeky thrall reflects badly on me also."

"Nonsense! Go ahead infuriating her, Brak," Skalgr said, in a pleasant glow from drinking too much. "If she had any sense at all, she'd give Ingvold back to you and send you packing. She ought to realize—but she doesn't—that the closer she keeps to you, the closer she is to her destruction. You're the great rock that her fate will be wrecked upon."

"And you're a great fool, Skalgr," Brak growled. "Why don't you be quiet and go to sleep?"

Brak spent the day prowling up and down the length of the great hall, seeing only dim cracks of light seeping between door planks. A muffled guard leaned against the door outside, probably sound asleep but certain to awaken if the door were opened. Brak flung himself down to sleep ten times, between intervals of aimless stalking around feeling miserable and angry, before he finally fell alseep to dream horrible dreams of falling into a huge pit, descending helplessly toward an inevitable doom at the unseen bottom.

He awakened instantly when the servants began stirring in the late afternoon; they were creeping around like furtive mice, shaking up the fires and eyeing the four guests in the hall with uneasy surmise. The animals in the barns adjoining rattled their halters and announced in various languages that they expected to be fed at once. More guards gathered at the doors to forestall the unhappy chieftains besieging the hall with grievances. Tyrkell slunk into the hall and stationed himself by the fire, where the steam rose from his snow-covered clothes with a smell like that of a wet dog. He leered and snarled at the visitors with undisguised hatred until Hjordis made her appearance, whereupon he almost groveled in humility, begging to know if he could be of service.

"We're going into the tombs," Hjordis said. "Fetch some torches and men to carry them, and don't be slow about it." Her tone was snappish, and she leaned heavily on her servant and a stout walking stick. Brak stared at her intently, hoping she would die as soon as possible and thus be out of his way. She glowered at him, as if knowing his thoughts, and limped across the hall to the rear wall, which was the native stone of the mountainside. With her stick she battered down several hangings, exposing a large door fitted into the stone. In a grim tone she said, "We Dokkalfar must have our bolt-holes, like all underground creatures who are not safe on the surface of the earth."

"Then you should stay below," Brak replied. "No one invited you to come up and attack our hill forts and kill our people."

Hjordis was spared the necessity of answering. Tyrkell and six men with torches stamped into the hall and slammed the door in the face of the petitioners, whose dissatisfaction was greatly augmented by a new development. Tyrkell's sinister features looked even more grim than usual.

"What's the disturbance?" Hjordis demanded, clenching her stick with her claw of a hand and hobbling forward. "Is it the draugar? Have they advanced?"

Tyrkell nodded. "To the glacier. Tomorrow night they'll be at our walls. Myrkjartan himself sends word that he wants to discuss the terms of surrender."

Hjordis emitted an ugly laugh and looked at Brak. "Tell him we're not interested in his surrender. Tell him he's going to be utterly crushed and his draugar beaten to dust if he presses his attack one step farther. Tell him that the Scipling and I have come to terms about the dragon's heart. Give that torch to Brak and go deliver my message."

Tyrkell surrendered the torch with bad grace and strode away. Hjordis commanded that the door be opened and drew her black cloak around her more securely. A gust of deadly cold air flattened the torches' flames and shook the remaining hangings on the walls until the air was full of dust and bits of rotten weaving.

"It will be a privilege for you outsiders to see where the kings and queens of the Dokkalfar have been buried for countless years." Hjordis directed two of her men to precede her into the windy darkness. "This cavern was once a great mine, which did its part to enrich the Dokkalfar kingdom before the springs of the blue flame were tapped and the mining brought to a halt. At one time, the flame was thought to be sacred, and the dead were buried there to be near it. But a more practical soul discovered that enemies thrown into the flame were quite well disposed of." She looked at Brak as she spoke.

Brak stepped forward as she led the way toward the tombs. "What has this to do with Ingvold?" he demanded. "You said she was alive and unharmed. If you've thrown her into the fire—" He stopped before his words choked in his throat to betray his fear and fury.

"No, she's alive, as I've told you," Hjordis said, "but she is very much connected with the blue flame. Follow me and you'll see for yourself. Walk in single file, if you please, close to the wall. Some of the steps have broken and are quite dangerous. A few unlucky souls have fallen into the pit, and it's a very long drop to the bottom. I realize you don't trust me not to arrange an accident, but I urge you to stay close to me for your own protection. There is another circumstance about the tombs which you will soon discover."

"I wonder that you trust *us* not to cause an accident, as you call it," Kolssynir suggested, lighting the knob of his staff.

Hjordis chuckled dryly. "Kill me and you'll never get Ingvold back. She exists suspended in a very delicate spell. You'll see for yourselves, once we reach the bottom. Remember what I have said."

Pehr hung back reluctantly, until Skalgr had to give him a shove into the tunnel beyond the door. "It stinks in here!" he said indignantly to Skalgr, who told him to be more respectful, since it was the dust of Dokkalfar royalty he was smelling.

The underground architecture of the Dokkalfar was far more grand than anything Brak had ever seen above ground. The heart of the mountain had been mined away in descending rings, leaving huge, arched galleries and pillars overlooking the vast pit. An eerie blue reflection shuddered like lightning on the rocky walls, vanishing to a reflected glow far below, as if the source of the light were deep inside a well. By a series of ramps and galleries, the group descended in smaller rings, although the upper tiers were so vast that the difference was hard to discern. Along the walls and in every niche were the tombs, some still neatly sealed with rock and mortar, others half open and crumbling. Kolssynir and Hjordis discussed famous Dokkalfar kings and queens as they walked, pausing at the tombs of the most notorious to look in at the remains, long since turned to dust, leaving nothing but rags of rotted cloth, leather, and metal, with jewels winking through the sad decay. Bones and skulls of lesser importance often lay scattered underfoot, crumbling and crunching in a most distressing manner when trod upon.

The sinister blue reflections intensified as they descended. Brak risked a plunge into oblivion for a look downward at the source of the flares. A brilliant blue fire leaped up at him, bathing him in a blast of icy air and subsiding to a sullen, steely dance far below in the darkness. Ice glittered on the rough faces of each level of rock, festooning the tiers with beards of ice and glittering pillars.

They were deep into the pit and breathing the cold, rare air of the blue flame, which now leaped high over their heads to lap at the icy rocks with an intense, burning cold. Bare flesh felt seared, so they kept themselves covered to the eyes. The damp earth underfoot became slippery with hoarfrost, and frequently falling spears of ice shattered over them in a frosty shower of flying crystals. The throaty, hissing roar of the fire filled their ears and made it difficult to speak in anything but a shout when the fire was leaping high; then it would inexplicably sink away to almost nothing, and the tremendous cavity echoed with their footsteps and voices.

Hjordis gazed around often, listening, as if expecting something to happen, and Brak became wary. Once or twice he caught glimpses of her face in the torchlight and silently observed that the curse had progressed rapidly in obliterating anything that had been human in her features.

Something stirred across the pit in the dark gloom of a great, arched gallery. Hjordis stopped at once, also hearing a rustling sound and a grinding of stones. A light flickered behind the curtains of ice, a warm, golden glow that made the ice hiss and expand with sounds of creaking and groaning, like some hoary old beast in pain.

"What's that?" Brak demanded sharply. "Who's there? Hjordis, if this is a trap you've planned, I warn you I'll take this dragon's heart and throw it into your precious cold flames rather than let you have it!" He yanked the little casket from its chain around his neck and took a stride forward as if he intended to suit action to word then and there.

"No!" Hjordis shouted, closely echoed by Skalgr, who rushed forward to grab Brak's cloak, taking care not to get too close to the edge of the pit. Hjordis flung out one hand to stop him and quickly hid it again.

"It's nothing that I have planned," she said in a savage tone. "But if you want to see your Ingvold again, you'll have to lend me the assistance of that heart. Come forward a little way and you'll see what I mean."

"I'm not sure we should trust her," Pehr said, accompanied by a cold, nervous chattering of his teeth. "This place feels like the very death to me."

"Come along," Kolssynir said firmly, his voice echoing. "We have no cause to be afraid, have we? Hjordis has more to lose than we do if some unfortunate betrayal takes place." He gave Skalgr a prod in the back with his staff and shouldered Pehr forward.

They descended a steep, rubbly ramp more narrow than the previous passageway. With no more pillars of stone or supporting abutments to obstruct the view, the bottom of the pit was now visible. It was a wasteland of ice and frozen rock jumbled together, with wisps of blue flame gleaming in every crack and crevice, rising and sinking in an eerie dance. Dazzling blue needles surged upward a hundred feet to explode into frost and come tumbling down with a brittle, tinkling note—delicate and deadly.

Brak put the heart into an inside pocket and shook the frost from his beard. "Where is she?" he demanded into a momentary lull.

Hjordis pointed across the fire to the far wall, sheathed in festoons of ice which had nearly covered the portal of a tomb, a small one half concealed behind a great crag of rock. The flame licked at the crag, whitening it with frost, and Brak knew he had no chance of getting through the flames alive to rescue her. Then his eyes traveled to the crag above as his thoughts turned to the idea of climbing down to her somehow. A sudden flash of light arrested his gaze. Startled and suspicious, he looked up toward the top of the crag. In a surge of lurid light he saw something perching there, an enormous ragged bundle of scraps and tatters clinging batlike, to a small ledge on the rock. Even in the strange light, the familiar outline of Skarnhrafn's helmet was unmistakable. Skarnhrafn spread his motley cloak like huge wings and greeted his old enemy with a sepulchral chuckle. He raised his visor and darted a fiery glance down at Brak and his company, sending them scurrying for shelter. Ice exploded and melted, freezing almost instantly into new, tortured shapes.

Skarnhrafn chuckled and muttered to himself in mindless glee. Then he gave a great hoarse bellow. "I am disgraced in Myrkjartan's eyes, but this will be my redemption! I shall take the girl to Myrkjartan, even so!"

Chapter 19

❖❖❖❖❖❖❖❖❖❖❖❖❖❖❖❖❖❖❖❖❖❖❖❖

"Skarnhrafn, you're a useless bag of old dust!" Hjordis shrieked at the draug, drawing the sword and shaking it at him. "I defy you to come down and fight me like a man, instead of like a fireship! You're a coward not to fight me for Ingvold. Come down here, and we will see who shall possess her."

Skarnhrafn chuckled slyly in response and shot another bolt of fire at the ice above, causing a small avalanche to come rattling and crashing down to the bottom of the pit. "I may be dead and dusty, but I'm not quite a fool, Hjordis," he wheezed. "You've got that Scipling with the dragon's heart with you, too, haven't you?"

Brak warily replied, "Yes, I'm here, Skarnhrafn, and I intend to take Ingvold out of this place as soon as I can. You won't be able to stop me when I decide to do it."

"So the Scipling and the witch-queen are allies now, eh?" The draug fell into a fury of croaking and gasping that might have been black mirth or a fit of temper. "Then I must see if I can change that by taking Ingvold away to Myrkjartan—yes, and that would restore me in his esteem once again. Oh, yes, it must be done; he commanded it.

Hagsbarrow, Hagsbarrow! A draug without a master is as good as old dust and bones—dust and bones!"

"I won't allow it!" Brak shouted back at Skarnhrafn furiously. "You've chased her and hounded her and nearly driven her insane, and I'm not going to let you take her back to Myrkjartan! You wretched old skeleton, you ought to be burned or buried where you won't be such a nuisance to the rest of us. I warn you, you'll be destroyed if you don't take this chance to escape now. The Rhbus are behind me, Skarnhrafn, and they won't allow one old draug to stand in their way."

"Rhbus, bah!" Skarnhrafn hissed. "They're using this girl to lead us all a merry chase. If the heart was in Myrkjartan's hands, the Rhbus would be helping him!" The notion sent him into a paroxysm of cackling and croaking.

"Have you seen enough yet?" Hjordis demanded, lumbering closer behind Brak. "He's been here since we put Ingvold in the tomb and won't let anyone near her. Nor will we let him out—not that he has really tried to escape yet. I suspect the flames hold him at bay as much as they do anyone else. Come, you've seen as much as you can see; let's go back to my hall and discuss some terms."

Brak opened his mouth to protest, but Kolssynir took him by the arm. "She is right, much as we hate to admit it. Let's go back to the hall before we freeze."

"Freeze? What about Ingvold?" Brak shook off the wizard's hand. "I haven't seen her; all I've seen is a hole in the rock and a worm-eaten draug hovering over it. I want to see Ingvold, and I won't leave until I do."

Hjordis sighed and began groping for a pouch tied to her waist. Her bandaged hands were more like huge swollen paws, and the folds of her gown seemed to conceal strange contours for a human form. Brak stared at her, almost certain he had seen a massive clawed foot beneath the hem of her cloak, and another bulging mass that he could not explain at all unless Hjordis had grown a tail. He was appalled, but mastered his revulsion and stepped nearer when she held out something in her hand to show him. It was a glass sphere somewhat larger than an egg, shot with swirls and bubbles that seemed to change shapes in the light offered by the blue fire.

"It's a seeing globe; you needn't be afraid of it," Kolssynir said as Brak hesitated to draw any closer. "Look into the sphere and you'll see her. It's quite all right."

Brak gazed dubiously into the sphere, seeing nothing but a thousand reflections of the flames knifing through it, surrounding the image of his own face, distorted by the curve of the glass. For a few moments he experienced the giddy dizziness and heart-pounding effects he associated with the consumption of the dragon's heart.

"She's inside the tomb, but she's only sleeping," Hjordis was saying. "It's just a spell, remember, and I'll take it off when I bring her out of the flames. I'm the only one who knows the secret of braving the fire, so you won't want to think about killing me when I've given you Dyrstyggr's sword. There, you see her now, don't you? She's quite comfortable, actually, and not feeling the cold at all."

He saw her in the tomb, lying on a stone shelf swept clean of the litter of past inhabitants. She lay in a curled position with one arm folded under her cheek as a pillow —a natural and familiar pose. Her face was pale and peaceful, framed by delicate wisps of her unskillfully pruned fair hair. For a heart-stopping moment he was sure he was seeing the tragic beauty of death, but then she shifted to a more comfortable position, drawing her eider closer under her chin and breathing a sigh he could hear as plainly as if he were standing beside her.

"Are you satisfied now?" Hjordis' voice grated in his ear. The image in the glass disappeared, and the globe vanished into Hjordis' pocket. "If you're reasonably satisfied she's still alive, then let's get out of this beastly cold before it's the death of us."

Brak stared at the hole in the wall, draped with ice and shimmering through the lapping of the blue flames. "Kolssynir, did you see her, or was I imagining it? Hjordis could have conjured such a simple spell to fool me, couldn't she?"

Kolssynir shook his head. His beard was so frosted by his breath that it looked entirely white. "She didn't conjure a spell; I'm certain of that much. These globes have a way of showing things to people exactly as they are. I'm sure I saw something quite different from what you saw, but it's no matter right now. Come along, let's get out of here before we freeze to the spot. Your ears are starting to look positively frostbitten." He tugged at Brak as he spoke, pushing him along in an upward direction ahead of Hjordis and motioning Pehr and Skalgr to hurry. Brak had never seen Kolssynir behave in such a flustered, almost frightened manner. The wizard hurried along at their heels, darting nervous glances over his shoulder and keeping himself between them and Hjordis.

Skarnhrafn swooped from his perch to follow them upward, alighting to start the echoes repeating his chuckles, coughs, and wheezes. The only consolation Brak could draw from the situation was the fact that Skarnhrafn could not get to Ingvold, either, because of the fire. With reluctance Brak allowed Kolssynir to hurry him toward the hall, but he looked back as often as he could to see the great crag that marked Ingvold's cell. He would rather have remained as close to her imprisonment as he could endure, crouching among the icy boulders and staring into the hypnotic blue flames.

When they regained the warmth and light of the hall, Hjordis left them alone to banish the deadly cold of the tombs with ale and food. Pehr and Skalgr began to be almost cheerful, but Brak could not forget the cold isolation of Ingvold far below. The comforts of Hjordisborg only served to deepen his feeling of desolation.

Kolssynir also seemed to be nursing some unpleasant and private thoughts of his own as he sat watchfully by the fire with his staff across his knees. He and Brak met each other's eyes often as they waited out the night, listening to the wolf-fylgur of the Dokkalfar howling around the walls of Hjordisborg and skirmishing with the draugar surrounding the fortress.

At last Brak broke the silence, long after the effects of the warmth and ale had rendered Pehr and Skalgr unconscious and blissful. Skalgr was curled up like a bony old hound beside the fire, with his cup in his hands, and Pehr leaned against the wall, where he had tried to keep himself awake by knocking his head against it periodically.

"What did you see in that glass of Hjordis' that frightened you so?" Brak asked in a low voice.

Kolssynir raised his eyes to glance around the hall, particularly toward the doors which were barred from inside.

Frequently they heard a deep, inquisitive sniffing, a whine, and the raking of strong toenails on the wood.

"I saw Hjordis," Kolssynir replied. "Only it wasn't quite Hjordis. I'm not sure what I saw. The only thing I'm sure of—" He paused and gazed into the fire. "—is that she has nets and toils spread for you and the dragon's heart that we haven't even dreamed of. Don't lower your guard for an instant. In spite of this curse, she's still terribly powerful. She's a monster, Brak."

"But is Ingvold really sleeping under a spell in that tomb, then?"

"Yes, I'm certain of it, or Skarnhrafn wouldn't be there waiting to steal her away somehow. Sit down; you needn't get excited. Just be cautious about what you accept from Hjordis."

Brak was not satisfied, but Kolssynir refused to say any more.

They did not see Hjordis until the following evening, long after the reports began arriving at the hall, describing the new advances of the draugar. Myrkjartan demanded to see Hjordis repeatedly, and Tyrkell slunk in and out, getting no nearer to Hjordis than the solid planking of the doors of her chambers at the far end of the hall. At each rebuff, he glowered furiously at Brak and Kolssynir, as if it were entirely their fault.

Finally Hjordis herself appeared, walking with difficulty and leaning heavily on two servants. She was muffled and bandaged as before in quantities of black worsted cloth, which, in combination with the dim light from the fires, made her loom like a large mass of shadow on the dais at the end of the hall. She waved away her servants and commanded Tyrkell to remove the inside guards and to make certain that no one disturbed her by hammering at the door, demanding to speak to her. Tyrkell took his orders and departed with his usual skulking bad grace, eyeing Brak as if he were cherishing hideous plans for revenge.

Brak kept his eyes on Hjordis, waiting for her to speak first. She looked back at him from the shadow of her coverings, and they glared at each other in a silent battle of wills.

At last Hjordis looked away from his accusing stare. "I

believe you're ready to listen to my offers now, are you not? You're expecting me to demand an exchange of the heart for Ingvold, or some such ridiculous request, but I won't make any demands of you. I realize the time is very short indeed. There's no use in my fighting it any longer. I know when I am defeated."

Brak could scarcely believe his ears. "Then you've decided to free Ingvold? Surely you have some conditions?"

Hjordis loomed forward with a creaking of her chair. "No conditions. The journey down to the fire put something into my very bones, and I know I'll be going back there before long, never to return. You may take your Ingvold and depart. And what's more—" She stood up painfully and hobbled forward. "I shall give you the sword of Dyrstyggr. Here, take it now as a surety of my word that you are free to leave whenever you wish." She unbuckled the belt from her waist and gave the sword to Brak. He came forward and accepted it gingerly, not quite certain it wouldn't burn his hands. Without removing his eyes from her misshapen figure, he backed away to rejoin his friends.

"Kolssynir, did I do the right thing?" he whispered. "Is this real, or is it another trap?"

"Don't take it!" Pehr whispered sharply, elbowing Skalgr, who could barely contain his excitement.

"Oh, take it, take it!" Skalgr hissed. "It's plain to see she's dying from the effects of Dyrstyggr's curse. What an excellent curse! A marvelous curse! Take it, take it!"

Kolssynir only shook his head slightly, as if he were seeing something fearful in his mind's eye. "When will we be able to leave?" he asked, turning to Hjordis.

Her voice, as she replied, was rich with irony and triumph. "As soon as Myrkjartan is cleared out of the way. But, as you must know, the fortress is completely surrounded by draugar, and Myrkjartan would never let you escape from him. The heart and the sword together are too great a prize for him to resist. It looks as if there's no other way for you to depart except by killing Myrkjartan. You have the sword and the heart. You can do it." She gave a signal then, calling Tyrkell's name, and the large outer doors burst open with a crash. A wave of Myrkriddir poured into the hall, carrying with them a host of Dokkalfar swinging axes and hewing with their swords against the axes, helmets, and shields of the Myrkriddir. In a moment Hjordis was surrounded by a tiny knot of Dokkalfar determined to die defending her against a score of grinning Myrkriddir. Another score skittishly pranced around Brak and his companions, eyeing the sword in his hands and keeping well out of reach as they threatened and menaced with their weapons.

Then into the midst of the uproar strode Myrkjartan, silencing the noise immediately. The black cloak with its red lining billowed around him in the cold wind that swept into the hall at his heels. He halted to look at Brak and the sword, with not a flicker of surprise on his face.

"Well, Hjordis," he said agreeably, "I believe you've set a trap for me, a most cunning trap. It was foolish of me to believe that you wanted to reconciliate, as your message implied. I am forced to respect you again, just when I had wrongly assumed you were defeated."

A cruel chuckle was his reply. "Your mistake will be your death, Myrkjartan. I have given the Scipling the sword as a gift, and I have promised that he can leave as soon as you and your wretched draugar are out of the way. I shall awaken Ingvold from her sleep behind the blue flames and he will take her with him—after he has done with you."

Myrkjartan looked at Brak again. "I should have killed you long ago when I had the opportunity. I knew it then, but you seemed so fat, innocuous, and absurd that I couldn't believe I should bother. But now I realize my mistake. You have changed, and it will be more difficult." He swept back his cloak to draw his sword.

"Difficult!" Hjordis laughed. "Impossible, you mean. He has the Rhbus to help him, and now he's got that sword. He'll kill you, Myrkjartan."

Brak measured his opponent. Myrkjartan compared with him like a well-picked old bone would compare with a strong viking's arm, well muscled from rowing and swinging an axe. Brak hesitated, ignoring the advice Pehr and Kolssynir were whispering into his ears and the assurance of pats and nudges from Skalgr, who was pattering around him with encouragement and anxious glimpses into his face. Familiar red and black images seemed to hover on all sides of him as someone stirred up the fire to make more light for the duel.

"Are you ready?" Myrkjartan sheathed his sword and took a good grip on his staff.

Brak slowly nodded. The sword of Dyrstyggr felt familiar in his hand. "Yes, I'm ready—Dyrstyggr." He spoke more to himself than to his opponent, as if he were listening to a remote inner voice, and his eyes were wide and glazed. He took two steps forward and made a lightning thrust at Myrkjartan, who narrowly warded it off with his upraised staff and leaped backward hastily, losing his complacent expression rather suddenly and setting the nearby Myrkriddir into squawking flight. Brak plowed through them after Myrkjartan, upsetting benches and a table without sparing them a glance. The sword was alive in his hands, each stroke alive with the vengeance of Dyrstyggr. Myrkjartan's spells failed to touch him, rebounding from the sword or shattering until the floor was slick with slime as they melted.

Kolssynir circled the fight, halting any treacherous interference from the Myrkriddir with bolts of fire that filled the hall with smoke and thunder, blinding the Myrkriddir and sending them scuttling for safety. His staff lit up the darkness at once when Myrkjartan extinguished all fires and lamps with a spell, and its bright light pursued the battle around the hall. Myrkjartan flung his staff aside and drew his sword, but his skill was no match for the fury of Dyrstyggr's revenge. Brak wounded him several times superficially, and he could see the sweat pouring down his opponent's face. His own eyes burned with a salty sting, and his muscles warned him that he was nearing exhaustion.

With a wicked twist, Brak hurled Myrkjartan's sword across the hall into the midst of some Myrkriddir. He lunged at Myrkjartan without hesitation, intending to kill him, but each thrust of the sword met only the fabric of the cloak, and Myrkjartan leaped away unscathed each time, although Brak was certain the blow would kill the necromancer. At last Brak brought the necromancer against the wall to finish him with a final stroke. The sword struck flesh and bone glancingly, and Myrkjartan went down with a roar of pain. Brak raised the sword to end the battle, bringing it down relentlessly and meeting nothing but the wood planking of the floor as the image of Myrkjartan vanished with the words of the escape spell on his lips, leaving behind a mocking chuckle.

"Coward! Nithling! Come back and finish it!" Brak bawled in a fury at such an underhanded cheat. He jerked the point of the sword from the wood and rushed at the slinking Myrkriddir, who only wanted to escape. He realized his strength was gone as the fury of Dyrstyggr's revenge ceased to burn in his blood, and he also realized, with despair, that he had lost his chance to kill Myrkjartan and that Ingvold would remain in her tomb until Myrkjartan was dead. The villainy of Hjordis' supposed unconditional surrender burst upon him with staggering clarity. He collapsed under the joyous assault of Pehr and Skalgr while Kolssynir leaped to close and bar the door, admitting no Dokkalfar except Tyrkell, who scuttled inside as quick as a weasel and posted himself at Hjordis' side with a defiant leer.

"Well done, Brak, well done!" Kolssynir gasped, sinking down on a bench to mop his face and catch his breath.

"We almost had him!" Skalgr exclaimed. "He was pinned to the wall and would have been killed, if not for the escape spell. The coward! No honorable wizard runs away from a fair fight."

Brak shook his head angrily and pushed himself away. "But I didn't kill him. Why couldn't I kill him? He ought to be dead."

"It was the cloak," Hjordis answered in a grim voice from her dark corner. "It protects its wearer from death. If you want Ingvold, you'd better see to it that Myrkjartan's luck runs out. With the dragon's heart and the sword, you ought to be able to kill him somehow."

Brak glowered at her. "You arranged to bring him in here to fight with me, didn't you? You told him you wished to discuss terms and you put the sword in my hands to kill him. You're deceiving me into helping you, Hjordis— whether I want to help you or not, everything I do to free Ingvold from her captivity is going to benefit you."

"Yes, indeed, I've been clever," Hjordis replied. "Between the two of us, we shall make a trophy out of Myrkjartan, as he has done with his old enemies. His luck will run out, and we will overwhelm him. You must ask your

Rhbus for their assistance the next time we meet with Myrkjartan."

"If we have the opportunity, that is," Brak said. "Listen to that uproar outside. It sounds as if the draugar have attacked the walls. If your Dokkalfar don't hold them off, we may be the next ones to join Myrkjartan's collection of skulls." He spoke grimly, listening to the clamor of swords and shields outside the main gates of the hill fort. Mingled with the sounds of battle was the howling of wolves.

Skalgr hugged his sides in high glee. "Listen to them tearing one another apart. Myrkjartan must be beside himself with rage. I knew he'd take it amiss that you tried to kill him." He added an injudicious giggle, and Tyrkell directed a mighty kick at him, the Dokkalfar's little red eyes gleaming.

Brak intervened menacingly, and Tyrkell backed away to take a defensive stance beside Hjordis. Her eyes gleamed at Brak like two red sparks in the darkness as he said, "I don't see how we can kill him now, since he knows that's our objective. He's not going to allow us to get near enough. And the worst of it is, how do we know where he is now? He vanished within these walls and, for all we know, he's still here somewhere. Perhaps he's searching for Ingvold."

Kolssynir stepped forward, scowling and pinching his lips. "It's more than likely—it's almost inevitable. Perhaps he has vengeance in mind, but I'd say he knows as well as any of us that once Ingvold is removed from Hjordisborg, Hjordis' hold over Brak is also removed."

Hjordis and Brak continued to measure each other. "Then Myrkjartan must be found," Hjordis said. "If he is still lurking inside the fortress, we can't allow him to get near Ingvold. I know he must be here, hiding in one form or another, perhaps disguised as one of the Dokkalfar or as a louse in somebody's beard, if he's clever enough. He's waiting and watching for his chance to strike me down and seize Ingvold, but I shall see to it myself that if he attempts to steal her, he'll be putting his own head into a noose." With ponderous creaking and shuffling, she rose to her feet. "As you see, I am no longer fit for defending Hjordisborg and leading my armies. The curse—I need not explain. Suffice it to say that Dyrstyggr has triumphed, wherever he may be. Tyrkell, do you see this Scipling?"

Tyrkell replied with a grunt and a bristling of hackles. "From now hence, you are to obey him as if his words were mine, although I shall be gone. He is standing in my place, with the sword I used to call mine. I command you to follow him and obey him, and to carry these instructions to my chieftains and warriors. The penalties for disobedience will be very severe."

Tyrkell looked desolately from Hjordis to Brak. "If you command it," he growled, "then I shall do it or die in the effort, no matter how repugnant I may find it. If you want me to be commanded by a Scipling, then I shall be." The sounds repressed within him intimated that the idea might be having negative effects on him already.

"Good. Then I shall bid you farewell. I don't believe anyone will see me again this side of that door." She gestured toward the door leading to the tombs. Limping heavily, she hobbled toward her rooms, dragging herself with difficulty along one wall for support.

Brak started to follow her. "Wait a moment. I don't want to command Tyrkell or any other Dokkalfar," he protested, hesitating when he saw her eyes fastened on him, glowing in that horribly unnatural manner. Then she turned again and shuffled away into the dark. Brak was reminded of a wounded bear crawling into its den to die, so he did not pursue her any farther. She closed the door, and he returned to the dim light of the fire.

Tyrkell confronted him with a ferociously surly expression. "What does our leader propose to do about the threat of Myrkjartan somewhere within our walls?" he rumbled, watching Brak with a sly, red eye.

Brak returned Tyrkell's challenging stare. "We will search for him. The door to the tombs must be placed under heavy guard so he can't get through to Ingvold. We need to fortify the walls and the gate in case the draugar make an attack. I don't think it's wise to spread the word that Hjordis is dying just yet, or the chieftains are likely to give it up entirely as a bad cause and go back home. We'll say she's very sick, or some such tale. In the meantime, we'll search the fortress for Myrkjartan every hour of the night and day, if we have to, until he shows himself. Tyrkell, I'll leave it to you to appoint the men to search. Every house and stable within the walls must be watched, if

Myrkjartan is as clever at concealing himself as Hjordis says he is. Everything depends upon discovering Myrkjartan before he discovers Ingvold."

"How can Hjordis desert us at a time like this?" Pehr demanded, looking around the hall a little wildly. "We haven't even got weapons, thanks to losing them at Hjalmknip. Myrkjartan could be in any crack or shadow, waiting to break our necks when our backs are turned. I don't know how we can even close our eyes for a moment to sleep if he's inside our walls somewhere." He stepped closer to Brak and spoke in a lower tone, intended for his ears only. "Brak, now that we have that sword, we can leave here at any time we choose and none of these Dokkalfar will dare to stop us. Don't you think this—this obsession of yours for Ingvold is needlessly complicating things? Haven't you ever, even for a moment, considered just leaving her behind and going on to do whatever the Rhbus want done?"

"No. Never."

Pehr was the first to look away. "All right, I'm sorry I said that. We'll stay here with you until Ingvold is freed, won't we, Skalgr?" He poked the old rascal with his elbow, sharply.

"To be sure we shall," Skalgr said a little faintly. "But I wonder how we'll ever break that spell of the blue fire to get at her if Hjordis dies without doing it or telling us how."

Brak looked dubiously toward the dark end of the hall. "I'll get it out of her somehow before she dies." Then he dispatched the glowering Tyrkell to secure the hill fort and begin the search for Myrkjartan.

The Dokkalfar searched gingerly for three days, leaping in terror whenever the fire crackled or a shadow moved. Not only were there turf houses and barns to search above ground, but Brak learned of the existence of a maze of tunnels underground leading to old mines, storage chambers, and secret exits to the outside. Myrkjartan could be hiding in any one of a thousand places, thanks to the Dokkalfar penchant for dark, underground hiding places and a basically suspicious, secretive nature that expressed itself in tunnels and secret passageways.

Hjordis was another source of exasperation. When he was in the hall, Brak often heard her moving about in her rooms with thumps and frequent rending crashes and a good deal of muttering and moaning. Her three physicians camped outside her door, but she fiercely rejected their offers of assistance. She consented to speak only to Brak or Tyrkell through the locked door as long as neither made a reference to allowing the doctors to see her. She seemed resigned to her fate and listened to the reports of the search with stoic calm.

Ten more days elapsed, with no results. The searchers combed every inch of the hill fort above ground and below, repeating their search three times before deciding by general consensus that Myrkjartan was not hiding inside Hjordisborg. They began to grumble about missing the fun of the nightly forays against the draugar, who surrounded Hjordisborg completely and seemed to be waiting for the Dokkalfar to make the next move. Or, as Hjordis suggested through the door, they did not know what else to do without Myrkjartan to lead them.

"I'd like to do some searching myself," Pehr suggested, stalking restively around the hall one wintry afternoon. The days were very short and gloomy with the advance of winter, and it was already dark enough outside for the Dokkalfar to be stirring around. He awakened the seven stout Dokkalfar whose job it was to guard the door of the tombs, and they rewarded his vigilance with ill-natured growling and glaring, as if they considered wakefulness an imposition.

Tyrkell, more morose and gloomy than ever, sighed and shook his head. "Myrkjartan isn't inside Hjordisborg, and no amount of searching and prying is going to turn him up. We'd do better to spend our time chopping up draugar." He mentioned it as if it were as commonplace as going out to chop wood.

"Come on, you old devil, let's take a walk down some of those old, musty tunnels again," Pehr said, tossing Tyrkell's cloak at him and roughing up Skalgr in passing. "You, too, Skalgr; you're sitting around too much and getting fat. I can scarcely see your bones anymore, and you're even starting to look healthy. You must not be getting enough fear in your diet."

Skalgr's indignant reply and subsequent getting ready to go out roused Brak from his gloomy contemplation of

Hjordis' latest refusal to talk to him about the spell over Ingvold. She was talking less and less, and he was giving more orders to Tyrkell, who was becoming more bristling and glowering with each order. Brak certainly didn't relish Tyrkell's company, but doing something besides brooding would do him good; even a walk half stooped-over in a dank, dripping Dokkalfar mine tunnel was better than wondering what would happen to him and his friends when Hjordis finally died.

Kolssynir consented to join them, leaving the seven sullen guards a final warning that he would have their ears if he came back and found them sleeping. "Not that it'll frighten them into staying awake," he said gloomily, "but there's precious little else I can do right now. You, Brak, at least can wear that sword around and impress the Dokkalfar with your importance, but they've seen plenty of wizards."

They prowled the old tunnels for several hours, lighting the way with Kolssynir's staff, until everyone's spirits were sufficiently chilled by the damp and darkness to cause them to look forward to a return to Hjordis' cavernous hall. When they emerged from the hillside entrance, the nipping wind peppered them with snow and whitened their cloaks. The scene inside the gates of the fortress looked almost cheerful, with firelight glowing through the snowy night from the clustered turf houses, which might have been any Scipling hill fort, except for the occasional flitting forms of long-legged black wolves darting away into the darkness.

"I hope you're satisfied now," Tyrkell grumbled as they walked through the new snow. "We've looked into every tunnel and searched every corner of this fort, and there's no Myrkjartan. I wonder what your next idea will be." He looked slyly at Brak and pounded on the door of the hall. When it was not opened immediately, he kicked it angrily, muttering about the guards probably being asleep inside with the door barred. The door yielded to his assault and fell open a little way.

"Hello, what's this? They locked it after us," Kolssynir said, raising his staff warily.

Tyrkell drew his sword and gave the door another kick to jolt it farther open. With an oath he jumped back, scattering the others behind him into a defensive array on either side of the doorway. Brak knelt and peered into the dimness of the hall. In the light of the dying fire in the central hearth lay the seven guards, weapons clasped in lifeless hands, sightless eyes staring dully at nothing. Beyond their bodies the door to the tombs stood open, breathing deathly cold into the hall and faintly illuminating the walls with an eerie blue flicker. At the other end of the hall, the door to Hjordis' chambers also stood open, splintered and wrenched from its hinges.

Tyrkell gave a strangled gasp. "He was here! He was here, and he's killed Hjordis!"

"And now he's down in the tombs," Pehr said, clutching his axe. "What do we do now?" He looked from the open doorway to Brak and Kolssynir.

Brak answered without hesitation. "We'll go after him."

Chapter 20

◈◈◈◈◈◈◈◈◈◈◈◈◈◈◈◈◈◈◈◈◈◈◈

Tyrkell was sent for reinforcements, and Brak was glad to be rid of him for a few moments. He chewed a small shred of the heart and implored the Rhbus for their direction. He only had time for a brief assurance and a few jumbled visions of the pit spiraling downward, Myrkjartan, and some other images he did not understand; then Tyrkell was back with ten anxious-looking Dokkalfar.

"Only ten?" Kolssynir exclaimed. "It's Myrkjartan himself we're going after, and all you bring to help us is ten men?"

Tyrkell scowled. "It was the best I could do. Everyone else is on the walls or outside fighting the draugar. They made a rush at us, so almost everyone is busy fighting. Ten was all that could be spared, and that's probably more than I ought to have taken."

"This is madness," Pehr said as they entered the cold, black caverns. "He could be anywhere, hiding behind pillars or rocks, waiting for us." He shivered, peering around at the crudely hewn columns and galleries barely and fleetingly illuminated by Kolssynir's staff.

"He's down below," Brak said with scarcely a glance to the right or the left. "It's Ingvold he's going after."

The blue flame far below sounded a guttering roar as they descended at Kolssynir's heels, with the Dokkalfar crowding close behind, peering suspiciously into every dark tomb before hurrying past it to encounter the next, as if expecting each time to find Myrkjartan lying in wait.

When they were about halfway down the sides of the great pit, Brak suddenly paused near the entry to a large side tunnel where the miners had made an unprofitable test excursion laterally into the heart of the mountain. The belated effects of the dragon's heart had unexpectedly caught up with him; his knees felt weak and his throat was burning like fire. The images of Kolssynir and the Dokkalfar blurred before his eyes, distorted into one great dark mass with dozens of curious eyes gazing at him. He steadied himself by leaning against the rock and shutting his eyes. Opening them, he peered into the perfect blackness of the side tunnel, waiting for the dizziness to pass and cursing himself and the heart. The gloom of the tunnel seemed to swirl around him, gathering itself into a massive dark shape that loomed over him silently, waiting for him to move away. Startled, Brak looked at it more attentively, knowing he couldn't be seeing what he thought he was. Whatever it was, it was very close; as he looked upward to where its head would be, he saw two tiny red eyes gleaming at him like two sparks.

Brak stepped back, grabbed Kolssynir's arm, and pointed, without taking his eyes off the thing, but it wasn't there when Kolssynir thrust his glowing staff into the tunnel.

"Nothing here but rocks," he said. "Rocks and more rocks. If you're feeling all right now, let's get going."

Before they had descended much farther, a bolt of bright fire swept the walls nearby, causing sheets of ice to crackle and explode. Rocks came crashing down, tier by tier, into the blue flame below. Skarnhrafn greeted them with a rusty chuckle from his perch on the crag and took to the air with a noisy fluttering of his ragged attire. He alighted in a more advantageous position and blasted them again with golden fire. More ice thundered down into the blue flame, which leaped to new heights, as if it fed upon ice gladly, and roared louder in the vast shaft.

The Dokkalfar tumbled into an open tomb for shelter. Kolssynir shoved Brak, Pehr, and Skalgr after them and took a position behind a heap of debris near the edge. Skarnhrafn's gaze swept over them, almost burying them in ice dislodged from above. With more maniacal chuckling and croaking, Skarnhrafn flew to another place higher above, poising himself on a rough abutment near the tunnel where Brak had suffered his attack from the dragon meat. Brak was not a person who was given to presentiments, but he felt impelled to crowd Skalgr aside to lean out of the tomb and peer upward to where Skarnhrafn sat preening himself, bathed in the unearthly light emanating from the helmet. Even at such a distance, Brak saw the massive shadow swelling behind the draug, hovering a moment, then making a pounce. Skarnhrafn at that instant launched himself into the air, unaware, and floated like a huge bat back to his favorite roost.

"Did you see that?" Brak demanded of Kolssynir, half disbelieving.

Kolssynir beckoned to the Dokkalfar to follow. "He's tired of harrassing us for a while. Come on, you great dolts, he can't reach us if we keep back from the edges."

"Something is up there, following us," Brak said in a low voice to Kolssynir. "I think the Rhbus tried to warn me about it."

Kolssynir looked upward for a few moments, then down at Skarnhrafn on his crag and at the blue fire below. "Myrkjartan is down there waiting for us, perhaps even now breaking Hjordis' spell over Ingvold. Whatever is lurking in the upper tiers will have to wait until we've dealt with Myrkjartan."

As they entered the last rough switchbacks to the bottom, Brak saw Myrkjartan outlined against the blue flames and pulled Kolssynir aside. "It's my duty to challenge him, so let me lead now. I have to finish the battle I began in Hjordis' hall."

"I could blast him," Kolssynir suggested, reluctantly allowing Brak to trade positions with him. "The two of us could kill him, I think. The magic in that cloak can't be stronger than both of us."

Brak only shook his head doggedly. "I'm going down there alone, and I want the rest of you to stay here, where it's safe. If I'm killed, then you must attack Myrkjartan before he gets possession of the sword and the heart. Pehr, I'll expect you to take my place if it comes to that, and to get Ingvold out of that tomb. You'll do it, won't you?"

Pehr stammered, "Well, I would certainly do my best— but it would be a better idea if you didn't get yourself killed, because I don't think I have the same sort of courage as you do, Brak. I can scarcely believe I once thought you were a coward. You'll be careful not to get killed, won't you?"

"Yes, we don't want to explain it to Ingvold," Skalgr added.

"We'll take a position to make sure we can protect you if you need us," Kolssynir said grimly, eyeing the Dokkalfar, who looked as if no one could induce them to take one more step toward Myrkjartan and the source of the blue fire. They had their faces wrapped against the cold, so that nothing showed except their eyes.

Brak descended alone, moving carefully over the exposed icy ledges. Skarnhrafn marked his progress with cackles and muttered asides to himself and Myrkjartan, and an occasional fiery blast directed upward, which resulted in avalanches of ice and rocks sluicing down into the fire.

"Myrkjartan!" Brak's voice echoed in the ancient mine shaft.

The necromancer raised his staff in welcome, his cloak billowing in the icy breath of the fire. "Is it you, Scipling, and alone? Have you come to finish the holmgang we began in Hjordis' hall?"

"Yes, I have. One of us will become fodder for the fire before the night is out."

"That would be a terrible waste. You'd be wiser to come down here to listen to what I have to say. Neither of us has the power to walk through those flames to reach Ingvold, so perhaps we ought to make a plan together."

Brak reached the lowest level, where the flames crept from between the rock, whitening them with incredible cold. He kept his hand on the sword, but Myrkjartan's demeanor remained peaceful. "Hjordis was clever," he said when Brak stopped at a wary distance. "She was the one to see the true worth of Ingvold—a stalking-horse for you and the dragon's heart. Whoever possesses Ingvold controls the wielder of the sword and the heart. A dangerous weakness in you, but admirable in you for your loyalty. If Hjordis had been more sensible and had kept Ingvold in a more inaccessible place, she might have used your power for many happy years of slaughter and destruction. But I suppose Dyrstyggr's curse is getting to her brain and she's weakening. It's just as well to have one less greedy enemy to worry about at this point."

"Then you don't know where she is?" Brak asked, remembering the shattered door with an uneasy twinge of vertigo.

"Dying, or so I've heard," Myrkjartan answered, annoyed. "But I'm not here to discuss the health of Hjordis with you. You and I must reach an agreement. As I said before, neither of us has the power to walk unscathed through the fire nor the power to negate the flames into abatement. We both want Ingvold removed from her cell behind the wall of fire, don't we?"

"I don't think you have the ability to get her out," Brak said. "Your powers are of the dusty sort having to do with corpses. Without your armies of draugar, you're not much to contend with, Myrkjartan. If not for that cloak, which is Dyrstyggr's, I would have killed you, and you know it."

"Of course, of course, but the fact remains that I have the cloak and its accompanying virtues," Myrkjartan replied. "And I also have a plan for getting Ingvold out." He glanced upward and called, "Skarnhrafn! Come down here. You're very slow."

The answer was a remote chuckle and another fall of ice and rocks as Skarnhrafn's gaze swept around the chamber. When the racket subsided, the draug's voice rumbled, "There are more things in this dismal hole than dead bones and blue fire, Myrkjartan. More than Sciplings and a handful of frightened Dokkalfar and one dusty old draug." The idea seemed to engage whatever sense of humor a draug might possess, and he fell into fits of cackling and wheezing.

"Hurry yourself down here, Skarnhrafn!" Myrkjartan commanded in an irritable shout. "If you want to restore my opinion of you, you'd better come down immediately!"

Brak fixed his eyes on Myrkjartan incredulously. "You think Skarnhrafn can fly down to her and carry her out? She could be killed in the flames. Even if your scheme does work, what about the sleep spell Hjordis has put on her?"

Myrkjartan shrugged. "Those things are easily broken, no matter what lies Hjordis has told you. She lied to you so you wouldn't kill her the moment you laid hands on that sword. Skarnhrafn! What are you waiting for, you fool? We've got victory within our grasp!"

Brak drew the sword and flung away his cloak. "You haven't consulted me about your supposed victory, Myrkjartan. I want nothing of your plans. I'm heartily sick of being trapped in the middle of the evil designs of creatures like you and Hjordis, who seem to think I'm nothing but a pawn to be pushed around for your benefit. I came down here to finish the duel we began—which you fled from in such a cowardly manner. Defend yourself, Myrkjartan, unless you're a complete nithling!" He advanced, scarcely feeling the cold blast of the flames as Dyrstyggr's revenge warmed his blood.

Myrkjartan drew his sword. "You leave yourself no alternative but death. Perhaps the other Scipling is more reasonable than you. Skarnhrafn! Don't allow the others to escape! They're hiding like rats in the wall above us. Skarnhrafn! I command you to assist me, or I'll tear you to pieces!"

Above on his perch, Skarnhrafn answered with a rusty chuckle and beamed fire recklessly from side to side, causing more ice to come crashing down, narrowly missing the Dokkalfar and covering the lower end of the walkway in rubble.

Myrkjartan did not flinch or take his eyes off Brak and the sword. "Skarnhrafn!" he thundered in a voice of menace. "Come down here at once! I command you!"

The answer was another rockfall on the ledges above.

Skarnhrafn swept the upper levels with fire, dislodging more ice and rocks.

Brak seized the advantage and lunged to the attack. Myrkjartan defended himself aggressively, but whenever he disengaged himself, he looked up for Skarnhrafn and shouted curses at him as more ice and rubble clattered down. Skarnhrafn skirmished about the galleries near the halfway point, then suddenly took to the air with a typical Myrkridda shriek, narrowly avoiding immolation in the surging blue flames. With more shrieks, the flapping black figure circled higher and vanished into the darkness.

"Skarnhrafn! Deserter! Nithling!" Myrkjartan bellowed in fury, lashing at Brak and coming very close to wounding him seriously, in spite of Dyrstyggr's sword.

"He's gone!" Skalgr's voice chortled from a little way above. "Even the draugar know a lost cause when they see one. This time no escape spell will save you. Go to it, Brak!"

Grimly they battled. During a pause, everyone heard several rocks fall from above, clashing and clattering on subsequent ledges. Something grated heavily, like a large boulder being pushed over another. It ground its way steadily downward, dislodging rocks as it came.

Kolssynir stepped from his cover behind a large shoulder of rock. "I think we'd better stop the holmgang for a short time while we decide what's making that disturbance."

Myrkjartan leaned on his sword and listened. Far above, Skarnhrafn sounded his wheezy chuckle and called faintly, "Halloo, Myrkjartan! You'd better follow my example and fly out of there! The very rocks are alive in this horrid place, with eyes and claws and teeth! I can't do anything with them—they just keep creeping along!"

"What on earth!" Kolssynir looked at Myrkjartan, and they exchanged a shrug. "It could be a rockslide, perhaps. Skarnhrafn evidently saw something out of the ordinary."

Myrkjartan shook his head, panting for breath. "He's mad—that useless draug. Wits weren't very strong to begin with. Never should have given him that helmet."

Glad for the opportunity to rest, Brak listened to the grinding sounds approaching. Their progress was marked by periods of silence, during which they all could hear Skarnhrafn muttering to himself far above. Kolssynir ordered several of the Dokkalfar to investigate, nearly on threat of their lives. While everyone's attention was fastened on the Dokkalfar, Myrkjartan suddenly raised his sword and renewed his attack on Brak. Not wholly unsuspecting, Brak managed to deflect an almost certainly fatal blow and stumbled backward, unable to recover his footing on the frost-rimed rocks. As he slipped and fell, he saw two red orbs gleaming in the darkness behind Myrkjartan. An immense dark mass suddenly reared upright with an inhuman scream and plummeted from the ledge above into the midst of the blue fire like an avalanche. The chamber was momentarily blackened as the fire was smothered in ice and rocks, but presently it burst into more brilliant life than before.

Brak leaped to his feet and dived for shelter. Something towered over him, black against the light of the fire. He heard Myrkjartan's sword clang against stone repeatedly. Then, with a horrible, snarling, worrying sound, the creature engulfed Myrkjartan in a monstrous bear hug. Brak winced in the fiery flash of Kolssynir's fire bolt, glimpsing the enormous lumpy thing that gripped Myrkjartan in its thick arms. He seemed powerless to escape, perhaps unconscious or dead. Kolssynir and Pehr led a charge of Dokkalfar at the monster, tripping over Brak as they went. Roaring and bellowing, the thing tossed its attackers aside as if they were mere flies. Tiny red eyes glared furiously as it shook Myrkjartan's limp form in its teeth. Brak leaped up to slash at it with the sword and was rewarded with an arm-jarring concussion and a shower of sparks, as if he had struck a boulder. The creature recoiled, hissing and growling, lashing at the sword with a massive black paw tipped with heavy claws.

Over all the din Brak heard Skalgr screeching as he dived at the creature in attack and went yelping in retreat. He uttered one continuous yell of defiance and weird exultation, sharpened now and then with terror. As Pehr, Brak, Kolssynir, and the Dokkalfar pounded with all their might at the unyielding thing, Skalgr capered through the scene, out of his mind with excitement as they struggled to pull the creature's quarry from its grasp.

"Get the cloak! Get the cloak!" Skalgr screamed a hundred times, keeping his distance.

The creature shook the body of Myrkjartan like a rag, roaring defiance at the swords clanging on its scales without making a dint. It lashed its short, heavy tail at its attackers; Skalgr leaped over it and actually scaled the monster's back, yelling and stamping with both feet. The beast ceased its mauling of Myrkjartan and snapped ineffectually at Skalgr, rearing aloft to dislodge him. Brak saw his opportunity and rushed forward to seize Myrkjartan by the legs with a mighty yank and to haul him out of the creature's grasp. Instantly it turned to retaliate, meeting Kolssynir's fire bolts with no visible damage. It retreated a pace, and Skalgr swooped in, scuttling so fast and bent into such a contortion that scarcely anyone recognized him until he paused to rip away Myrkjartan's cloak and go bounding off with it clasped in his arms.

Brak attempted to drag the necromancer's body to safety, but the beast perceived his intent and lumbered at him with a savage growl, so he backed away toward Pehr and Skalgr. Kolssynir also backed away, hurling bolt after bolt, which exploded harmlessly against the beast's heavy plating. Slowly they retreated before its advance. The creature pressed forward until they were forced onto the walkways leading upward. Then it halted and glared at them for a while, uttering shuddering growls as a warning before it withdrew slightly, ignoring the small heap that was Myrkjartan.

Kolssynir wiped beads of sweat from his face, and Brak found that his knees were trembling. "This won't do at all," Kolssynir said. "If Myrkjartan is dead, his body must be carefully burned and the ashes scattered to prevent his draug from ever walking. His power would be ten times greater, were he dead."

"But we've got the cloak!" Skalgr exclaimed. "Let's just leave him here to the tender mercies of that monster. You can seal the door above and they can stay here enjoying each other's company forever."

"I agree," Tyrkell growled fervently. "In a few moments there'll be no keeping my men down here for another instant. Myrkjartan is dead and so is Hjordis, so let's leave it at that and get out of here while we're still alive."

At the time, it seemed like eminently good sense to everyone but Brak. "What about Ingvold?" he demanded bitterly. "Are we just going to abandon her?"

Tyrkell replied over his shoulder, "You can stay here with her if you like, until you freeze to death. We're leaving!" Without looking back to see if the others followed or not, the Dokkalfar hurried away in the dark, using their native instincts for guidance in the absence of torches to light their way.

"Come on, Brak, there's nothing we can do for her now," Kolssynir said. "We'll go back to the hall and decide what to do."

Reluctantly, Brak let himself be drawn away from the pit and the fire. He stopped and looked back often at the great beast crouching there, mindless of the fire's searing cold. It seemed to watch him, too, agreeing with his silent promise to it that he would be back—soon.

Skarnhrafn chose to keep reminding them of his existence by scourging the galleries with fire. The Dokkalfar hailed him with arrows and rocks, driving him back to his usual perch on Ingvold's crag. He glared at them and raked the creature below with flames, eliciting angry roars and screams until the underground vault rang with its hideous cries, echoed by Skarnhrafn's mocking shrieks.

The strain suddenly seemed to catch up with Skalgr. He leaped up, shaking his fists, prancing around in a bizzarre dance and screaming, "It's your turn next, Skarnhrafn! You pile of barrow dust, you cackling ninny, you usurperous vermin—" He might have continued, but Pehr knocked him down and muffled him under Myrkjartan's cloak, muttering something about forcing the little nithling to swallow it if he couldn't keep himself quiet.

Long after they reached the safety of the hall above, Skalgr was in a state of delirious triumph, as if he personally had killed Myrkjartan and Hjordis and was making plans for wrenching Skarnhrafn's helmet off his shoulders with his own hands. Brak was too consumed with his worry for Ingvold to pay him much heed when the old scrounger draped Myrkjartan's cloak over Brak's shoulders and stepped back to admire the effect. Tyrkell and the Dokkalfar were suitably impressed, and skulked around the hall with a most deferential attitude.

Two days elapsed before Brak persuaded Kolssynir and Pehr and Skalgr to return to the lair of the beast below. Pehr in particular was not anxious to renew his acquaintance with it and required a great deal of persuasion before he consented to accompany the others.

They found that nothing had changed, except that Skarnhrafn had taken up a perch closer to the bottom of the cavern. He raked the intruders with fire and set up an unearthly din of screeches and jeers and seemed purposely to melt huge blocks of ice from their moorings to go crashing into the fire.

"The beast will be amply warned of our approach," Kolssynir said grimly as they crouched behind a sheltering heap of stone.

When Skarnhrafn tired of his game, he flew back to his roost to sit chuckling his satisfaction, with a good view of the area below. To Brak, the black, untidy figure of the Myrkridda hovering over Ingvold was almost intolerable, like a vulture of the most loathsome sort.

"Scipling!" the draug called. "Halloa, Scipling!"

"What do you want, Skarnhrafn?" Brak replied warily.

"To talk. To bargain. To get out of this place." He added a nervous cackle as the rocks moved at the bottom of the shaft. "There are thousands of draugar outside with no leader, now that Myrkjartan is gone. Draugar aren't bad fellows when you get used to them, and you'd find the Myrkriddir quite witty and charming, once you really got to know them. I can get Ingvold out of her tomb, no question of that. What I need is someone to call Master, someone who will lead the draugar and the Myrkriddir. We can crush these impudent Dokkalfar, with you to lead and me to follow. It would be glorious, eh, Scipling?"

"Deliver Ingvold unharmed to me, and we might talk," Brak replied. "How do you propose to get her out of the fire without being touched by it? A draug doesn't feel the heat or cold, but a living creature will perish instantly at a touch of that fire."

Skarnhrafn gave a wheezy chuckle and thumped himself on the chest with a hollow, dusty sound. "I can do it, Master. You shall be the leader of thousands of draugar. You must forgive me if I occasionally forget and call you Myrkjartan. In that cloak you look very similar."

"Skarnhrafn," Brak began in annoyance. "I'm not Myrkjartan and I don't ever intend to be Myrkjartan. These are Dyrstyggr's weapons. Myrkjartan and Hjordis are dead, and so is the quarrel between them. It would be a fitting gesture from you to relinquish Dyrstyggr's helmet and to bring Ingvold back to safety. Then all this fighting will be done with and we can all go back to our homes in peace."

"Dead!" Skarnhrafn cackled with glee. "Oh, no, not dead! Not dead at all! You haven't been down here watching and listening, have you? No, of course not. You should know by now there's no such thing as dead—really dead. Anything can be revived again, just as I was by Myrkjartan. There's nothing dead about being dead, nothing at all, once you get used to it—"

"He's perfectly brainless, you know," Pehr remarked in disgust, teeth chattering. "How much longer are you going to stay down here, Brak? Haven't you seen enough?"

Brak listened to the sounds of rocks grinding together down below near the fire. "No, I haven't seen enough. I want to be certain Myrkjartan is dead, for one thing. We ought to burn him if we can."

"It isn't enough that a monster the size of a mountain has eaten him, perhaps?" Pehr asked hopefully.

"Come on," Kolssynir snapped, giving him a push.

Skalgr lingered a moment to look across the void at Skarnhrafn. "You're the next, you great jabbering horsefly. We'll knock you to shreds. We'll pound you to dust. You've no more right to that helmet than that monster has. Make a note of yourself, Skarnhrafn; very shortly you'll cease to exist."

As they crept cautiously down the ramps toward the bottom, a huge black form rose between them and the fire and gazed down on them with small, glowing eyes. They stopped and returned its stare. It lifted one heavy paw and seemed to beckon them closer. When they did not move, it beckoned again, unmistakably indicating that they should draw nearer.

"I'd assumed it was an animal of some kind," Kolssynir said, standing up fearlessly to examine the creature. It was twice as tall as a man and ten times more stout. In the light of the fire it looked as if it were formed of rough stones, made either to stand upright, as it was presently doing, or to go on all fours. "I think it must be a rock troll," Kolssynir continued. "A pet of Hjordis', I suppose.

Rather cute little beasts as infants, but they do have an unforgivable tendency to grow larger—much larger."

The rock troll eased a step closer with a heavy grinding of its rocky scales. Kolssynir promptly abandoned his scientific study and dived behind a rock. The creature began to hiss and rumble, as if it were clearing its throat for a roar.

Instead, a small voice said, "Don't be afraid. I mean you no harm. I have to get close so you can hear me speak." The voice was very faint and hoarse.

Brak unsheathed Dyrstyggr's sword and took a tentative step closer. Behind him, Skalgr had fallen into some kind of fit, giggling and hugging himself and rocking to and fro as if he couldn't hold still. Brak ignored the disgraceful behavior of his friend and looked up at the enormous thing towering above him like a living wall of stone.

"Who are you, and what do you have to say to us?" he demanded. "You nearly killed us, and you did kill Myrkjartan. We thank you for that service, but we'd like to know what you're doing here. Did Hjordis tire of you and put you down here?"

The creature's eyes were upon him. "I didn't expect you'd recognize me in this loathsome aspect, but you might have known my voice, Brak. I am Hjordis. What you see before you is the complete working of Dyrstyggr's curse."

Brak's fear melted away into a different species of horror and revulsion. "Hjordis! I can scarcely believe it—but we all saw the change taking place before our eyes. I realize you must be right. You came out of your rooms and followed Myrkjartan down into the tombs. We passed you at the side tunnel about midway. There's nothing left of you that once was—as you were before?"

"No, nothing. You are understandably disappointed that I am still alive, are you not? You'd hoped to end the fighting against the Ljosalfar, once you'd got the helmet back from Skarnhrafn. I must say you look quite natural in Myrkjartan's cloak. You'll look well leading the Dokkalfar to victory against the Ljosalfar."

"You said you would free Ingvold when Myrkjartan was dead. You saw to that yourself, so I now remind you of your promise. Are you going to honor it, Hjordis?" Brak tasted the bitterness of sickening hope, knowing it was futile even to ask.

"I will honor it when the day arrives that I need you no longer. When the Ljosalfar have vanished from the surface, and the sun is not so bright and arrogant in the sky, and there are no more battles to be fought, then you and Ingvold shall be freed."

"What do I care for your promises! You never intend to keep them. It would be better to destroy this heart now in the flames." He groped for it and would have thrown it into the fire, but Skalgr leaped forward and caught his arm.

"Don't be hasty!" Skalgr exclaimed, holding on like a leech as Brak tried to shake him off without much gentleness. "Sometimes these things aren't as bad as they sound —or as permanent. Be patient, won't you, and give yourself a little time to get used to the idea. Surely you can think of a better way to outwit her than to destroy the heart so impulsively."

"But of course, be sensible," Hjordis said. "You'll have positions of power and respect among the Dokkalfar—not to mention wealth. As you see, I'm in no fit condition to rule, so you shall be my voice and my arm to wield the sword. You'll have almost unlimited power over thousands of Dokkalfar, caverns of the earth's treasures, and so much domain you'd never know where it began or stopped. The Dokkalfar would be grateful to you for leading them to such triumph. It would far surpass anything you might expect in the Scipling realm, even if you weren't a mere thrall. You'll have anything you've ever wanted. Ingvold will be here, where no one else can take her away, and you can look at her any time you wish with my seeing sphere. She'll never grow old and shrewish as long as she's in my spell."

Brak looked at the ice-covered tomb where Ingvold lay. "She'd be better off dead than spending her years asleep under a spell," he said bitterly.

"Now don't be hasty," Skalgr interrupted. "Take a moment to accustom yourself to the idea, and you'll see that you needn't leap into any irreversible decisions just yet. It won't hurt Ingvold to sleep for a while longer."

"If you prove your loyalty to me," Hjordis said, "I'll release her before all the Ljosalfar are destroyed—provided

I think you'll still remain to help me. You see, I'm a reasonable person, in spite of my frightful exterior. I shall be fair with you if you are faithful to me."

"And don't say you'd rather die first," Skalgr said to Brak, anxiously giving him a little shake to get his attention. "You're no good to yourself or anyone if you're dead. As long as you're alive, no matter how wretched and starved—or rich and powerful—there's always a chance you can overpower her. You may have to descend to the depths—if you agree to assist the Dokkalfar for a time, no lasting harm will be done to the Ljosalfar. They've been fighting the Dokkalfar since the very beginning, when the maggots from Ymir's body became dwarves and Dokkalfar, with no victory in sight for either side. Just remember—as long as you're the least bit alive, there's always the chance for vengeance, vengeance, vengeance!" He spoke so fiercely that his voice shook and his eyes burned with a feverish light.

The rock troll rumbled menacingly and swiped at him with one huge paw. "Vengeance against me! From a vermin like you, that's not likely. I'll not tolerate the sight of you again. You remind me too much of an old enemy I squashed into wretchedness. If you were a bit fatter and better curried, you might even look more like him." She blinked her red eyes scornfully. "Who is there on earth who could kill me now? Even the Rhbus withdraw from such a notion."

Brak looked at the sword in his hand, debating trying it once more against her flinty scales. Hjordis chuckled. "Go ahead and try it if you wish. I know you can't kill me—no yet anyway. Not as long as Skarnhrafn is flitting around with your helmet. I believe I shall keep the helmet out of your hands, as a little insurance. You won't have all your powers as long as it is missing, but what you have should be sufficient. Now, then, are you ready with your answer?"

Chapter 21

❖❖❖❖❖❖❖❖❖❖❖❖❖❖❖❖❖❖❖❖❖❖❖❖

Brak looked at the monster loweringly. It had suddenly come to represent every thwart and disappointment he had ever suffered in his life, beginning with his misfortune to have been born a thrall and culminating in the refusal of the Rhbus to destroy this horrible, unjust creature called Hjordis, whose very existence was a deplorable abomination.

Furiously he launched himself at the beast, battering at its small, craggy skull with the sword until the sparks flew. He hammered at it until his arms were almost numb, and the monster crouched under his attack, patiently waiting until he had exhausted his fury and could hardly find the strength to lift the sword and let it fall.

Then Hjordis reared to her full height, towering over Brak. Pehr gave a shout of alarm and darted forward to seize Brak and haul him against his will to a safer place. Hjordis made no pugnacious moves and watched with contemptuous indifference.

"You see how futile it is to try killing me? Dyrstyggr may have done me a favor by changing me into a rock troll. I will probably live forever, thanks to this curse."

"No!" Skalgr shouted, abandoning his hiding place to shake his fists at her. "Vengeance, vengeance, vengeance!"

Kolssynir silenced him with a rap from his staff. "As arbitrator in this affair, I tell you, Skalgr, to shut your mouth and keep yourself out of sight. Hjordis, we aren't ready with an answer yet; you must give us a bit more time."

Brak shook off his friends' restraining hands to confront

Hjordis again. "No, I have the answer now," he began, taking a defiant stance, but Kolssynir refused to let him finish.

"No, not now. As arbitrator, I refuse to allow you to speak. We'll return later with our answer, after we've discussed it carefully. There's more to be considered here than meets the eye." He looked at Brak sternly until Brak reluctantly sheathed the sword and backed away.

"Ten days," Hjordis said. "I won't see any of you before that time is up, no matter what your answer." She ponderously turned her back to indicate that the conversation was over and lumbered through the flames to her lair near Ingvold's tomb.

The passage of the next ten days was not without difficulty. The wizards of Hjordis rose in rebellion and had to be put down with great severity by Kolssynir. Several of the survivors escaped from the hill fort to take their chances among the draugar rather than join their cronies in imprisonment. The draugar discovered and occupied the main escape tunnel under the mountain, which rendered the morale of Hjordisborg very low and grim. The wolf-fylgur of the Dokkalfar shredded a hundred draugar nightly, but the creatures kept attacking and coming on by force of sheer numbers. Even Kolssynir was concerned and astonished at the number of the draugar, and more particularly amazed when Tyrkell humbled himself and begged Brak to lead the Dokkalfar against the draugar in a campaign to destroy them once and for all. Brak was more disposed to let the draugar overwhelm Hjordisborg, but Kolssynir, Pehr, and Skalgr were certain it would not be to their best interest, not to mention the fact that it wouldn't benefit Ingvold in the least. Finally he was persuaded to lead out the Dokkalfar to battle, after trying in vain to find the Rhbus for their advice. To his great and bitter dismay, even Gull-skeggi seemed to be eluding him, and he wondered what he had done to merit their desertion of him.

The Dokkalfar's spirits lifted euphorically after their rout of the draugar armies, whose tattered remnants were scattered for miles surrounding Hjordisborg. Brak detected no assistance from the Rhbus, but the very sight of him with the cloak, the sword, and the heart stirred the power-greedy Dokkalfar to implacable ferocity, and for days after the battle with the draugar no one talked of anything else but the next attack upon Miklborg and how differently it would turn out this time. The remains of the draugar kept the Dokkalfar pleasantly employed for several days in the loading of them into wagons and carts to haul to the hill fort for firewood.

The battle with the draugar, however, was not finished. Small bands of draugar attacked the wagons frequently, and larger groups skulked in the hills. Tyrkell's initial elation faded as he and everyone else realized that their predicament with the draugar would not be solved quite so easily. Brak discovered that worrying about the draugar was a welcome relief from worrying about Ingvold, and the ten days passed more quickly than he had once thought possible.

The answer he gave to Hjordis was a different one from what he had also thought possible ten days before. Skalgr and Kolssynir had nagged him into the realization that time might change the situation in their favor and that he could do nothing to Hjordis herself without the additional power of the helmet. Resignedly, he promised to be patient and refrain from any impulsive heroic actions that might jeopardize their future chances of rescuing Ingvold themselves.

Thus it was, when he again confronted Hjordis in her lair at the bottom of the cavern, that he said to her, "We choose to remain. We'll abide by your terms—on one condition."

"Condition?" Hjordis shifted so that she could glare at him loweringly. "Should I be obliged to listen to conditions? Daily I am becoming more convinced of my absolute power. Perhaps the Dokkalfar would rather have me for a leader after all. I could be very useful at battering down the walls of hill forts. But go ahead and state your condition, and I shall consider it."

"What arrogance," Brak muttered between his teeth to Kolssynir. To the rock troll he answered, "We'll assist your cause as far as we are able, with only one exception. We refuse to bear weapons against the Ljosalfar. When it comes to shedding blood, let your Dokkalfar earn the infamy for themselves."

Hjordis gave a snort. "It's of no consequence to me. If you lead the Dokkalfar, most of the infamy will be yours anyhow. However, I'm glad you decided to be sensible. You won't regret it, I assure you."

Skarnhrafn, roosting up above on the crag, amused himself throughout the interview with mutterings to himself and sepulchral chuckles. "You won't regret it, I assure you!" he mimicked. "The Scipling is assured of nothing but a treacherous death if he believes any assurances of yours. He'd be better off to join the draugar and be called Master than to be your slave today. I can get Ingvold out of that tomb any time you command it, Scipling."

"You witless lump of carrion," Hjordis growled. "If you get within my reach, you'll be nothing but dust in a very few moments. What is a pack of crumbling draugar compared with the Dokkalfar? Bah, get out of my sight!" She struck at Skarnhrafn as he dived at her from above.

Skalgr, who had insisted upon accompanying them on the provision that he wouldn't betray his presence to Hjordis, crept out of his hiding place and studied Skarnhrafn and Hjordis, his eyes glowing with anticipation. "Skarnhrafn! You're already beaten. There are no draugar for Brak to command, even if he wanted to. The Dokkalfar have destroyed them all."

Skarnhrafn greeted the news with an awful shriek, followed by groans and howls and the ripping out of several large tufts of matted hair or beard, which the fire devoured in a shower of bright sparks. Then he blasted Hjordis with fire until her scales glowed red-hot. Still she was undiscomfitted, roaring and slapping at him as he passed overhead.

"Destroyed! Destroyed! Years and years of the Master's work!" Skarnhrafn screamed. "I'll have my vengeance on you, Hjordis! All destroyed, all the beautiful draugar and Myrkriddir!"

"Not quite all," Skalgr said cunningly. "There are still enough draugar left to conquer Hjordisborg, if they had the proper leaders. It would be a most fitting revenge if you snatched Ingvold away from Hjordis. Brak, of course, would follow with Dyrstyggr's weapons—"

A terrifying roar from the rock troll sent him scuttling without bothering to finish. "You! It can be no other!" Hjordis thundered, making a lunge at Skalgr as he fled up the ramp, but he was safely out of her reach. Hjordis dragged down a huge armload of rocks instead of her intended quarry, who selected a perch high above and proceeded to exasperate Skarnhrafn into a frenzy for vengeance. The draug bathed Hjordis in orange flame until her stone scales were hotter than any forge. She bellowed and slapped at him as he circled above her.

Kolssynir seized Brak's arm and dragged him up the ramp. Pehr needed no encouraging. They ran upward at Skalgr's heels, dodging the frequent cascades of ice dislodged by Skarnhrafn's glancing eyes. The first shelter that offered itself was a large, crumbling tomb, and they tumbled inside without hesitation. Fortunately, it also provided them with an excellent view of the battle between Hjordis and Skarnhrafn.

"You fool," Kolssynir snapped to Skalgr. "What do you mean by inflaming them against each other? You might have got us all killed!"

Skalgr clutched a handful of Myrkjartan's cloak, hugging it in his arms and bursting out in fresh cackles and wheezes of mirth. "Oh, isn't it just too lovely? I can scarcely bear it! It's too much. How I wish—" But he went into a coughing fit before he could say what he wished, and no one really cared to pursue it.

Skarnhrafn's fire blasted Hjordis at greater intervals, as if he were beginning to realize the futility of attacking her impervious armor. With a last withering blast, he retreated to the top of his crag to peer down at his adversary. Hjordis gazed up at him steadily, waiting for his next swooping attack.

Skarnhrafn chuckled hoarsely. "Scipling, are you still there? I shall rescue your Ingvold, and you shall become the Master of the draugar and Myrkriddir. Myrkjartan gave me this plan. It is only fitting that I should enact it for the new Master. Are you watching, Scipling?"

Brak left the shelter of the tomb. "Skarnhrafn, are you sure you can do it without harming Ingvold?"

Skarnhrafn uttered a mirthful shriek. "It will be easy, Master Scipling, with no danger to the lady."

An answering rumble from the rock troll gave Brak cause to think otherwise. Skarnhrafn left his perch and flew higher, scathing the cliffs with his gaze. Rafts of ice plummeted from their moorings, jarring more ice and rocks loose to swell the tumbling mass to avalanche proportions. Brak gave a shout of alarm and dived back into the tomb. The roar of falling ice and rock filled the cavern until it seemed the entire excavation was collapsing. From what Brak could see through the dust and ice particles, all the ice on the galleries and cliffs and crags was falling into the blue fire, which leaped high and bright. Then it began to sink, until the entire pit was a well of darkness. The last of the ice crashed to the bottom; then silence reigned absolute.

Kolssynir lit his staff. They crept warily to the edge of their level and peered down into the darkness without seeing the bottom. Kolssynir discharged several fire bolts to illuminate the area, which was drastically altered by heaps of jagged rocks and blocks of ice. The blue fire was smothered under the avalanche, and presumably the rock troll also. Ingvold's tomb seemed undisturbed; the crag had protected it from most of the rockfall.

Skarnhrafn chuckled from above, his fiery gaze beaming before him as he floated downward like a large flake of soot to alight near Ingvold's tomb, exulting in the downfall of his enemy.

Warily Kolssynir led the way downward again, picking a difficult path over the loose stones and ice. Brak scarcely dared to hope that the rock troll could be defeated so easily. He hurried, ignoring Kolssynir's injunctions to be careful, leaping over the parapets of ice in reckless fashion until he came to the bottom. Skarnhrafn ceased his capering and jeering to salute him. As Brak reached Ingvold's tomb, small spears of blue flame began lapping feebly between the rocks. He clawed at the rocks sealing her tomb and discovered they were mortared together with ice. He summoned Skarnhrafn, who unvisored himself and melted the ice at a glance. Before they were cool enough to handle safely, Brak was tearing the rocks away, with Skarnhrafn hovering at his shoulder and cackling encouragement. The flames reached a little higher, appearing in more places. Kolssynir shouted angry warnings as he descended the rockslide at a more sensible speed, and Skalgr also screeched something about the helmet, which Brak also chose to ignore, knowing he could get it with only ordinary difficulties after he had freed Ingvold.

The stones blocking her tomb stubbornly resisted his efforts to drag them away, and the flames filled the bottom of the pit with their light. Skarnhrafn circled overhead anxiously as Kolssynir strode through the needles of blue fire.

"Brak, you've got to come out of here before the fire returns, or you'll be trapped!" he roared. "Those stones were put together by magic, and you haven't the power to tear them apart!"

Brak drew the sword and attacked the stones with it in helplesss fury. Kolssynir tried to drag him away before it was too late, but Skarnhrafn bounded from his roost on the crag and struck a threatening blow at the wizard with his rusty axe. Kolssynir leaped back in surprise, and Skarnhrafn lunged after him, snarling, "Get away with you and your interference! Let him be trapped by the flames and die, if he wishes. I will continue Myrkjartan's dream myself when I possess Dyrstyggr's weapons, without the nuisance of troublesome Sciplings and Alfar maidens. What harm do you think Dyrstyggr's cursed sword can do to me?" He laughed in his chilling, maniacal fashion and made another feint at Kolssynir.

Brak abandoned his useless scrabbling at the stones, more angry at his own credulity than at Skarnhrafn's duplicity. He hewed at the draug, driving him away from Kolssynir. Skarnhrafn paused to laugh derisively, situating himself between Brak and any retreat to safety. In that instant, the ice and rocks suddenly heaved almost at Brak's feet. The rock troll rose from the avalanche, shaking the ice and rocks from her back as if they were almost nothing to her, rising with a roar of terrible rage and lumbering through the fire that whitened her scales with ice. She ignored Brak, who took the opportunity and ran for cover with Kolssynir, leaping over the flames and dodging around their larger pillars as the fire gathered strength. With one mighty buffet she sent Skarnhrafn and his wraith horse spinning, screaming in terror as they took flight, with Skarnhrafn barely clinging to the wretched beast. The damage it had suffered from the rock troll suddenly became evident as it began to disintegrate in Skarnhrafn's grasp. They both plunged into the midst of the rising flames and ignited with a loud crackling, much like grease in a conventional hot flame. The fire tossed them aloft crazily, as if savoring a particularly combustible tidbit; then the remains of horse and draug fell gently in a sifting of large, dirty flakes of frost. One glided to a landing on Skalgr's cloak, which he beat away with desperate horror.

The rock troll watched the remains of Skarnhrafn raining down, making note of the place where the helmet fell with a rattling clank. Ignoring the flame frosting her scales with deadly ice, she ambled toward Ingvold's tomb for a look at the damage and returned to gaze at Brak, blinking her little, red eyes through barnacles of frost. They exchanged a long, intelligent look. Hjordis shuffled through the remains of Skarnhrafn until she found the helmet, whitened with frost. She held it awkwardly in her outsized paws. "I hope you have learned a lesson from this exercise. I am indestructible. There's nothing you can do to escape my power, unless you choose to let Ingvold die, which she will certainly do if you are not nearly to protect her. I am distressed by your apparent treachery with Skarnhrafn, but no harm has been done by it. Quite the contrary; I have gained the helmet with very little trouble. Don't look so downcast; it will one day be yours when I am certain you can be trusted with it. You may carry the news above to my Dokkalfar that Skarnhrafn is vanquished and that I am alive and stronger than before. No doubt that chattering magpie Skalgr will be glad to spread the gossip."

Skalgr peered cautiously from his hiding place. "If I might venture to add, I'd say that a protracted sojourn in your native element, the dark underground, has been most beneficial to your health and that you expect to rejoin your devoted subjects as soon as you regain your former strength."

Hjordis chuckled maliciously. "That sounds well, even coming from one such as you. And now, my gallant swordsman, I have some orders for you."

Brak raised his head to look at her. His customary stoic calm had overcome his ferocious disappointment, so he was able to present the outward appearance of unflinching composure. He sheathed the sword and folded his arms beneath the cloak as he waited for her orders. Pehr kept staring at his expression, which could only be described as flinty and somehow older than the face Pehr remembered from Thorstensstead. Brak looked decidedly fierce, Pehr realized, and wondered how he had failed to observe such a drastic change.

Hjordis took a moment to gather her thoughts. "I want you to destroy Miklborg before spring. Send couriers to all the chieftains who are obligated to me and bring them back to Hjordisborg for a council. Let the couriers carry the word that I have command of all Dyrstyggr's weapons now, and that Myrkjartan and Skarnhrafn are no longer of any consideration to the Dokkalfar. When all the chieftains are assembled here, you may return to me and ask for further instructions. I have nothing more to say to you until what I commanded is done."

"Then I will do my utmost," Brak said, with a parting glance at Ingvold's tomb. His voice was grim, and his manner was equally stern and unbending after their return to Hjordis' hall. As Hjordis had directed, Brak dispatched the messengers and announced the downfall of Myrkjartan and Skarnhrafn. He declared that he would be the spokesman for Hjordis until she returned, which was not to the liking of Tyrkell in the least. His expression became more sour and his slinking more pronounced, almost to the point of eavesdropping on everything said among Brak and his advisers. With grudging respect the Dokkalfar accepted their new leader, and the chieftains from the surrounding hill forts began arriving at Hjordisborg.

No one talked of anything but the coming assault of Miklborg. The short, gloomy days of early winter would soon decline into several months of almost perfect darkness, when the powers and ambitions of the Dokkalfar and every other creature of the dark would be at their apogee. As the days darkened to mere twilight, Brak's spirits correspondingly declined and his aspect became even more unfamiliar and forbidding. In his darkest thoughts he considered various desperate escape plans, hoping none of the grim Dokkalfar chieftains could read his mind. They looked at him with that mixture of awe and aversion reserved for turncoats of all types, eyeing him with their own opinions carefully veiled behind bristling black beards and drooping hoods.

As the fatal day for Miklborg's demise approached, Dokkalfar from all the hill forts obligated to Hjordis poured into Hjordisborg, which spoke well for Brak's powers of persuasion, but he found no satisfaction in it. Hjordis had told him the weak points of each chieftain and how to take advantage of them with subtle threats and effusive promises from Hjordis, until Brak began to loathe his position. With increasing gloom he watched the Dokkalfar practicing and planning while the nights lengthened. On the first daylong night uninterrupted by the briefest appearance of the sun, the Dokkalfar would attack and fight without ceasing until Miklborg was a hollow-eyed ruin and all its occupants dead or captive.

Still the Rhbus had given Brak no sign. His efforts earned him nothing but dizziness and a burning throat and mouth, and the visions merely tormented him with halfseen images and suggestions of ideas which he could make no sense of.

"I don't think you should distress yourself needlessly," Skalgr lectured to him, observing his dissatisfaction with the Rhbus. "If the Rhbus wanted to tell you just to remain where you are for a while, what better way than to simply ignore you? Come, they'll help you when the time arrives. Don't look so glum and bleak. No one has died yet, not a single arrow or spell has been flown, and here we are, well fed and safe from our enemies. While we're not exactly reposing in the bosom of our dearest friends and allies, we're far better off now than other times I can think of." Skalgr had grown almost glossy from stuffing himself at every opportunity, and a set of new clothes made him almost unrecognizable as the scruffy old villain who had begged for his supper one night south of Hagsbarrow. Nothing, however, could change his long, opportunistic nose and his avaricious eye, although his scroungy beard had grown out quite decently.

Brak did not reply to Skalgr's logic. He only sighed and shook his head, continuing to pace like a prisoner awaiting execution.

Skalgr sighed also and hitched himself a little closer to the path where Brak paced. "Every good purpose has its own time," he said earnestly. "You mustn't try to hurry it. I assure you, this waiting and delay is as irksome to me as it is to you."

"You're making the most of it, though," Brak said, giving Skalgr's ribs a pinch to emphasize how much new padding had grown thereon. Brak's brooding about Ingvold and Miklborg had rendered the remaining softness from his frame, much like snow melting away from a craggy mountain of granite. "I don't suppose I blame you. None of us would be here now if not for my stubbornness about Ingvold. I wonder if I shouldn't send you away from here before something happens to you, when Hjordis tires of tormenting me with Ingvold."

Pehr wearily renewed his oldest argument. "If you'd let me, I'd go to Miklborg for help. I've suggested it a hundred times."

"Well, consider it rejected a hundred and one times," Kolssynir replied testily. "What would you have them do, attack this place and hasten their destruction? If you want to make yourself useful, think of a way to get that helmet from Hjordis. Then we can go in search of Dyrstyggr and get him to free Ingvold by killing that monster."

Brak only shook his head. They had discussed the matter around and around, and he would never agree to deserting Ingvold long enough to find Dyrstyggr. At first they had collaborated fiercely to discover a plan to kill Hjordis and escape with Ingvold. But each subsequent visit to the rock troll's lair convinced them of the futility of their plans. She seemed to grow larger and more solid every day, until attacking her made as little sense as attacking a rocky mountainside. Skarnhrafn's swift death had shown them her deadly speed and strength, as well as the withering fury of the blue flames. They briefly considered lowering someone with ropes to Ingvold's tomb, but the effort would be too slow and cumbersome, not to mention the time it would take to chisel away the ice between the stones that sealed her up.

"Avalanches won't crush Hjordis," Brak said. "Swords can't touch her. Fire can't burn her. Haven't you got a spell for killing rock trolls, Kolssynir?"

"For the thousandth time, no. Haven't I explained to you that we wizards are by no means perfect?"

"And rock trolls are?" Pehr demanded.

Kolssynir looked at his satchel and staff in distaste. "It's hard to improve upon solid rock, my boy. I've never felt so useless in all my life."

Skalgr nudged Brak sympathetically. "Don't be discouraged. Just be patient. All we need is Dyrstyggr's helmet and the Rhbus will listen to us again."

Brak hardly heard him. "It's time we went below to see Hjordis. Someone tell that renegade Tyrkell to guard the hall while we're gone."

The winding journey downward never ceased to chill them to their hearts. Brak thought about Dyrstyggr on the way down, wondering how much old Skalgr really knew about him, and if aid could come from that unknown quarter. Skalgr was unhelpful on the subject, saying only that Dyrstyggr was yet a long way off. Brak touched the little case containing the heart. He hadn't appealed to the Rhbus at all lately, after two unpleasant disappointments. When no one was watching, he removed a small thread of the meat and began to chew it. By the time they reached the lair of Hjordis, his knees were weak and his mouth was inflamed. He silently presented himself to Hjordis, looking into her small red eyes as if they were two seeing globes. She looked back at him with suspicion and considerable fear.

"The sphere again, I suppose," she greeted him. On each visit Brak asked to see Ingvold in the globe, sleeping peacefully in her tomb. The enormous paws of the rock troll would proffer him the fragile glass sphere, and each time he would study it until Hjordis became impatient and took it away. Each time he feared the glass would shatter in her granite hand, but she always managed to place it on a high ledge in the stone without breaking it.

Brak stared into the sphere, sternly quelling the trembling in his limbs and the blurring of his vision. If he could see Ingvold and call upon the Rhbus at the same time, they might hear his plea and decide to help him.

The clouds in the sphere cleared away, showing him a small stone cell and a stone shelf for a resting place, but Ingvold was not sleeping upon it. He saw a figure crouching discontentedly in a corner, glaring at him with all the frenzy and hatred of a fox with one foot in a trap. With a wild lunge the ragged creature sprang at him, mouthing unheard curses, eyes blazing as he fell flat at the end of a chain tether. He lunged up again, foaming and raving, before the mists obscured him once more, and the immense black claws of Hjordis plucked the globe from Brak's fingers.

"You see she's quite all right," Hjordis rumbled. "When she is awakened depends upon you. The time is not far distant, I hope?"

Brak blinked, still seeing the image in the glass. "No, not far," he heard himself answer distantly. He was certain the shaggy old wretch struggling with his chain was either a vision of himself in years to come or Myrkjartan, still alive and being kept as Hjordis' prisoner.

Chapter 22

◇◇◇◇◇◇◇◇◇◇◇◇◇◇◇◇◇◇◇◇◇◇◇◇◇

"Myrkjartan, still alive?" Kolssynir whispered incredulously when they had returned to the hall. "But that's unbelievable, after what we saw. What purpose could she have in mind in keeping him alive?"

"She has more possibilities for him if he's alive," Skalgr said. "Or perhaps she enjoys keeping him captive, like a wolf on a chain."

"If it really is Myrkjartan," Pehr added worriedly. "If the image Brak saw is himself in years to come, that sort of development doesn't auger well for the next heir of Thorstensstead. My father would never know my miserable fate."

Brak paced up and down, glancing at the sword and cloak where they lay on the table, and at the small case containing the heart in his hand. He knew the tunnels under Hjordisborg were virtually stuffed with Dokkalfar waiting to attack Miklborg. The first dayless night was only a matter of half a dozen weak final appearances of the fading sun; it rose briefly at midday and lost no time in sinking away again into oblivion. The Dokkalfar established camps and outposts in preparation for their attack, scarcely bothering to avoid such a contemptible sun. All that remained to be done was for him to appear wearing the cloak and bearing the sword, and the Dokkalfar would sweep forward to the attack, eager for vengeance and destruction. Even without Brak to lead them, they were a formidable force with excellent chances of defeating the men of Miklborg, who might not be so well prepared, although they couldn't help knowing of the arrival of large numbers of Dokkalfar from the surrounding Dokkalfar enclaves.

Brak spent the last days restlessly pacing or brooding, and gazing in despair at the fading sun. When it at last failed to show itself over the horizon, he knew the time had arrived. Amid tumults and exultations the Dokkalfar saddled their horses and began the marches to take up their positions. Brak and his friends delayed, accompanied by the ever lowering Tyrkell, who had sharpened all his weapons ten times in the past six days. Tyrkell grumbled impatiently as Brak sat brooding over his awful charge, watching long, dark lines of horsemen, warriors, and fylgurwolves loping away under the sheaves of brilliant winter stars.

"It's time we were off," Tyrkell said. "Our horses have been waiting for hours, and the chieftains who were going to ride out with you gave up waiting and left long ago, so you won't have much of a procession when you do finally decide to go. Just the five of us," he added with a snort. "I only hope no one starts the rumor that you're afraid."

Brak stood up, shaking out the cloak impatiently. "I'm going below to see Hjordis again," he said. "The rest of you may start ahead of me if you wish, and I'll catch up to you after I've talked to Hjordis."

Kolssynir scowled. "What do you want to see Hjordis for? We've been down there almost every day for the last six days. We've gone over her plans a hundred times, and everyone from the chief warlords down to the least potboys are out there bristling with arrows and lances and swords. What more could you have to say to her?"

Brak made no answer, except a scowl of his own. Skalgr grabbed up his cloak and fastened it hastily as he followed

Brak toward the door to the tombs. "You're going to ask her again for the helmet, aren't you? I admire your perseverance, Brak, although I doubt that she's changed her mind."

"Changed her mind? Not likely!" Pehr exclaimed. "She was furious last time when you asked. Don't be a fool, Brak. I wouldn't ask her for it again for any amount of money. You don't really intend to drag us all down there again, do you? Hjordis puts me so far out of spirits it takes me two days to recover, and that's no frame of mind for battle."

"I'll go with you," Skalgr said. "I find Hjordis rather entertaining when she's in a fury."

"I'm going alone," Brak said. "I want the rest of you to ride ahead. You can wait for me on Baldknip. Now that the sun no longer rises, a matter of a few hours will make no difference to the execution of our plans. Tyrkell, you can go farther ahead and carry the word that I'm on the way—with or without the helmet. Kolssynir, I'll leave it to you to keep Pehr and Skalgr out of the path of the fighting. Baldknip is the safest place for you, and you ought to have a good view of the glorious Dokkalfar attacking Miklborg."

"I'll stay with you," Skalgr insisted, darting around Tyrkell, who was distributing his weapons, sheaths, and quivers about his bulky person with grim satisfaction. "Brak, you shouldn't go down into that horrid place alone. You might get injured or—"

Tyrkell collared him and gave him a shove toward the outer doors. "What use would you be to anybody, you old, dried stick? Get your weapons together, if you dare use any, and we'll all have the pleasure of one another's company as far as Baldknip."

Kolssynir dressed against the cold and hung his weapons on his belt, watching Brak uneasily all the while. "You won't be long, will you? If you take above three hours, I'm coming back for you."

"Enough talk," Tyrkell said roughly, half hauling Skalgr to the door with him. "When there are battles for fighting, it's no time for idle chitchat. If you weren't such dolts, you'd know that he only wants a last squint at his precious Ingvold before he goes off to fight. Perhaps it will strengthen his courage—I certainly hope so."

Brak turned quickly, putting his hand on the sword, but Tyrkell read his expression instantly and whisked himself out of Brak's reach by diving through the open door, which gave Pehr an excuse to jeer as they rode away, abusing Tyrkell for his stupidity.

Brak barred the door and sat down at the table to stare into the tallowy flame of the lamp. Slowly he chewed a small shred of the dragon's heart. If the Rhbus did not want Miklborg destroyed, this was their last chance to help him. He stared at the flames, his vision blurring, and he saw the image of Skarnhrafn's helmet where it rested in the midst of the blue flames on a cairn of stone which Hjordis had piled up to remind herself of the death of Skarnhrafn. The flames lapped at it and feathered it with frost, winking through the grim visor which had once contained the fiery fury of Skarnhrafn's gaze. What use was the helmet against Hjordis, Brak wondered irritably, when its powers couldn't harm her rocky scales—even supposing his own gaze would be turned to fire, which he could not imagine under any circumstances. This was supposing, of course, that he could somehow snatch the helmet from its icy cairn and bring himself to put it on. He shook his head and rubbed his eyes to clear them of the image of the helmet. When he looked up again, he saw across the table from him a dark figure which he took for that of one of the servants who kept Hjordis' hall in readiness for her imagined return.

"There's nothing more to be done tonight," he said. "You can go watch from the walls, where everyone else is watching the departure of the armies." He kept his eyes hidden, not wanting a servant to see how strange they looked when the dragon meat was working.

"But I wouldn't like to leave you alone now," a familiar voice replied, and Gull-skeggi sat down on the opposite side of the table, facing him over the smoke and glare of the tallow lamp.

"Where have you been?" Brak demanded, half laughing, half angry, with relief and exasperation. "You can't imagine how I looked for you and how I waited, wondering if anything could be done to put a stop to this entire wicked twist of fate. But now—why didn't you appear sooner? It's too late now for Miklborg, and Hjordis—"

Gull-skeggi lifted one hand and shook his head gently. "I've always been here, quite close to you, disguised in this old cloak to look like one of the servants. While you were pacing and fretting, I was hauling your firewood or feeding your horse. I have watched you with great care, and the changes in you are wonderful. You haven't really required my assistance, but you are aware of that."

"Am I?" Brak said, astonished and indignant. "What am I to do about Hjordis? Fire won't touch her, nothing can smash her, and a sword would break against her—why, I defy even the Rhbus to think of something more powerful than she is. You're supposed to know everything, so why can't you tell me what it will take to kill Hjordis and free Ingvold?"

"I can, and I will," Gull-skeggi said, "but you already know it yourself. You possess all of Dyrstyggr's weapons but one."

"The helmet? What good is that to me? I can't throw fire by just looking; I don't have the powers Skarnhrafn once had." Brak rose to stalk back and forth.

"But the helmet's absence gnaws at you, doesn't it? Don't you feel somehow incomplete without it? Even as useless as it seems to you, you know you must go after it and get it from Hjordis somehow; otherwise, would you be here now, working up the courage to confront her once more and demand it from her?"

Brak sat down gloomily. "I'd told myself I was going to say farewell to Ingvold. That idea makes more sense than angering Hjordis again. I've asked her for it twice, and she refuses to give it to me. If I go down there and make an attempt to seize it, I'm sure I'm going to be killed, which is perhaps the best plan after all. I only regret the loss of good Alfar men defending Miklborg—and Ingvold, of course. Perhaps she—we'll be together soon enough, I suppose, once Hjordis realizes there's no sense in keeping her alive any longer."

"Together in death. I'd rather see you together in life," Gull-skeggi said with a sigh and a shake of his head.

"Then do something!" Brak flared. "If you really care about us or about Miklborg and the Alfar, tell me how to kill Hjordis!"

Gull-skeggi spread out his hands imploringly. "I can't

tell you what you already know—what you must know—or all our careful plans will come to naught. The Rhbus will have made a dreadful mistake, and the Rhbus simply never make mistakes. You Sciplings have a curious tendency to struggle against your own knowledge, and that has made this endeavor a most ticklish one for us. You can't begin to know how we've worried over you. An Alfar does what he knows he must do, no matter how senseless it may seem, and all is ultimately well, no matter how long it takes for the consequences and results to sort themselves out in a sensible fashion. But you Sciplings are stubborn and headlong creatures. You are like the rocks rending the smooth currents of a river, certain your destiny has nothing to do with that of anybody else. You have such a great and solemn sense of your own importance that you are almost unable to move. You must decide, Brak, whether to wait any longer or to do what your conscience tells you."

"It still makes no sense, but I'll try for the helmet. No, I'll get the helmet and you'll see how useless it is," he added in a bitter tone.

Gull-skeggi silently accepted his challenge and followed him into the cold darkness and the death and decay of the rows of tombs, the arches and galleries of the old mines, and the deathless flicker of the blue flame below.

Brak looked back at Gull-skeggi many times before he reached the bottom of the pit. When Hjordis heard their approach, she crawled from her lair and reared to her full height beside the fire with a heavy grinding and creaking of her massive scales. Brak glanced back at Gull-skeggi with an ironic smile to make certain the Rhbus understood the impossibility of the task before him. Gull-skeggi looked gravely at Hjordis and motioned Brak to continue onward, and he followed at Brak's heels, pegging each step with his staff.

When they came into view of Skarnhrafn's helmet on the cairn, Gull-skeggi stopped. "I shall go no farther with you," he said, "but you won't be needing any help, now that you've come this far."

"Perhaps not," Brak answered, dividing his attention between Hjordis and the cairn with Skarnhrafn's helmet. He knew how fast she could move when she wanted to, and wondered if a sudden rush for the helmet would confuse her long enough for him to escape with it.

"I thought you would be back," Hjordis rumbled. "You've come to demand the helmet again, haven't you?"

"No. I've come to take it." He made no move toward it, keeping his eyes fixed on Hjordis.

"I won't let you have it. Not now, possibly not ever."

"You're afraid of what might happen if I get it, aren't you?" Brak advanced a step closer to the cairn, and Hjordis also creaked a bit closer. It stood between them, slightly closer to Brak. He took another step, and so did she, grinding the ice underneath her.

"You're not a Skarnhrafn," she said. "Your gaze won't be fire. You've seen how little fire affects me. You can't hope to be more powerful."

"I don't," Brak replied, taking another step.

"Then the Rhbus must have told you something. What a nithling you'd be if not for their interference. You couldn't have done anything on your own. Where have you been hiding them?" She gazed around the great cavern without seeing Gull-skeggi in the shadows nearby.

"You don't see anyone else here, do you?" Brak came closer, almost to the foot of the cairn. The helmet was just out of arm's reach. He would have to make a short scramble for it.

"Wait. I thought you were reasonably content with your power over the Dokkalfar. Is it more power you want? I can arrange to have you taught in the Dokkalfar method of magic. There are spells for extending one's life span. You could live forever if you wanted to, instead of growing old and dying so soon, as you Sciplings usually do."

Brak shook his head. "I don't want any more of your promises. Each promise of yours is wrapped in lies. I've seen the wretched creature chained to the wall, and whether it is myself or not, I no longer wish to submit to your tyranny."

Hjordis responded with a roar and a lunge, aiming a deadly crushing blow with one massive paw. Brak sidestepped and dived around the cairn to use it for protection while he scrambled up its slippery boulders. With the end of his sword he hooked the helmet down from its perch, aware of the blue flames whitening the fabric of Dyrstyggr's cloak. As he leaped down from the cairn, Hjordis slapped at the helmet and struck it away among the rocks and ice with a resounding clamor. Brak dodged her again and leaped in the direction of the helmet. He managed to pick it up, but it was so fearfully cold that his hands were instantly seared and he dropped it quickly, as if it were scorching hot. Hjordis lumbered after him, so he gave the helmet a kick to keep it out of her reach, which also diverted her from striking another blow at him. She scooped up the helmet in her claws with a triumphant roar, but Brak came after her, using Skalgr's old trick of running up her back as if she were a large mound of rocks. He had time only to deal her a single ringing chop with his sword before she shook him off and whirled around. He struck the helmet out of her grasp; for an instant, he thought he would be crushed as she lunged after it, nearly grinding him against the surrounding rocks. Nimbly he climbed up her scales, finding easy handholds among the rough stones that formed her armor. She bellowed in fury and tried to shake him off or crush him again, but he scrambled down her other side, prepared to knock the helmet out of her claws again. She seemed to have forgotten it for a while in her rage against him. She charged at him, lashing her tail from side to side to discourage another attack on her back. In the bright light of the fire he saw a spreading black stain oozing down what could be called her shoulders, and his own hands were sticky. It had to be blood. For an instant, he thought he somehow was wounded, but his alarm turned swiftly to savage glee. He had discovered a weak place in her seemingly impervious armor, and it must be in the region of the back of her neck. His suspicions were confirmed by the way she furiously defended her back from him now, sidling around to keep it to the fire or against the wall. She hissed and snarled at him in greater fury, as if knowing he had guessed her weakness. The helmet lay forgotten, occasionally swept out of the way by a powerful stroke of her lashing tail. She would have retreated into the fire, where Brak could not get at her, but he had managed to back her into a small blind gallery and barred her escape to her lair. With short rushes she tested his resolve to stand his ground against her, but each time she placed her forepaws on the earth for a charge, she opened her back to attack. Twice Brak seized a handhold and dealt battering blows to the back of her skull and neck, one of which was telling. Her shriek echoed from the cliffs and galleries above, and her convulsive plunging shook Brak off as if he were a gnat. He scuttled to safety to watch for a moment as she writhed and clawed the ground, unable to rise. Seizing the opportunity, he darted in again, avoiding her raking claws. He leaped over her tail, which could only twitch and shudder; he climbed up her back, slipping in the gore, and rammed the sword underneath the overlapping scales on the back of her neck into flesh instead of stone. It was only a small area where one rocky scale allowed a gap in her armor by not fitting properly, but it was enough to ensure her doom. Slowly she sank into a heap, gasping for breath and regarding Brak with her small red eyes. As their light dimmed, the blue flames began to sink.

"Hjordis! You can't die without telling me how to release Ingvold from your spell!" Brak exclaimed, coming as close to her face as he dared. "Hjordis! Can you speak?"

Her eyes flickered a little. She wheezed, trying to speak. "I was the last of my father's line. The flame dies with me." The light in her eyes became unfocused and faded away.

Brak knew death when he saw it. He turned to look for Gull-skeggi, who was descending the pathway with his lighted staff in hand. By the time they met, the light of the blue flames had faded to a few pale embers fluttering in the frost. Gull-skeggi held his staff aloft to look at Hjordis for a moment, but Brak tugged him away impatiently toward Ingvold's prison. The blocks of stone came away grudgingly as he worked frantically at them. Before he had forced an entry, he heard a faint cry on the other side of the stones.

"Ingvold!" he shouted, awakening the echoes in a derisive chant.

"You'd better let me help you," Gull-skeggi said, wedging his staff into a crack. He turned up his embroidered sleeves and pushed and pulled at the rocks alongside Brak until an opening was made, with Ingvold shoving from the other side with all her might. Laughing, crying, and shivering, she wriggled through the small hole and flung her arms around Brak's neck and kissed him, too, but he wasn't quite sure he hadn't imagined it.

"Faithful Brak! I knew you'd be here!" she exclaimed. "You are real, aren't you, and not another dream?"

"I'd be a nightmare if I were," he said, aware that he was smeared with blood from Hjordis and very muddy from opening the tomb. "Look at you shiver; Hjordis didn't bury you properly—with a cloak and warm boots. I'd be insulted, but she's dead—quite dead." He looked around in the dark suddenly, thinking he had heard the rattling of a chain echoing his words. "It's time we got out of here. Gull-skeggi, you go behind with the light, and I'll carry Ingvold."

"You'll get tired," Ingvold protested as he picked her up and wrapped her in the folds of the cloak, still shivering.

"Nonsense. It will be much quicker and easier this way. Gull-skeggi, you'll have to walk a little faster than that if you're to keep up with us." He strode over the former bed of the blue flames, his foot striking something metal as he passed.

"The helmet," Gull-skeggi called, stopping to pick it up. "I shall carry it for you."

The clatter of the helmet made Brak think of chains rattling. He walked a little faster, scarcely minding Ingvold's weight in his arms. If the cloak had any power in it, it must have added to his strength. He climbed the spirals of the huge cavern and passed the side tunnel where he had first seen Hjordis as the rock troll; he passed all the tombs of her crumbling ancestors, fitfully illuminated by Gull-skeggi's staff, and did not stop until the door to the tombs was securely barred behind them and a table shoved against it for good measure.

Gull-skeggi poked up the fire into a cheery blaze and sat down to look at Ingvold, who was still wrapped in Myrkjartan's cloak. She suddenly recognized it and turned pale, and paler still when Brak gave the helmet a careless nudge with his foot to move it as he returned from Hjordis' rooms with an armful of boots, cloaks, gowns, and anything else that looked useful and portable.

"I don't know which of these you'll want," he said, dropping the lot beside her on a bench. "Dress warmly. We'll be riding fast and far tonight. Kolssynir, Pehr, and Skalgr are waiting for us on a hill about two miles from here— will you please hurry, Ingvold? This will be our only chance to escape and save a few lives from Miklborg."

Ingvold had knelt beside Skarnhrafn's helmet, turning it over gingerly, half expecting to see a dusty draug head leering out at her.

"Well, then, that takes care of Skarnhrafn. What about Hjordis? Is she dead, too?" Ingvold quickly pulled on a pair of Hjordis' boots and leggings, her eyes on the sword at Brak's belt.

"She is dead," Gull-skeggi replied, assisting her with a cloak.

"And who are you, by the way? You've been very helpful. Are you coming with us?" she asked.

"We'll tell you everything as we travel," Brak said. "He's Gull-skeggi, one of the Rhbus. I hope there are horses for all of us. Here are some of her weapons for you; I hope we won't need them, but since coming to this realm, I've learned to expect the worst at every turn. Are we ready now? Come, let's go, then."

A hurried search of the stable revealed that, besides Hjordis' Dokkalfar charger, only old Faxi remained as the last able-bodied horse in Hjordisborg. Brak saddled him and tossed Ingvold onto his back. "We'll have to double up," he said to Gull-skeggi, but the Rhbu smiled gently and shook his head.

"You'll be going on alone," he said. "But I'll be watching you until the final steps in our plan have been executed. You've done extremely well so far, Brak, but you mustn't leave without this." He held up the helmet.

Brak took it and fastened it to his saddle. "You were right about its being the key to Hjordis' doom. What would have happened if I had put it on?"

Gull-skeggi looked thoughtful. "It's very fine workmanship, but I doubt you would have noticed anything except that it might be rather more difficult to breathe inside such a contraption. Skarnhrafn, you must know, had his eyes long before he ever wore this helmet. Now I've delayed you long enough. Farewell, dear friends, farewell!"

They let themselves out the main gate, under the astonished eyes of the two gatekeepers. "It's the queen!" one hissed to the other. "Isn't this going to be a lift to everyone's spirits!"

Without pausing, they urged their horses forward at a gallop through the chopped and dirty snow, where the armies had marched. Faxi extended himself and ran as if his heart were in every stride, keeping his head down to watch his footing, and his ears flattened in utmost concentration. By the time Baldknip came into view, vapor poured in clouds from the horses' steaming hides, but Faxi never offered to slacken the pace.

Three riders came down to meet them, slowly at first, then charging forward in a wild rush. They clustered together for an excited greeting, which was not without emotion, since old Skalgr couldn't seem to stop dripping tears on every hand he shook.

Their plan was to cut around behind the waiting troops, taking the long way to the north side of Miklborg, where they had a good chance of approaching the hill fort unseen by the Dokkalfar. However, as they advanced, they couldn't help meeting up with small groups of Dokkalfar, and several times they rode through camps because there was simply no other way around. The word of Hjordis' return electrified the Dokkalfar, although most kept a respectful distance as she passed. Those who did approach got near enough only to see a white-cloaked figure, and a very clear view of Brak scowling at them and commanding them to wait until he had given the signal. The deception worked so well that they proceeded in a more direct line toward the front and congratulated themselves on their success, until they encountered the group of warriors that included Tyrkell. After giving his orders, Brak led his friends away, but he looked back to see Tyrkell staring after him.

"Do you think he suspects something?" Brak whispered to Kolssynir.

"Let him suspect whatever he wants," Kolssynir snapped. "He knows you have the right to change your mind about leaving us on Baldknip. What concerns me more is three days of pitch-blackness between us and Miklborg, strewn with hundreds of battle-anxious Dokkalfar and I don't know what manner of cliffs and crevices. It's a mercy we've studied enough maps in the past month to find it almost in our sleep, but it's confounded dangerous."

After pausing a moment to allow him to examine the directions with a ley pendulum and squint at the stars with the assistance of some curious instruments, they forged through the snow steadily, with several halts to find the ley-line. They passed the foremost of the camps, where the Dokkalfar and their horses were ready to plunge forward at a word from Brak. Waiting any longer was a grievous disappointment to them, and they muttered their dissatisfaction.

All the shadows seemed alive. Brak strained his ears, listening for sounds of pursuit, but all he heard was the heavy breathing of the horses, the creak of leather, and the hiss and squeak of the snow as their hooves plowed through it. He glanced often at Ingvold, hunched in her saddle, and she, too, was listening.

Skalgr, riding ahead and to one side, suddenly halted and raised a warning hand for a moment, which soon lowered itself to point to the south. Parallel to their course, a long, moving line bobbed in and out of the stunted trees, soundlessly passing their position and disappearing into the shadows of the fells.

"Fylgur-wolves!" Brak exclaimed grimly, loosening the sword in its sheath. "It must have been Tyrkell who set them off. I had a feeling he knew something was amiss."

Skalgr's voice trembled as he spoke. "I haven't come this far to be thwarted by some hairy-faced son of a she-wolf! He'd better not get in my way now, or he'll regret it most bitterly."

"Tyrkell has waited for this moment a long time," Kolssynir said. "I'll bet my satchel and staff it's pure jealousy."

Chapter 23

❖❖❖❖❖❖❖❖❖❖❖❖❖❖❖❖❖❖❖❖❖❖❖❖

They urged more speed from the tiring horses. Suddenly, directly ahead, a wild howl pierced the brittle night. At once Kolssynir halted to listen, but all they heard was the labored puffing of the horses. Quickly he dismounted to test the ley-line. Without a word he remounted and set off at a faster rate than before, altering their course slightly to the north.

Another fierce, exultant cry echoed behind them. Brak glanced back and saw more fylgur-wolves padding along in single file on the trail of their quarry with no attempt at concealment.

"I'm sure we'll be using them presently," Kolssynir called a halt. Skalgr gasped, "The beasts are all around us! We can't escape!"

"Don't be absurd," Ingvold retorted. "We've got Brak to defend us with Dyrstyggr's weapons."

"I'm sure we'll be using them presently," Kolssynir added. "I never thought I'd see the day when I'd be in the protection of any thrall of mine. Be on your guard, everyone, and when we're attacked, keep close together. Solitary prey is easy prey for wolves."

The howling occurred at closer intervals. Skalgr crowded as near to Brak as he could get, glancing often at the sword which Brak was carrying across the pommel of his saddle and reassuring himself by frequently rubbing a fold of the cloak between his fingers.

"Dyrstyggr's revenge has carried us this far," he muttered. "It will carry us to Miklborg and safety if we have to carve a trail through a forest of fylgur-wolves."

As the steaming horses plunged down a steep hillside, wild-eyed and snorting at the smell of wolf, Ingvold shouted the first alarm as a dozen wolves suddenly appeared almost under the horses' noses, snapping and snarling. Others dived for the horses' heels, and more leaped at the riders in a concerted effort to drag them down. Pehr's horse slipped and fell with a scream of terror. Brak brought his horse under control with a yank on its iron jaw and a smart rap between the ears; then he began scything at the wolves with Dyrstyggr's sword. Several perished in wizard flame, dashing away like torches to roll uselessly in the snow, bursting into flame anew each time the flames seemed to be out. The sword made short work of many others, dyeing the snow black with their blood. Dyrstyggr's revenge burned as hotly as ever. The wolves took to their heels, what few were able to flee. Brak plunged after them and cut one down; wizard fire caught another, reducing their number by half.

Pehr's horse was bleeding but not hamstrung, so they collected themselves and rode on at a fast pace toward Miklborg. Its distant lights twinkled invitingly, seeming impossibly far away. On all sides, the gaunt black shapes of fylgur-wolves lurked, peering at the riders with glowing red eyes and disappearing into the shadows and crevices. Their howling took on a note of rage that made Brak wish for strong walls and stout doors between themselves and the vengeful Dokkalfar. He kept Ingvold and Faxi close to him, hoping to stand between her and the wolves when they attacked again.

Silent and swift, the wolves gathered around them, gradually closing like a great net and bringing their quarry to a halt on a windswept knob of hillside. The horses stood with their heads down, their ribs heaving and steaming. Not far beyond waited the circle of fylgur-wolves, taut with impatience and the lust for blood.

Kolssynir commanded everyone to dismount and take shelter in an inadequate jumble of boulders at their backs. Brak spared Faxi a brief pat before he pushed him away, knowing this would probably mean the death of all the horses. He took his stance with his friends and waited, weapons ready, while the wolves milled around, snarling and snapping just out of sword reach. They kept a healthy distance from Brak, who had put on the helmet to intimidate them, hoping they wouldn't have the wit to realize its marvelous fiery powers had perished with Skarnhrafn.

The Dokkalfar never observed any deficiency; the instant Brak raised the visor for a breath of air, Kolssynir blasted them with fire, abandoning his sword for wholesale fire wizardry, summoning up walls of flame, fire bolts, and showers of fiery daggers and other flaming torments to baffle the fylgur-wolves. Several hurled themselves through the flames to die on the points of swords or from the axe Ingvold wielded. After a brief and costly encounter, the wolves retreated over the carcasses of their dead and dying companions. They conferred together as no natural wolves would do, and it was then that Brak noticed that some of them had restored their forms to those of men, probably for the final encounter.

With greater caution, the wolves crept forward on their bellies, baring their teeth in horrid, snarling grins and halting to snap and howl and whine. Taking care to stay out of sword range, they harried and skirmished relentlessly, but Brak immediately saw that they were only offering diversion from the other Dokkalfar creeping closer with their swords and axes. Pehr proved that he was not deceived by shooting a few warning arrows among the Dokkalfar to send them scuttling for cover. Kolssynir's attention was also on the Dokkalfar when a single wolf darted forward, head low; instead of leaping high for a throat-hold as the other wolves had been doing, he dived in low and fastened his teeth in Brak's leg below the hem of Myrkjartan's cloak. Thrown off balance by the sudden pain and shock, Brak staggered and fell, shouting a warning and flailing around desperately with the sword. A flurry of snapping fangs and raking paws overwhelmed him. Hands tore away the cloak and the helmet and the heart around his neck. A heavy blow on his head made the stars swim, and the moment his hand relaxed its grip, the sword was snatched away also. Throughout, he heard the wild yelling of Skalgr.

Once the Dokkalfar possessed Dyrstyggr's weapons, the rest of the battle ended quickly. The wolves vanished, replaced by scowling Dokkalfar surrounding their captives with a fence of sharp swords and axes. Ingvold knelt beside Brak, anxiously examining him for signs of life, and

Pehr and Kolssynir stood over them, making menacing gestures with their swords at the Dokkalfar. When Brak's vision cleared and he was able to rise to a shaky crouch, the first object he saw was the hairy countenance of Tyrkell, illuminated by a guttering torch that caused his twisted face to writhe with squints and scowls.

"I wasn't fooled by your tricks," Tyrkell growled, with a sidelong glance at Ingvold. "I know the way Hjordis sits a horse, and I also know there's no such speedy recovery from a curse like hers. So I knew it had to be the Alfar chieftain's daughter and that you had used some sort of treachery to steal her away. Perhaps you even killed Hjordis. However it was, I've thought for a long time that having a Scipling lead the Dokkalfar to battle was a shame, when there are other loyal Dokkalfar that Hjordis ought to have chosen and given more recognition to. As you see, the leadership of the Dokkalfar shall soon change, now that I possess the weapons of Dyrstyggr. No one will dare dispute it."

Brak shook his head doggedly. "You're a fool, Tyrkell. If you knew the curse on that sword, you'd die before you'd touch it. You never knew what it did to Hjordis. Do you remember that beast that killed Myrkjartan?"

"Stop, I don't want to hear another of your treacherous words. I wouldn't lend them a moment's truth. I don't intend to waste any time with you, not when I'm about to lead our armies against Miklborg. It's a pity you won't be alive to see the glory I shall receive. I ought to thank you for your destruction of Myrkjartan and Hjordis and Skarnhrafn, which will only benefit me." He motioned, and the waiting Dokkalfar readied their swords.

"Just a moment, Tyrkell," Kolssynir said, stepping forward. "You're not a fit leader. All you're good for is second in command to someone like Hjordis or Myrkjartan. You're simply too common and dull to be the leader of anything, except maybe a small band of thieves. I assure you, as an adept fire wizard, that it will be costly in terms of your men to kill us. Look how many of your friends and kinsmen you've lost already. Good chieftains and warlords don't like to lead their neighbors, friends, and relatives to slaughter. It causes very bad feelings among the survivors, and the person they will blame is you. There's too much of the berserkr about you for you to last long as a leader, Tyrkell."

Tyrkell glowered. "The Dokkalfar will follow anyone with Dyrstyggr's weapons, or they'll be dead Dokkalfar. You can spare your arrogant speech, wizard, because I'm resolved on the course I've chosen, and nothing shall stand in my way." He stepped back. "You can defend yourselves for as long as you wish, but in the end we'll kill you."

He gave his men their instructions—no one was to be spared. They began circling and feinting. Kolssynir handed his axe to Brak, and the four of them put their backs together.

"Skalgr is missing," Brak said without lowering his guard. "Was he killed?"

"No, the wretched coward," Pehr growled. "He ran away to save his own neck and took the last good horse with him. Your Faxi survived, only to be stolen by a mincing, slinking, lying, thieving—" He angrily bent back a swift sword thrust, wounding the Dokkalfar superficially besides.

The Dokkalfar closed upon them in deadly earnest, and the massacre would have been swift and sure if not for Kolssynir's extraordinary spells. He conjured fiery clouds to hail their assailants with hot, blinding sparks, driving them back twice, much to the fury of Tyrkell.

"Where's Bjorn? Bring me the helmet and sword!" Tyrkell bellowed in a fury. "I'll use their own powers on them, and I'll do the job myself, you nithlings! Bjorn! Answer at once!"

The Dokkalfar fighters began peering around in uneasy surprise when no Bjorn was forthcoming. Tyrkell strode through them, roaring for Bjorn.

"I saw him riding away not long ago," someone ventured, taking care not to get too close to Tyrkell, whose rage might easily overtake any bearer of bad news.

Tyrkell clenched his powerful fists and glowered from side to side like a savage wolf deciding which throat to tear out first. Then, with a roar of uncontrolled fury, he hurled off his own helmet and buried his hands in his hair as if he wanted to tear it out by the handful, adding several more bellows and shrieks of passion.

"Then Bjorn has stolen the weapons of Dyrstyggr?" A

burly Dokkalfar dressed as chieftain stalked forward to confront Tyrkell. "You promised me rewards if I called my men to follow you in this wild scheme. Now you've lost the weapons, and I've lost so many men that I won't dare go home again. How are you going to repay me, Tyrkell, and the families of these dead men?"

Tyrkell whirled around, his eyes narrowing vindictively, as the men began to mutter and put up their swords. "You can't desert me now, you cowards. Bjorn is one of yours, so you must find him and bring him back to me. If you think to acquire Dyrstyggr's weapons by this trick, you're fools. Fools!" he added in a screech as the chieftain contemptuously turned his back and strode away, calling to his men, whose departure reduced the number of Tyrkell's followers to far less than half. Enough remained, however, to prevent any hope in the hearts of the captives.

"Fools!" Tyrkell thundered again, when they were safely gone.

"Who's a fool?" a voice demanded sternly from the shadows of the rocky hillside. A lone horseman rode forward, lashing the sunken flanks of a limping, exhausted horse. He dismounted as the poor beast stumbled, nearly collapsing. The stranger bent a long look at Tyrkell's captives before turning to Tyrkell. "You're the great fool!" he cried, thrusting Tyrkell aside. "You lost Dyrstyggr's weapons! You entrusted them to an avaricious rogue similar to yourself and he absconded with them, right from under your nose. You might well start calling yourself the fool, you blundering ass."

Tyrkell drew his sword. "You're rather bold and insolent, whoever you are, but I'm not frightened by idle chatter. If you've got a weapon, you'd better find it, or you shall die with your hands empty and your name unknown. No one calls Tyrkell a fool—"

His words caught in his throat as the stranger drew back his hood to reveal his face. "I don't need to make my name known," he said with an unamused chuckle.

"Myrkjartan!" Tyrkell spoke in an altered tone. "Or is it his draug? We thought you were dead."

Myrkjartan's face was twisted with recent scars, and his long, matted beard and hair blew wildly in the wind. "Dead! So you and others had hoped," he retorted, turning his burning eyes toward the captives. "With Hjordis dead, I was able to work small spells undetected, grinding away at the stones and the chains without rest, sustained by my lust for revenge. Dead, indeed! What fools!"

Kolssynir gripped his staff and advanced a pace. "But what can you do now, since the clever Bjorn has stolen your cloak, with most of your dreadful powers? Your armies of draugar are neatly stacked in the tunnels under Hjordisborg, and the good housewives warm their soup daily with the best of your followers. Skarnhrafn is reduced to nothing, and Hjordis is dead. The attack on Miklborg has excellent chances of succeeding, I must admit, because I helped plan it, but no one can say for sure what will happen where the Rhbus are concerned."

Myrkjartan gave Tyrkell another shove, spurning his apologies and protestations of loyalty. Stalking forward with a painful limp, he confronted Kolssynir and Brak. "You very nearly succeeded in your plot to turn Hjordis and me against each other. It seemed that wherever any of you appeared, more difficulties arose. Such cleverness and sheer guile are deplorable. But now, in the end, I have come to avenge Hjordis' death on the ones who led her to it—the Sciplings, the girl Ingvold, Kolssynir, all the Alfar the Dokkalfar can possibly destroy, the Rhbus themselves, if I can find them—and most of all, that skulking, thieving old scoundrel you call Skalgr. It was he all along. I should have recognized him; the fault lies in that mistake alone. It was for the opportunity of finding him once more in my power that I worked to escape from the cell Hjordis put me into, and when I found her dead, I knew it was he who had caused it." His fevered eyes blazed, and he shook his fist in a spluttering, spitting fury. "Where is Skalgr? Don't attempt to hide him from me!"

"Skalgr!" Brak said with contempt. "He sneaked away like a coward. He's not the one who killed Hjordis. You must be mad. I am the one who killed her."

"Gone!" Myrkjartan stood still, while Tyrkell sidled closer and ventured to tweak the hem of his ragged old cloak, cringing away when Myrkjartan whirled on him.

"But the cloak and the sword, Master. We should follow that wretched dog Bjorn and —"

Myrkjartan laughed. "Wretched dog yourself. Bjorn no

longer has the cloak. He hasn't much of anything. I passed him on my way here. He's lying on the next hill over with his head smashed and not a trace of the weapons with him. Nothing but hoofprints."

Tyrkell's swarthy face blanched in the moonlight. "Then who has the cursed stuff?"

Myrkjartan's reply was a furious howl, and he dived at Tyrkell with outstretched hands, but Tyrkell sprang away more adroitly than Myrkjartan's lame leg could follow.

"Fool! Nithling! To think that you could take my cloak!" Myrkjartan glared first at Tyrkell, then at Brak. He drew a sword, but the pain in his leg compelled him to sit down suddenly and clutch it. "At least I shall have the satisfaction of seeing you die for your presumption, Scipling. No one takes my cloak and lives."

"It's Dyrstyggr's cloak, not yours," Ingvold replied. "Hjordis' and your own greed for power have led us all to this pretty pass. I hope you never get it back again, you old carrion crow."

Myrkjartan snarled in pain, still grasping his leg. He beckoned imperiously to the remaining Dokkalfar, who hastened forward to a respectful distance. With a lowering eye Myrkjartan surveyed them, twenty-two stout fellows with frost whitening their beards and rough outer garments.

"What the Dokkalfar must have is a leader," he said with a contemptuous sneer in the direction of Tyrkell, who looked very abject. "I propose to be that leader, for a time until a suitable Dokkalfar is chosen. We shall destroy Miklborg, so that not a stone is left standing. We shall— But first you will kill these intruders to prevent more of their interference. Dokkalfar, ready yourselves."

Brak and his companions prepared themselves likewise, hearing as they did so the choruses of howling rising from the distant troops of Dokkalfar, signaling to the various parts of the inexorable machine that was soon to close on Miklborg.

"They've decided to attack," Brak said to Ingvold. "We've failed in everything we tried to do."

"No, never say that. Even if we must die, it only means that the Rhbus have a better plan," Ingvold said sorrowfully. "But I'd really hoped for better times for you and me, Brak."

"There are only twenty-two of them, not a hundred," Pehr declared, swinging his sword almost eagerly. "Come, you great nithlings, let's get it done with!"

The Dokkalfar skirmished at them, dodging Kolssynir's spells, which Myrkjartan weakened with counterspells. Then Pehr wounded one of the Dokkalfar, which gave them the resolve they needed to charge forward as a body, swords and axes upraised to finish their act of mayhem.

Before they exchanged a dozen blows, their brutish faces were suddenly bathed in brilliant, fiery light, and four of them collapsed, hissing and steaming like melting ice. With a yell of mortal terror, the Dokkalfar nearest them dropped their weapons and ran for their lives, while the others stood still, gabbling among themselves to find out what had happened. A swath of bright light trimmed away a few more of their number before they decided to flee, ignoring Myrkjartan's furious shouts. An ice bolt broke over their heads, which halted a few and sent the more sensible ones scrambling away at a faster rate than before. Limping forward with his sword in one hand, Myrkjartan dragged Tyrkell after him, roaring incoherent challenges. The captives ranged themselves for an attack.

"Dyrstyggr!" Myrkjartan bellowed, pausing to unleash a furious blast of icy power. "I know it's you! Thief! Nithling! Traitor!"

A wave of white light glared on the necromancer, causing Tyrkell to dive behind him for protection. "You're the thief, Myrkjartan. Who was it who stole my equipment from me and parceled the pieces out to your brigand friends? My vengeance has followed you a long while, and now it has caught up with you at last. Surrender yourself, Myrkjartan, to the judgment of Elbegast, or shall I be forced to take you before him piecemeal?"

A cloaked rider urged his horse nearer, carrying the sword in a ready position and keeping Myrkjartan squinting in the bright light that poured from the open visor of the helmet. A motion of the sword invited the former besieged captives to close around Myrkjartan and Tyrkell. Myrkjartan glared at Brak and Pehr.

"Surrender myself to such as these?" he snarled, hitching himself painfully around to confront them. "I'll see them tormented by my draugar for the rest of their days! I despise them, and I despise you, Dyrstyggr! I'll avenge myself on all of you!" He raised his staff for a spell, but Dyrstyggr knocked it from his hand with the sword. Kolssynir at once seized the opportunity and sprang onto the necromancer's back, carrying him down immediately. Tyrkell did not waste a moment in coming to his former Master's aid; he somehow tumbled away from Brak and Pehr, resuming his fylgja form in the process, and went streaking away with a desperate howl.

Kolssynir bound Myrkjartan's hands behind him with a soft little cord that seemed to put an end to Myrkjartan's blustering, reducing him to a miserable, terrified old wretch who reminded Brak of old Skalgr in his worse days.

Brak turned away from Myrkjartan's helpless snarling and ranting of useless curses. For the first time he realized they were surrounded by a hundred Miklborg Alfar, who were making short work of any Dokkalfar who lacked the sense either to surrender or to flee. Watch fires blazed on the walls of Miklborg.

"We're saved! Miklborg is saved!" Pehr roared unnecessarily into Brak's ear, shaking him, punching him, and giving him a crushing bear hug.

Kolssynir turned his prisoner over to the Ljosalfar chieftain and threw himself at once into the marshaling of the warriors against the Dokkalfar. Myrkjartan was taken away, and word was carried back to Miklborg regarding the positions of the Dokkalfar and what their plans were. Throughout all the confusion and activity, Dyrstyggr and his horse stood watching from the hilltop.

Brak slowly began to relax his guard and lowered his borrowed axe to the ground, realizing that the great weight of a terrible responsibility had lifted from his shoulders. He was free to go back to Thorstensstead and resume his old life of pitching hay, tending sheep, and good-humoredly allowing Pehr to make a fool of him. He felt almost light-headed with relief. He also was beginning to feel rather useless, standing around gaping while all the Ljosalfar were arraying themselves for battle.

Ingvold tugged at him, breaking his reverie. "Come on, let's speak to Dyrstyggr before he's gone. He'll be busy leading the Ljosalfar, and we mightn't have another such opportunity." She pulled the ring from its string around her neck and confidently approached the silent dark figure, drawing Brak after her, though he wasn't at all sure the famous hero wanted to be disturbed.

"Dyrstyggr, I came to return your gift to my father Thjodmar," she said, holding up the ring to him as he raised his visor to shed a warm, golden pool of light upon them—sunlight, which made Brak think of early summer days, green fells, and peace. Ingvold continued. "We were searching for you to give you the dragon's heart and to ask your help. We're grateful to you for coming to us, and we'll never forget how you saved us from Myrkjartan and the Dokkalfar."

Dyrstyggr held up one hand to stop her. "No, it was you who came to my rescue, you and two Sciplings—two brave, generous young men who deserve my deepest thanks for regaining my weapons from the treacherous enemies who stole them. I was powerless to help myself, thanks to the great punishments I received from Myrkjartan and Hjordis. Now, thanks to all of you who came to my rescue, I am restored to my old status. When I return to my home, I shall see to it that you are suitably rewarded."

"We don't wish to be rewarded," Pehr began handsomely, but he stopped when Dyrstyggr slowly shook his head at him.

"You shall all be rewarded, whether you want it or not," he said. "Ingvold, your father's ring is your ring, not mine. And as for you, Brak, skulking behind the others and keeping silent, I have something to restore to you to repay in part the tremendous debt I owe to you."

Brak stepped forward reluctantly. "I'm nothing but a thrall," he said with difficulty. "There's no debt an exalted person such as yourself could ever owe to me. I fear we're delaying you in leading the Ljosalfar against the Dokkalfar."

"That privilege is not meant for one of my advanced years. It's time I went on to other things." Dyrstyggr sheathed the sword and placed sheath and belt in Brak's hands, despite his reluctance to accept them.

"The sword," he said gruffly. Then he unfastened the brooches of the cloak and draped it with a flourish around Brak's shoulders.

"The cloak." From his neck he detached the little case

that held the dragon's heart and placed it around Brak's neck.

"The heart. Keep it close to your own." Next he dismounted and placed the reins in Brak's hand.

"Your horse." He added a chuckle—and to Brak's astonishment, the horse was old Faxi, rather ragged and caked with blood from his own wounds and those of others; but his eyes were still fiery from his recent honor of bearing a hero so famous.

"Your helmet." Dyrstyggr removed it from his head and tucked it under Brak's arm, which seemed to have lost the power of voluntary movement, so great was his astonishment.

"And finally, the most useless present for the last." Dyrstyggr knelt unexpectedly at Brak's feet. "Your servant. I am old, and now that my enemies are dead or captured, it's time for me to pass the weapons along to someone young and strong who will grow old with them, as I have done, and who will do much good with them for the causes of the Ljosalfar people. They're yours, Brak; you've earned them and paid for them with your loyalty, courage, and labor. I couldn't wish for a better man to have them."

"I agree," Ingvold said.

Brak slowly shook his head in wonder, looking at the weapons. "But I'm still only a thrall. I'm not at all worthy to take these, any more than I am free to do so."

"Not any longer," Pehr said gruffly. "I'm your chieftain, and I release you, Brak. You're a freeman now, as good as any man, and much better than many."

Brak raised his eyes to Dyrstyggr, who stood to face the pale moonlight, showing his features for the first time. Brak stared at the familiar avaricious nose, knowing there could be no mistake. "Skalgr!" he gasped in shock. "You're Dyrstyggr! It was you all the time! And to think," he added in sudden, horrible mortification, "how we teased and abused you!"

Dyrstyggr only laughed and assumed his old stooping Skalgr self, looking unspeakably sly.

"I didn't mean all those nasty things I said," Pehr began. "I say wretched things like that all the time—I'm such a great fool. I beg your forgiveness, Skalgr—I mean to say, Dyrstyggr."

"I'm so ashamed," Ingvold said, shaking her head. "If only you'd told us from the start—"

"You'd never have believed me," Dyrstyggr said, looking at his friends fondly. "I enjoyed your insults because they were so sincere. A famous and pompous old stodge like me hears a lot of flattering in his lifetime, and it doesn't hurt anyone to be taken down a few pegs once in a while. It was a good disguise, wasn't it? Genuine hunger and shivering added to it greatly, I suspect. However," he continued more earnestly, "I must ask your forgiveness for leading you astray so many times. I hated to play the traitor, but I knew we could conquer them only by turning them against each other. Let the strong defeat the strong, I always say, and leave the weak to aggravate them. They had taken away my powers, not to mention turning me out to perish, homeless and lordless in a very unfriendly land. Revenge alone kept me alive until the Rhbus brought me to you. I knew then I'd recover my powers and my weapons, but by the time I was given the opportunity to take them from Bjonn, I knew they were no longer rightfully mine." He sighed, then immediately brightened. "Come, Brak, you shouldn't be just standing there. Fasten that sword belt and smarten up your cloak a bit. You're the one who will be leading the Ljosalfar, and I hope you lead them right up to the gates of Hjordisborg."

"Skalgr." Ingvold went to him and put her arms around him. "You'll always be Skalgr to me, and I hope as dear a friend as you ever were to my father. You've suffered for us. He always said you were the finest of all the Ljosalfar."

"I only wish I'd escaped in time to save him," Dyrstyggr said with a break in his voice. "But Thjodmar would be proud of his daughter. Proud to bursting."

Someone sounded a hoarse blast on a horn nearby, and others began sounding their doleful notes far and near. Dyrstyggr looked at Brak expectantly. "Well, it's you they're waiting for. This time you're on the right side, and you know everything about the Dokkalfar down to the last foot soldier and what he's had for supper. You'll be teaching them a lesson they'll not soon forget."

Brak could find nothing to say that wouldn't sound absurd. He solemnly shook hands all around, trying not to notice when Pehr tightened the girth on Faxi's saddle for him. When he took Ingvold's hand, he was reluctant to let it go until he had cleared his throat and extracted a promise from Pehr that he would guard her with his life until Brak came back to claim her.

As Brak was mounting his horse, Kolssynir halted himself in the midst of an important dash and began to address Brak as Dyrstyggr. When he realized his mistake, he looked slowly from Brak to Skalgr and back to the unmistakable equipment Brak possessed. Dyrstyggr stepped forward and shook his unprotesting hand. "I'll pay you back your fifty marks as soon as I get back to Snowfell. You understand I was in rather bad straits."

"Think nothing of it," Kolssynir said, at last regaining some of his composure. "Skalgr! But couldn't you have trusted us with your secret—Dyrstyggr?"

"Yes, and it wouldn't have worked half so well," Dyrstyggr said contentedly.

Chapter 24

◇◇◇◇◇◇◇◇◇◇◇◇◇◇◇◇◇◇◇◇◇◇◇◇

Before Brak and Kolssynir returned to Miklborg, the sun had come back from its winter exile, and the harsh cliffs and walls of Miklborg were green again. The resolve of the besieged survivors of Hjordisborg seemed to melt along with the ice and snow, and they surrendered themselves to Brak and the Ljosalfar. Among them was a most anxious and fawning Tyrkell. When Brak made his crimes known, he was hauled away in chains and further distinguished by being exported with the rest of the warmongering chieftains to the farthest northern reaches of Skarpsey, where the darkness and trolls abounded. They were set ashore with enough supplies and food to keep them alive until the northern Dokkalfar discovered them, and sternly warned never to come south again.

After the destruction of Hjordisborg and the punishment of the instigators, the rest of the Dokkalfar hill forts and outposts sent conciliatory messages and offers of peace. Several of the nearest removed themselves northward, and the remaining Dokkalfar chieftains endeavored to be as polite as possible.

The most welcome news to Brak was the death of Myrkjartan. After several very near escape attempts during his lengthy trials, he ultimately escaped by hanging himself in his cell, much to the dismay of all his captors. The draug of a suicide was a much-dreaded apparition, certain to be yearning dangerously for revenge. To prevent such an occurrence, the wizards of Miklborg staked the body down in a bog in an undisclosed location and wove spells to prevent the draug of Myrkjartan from rising to exact his vengeance.

The celebrating of the victory was merry and extensive. Dyrstyggr was perhaps the merriest, delaying his long-anticipated return to Snowfell so that he could enjoy all the introductions and present Brak as his successor to chieftains, earls, and other people of no importance, but who were extremely interesting—all of whom treated the guests to several days of feasting, drinking, and singing.

On the day they returned to Miklborg to resume the business of living, a light, misty rain hung over the walls and fields of Miklborg, where a solitary plowman was toiling around a large rectangle of green, followed by flocks of screeling gulls. They all halted to look at the homely turf houses softened with mist and fragrant smoke curling from their roofs. Lambs scarcely a day old bleated after their mothers, and someone was pounding a horseshoe in the forge.

After a moment of silently surveying the little settlement, which had quickly abandoned its warlike appearances to resume the plowing and planting and the caring for the livestock important to human life, Pehr shook his head and suddenly said, "Brak, it's time to go home."

"Home?" Ingvold said sharply. "This is home, until Gljodmalborg is rebuilt, as we talked of doing so many times. Do you think you're going to abandon me now?" She spoke mostly to Brak, who looked in dismay at Pehr.

"Yes, it's time for the planting," Pehr said, "and you know how much help my father needs with the spring shearing and lambing. Then before you know it, it's haying time, and before much longer it will be autumn again."

"You mustn't stay if there's somewhere else you're always thinking about," Kolssynir replied.

Dyrstyggr disconsolately looked from Brak to Pehr. "But it's beautiful here, and you're famous heroes, both of you. Once you rebuild Gljodmalborg, you've got a virtual kingdom of your own, not to mention the benefits of being near to me and Kolssynir. Why, it would be a noble life you'd both have here if you stay."

Brak made no answer, gazing away with a frown to the west, and Pehr replied, "It's not that I don't like it here, and it's very tempting, but I just somehow miss Thorstensstead. There's something binding about the earth where a man is born, and it will all fall to me someday when my father goes into the mound. I suppose it seems like a small and unexciting place to want to go back to, but I've learned to care about it to an astonishing degree during these past months, although I'm sure it seems dull by comparison." He glanced at Brak. "But it's not so uninteresting to those of us who truly know and love it, is it, Brak?"

"No, indeed," Brak said gravely.

Ingvold looked down at the wet grass dampening the hem of her gown and cloak, and up at some interesting clouds overhead. "Well, I suppose I can't be too surprised, since I yearn with all my heart to get back to Gljodmalborg. I hope you can explain to Thorsten how you came to be absent for so long, and return with two different horses and such a quantity of Alfar gold rings and presents. And, Brak—" She waited until the plowman had jingled his way past them, turning over a great black curl of fragrant earth in the wake of his plow. She held out her hand to Brak, who was still watching the plowman slogging along in huge muddy boots with the rainwater dripping off the brim of a misshapen old hat. "All I can say is farewell—and thank you." Her voice seemed to fail her, indeed.

Brak took her hand, looking past her downcast face to the plowman, who had stopped his horses to rest a while at a convenient distance for staring affably at the returning heroes. He removed his old hat, flapped it as a gesture of homage and respect, and fitted it onto his head once more with a cheerful nod of recognition.

"Pehr has been my chieftain all our lives," Brak began, "and in spite of the fact that he has cast me off and declared me a freeman and henceforth responsible for myself, I'm not likely ever to renounce the bond of brothership between us. You'll always be my chieftain, Pehr—I'm not likely to have another in this realm—despite the distance that will come between us. I have always been loyal, but now there are other loyalties for me." He gestured toward Miklborg, and his hand came to rest on Ingvold's shoulder. "I've found my own place to belong, Pehr, where I'll be a man in my own right, and I am bound to it as much as you are bound to Thorstensstead."

Pehr gaped at him in dismay. "But Thorstensstead is your home, too, Brak, and it will be as long as I'm there. I didn't imagine you'd want to stay, I'll be lost without you. But I also realize—" He paused to look at Ingvold, who was suddenly radiant. "—you've got more of a life here than I could ever give you, thrall or free. You've got a name, and honor." He shook hands quickly with Brak and turned to walk toward Miklborg, followed by Kolssynir and Dyrstyggr, who looked unspeakably pleased as he glanced over his shoulder at Brak and Ingvold lingering behind in the rain.

The old plowman passed them twice as they stood talking, and the three watchers on Miklborg's earthworks were quite wet when Brak and Ingvold finally approached. A number of horses grazing nearby raised their heads and came plodding forward with friendly snorts and nickers, in the hope of finding a treat in someone's pocket. Brak spoke to Pehr over the neck of his new horse, a golden-maned chestnut of aristocratic breeding and training.

"I hope you'll stay long enough to see us married. You will, won't you?"

"Yes, of course." Then Faxi, with a flurry of nipping and kicking, shoved his way forward to his master's side, a position which he jealously guarded against all usurpers.

Brak smiled and thoughtfully rubbed the old horse's unlovely and recently scarred knobby hide. He looked back at the plowman, still toiling in the light rain.

"You aren't changing your mind, are you?" Dyrstyggr demanded.

Kolssynir added, "It's an easy thing to send you back, if that's what you really want. You've a hard life ahead of you as a leader of the Ljosalfar if you stay here. I promise you, it won't be all pleasant."

"There are already some sinister rumblings to the east," Dyrstyggr declared with relish. "It's old Glam, the great stupid bullish numbskull. I shouldn't be surprised if we had to march on him to convince him the fighting is over now."

Brak shook his head, still smiling. "No, I'm only remembering old times. I'm going to keep Faxi here in permanent retirement, to remind me always of how I came here and how I found Ingvold."

"I'm in no danger of ever forgetting," Ingvold said, her face as bright as the sun that was glowing behind the clearing clouds.

"And another thing I'm going to do," Brak continued, putting one arm around Ingvold, and with his other hand bestowing Pehr's stout shoulder with a comradely and probably painful squeeze. "I'm going to find that plowman and invite him to the wedding. I think he looks like Gullskeggi, the Rhbu."

"The Rhbu! Why didn't you say so?" Ingvold exclaimed eagerly. Everyone whirled around for a look, but the Rhbu, if it were he, was gone, muddy boots, old hat, horses, and all, leaving the newly turned earth to welcome the soft spring rain.

ABOUT THE AUTHOR

Elizabeth Boyer began planning her writing career during junior high school in her rural Idaho hometown. She read almost anything the Bookmobile brought, and learned a great love for Nature and wilderness. Science fiction in large quantities led her to Tolkien's writings, which developed a great curiosity about Scandinavian folklore. Ms. Boyer is Scandinavian by descent and hopes to visit the homeland of her ancestors. She has a B.A. from Brigham Young University, at Provo, Utah, in English Literature.

She now lives in the Rocky Mountain wilderness at Scofield State Park in central Utah. She and her ranger husband Allan write and photograph outdoor recreation articles. They met on a desert survival trip in the canyons of southern Utah. They share their home with two daughters, a Siamese cat, and a pet skunk named Chanel. Ms. Boyer enjoys backpacking, cross-country skiing, painting, and reading.

Enchanting
fantasies
from